LOST
TOMORROWS

LOST
TOMORROWS

A RICK CAHILL NOVEL

MATT COYLE

OCEANVIEW PUBLISHING
SARASOTA, FLORIDA

ISBN 978-1-60809-363-2

Cover Design by Christian Fuenfhausen

Published in the United States of America by Oceanview Publishing

Sarasota, Florida

www.oceanviewpub.com

10 9 8 7 6 5 4 3 2

PRINTED IN THE UNITED STATES OF AMERICA

For Carolyn Wheat,
who knows Rick Cahill almost as well as I do
and without whose input no one else would know him at all.

ACKNOWLEDGEMENTS

No book can make it onto bookshelves without the help of many people behind the scenes. My sincerest thanks to:

Kimberley Cameron for your continued guidance and friendship . . . and so many great meals.

Bob and Pat Gussin, Lee Randall, and Autumn Beckett for a great working relationship and always striving to put out the best book possible.

David Ivester and Ken Wilson for marketing efforts.

Jane Ubell-Meyer for innovative ideas and endless energy on how to build the brand.

Carolyn Wheat, Cathy Worthington, and Penne Horn for working out the kinks at the Saturday Writers Group.

My family, Jan and Gene Wolfchief, Tim and Sue Coyle, Pam and Jorge Helmer, and Jenny and Tom Cunningham for always listening and sibling marketing.

Nancy Denton for a vital early read.

David Putnam for advice on firearms and police procedures.

D.P. Lyle for answers on medical questions.

Patricia Smiley for help with nautical terminology.

Nick Welsh of the *Santa Barbara Independent* for an overview of Santa Barbara neighborhoods.

A sergeant on the Santa Barbara Police Department, who prefers to remain anonymous, for information on the Investigative Division and police vehicles.

Any errors regarding firearms, police procedures and vehicles, medical issues, boats, and neighborhoods are solely the author's.

LOST
TOMORROWS

CHAPTER ONE

Krista. Dead.

Krista Landingham, my training officer when I was a rookie, a boot, on the Santa Barbara Police Department seventeen years ago. The woman who taught me how to be a cop. How to walk the edge and not fall off.

I slumped back in my bed, stunned. The message on my voicemail was from her younger sister, Leah. She stammered when she said Krista's name. Her voice laden with emotion. She gave no explanation of how Krista died, just that the funeral was tomorrow at Trinity Episcopal Church in Santa Barbara at three p.m. Had she died on the job? An accident? From a long-standing illness? I didn't know because I hadn't talked to Krista in thirteen years.

I had thought about Krista every so often, but never tried to contact her. She was in the past. She was Santa Barbara, and I didn't want to go back there in my body or my mind. Ever. I wanted to find out how she died, but didn't want to call her sister. She'd sounded crushed on the voicemail message. I didn't want to make her relive today what she'd have to relive tomorrow at the funeral. And forever.

The short window until the funeral didn't give me much time to think things over. The drive from San Diego to Santa Barbara took about three and a half hours, plus or minus, depending upon the traffic and what time I left. I had a process server gig the next morning. If I got it done by ten a.m., I could make the funeral with time to spare.

If I decided to go.

Midnight, my black Lab, shifted his position at the foot of the bed to catch my attention. He still hadn't gotten used to my new routine. Or lack thereof. I had. Too easily. I got out of bed and Midnight snapped to attention, then pranced in place. Breakfast, finally.

I put on the same pair of shorts I'd worn yesterday, then grabbed my last clean t-shirt from the dresser. Midnight had already dashed from my bedroom and clattered down the staircase. I grabbed my phone and thumped down after him.

I fed Midnight and let him outside, then sat at my kitchen table and Googled Krista Landingham on my phone. A four-day-old article in the *Santa Barbara Independent*. Krista had been killed in a hit-and-run car accident on State Street, the main drag in downtown Santa Barbara. The driver and the car hadn't been identified. She'd been alone when she was killed at 2:17 a.m. on Monday morning, April 1st. Santa Barbara Police Department would not release the name of the lone witness to the accident.

Two seventeen on a Monday morning on State Street. Odd time to be out alone. My recollection of the bars downtown was that the latest closed at 2:00 a.m. Earlier on a Sunday night in early spring. I'm sure the SBPD detectives were all over it. Krista was one of their own. They'd solve this case, no matter how long it took. The investigation of a cop's death never went cold.

Krista had just turned forty-six on Saturday. Too young for someone I remembered as being so vital. Her mom, dad, brother, and sister, were listed as surviving family. Along with Tom Weaver, her ex-husband. Ex? I wondered when they got divorced. She'd been married, unhappily, when I knew her.

Krista had been on the job for twenty-five years and died with the rank of sergeant, having recently been promoted to the Major Investigation Unit. According to the paper, the unit, known as MIU, was created in 2012 and investigated all high-profile cases.

Killed crossing the street. Alone. Nothing heroic or romantic about that. Just sad. We'd been family once. The brother and sisterhood of blue. Closer than family, really. I should be there when she was put into the ground. But I'd have to walk the gauntlet of accusing eyes from the cops I once worked with and called friends. I was forever the cop who tainted the badge and the department's good name.

The cop who got away with murdering his wife.

My brothers in blue hadn't believed I was innocent back then. Why would they now?

Krista had been family, but we hadn't talked or had any contact in thirteen years. The familial tie broke soon after my connection with SBPD did.

Still, Krista was once a big part of my life. Going to her funeral would be the right thing to do. I'd spent every day of my life since my wife died trying to do the right thing. At least, my version of it. Not always the law's. Things sometimes turned out wrong. People died on my watch while I thought I was doing the right thing.

I wasn't sure what was right anymore.

I'd stay away from Santa Barbara and the pent-up scorn of people who once had my back. Let those gathered mourn in peace and not have my presence force them to battle rage and hatred through their grief. Maybe that was the right thing to do. Be a coward and let Krista's body return to the earth without paying my respects.

To the woman I slept with the night my wife was murdered.

CHAPTER TWO

MIDNIGHT BARKED FROM the backyard, then someone knocked on my front door. Hard. I looked at the time on my phone, 8:21 a.m. Once late for me to start my day, but always early for someone to knock on the door uninvited.

I grabbed a Smith & Wesson .357 Magnum off the top shelf of the hall closet and sidled up to the front door, gun arm bent at the elbow. I snuck a peek through the peephole from the side, then lowered the gun.

"Shit," I whispered to myself.

Another knock. Harder.

I opened the door.

Moira MacFarlane stood in the doorway with her hands on her hips. Five foot nothing, a hundred pounds, her presence took up more space than an All-Pro left tackle.

"Most people call before they drop by." I stared down at her.

"Cork it, Cahill. I've lost count of the number of times I've called you over the last few months." Her ice in a blender voice at full rattle. "But I know the exact number of times you've returned my calls. Zero."

"I've been busy."

"Doing what?" She glanced at the gun in my hand, then pointed her brown eyes back at me. "Indoor target practice?"

"Stuff."

She ran a hand along my cheek. "Growing a beard?"

"Maybe." Not really. I couldn't remember the last time I shaved. Or even looked in a mirror.

She pushed past me without invitation. Midnight spotted her through the sliding glass door in the living room and started barking again. Happy yelps. Moira went over and let him in. She knelt down and hugged him and he licked her face.

Moira surveyed the living room. Pizza and to-go boxes and beer bottles soiled the coffee table. And an end table. I looked at them, too. Actually, seeing them for the first time in too long. They'd become background wallpaper that I no longer noticed. The detritus of my new life.

"I thought you liked to cook."

"I do." But cooking required planning and cleaning the dishes. There were already plenty of dishes in the sink along with dirty pots and pans.

Moira shook her head and walked into the kitchen. She sat down at the table strewn with a week's worth of newspapers and a couple used cereal bowls.

"Jeez, Rick." She squished up her eyes and mouth. "You were never a neat freak, but you weren't a slob. This is worse than my son's apartment at San Luis Obispo. He's twenty-two. What's your excuse?"

I didn't have an excuse. I just knew that if I didn't change my life, it wouldn't last very long. Like too many people who came in contact with me. Letting things slide around the house was the best I could come up with so far.

"I'm guessing you had another reason besides playing my mother to come over here." I sat down at the end of the table.

"You're still an asshole. At least that hasn't changed."

"Thank you. The reason you're here?"

"I have a job I need help with." She pulled a manila folder out of her shoulder bag and tossed it in front of me. It landed on the sports page. From five days ago.

"Not interested." I tossed the folder back in front of her. Not sure of the date of the sports page it landed on. "Thanks, anyway."

"You didn't even look at it." She opened the folder and set down a photograph of an overweight middle-aged white guy in front of me. "Infidelity case. Your specialty. All you have to do is help me tail this guy. No contact. No guns. Nobody gets hurt."

We hadn't talked in six months. First, she avoided my calls, then after I'd stopped for a while, she started calling me, and I didn't answer. But she'd only needed one look at me and my house to figure everything out. More proof of what I'd always thought. She was the best PI in San Diego. And she could find plenty investigators other than me who'd be happy to help her on a case.

"I don't need the work and it's not what I do anymore." At least half of it was true. I tossed the photo back to her.

"Bullshit, Rick." She stood up and was about as tall as I was sitting down. "You can't get enough process server gigs or workers' comp fraud cases a month to make a living." She panoramaed an arm around the kitchen. "If you call this living."

She was right about my shrunken private investigator resume. I'd already broken into my savings to pay off credit cards. But I wasn't going back. I'd pick up wait shifts at Muldoon's Steak House before I took money to try to help people with real problems again.

Nobody died when you spied on people cheating the man. Or handed an envelope to an unsuspecting citizen and told them they'd been served. A thirty-second encounter and then you moved onto the next one. No entanglements. No feelings. No worrying about doing the right thing.

"I'm doing fine." I stood up. "Thanks for coming."

"No you're not. You're a mess." Moira slowly shook her head. "You need to get back on the horse. You're a good investigator. A good man. Some things are just out of our control. You can't blame yourself for every bad thing that happens."

"Just the things under my control," I whispered to myself. I walked through the cased opening into the living room and swept my arm toward the front door. "Thanks for dropping by. Let's have lunch some time."

Moira slammed her chair into the table and brushed by me, her shoulder bag sideswiping my stomach. She threw open the front door but turned to face me instead of leaving. The morning sun backlit her tiny body into silhouette, stretching her shadow long into the foyer. She took a couple deep breaths and relaxed her shoulders.

"I should have answered the phone when you called me last year." The edge in her voice smoothed off the gravel into pebbles. "I had to figure things out after you pulled me into your damage. You put me in a bad position, but I've forgiven you. I know you were trying to help me in your broken way. I didn't realize that you needed me as much as I needed to stay away from you. That was my mistake. I've tried to make up for it and help you, but you won't let me." Her big brown eyes held a cavern of pain. "I don't think I can try anymore."

She stepped outside and closed the door, pulling her shadow along with her.

CHAPTER THREE

THE WOMAN'S NAME I'd been given papers for at the process serving agency the next morning was Irene Faye. She was a cashier at a Vons in Pacific Beach. I sometimes shopped there and recognized her in the photo the agency showed me when they gave me the sealed document. A bit younger than me, late thirties. Red hair was always pulled back into a bun. Freckles across a button nose and bright green eyes. A big smile ever present on her face. Beautiful in an unconventional way.

All things being equal, I always chose her checkout line. Today would be the last time I did that. The last time I'd shop at that Vons. I considered not taking the job when I saw her picture. But I needed the seventy-five bucks, and if I didn't take the gig someone else would. Irene Faye was going to be served papers she didn't want, one way or another. I chose to be the one way so I pushed aside the warm feelings I had for her and took the job. If I gave up process server work, I'd never get close to making my monthly nut. I had a dog who needed feeding and a backyard to explore.

A middle-aged woman checked out in front of me in Irene Faye's line. She had a full cart. The kind of grocery shopping you did when you had a family to feed at home. The kind of shopping I thought I'd be doing by now. Getting enough groceries for a wife and two, maybe three, kids. That had been my path fourteen years ago. Before Colleen was murdered.

I've never filled an entire grocery cart up in my life. Today I had a hand basket with a couple of apples and bananas in it. And those were just props.

The woman ahead finally finished and loaded canvas bags of food into her cart. She paid with a check. I unloaded the fruit onto the conveyor belt. Irene Faye gave me a quick smile as the check bobbed up and down in her cash register. A rock turned over in my gut. I didn't know what document was in the sealed envelope in the pocket of my sweatshirt. I never knew. I didn't want to know. But it was never good news. Good news didn't arrive via a stranger verifying your identity and shoving a sealed envelope at you.

The woman with the full grocery cart and a family at home finally cleared the cash register. Irene Faye pulled my apples onto the scale.

"Good to see you." Huge freckle-faced smile. "Did you find everything you needed?"

"Yes." I couldn't force a smile. "Thanks."

The woman with the cart turned out of the aisle. One of her canvas bags shifted and a carton of eggs splashed down onto the floor.

"Clean up at register five," Irene said into her PA system. "Ma'am, I'll have the bag boy grab you another carton of eggs."

She pulled my bananas onto the scale.

"Don't," I said quietly and reached across and put my hand on top of hers. I'd do my job, but the props now felt like insult on top of injury. I grabbed the envelope out my sweatshirt pocket and handed it to her. "Irene Faye?"

"Yes?" She smiled, cocked her head, and hesitantly took the envelope. The rock in my belly grew into a boulder.

"You've been served."

"What?" Her eyebrows pinched up and she stared at me. "What is this?"

I looked for an exit, but the woman with the cart ahead blocked the way.

"I don't know. I'm sorry." I tried to step around the woman just as a bag boy arrived with a mop. He picked up the upside-down egg carton and it opened disgorging all its eggs.

"Oh my God!" Irene Faye shrieked and dropped the papers I'd served her.

I steered the bag boy out of the way and rushed toward the exit, slipped on goo, and almost went down. I bolted outside and made it to my car. Seventy-five bucks wasn't worth seeing the checker's face and hearing her shriek. Not someone I knew. Strangers were bad enough. I leaned back against the headrest and closed my eyes.

Somebody pounded on my window. I jerked my head and opened my eyes. Irene Faye stared at me through the window. Tears streaming down her face. I lowered the window.

"How could you do that to me?" Her face contorted in sadness and pain. "I thought you liked me."

"I do. It's just a job. I'm sorry. I don't even know what's in the envelope." I was embarrassed even as the words left my mouth.

"He's trying to take my children away from me. How can you help a man like that?"

"I don't know him. I just get paid to deliver envelopes."

"But you know me. How could you do that? What kind of a man are you?" She spun and ran across the parking lot, stopping at a sub-millennial Toyota Rav 4. She fumbled with her keys, finally got the door open, jumped inside, peeled out, and drove away. To her kids, a lawyer, or maybe just someplace else.

Irene Faye was a real person. Not a bit player in a life I was trying to ignore. And I'd just caused her pain. I knew I was only a conduit for the ruin coming her way. If not me, someone else would have served the will of her ex stamped with the authority of a municipal court. Irene Faye couldn't avoid the chin music life just threw at her. But I didn't have to be the baseball.

I was a private investigator. All actions I took had repercussions. On the innocent, the guilty, and me. I'd done things that would have put me behind bars if I'd been caught. All in a quest for the truth. Doing what I determined to be right without consideration of man's laws. Or God's. What scared me most was that breaking those laws bothered me less and less. The only way I could see to stop taking the law into my own hands would be to find a new line of work.

Irene Faye left before I could answer her question. *What kind of a man was I?* It had been rhetorical, but I had an answer. One I finally realized I couldn't live with anymore.

Krista Landingham was being put to rest in Santa Barbara today. I couldn't lie to myself anymore that it didn't matter whether or not I was there to say goodbye.

CHAPTER FOUR

I MADE IT to Trinity Episcopal Church in Santa Barbara at 2:50 p.m. Traffic had been worse than I expected on a Saturday. Lane closures due to perpetual road work on Interstate 5. I'd anticipated having time to get a hotel room and change into the slacks and blazer I laid out in my Honda Accord after I dropped Midnight with my next-door neighbor. Instead, I changed in the back of the parking lot across from the church.

Mourners were still streaming into the old stone gothic church when I emerged from behind my car. Luckily, I didn't recognize any of them. Of course, I was fifty yards away and hadn't seen anyone from the Santa Barbara Police Department in thirteen and a half years. I waited for the last of the mourners to enter the church before I walked up to the entrance. Hopefully, I'd slip in, pay my respects, and slip out without anyone from SBPD seeing me.

An older man in a black undertaker suit greeted me inside the foyer. If he was from SBPD, I didn't recognize him. Probably someone from the church or the mortuary handling the service and the burial.

"Would you mind signing the memory book?" he asked in a soft undertaker voice and swept his arm to a small wooden table with an open guest book bound by a ribbon. "It would mean a lot to the family to have a record of Krista's friends who attended."

I hadn't thought about a guest book. I didn't want my presence known anywhere in Santa Barbara. I just wanted to sit in the back, pay my respects, and leave before anyone I knew saw me.

I guess I could write John Doe or make up a name. But that would put me right back in the Vons parking lot with the wrong answer to Irene Faye's question.

The least I could be was a man who didn't lie at a friend's funeral.

I signed my name and walked into the nave of the church. Four rows of pews across and ten or twelve deep were full of men, women, and some children, all dressed in black and dozens of male and female cops in their dress blues. Cement-pillared grand arches separated the two outside pews from the two in the middle.

More cops and Santa Barbara sheriff's deputies stood lining the outside of the pews and all around the back. There were at least a couple hundred cops wedged into the church. This was one day the fire marshal would look the other way. Law enforcement personnel came from all directions when a police officer is lost in the line of duty. Krista's death had been an accident, but the outpouring of support from her brothers and sisters in blue showed how much she was respected. And loved.

I'd forgotten what it felt like to be a part of that family. The only memory I had left was my excommunication from it. I scanned the rest of the church looking for a soft landing. None. I decided to remain in the back behind the phalanx of law enforcement. Easy access to the exit to leave unnoticed when the service was over.

The undertaker type from the guest book solemnly walked over to me and led me through the rows of cops to the last pew in the far corner of the church. No one took much notice; all eyes were to the front. I hadn't seen an opening to sit, but sure enough there was a space next to the wall beside a young woman in a black skirt and sweater. I shuffled along the pew whispering "sorrys" and sat down. The organ started playing a dirge as soon as I sat.

The church, the music, the solemn black-wardrobed congregation. Colleen's memorial came rushing at me from the dark corner of my mind where I kept it hidden. The malevolent glare from her father, mirrored in her sister's eyes. Standing in the aisle because her family wouldn't make room for me in the front pew. Mourning in silence, fighting off tears, denied the chance to speak about the woman I loved. Not willing to show weakness in front of those who hated me. Who thought I murdered the daughter, sister, friend they loved. Who still think I did.

Even on the day Colleen was memorialized, my pride, my stubborn will, wouldn't let me express my grief in public.

That I did alone, away from Colleen's family, and even my own.

The priest began the service, and I pushed Colleen, her family, and my failings back into the darkness.

I scanned the backs of heads of Krista's mourners looking for familiar ones from over a decade ago and finally gave up and paid attention to the service. That's why I'd made the four-hour drive. To honor Krista's memory, not worry about the past.

Krista's brother, Stephen, made his way to the pulpit to speak. Tall and wide shouldered, he looked much the same as when I first met him at one of Krista and her husband's barbecues. Just less blond hair above his forehead. He was a Santa Barbara sheriff's deputy and spoke about how proud he was to follow his father and big sister into law enforcement. He spoke of a childhood when Krista was the toughest kid, boy or girl, on the block, and someone who never forgot a birthday and doted on his children, her nieces and nephew.

Santa Barbara Police Chief Kate Marks, thin, with short blond hair and a command presence came to the podium and called Krista a role model, not only for the female police officers on the force, but for all of SBPD. She spoke haltingly, like it took all of her will to hold her emotions intact. Tears filled my eyes as I struggled with the same fight.

Former Santa Barbara Police Chief Lou Siems was next. He'd been the chief while I was on the force and now owned a cop bar in town. Respected and well liked by the rank and file, Siems was also rumored to have been a bit of a player. He was on marriage number three when I did my short stint on SBPD. Siems' once jet black hair had gone mostly gray and his face was rounder, but he still had an infectious smile and spoke charismatically. He called Krista a cop's cop and a trailblazer for female police officers in Santa Barbara to follow.

Last to speak was Police Captain Ted Kessler. He'd joined the force a few years ahead of me. I never had much interaction with him on the job. I worked the streets and he worked the brass. He made lieutenant young, but his only command was Chief Siems' car. The chief's unofficial driver and official ass-kisser. He was in command of MIU and had been Krista's supervisor. I would have thought he'd be at least deputy chief by now. I guess Chief Siems retired too soon. In his early forties, Kessler still looked like a beach volleyball player. Tall, lean-muscled with a wedge of gelled blond hair on his head. He was smooth at the podium, but lacked Siems' charm.

Through all the speakers there were some tears, but more laughs. The stories made me remember the Krista I spent over a year next to in a patrol car on the streets of Santa Barbara. Smart, tough, charming, and just cunning enough to imperceptibly shade a police report to reveal the hidden truth. I suddenly missed the time we spent together and the thirteen years we never talked.

I owed her a lot. But I never forgave either of us for being together when I should have been with my wife the night she died.

People rising and exiting the pew in front of me brought me back to the present day. The time had come to pay final respects. The burial would be private. I was the last one out. The exit from the church was just across the way. I'd so far been spared the glares and not so low whispers that I'd be sure to encounter when someone recognized me.

I'd come to church and celebrated Krista's life. I'd mourned her quietly. I'd done everything a decent person does but pay my last respects. A right turn out of the pew and I'd be on my way home.

What kind of a man was I?

I exited the pew and turned left. Down the aisle toward Krista's closed casket.

CHAPTER FIVE

WHEN MY TIME came to stop in front of the casket, I bowed my head and said a silent prayer. I turned to exit through the front of the church and bumped into a solemn sheriff's deputy. There were at least fifty more grim-faced men and women wearing SBSO olive green uniforms behind him.

Shit. Wading through the deputies to escape out the front would draw just the kind of attention I wanted to avoid.

I turned back and followed my pew out through a side entrance that emptied out into a courtyard. Where Krista's family stood in a receiving line. The line of mourners in front of me was at least thirty deep. Beyond them, a group of eight or nine men in uniforms and one suit stood in a loose circle by the courtyard's exit onto the sidewalk. My escape. I recognized one of the men facing my direction. Tom Weaver. Krista's ex-husband.

Shit.

I stayed in the reception line, hoping Weaver would leave by the time I paid my respects to Krista's family.

I'd never met Krista's parents, but I knew her father had been a cop at SBPD before her. A man in his seventies was the first receiver in the line. His cop bearing would have been enough to tell me he was Spence Landingham. Krista's square chin left no doubt. Taller than me with broad shoulders, but hallowed out with age. I shook his hand and he gave me a weary smile.

"Krista was my training officer when I was a rookie a long time ago. She taught me a lot."

"That's nice to know. She enjoyed her time as a T.O. What's your name? Are you still on the job?"

I could lie, but then I'd have an answer to the question Irene Faye asked me in the Vons parking lot.

"Rick Cahill," I spoke softly and hoped no one else in the area heard me. My name answered both questions.

"Oh." His head jerked back a couple inches and he made a face like he'd been slapped. "Well, thanks for coming." Spence Landingham then turned his attention to the next person in line.

I stepped in front of Krista's mother who wore a hat with black lace covering her tearstained eyes. She could barely reign in her grief. I took her outstretched hands in both of mine and gently squeezed. "I'm sorry for your loss."

No need to tell her who I was. I and every other mourner didn't matter. Myriam Landingham had lost her daughter. No well-wishes or show of support could ever ease the grief of a mother who'd outlived a child. I moved on to Krista's sister, Leah Landingham. The reason I was in Santa Barbara. She was the baby of the family, seven or eight years younger than Krista. She had blond hair with blue eyes that glimmered, with Krista and her father's chin, but softer, and sharper cheekbones than her sister that blended together into stunning beauty. Even in grief.

"Rick." She stepped in to hug me. I politely hugged back. "I'm glad you could make it. Sorry for the short notice. I know Krista is happy you're here."

I'd only met Leah a few times at the barbecues. We'd probably talked a total of sixty minutes over two and a half years. I'd liked her in a I-have-a-wife-she-has-a-boyfriend sort of way. Nothing beyond that. She'd always been friendly, but the hug surprised me. And brought me unwanted attention.

"I'm sorry for your loss. Thanks for letting me know. Krista taught me a lot." Apparently, my go-to phrase for the day. I didn't know what else to say, especially with the eyes of her brother on me along with those of SBPD cops I couldn't see, but could feel.

She reached in for another hug, which was awkward. To not hug back would have been even worse. She pushed her mouth close to my ear. "I have to talk to you before you go back to San Diego. I'll call you as soon as I can." She released me and gave me a deadpan grief smile. I returned one even while my head swirled.

What could she want? We hardly knew each other.

I moved onto Stephen Landingham. He was a few years older than me, but we were both still young to the job and full of cop musk when we first met. Puffed-out chests and bull-legged swaggers back then. Life had beaten that macho out of me in the last fourteen years. I didn't miss it, but would have chosen a different journey to lose it.

"Cahill." Stephen Landingham didn't offer his hand but pushed out his chest like old times. His voice carried past the reception line to the circle of men by the exit. Heads turned. The eyes of Krista's ex, Tom Weaver, caught mine. He didn't look happy. I turned my attention back to Krista's brother.

"I'm sorry for your loss." I didn't expect a hug like Leah had given me and didn't offer my hand to force the issue.

"I'm surprised you're here." Landingham's blond buzz cut sloped from back to front like he was always speeding downhill. "I doubt anyone here will throw you a welcome-back party."

"I'm here to pay my respects to your sister. I'm driving home as soon as I leave."

My welcome reception made me change my plans. I already paid a mortgage in a city where half the people disliked me. Why rent a hotel room in a town where it was unanimous? I guess except for Leah Landingham, but I wasn't sticking around for that outlier. At least I had a dog who loved me in San Diego.

I turned from Stephen Landingham and headed for the courtyard's exit.

And the band of brothers in blue.

The circle of men broke into a line that blocked the exit. Except for the one man not in uniform who split off and headed to the street. I'd only seen the back of his head, but was pretty sure I recognized it. I'd seen it enough when Colleen died fourteen years ago and again eight years later when he tracked me down in San Diego.

Retired SBPD detective Jim Grimes. The man who arrested me for Colleen's murder and never stopped believing I was guilty. Not when the charges were dropped and I was released from jail and not when he tried to help pin another murder on me in San Diego.

Of all the people mourning Krista at the church who hated me, Grimes hated me the most. He'd never been shy about expressing his feelings before. Why leave now when he could have me in his crosshairs with a phalanx of brothers in hate to back him up?

Gift horse. No reason to check its teeth. There were still plenty of unfriendly faces staring at me. Tom Weaver, in dress blues, stepped in front of me and shoved his face into mine.

"Who invited you?" Weaver's once black mustache had thinned and turned gray, just like the hair on his head. He'd had ten years on Krista, which made him seventeen years older than me. When I knew him, he'd looked like the Marlboro Man. Now he looked like the Marlboro Man's jowly father.

"I didn't think I needed an invite to pay my respects to my ex-partner." I didn't want to put Leah Landingham in a jackpot with her ex-brother-in-law. But mostly, I didn't like people nosing into my business.

"Your partner?" Fumes from coffee laced with bourbon wafted across my face. "She was your T.O. and you were nothing but a boot. You always did have an exaggerated opinion of yourself, Cahill. Still do, even after the pile of shit you made of your life."

"She was my friend, Tom, and I came to pay my respects." I could have explained to him that Krista and I had been partners for a year after my training period, but I didn't feel like getting into a pissing match. Not today. Not at Krista's funeral.

"You've paid them. Time to go back to San Diego. You don't have any friends here." He double-barreled two fingers and poked me in the chest. I held my ground.

Weaver never showed me much attention good or bad when I partnered with Krista. I was just another boot to him. To be seen only when necessary and heard never. Now he hated me like every other Santa Barbara cop who thought I got away with murder and tainted the department's image. I got it. But even back when I was a suspect before my suspension and arrest, Weaver ignored me. I got plenty of nasty stares and whispers back then, but never from him.

Something had changed.

Maybe he knew. Maybe Krista told him about us. Maybe that's why they got divorced.

"I'm sorry for your loss." I'd said goodbye to Krista. There was nothing left to say to Weaver. It was time to leave. Except, he'd poked me in the chest. Hard. The sled dog in me growled on the inside. The harder you pulled on a Husky, the harder it pulled back.

I stood in front of Weaver and waited for the next pull. Or poke.

"Your sorrys don't cut ice up here, Cahill." His voice bellowed out on a cloud of bourbon fumes. Heads turned in the courtyard. "So put your tail between your legs and go the fuck back to San Diego before I do something you'll regret."

Weaver pushed two fingers at me. A hand shot in from the side just before I could grab it.

"Stand down, Lieutenant Weaver." Captain Kessler stepped in between us. He put his arm around his shoulders. Pals. "We're all friends, here. Right, Tom?"

Weaver relaxed his shoulders and the edges of his Marlboro mustache drooped lower. "Right."

"Rick Cahill. It's been a long time." Kessler released Weaver and thrust a hand at me. "Nice of you to be here. Krista was always in your corner."

I had been in a corner, like a fighter. Me against SBPD. I shook Kessler's hand. He shifted his hand to my back and stepped away from Weaver and led me through the courtyard gate onto the sidewalk. We stopped and squared up to each other.

"Thanks, Captain. I probably should have stepped off."

"Old habits die hard." He smiled a friendly, yet politician's smile. "Did you and Krista stay in touch after you left the force?"

He didn't say after I was fired. A nice touch.

"Unfortunately, no. We hadn't talked in years." Now I wished we had.

"In case you were wondering, we still work your wife's murder when we can allocate the time and manpower."

"Any new leads?" I asked.

"Sadly no, but I do believe Colleen's murder will be solved someday and her killer will be brought to justice. It's one of my top priorities."

He gave me a smile that was harder to read than the last. I couldn't tell if it was meant to reassure or target me. Was he the one cop in Santa Barbara who'd moved off me or did he think I was guilty like the rest? Now that I might need it, my alibi had died with Krista.

"Thanks." I think.

"You staying in town tonight or heading straight back to San Diego?" Again, I didn't know where I stood. Pleasant conversation ender or the town sheriff telling me to get out of Dodge.

"I'm driving home tonight." Nothing good could come from staying in Santa Barbara.

"Safe travels." Politician's smile. "You'll hear from me if anything breaks on your wife's case."

On the phone or in person with steel bracelet accessories?

Captain Kessler was a tough read. I was happy to be leaving town. We shook a final time, and I crossed the street to the parking lot that held my car.

I stripped off my blazer and threw it in the back seat. I'd paid my respects. Avoided a fistfight at a funeral. That's the kind of man I wanted to be. Not the one who shoved an envelope full of bad news at Irene Faye this morning or the one who slept with Tom Weaver's wife fourteen years ago. Or the one who sometimes used violence as a means to a good end.

But I wasn't done with Santa Barbara, yet. I hadn't paid all my respects. Or paid for all my sins.

I had one more stop to make before I drove back home to San Diego.

CHAPTER SIX

THE APARTMENT WAS only about a mile away from the church. It looked exactly as I remembered it. Same beige and white paint. Probably hadn't been repainted since I lived there. I hadn't been back since I moved out a week after a jogger discovered Colleen's body on East Beach. Lost two month's rent I couldn't afford, but I couldn't stay there any longer knowing Colleen would never walk through the front door again.

And knowing the last hour we spent together in that apartment was the worst hour of our marriage.

I parked across the street and stared up at apartment # 3 on the second floor. I'd not only carried Colleen over the threshold our first night as a married couple, but carried her all the way up the stairs to get there. Still trying to impress her even after I put a ring on her finger. I couldn't remember exactly when I stopped trying to impress her. Woo her. But sometime during the last three months of her life, I stopped.

I'd put the blame on Colleen during our weekly fights. Claimed she'd become too judgmental. But deep down, even as I accused her, I knew I'd been the one who'd changed.

I'd seen the parts of Santa Barbara that tourists never see. The gangs, the violence, the inhumanity. And I'd let it infect me. Taint me. Harden me. Us versus them. Every day a war. I brought the war and its nastiness home with me every night. I still hadn't learned how to shove the job into a compartment in my brain when I was off duty. The smart cops, the ones who lasted, figured that out in the first year or two. I was on year three and the battle raged 24/7. On the streets. In the bars woofing after my shift. At home with my wife who needed a husband, not a cop perpetually on duty.

I hadn't been back to Santa Barbara since SBPD released me from jail and eventually fired me. The department, led by Detective Grimes, was sure I killed Colleen. DA Levin dropped the charges and told SBPD to come up with more evidence and she'd take the case to court.

Apparently, Grimes never gathered enough new evidence to satisfy Levin. She was gone now and so was Grimes. He'd retired to become a private investigator like me. But not like me. Colleen's father hired him six or seven years back to work one case. His daughter's murder. When Grimes caught up with me six years ago in San Diego, I was still his only suspect. I doubt anything had changed for him or John Kerrigan.

After the TV show *48 Hours* did an episode on Colleen's murder, the whole country thought I was guilty. And I was. Just not for the crime I'd been accused of. I was still serving a life's sentence for another Thou Shall Not on God's list.

I sat across from the apartment for an hour and a half sifting through memories of Colleen. Zipping two sleeping bags together and sleeping in a tent on our honeymoon at Fallen Leaf Lake. And then repeating the experience our first night in the apartment because our new bed hadn't arrived yet and I'd forgotten to have the electricity turned on. I'd offered to stay in a hotel, but Colleen wanted to make an adventure out of it. Complete with lanterns for light. But the good memories only hovered for so long, eventually blown out by the storm of bad ones. The nightly fights late in our marriage. The shouting match and broken furniture that last night. Her body on the coroner's table.

I tried to latch onto the good memories and push back the bad that clung to their edges. Trying to hold back the rain.

A night in Santa Barbara had made sense when I packed a bag in San Diego and threw it in the trunk of my car eight hours ago. Not anymore.

No call yet from Leah Landingham. Probably still immersed in her sister's funeral. Hopefully, Krista had been laid to rest by now.

I remained parked across from Colleen's and my old apartment for another half hour waiting for Leah's phone call. Nothing. I finally pulled away from the curb and drove a couple blocks toward the on-ramps to Highway 101. North to the right, south to the left. A hotel and an overnight in the city of wrong memories or home to San Diego and the decision whether or not to abandon my career as a private investigator.

I turned left.

CHAPTER SEVEN

My phone rang just as I passed San Ysidro Road, the main entrance off the freeway into Montecito, the wealthiest town in Santa Barbara County. Or almost any county in America. Or the world. Home to Oprah.

I answered.

"Rick, it's Leah Landingham."

Shit. Hopefully, I'd be able to give her whatever she wanted over the phone. Santa Barbara was receding in my rearview mirror and that's where I wanted it to stay. Forever.

"Tough day." I didn't know what else to say.

"It is." Her voice, heavy. "I'd really like to talk to you."

"Okay."

"In person."

Shit.

"I'm already driving south on the 101." Almost free. "I waited for a couple hours . . ."

"Oh." Mournful, like the whole day was still pulling her down. "I should have called you earlier, but after we buried Krista, we went back to my parents' house for some time alone as a family."

"I understand." I felt guilty putting my aversion to staying in Santa Barbara over Leah's long day of grief. "You have me for as long as you need. I've got at least a three-hour drive ahead."

"If you're not in Santa Barbara anymore, it doesn't matter anyway. Thanks for coming all the way up here to say goodbye to Krista. That was sweet of you. Goodbye, Rick."

"I'll bet you haven't eaten all day," I said.

"I'm not really hungry."

"I am." I took the next off-ramp, circled over the freeway and got back on, going north. "There used to be a great little family-owned Mexican joint on East Haley Street."

"The Rose Café."

"That's right. Is it still there?"

"Yes." A lift in her voice. "I think they close at nine."

"I can get there in twenty minutes."

"I'll get us a table."

* * *

The Rose Café was a hole in the wall off the main track of downtown Santa Barbara. A perfect spot to not be seen. Krista took me there my first day on the job. Our first code 7 together. A lunch break. We'd have many lunches there together as T.O. and boot, partners, and later, as friends.

Leah Landingham sat in a vinyl chair at a two-top next to the front window. I sat down across from her in the small restaurant decorated with indigenous Mexican paintings on the walls. She smiled, but it took effort. Then the weight of the day returned to her face.

A middle-aged waitress slid a menu in front of me before I even said hello to Leah. I ordered chicken enchiladas with mole sauce and a Dos Equis. My favorite dish back in the day. I hoped they hadn't changed the recipe.

Leah skipped the food and ordered a glass of white wine to take the place of the empty glass sitting in front of her. She leaned forward, glanced at the ten or so other people enjoying their dinner in the restaurant, then looked back at me.

"I don't think Krista's death was an accidental hit and run. I think she was murdered." Just above a whisper, but the words struck me as if through a blowhorn. I blinked a couple times.

"Why do you think that?"

"A hit and run on State Street at two in the morning after a Sunday night? Krista didn't go to bars anymore. She stopped drinking six years ago. There was no reason for her to be there at that time of night."

Krista could drink most of her male counterparts on the force under the table back when I knew her. It wasn't always pretty.

"What are you saying? That she was killed somewhere else and someone dumped her body on State Street to make it look like a hit and run? Look, as you might guess, I'm not a fan of SBPD, but their crime scene reconstruction team would have sniffed that out in a second."

"No." She scanned the restaurant again and leaned closer. "But I'm wondering what she was doing standing in the middle of State Street, two blocks from any bar at two in the morning. Her car was parked in a lot fifty yards away and the one witness said she was walking from the car, not to it."

"Was there alcohol in her blood on the tox screen?"

"I don't even know if they ran one, but there wouldn't be." She squinted her left eye. "I just told you, she didn't drink."

Unless she hid it from those she loved.

"What does your brother think of the investigation? Your dad?" The waitress dropped off my Dos Equis and I hit it hard. I could have used a tequila chaser. Or three. It had been a long day and the night was getting longer.

"They have questions, but they're cops. They take the word of the police as gospel."

"You don't? You come from a cop family."

"Yeah, but I married one, too." She folded her arms and tilted her head to the right. "I know they're not all righteous do-gooders."

I was born a skeptic and my interactions with the police departments in Santa Barbara and La Jolla pushed me to borderline paranoia, but I also knew that it's always difficult for loved ones to make sense of an accidental death. We sometimes grasp for unlikely answers to ignore the obvious truth. I didn't know if that was the case for Leah Landingham. The least I could do was listen and ask questions.

"Have you shared your concerns with the investigating detectives?"

"Mitchell and Flora? They nod and smile and hustle me out of the station as fast as they can."

"Did Krista have any enemies that you know of?"

"No." Leah shook her head.

"How about a boyfriend? Does anyone know why she was on State Street at two a.m. on a Monday morning? Could she have been working a case?"

"She hasn't had a boyfriend for almost a year. Nobody knows what she was doing there. If Mitchell and Flora know, they're not saying."

"Did the police give you her phone with her personal effects?"

"Yes, but the phone was broken by the impact of the van hitting her." Leah's eyes slipped into a thousand-yard stare. She must have been reliving an accident she hadn't seen but had imprinted an image on her mind that she'd never be able to erase.

The waitress delivered the enchiladas mole. Their earthy smell reminded me that I hadn't eaten in twelve hours. I dug in. Mexican umami with a hint of sweetness. As good as I remembered. I felt guilty for enjoying the food so much on such a sad day.

"I'm sure the detectives are doing their best to track down the person driving the car. It doesn't really matter how they get there as long as they find the person."

"They won't if they're not looking in the right places." Leah finished her second glass of wine with a head snap. "They seem to have tunnel vision on it being an accident."

Which it probably was. But I understood her desire to find the truth. Now.

"What do you want me to do?" I dreaded the answer even as the question left my mouth.

"I want to hire you to investigate Krista's death."

There it was. Leah needed my help. Or thought she did. She didn't know the destruction that could bring. There was a long list of the people I'd tried to help. And a short one of people who'd died because of it.

"Why me? If you really want to hire a PI, you should get someone local. Someone who knows the terrain up here. Who can work with the police. Not someone the police hate."

"I already have, but I want you to help him." She reached across the table and touched my hand. "Please."

"Leah, if I thought I could help, you wouldn't have to ask me." I squeezed her hand and let go. It was warm. I hadn't felt warm in a long time. "You know my reputation up here. I'd do more harm than good."

"Krista always said you were the best partner she ever had. Even when you were a rookie."

"That was a long time ago. Before SBPD arrested me for murdering Colleen."

"I've read about a couple of the big cases you solved in San Diego, Rick. I want someone with fresh eyes, an outsider, to look into Krista's murder. At least talk to the witness."

If I said yes, could I walk away if the case got personal? Even more personal than investigating an old friend's murder already was?

Irene Faye, tears streaming down her face in the Vons parking lot this morning, came back to me.

"Okay. I'll do it."

CHAPTER EIGHT

A COUPLE YEARS ago, a vice president of the Best Western hotel chain hired me to get enough evidence of his wife's infidelities to break their prenuptial agreement. I got what he needed. Saved him a bundle. My reward, beyond my fee, was two weeks of free nights at any Best Western in the country. Tonight, I took my reward at the Beachside Inn across from the beach a quarter mile down from Stearns Wharf, one of Santa Barbara's iconic landmarks. I also broke the seal of the first Dos Equis from the six-pack I bought on the way from the restaurant to the hotel.

I sat out on the second story room's patio and stared at the lights on the wharf. Colleen and I had spent a few romantic nights out among those lights. Eating ice cream from the little shop on the pier, listening to the lapping water below. Arguing over the number of children we'd have and teasing each other with ridiculous names for them. We thought we had our whole lives to figure it out. We were wrong. A mile north of the wharf Colleen's body was discovered on the beach three months after out last trip together to the ice cream shop.

I went back inside the hotel room.

* * *

Someone knocked on my door at nine fifty p.m. Leah Landingham was the only person who knew I was staying at the hotel. I didn't know how many glasses of wine she had before I met her at the Rose Café, but she had one while I was there. Maybe my hand had felt warm to her as hers had to me. Or maybe there was one other thing she wanted to tell me in person about Krista's death.

I stood to the side of the door, leaned over, and looked through the peephole. Wrong on both counts. Horribly.

I opened the door. Retired Santa Barbara Police Detective Jim Grimes stared at me through cold steel-blue eyes. The same eyes I'd looked into when he read me my rights and arrested me for Colleen's murder.

"Cahill." Voice flat, eyes hard.

"Grimes." The last time I'd seen Grimes I'd laid him out with a sucker punch at a San Diego retail mall six years ago. He'd tried to connect me to a murder I didn't commit. We were even. According to my old set of rules. The one where violence was justified in the name of a good cause. Mine.

"We need to talk." Grimes eyed me, then the door I held as a barrier between him and me. The past and the present.

"That's your opinion."

"You always had to play it hard." He squinted and shook his head. "Even when your wife was on the coroner's table, you had to play it hard. That was a big mistake, Cahill. Cost the investigation time and focus."

"If you tracked me down to tell me I'm an asshole, Grimes, get in line. You got something else to say, we can do it from this distance."

"Leah Landingham hired me to investigate Krista's death and now she wants me to work with you."

"I figured that out when you knocked on my door." Leah was the only person who knew where I'd booked a room. Grimes was a PI. Of course, she'd hire an ex-homicide cop to investigate Krista's death. I just wish she'd told me it was Grimes. I would have given her a different answer. "I told her I'd stick around to interview the sole witness. If nothing comes from that, I'm on my way back to San Diego and you and I never have to see each other again. That cover everything you wanted to talk about?"

"Nope." He folded his arms across his chest. "Krista reopened your wife's murder investigation a week before she died."

I pulled the door wide and let Grimes in.

CHAPTER NINE

MY MIND AND heart raced against each other. There wouldn't be a winner. I hid it all behind a stone face. I sat in the office seat next to the small desk and let Grimes have the cushioned chair across the small hotel room. I didn't offer him a beer or a smile.

"Talk."

"Krista was a sergeant on the Major Investigation Unit. As such, she oversaw cold cases. She personally reopened Colleen's murder investigation." Grimes eased back into the chair, comfortable dispensing information. He liked to be in control. "Naturally, she wanted to talk to the original detectives who investigated the murder. Craig Byers died of cancer six years ago. That left me. Of course, I was the lead anyway."

"Why now?"

"Why now what?"

"Why did she decide to open the case now and why was she personally investigating it?" Being my alibi might put her in an awkward position.

"She'd just been promoted to MIU a few months ago." Grimes eyed my beer and ran his thumb and forefinger over his gray mustache. "The chief is all about community handholding and has allocated a lot of manpower to photo-op policing and MIU was stretched thin. Krista didn't want the cold cases to sit any longer than they had to. She picked Ms. Cahill's first. Maybe she put a team on it, but when she talked to me, she was running solo."

"Do you think there's some connection between Krista looking at Colleen's murder and someone running her down in the street?"

"I haven't seen anything that connects the two."

"Did she learn anything new about Colleen's murder?"

"Maybe. She picked my brain and didn't give me back much. She did eliminate one suspect, though." Grimes thrusted his chin at me. "You."

"You should have figured that out fourteen years ago."

Grimes shot out of the chair, but stopped short of attacking me. He aimed a loaded finger at me. "Don't give me that bullshit, Cahill. You had an alibi. You could have cleared yourself the first night. We would have shifted the focus of the whole investigation and might have found Colleen's murderer!"

He was right. I'd kept Krista's and my dirty little secret a secret when Grimes had me in the small square room under the white lights. I took it with me to jail. Not just to play hero to protect Krista, but to protect my own reputation. With my family. Colleen's. And the public.

And with my family in blue. Cheating with another cop's wife happened, but it was a betrayal and hard to come back from. I'd put my cop family ahead of my own, but betrayed them both.

Krista wanted to come forward even though it would ruin her marriage and probably her career. I told her to wait and toughed out a week in jail. I couldn't have lasted much longer. I would have told the truth before there was ever a trial. All of it. Turned out I didn't have to.

But the joke was on me. I'd lied to protect my reputation, gotten released from jail but never exonerated and would be forever known as the ex-cop who got away with murdering his wife. Except now the one person who'd wanted to see me in the gas chamber as much as Colleen's father knew the truth.

And he had a right to be upset about it.

"You're right." The guilt, the sadness, the horror of that night came back at me. I wanted to run. Away from Grimes. Santa Barbara. My past. But I'd already been running for fourteen years and hadn't gotten very far. The past never goes away.

"Your mea culpa doesn't do either of us any good now, Cahill." Grimes sat back down.

"Then why are you here? Just to watch me twist? Fine. Let me know when you've seen enough so I can get on with my life."

"Believe me, asshole, I'd rather work with anyone but you. I haven't forgotten about the stunt you pulled in San Diego." Grimes gave me his cop glare. His hair had grayed since his days on the force, but his glare could still run a chill down a suspect's back. "However, I was hired to do a job and I'm going to do it. You were forced on me and I'm going to work through that. It's called being a professional. Pay attention, you might learn something."

"Maybe." I emptied the rest of beer number three down my throat. "Does SBPD have a lead on the car or driver?"

"Vehicle was described as an older white panel van." Grimes lost his attitude while in detective mode. "Like a painter's van. SBPD sent paint chips from Krista's clothing to the forensic lab. They should get results back soon."

"So it could belong to a painter, a maintenance man, or your run-of-the-mill serial killer. I don't imagine the cops tracked down every white van owner in Santa Barbara County."

"They're about halfway through them." The cop slow burn.

"What about body work being done on any of these vans after April 1st?"

"Brilliant, Cahill. The veteran detectives who've spent twenty-plus years on the force, not three whole years like you, didn't think of that."

"Humor me, Grimes. If we're going to work together, for however briefly, I need to know as much about the case as you do. Did you get a copy of the police report?"

"Yes."

"Did you make me a copy?" I asked.

He let go a breath. "I'll get you one tomorrow, but keep it to yourself. I'm not even supposed to have one."

"What's your read on Detectives Mitchell and Flora?" I grabbed two beers from the mini fridge and set one down in front of Grimes.

"They work for MIU." Grimes took a swig of the beer. "They were under Krista's supervision. They're good cops and are working the case methodically, as they should. They'll do everything they can to catch this sonofabitch."

"Then why didn't you talk Leah into believing in the detectives and not take the case as a PI?"

"I don't have to explain myself to you, Cahill." Grimes gave me the look, but I stayed all in on a game of blink. He finally spoke again. "Krista deserves justice. It can't hurt to have some extra eyes on the case. I'm doing this pro bono, in case you thought I was doing it just for the money."

I took a check from Leah because I needed the money. A day's retainer. Maybe that made Grimes a better man than me. Maybe a lot of things did. But I was going to give Leah her full day's worth and not take everything the cops deigned to share with Grimes as the unvarnished truth.

"Actually, the thought never occurred to me. I know you'll bloodhound the case because that's the kind of detective you are."

"Anything else?"

"How does SBPD feel about you peeking over their shoulder?"

"They're okay with it as long as I share everything I find with them." He folded his arms across his chest. "And that's what I intend to do."

I doubted the police department would give me the same welcome they gave Grimes.

"Does the sharing go both ways?" No way it could, but I wanted to see if Grimes would start our brief partnership with a lie.

"Within reason, Cahill. They have badges, we don't. They'll tell me what they can, but there are certain lines Mitchell and Flora won't cross even for a retired cop."

"What do you know about the witness?"

"His name's Dustin Peck. Thirty-four. Bar manager at Joe's Café. He's been out of town with his family the last couple days and is supposed to be back at work tomorrow. I plan to talk to him then."

"What do you think Krista was doing down on State Street at two a. m. on a Monday morning?" I asked.

"I have no idea. Closing down a bar, maybe."

"Leah said she quit drinking six years ago."

"People fall off the wagon."

"Or maybe she was meeting someone. Leah said Krista's phone was broken by the impact of the van. Did SBPD get phone records from her cellphone carrier? If she was meeting someone, maybe there's a record of a call or text on her phone records."

"I'm sure they did, but don't blow this up into a grand conspiracy, Cahill. This case will be solved by the information that comes back from the lab about the paint transfer onto Krista's coat. We're here to back up the police."

"I thought we were here to investigate and see if the cops missed something."

"That's what I just said."

I took a swig of beer. Grimes hit his beer, too. Détente. Putting aside our differences for the greater good. For now.

"I guess we're meeting at Joe's tomorrow to talk to Dustin Peck."

"Let's meet at the corner of State and Gutierrez at 10:30 a.m."

"Crime scene?"

"Yep." Grimes stood up and set his beer down on the small hotel bureau. "It won't hurt to have another set of eyes look at it before we talk to Peck."

He walked over to the door and exited the hotel room. No good-bye. No sticking around to finish the beer. A show of disrespect? Asking me to look at the crime scene was the opposite.

Half empty, half full. Best I could hope for.

I took another gulp of beer. Went down easy. The six-pack would be empty by the time I crawled into the hotel bed. Everything about Santa Barbara made me want to drink. Memories of being a cop and hitting a bar after end of watch. Drinking more when I got home and complained about mankind to Colleen. Going home to an empty new apartment after she was dead. Santa Barbara would always be about the past to me. And what might have been.

I was going back to San Diego tomorrow night. Whether Grimes and I tracked down Dustin Peck or not, I was going home.

CHAPTER TEN

THE SUN WAS still hiding behind the morning haze when I hiked four blocks up State Street to meet Grimes. I arrived fifteen minutes early, but he was already there. He stood in front of an empty retail building on the corner. No handshake or even a hello offered by either of us when I stopped next to him. He handed me a manila envelope with the police report in it. I fingered through until I found the accident reenactment diagram. I'd read the rest later.

The diagram had the POI—point of impact—about twenty feet up from where I stood in the middle of the street. Krista had been knocked out of a shoe, and her POR—point of rest—was thirty-seven feet behind me, next to the curb. Estimated speed of the vehicle at impact was thirty-five miles an hour.

Grimes walked up the sidewalk parallel to the POI. I followed. He pointed to the middle of the street. Morning tourists passed by us on either side, unaware they were right in the middle of a crime scene where a good cop had died.

"Was Krista wearing dark clothing?" I asked.

"It's in the report." A scowl.

"Humor me."

"Jeans and a leather jacket."

"So it's possible the driver didn't see her at night."

"Yep." Grimes pointed to the street. "One of her tennis shoes was recovered in the middle of the street. Son of a bitch knocked her right out of it."

I looked into the street. No bloodstain on the asphalt that I could see. Thank God. But something was missing that should have been there.

"No skid marks?" I asked.

"No."

I walked back down to the area next to the curb where Krista's body had come to rest. No skid marks anywhere along the path, which meant the driver didn't even slam on the brakes after impact when he realized he'd struck something.

"Whoever was driving the van never hit their breaks. Is that in the report?"

"Yes." He tilted his head like he was talking to a child. "The report is very thorough. Jake Mitchell is a good detective. Nobody's slacking off. Every cop on the force is working overtime. Some on their own dime. Believe me, SBPD wants to catch Krista's killer more than you do. You don't get to come up here and play hero. Not in Santa Barbara."

"Let's just try to get through the day, Grimes. I'm doing what I was hired to do. Did they get anything off security cameras?"

"No. The nearest business that has a camera is four blocks away."

"And none of them caught a white van going south on State Street at two fifteen that morning?"

"Nope."

"So, the witness was a block and two-thirds or three-quarters from here?" I looked east down State Street toward Joe's Café where the witness had been when he saw the accident.

"What's your point?"

"That means the van was either parked on State Street at the most a block and three-quarters away from the impact zone or it turned off a side street in the same area and accelerated up to thirty-five miles an hour before it hit Krista without braking. Does that sound like an accidental hit and run to you or does that seem like someone acting with malice?"

"That sounds like someone who was blatto drunk and ran after they realized what they'd done."

"All the while never braking?"

"We don't know whether or not they braked. Only that they didn't slam on their brakes and leave skid marks. A lot of DUI accidents occur without the drivers using their brakes. They hear the thump before they see anything."

"Yeah, but after the thump they usually slam on their brakes."

"Not always." Dismissive.

"How far back did the detectives watch the security cameras' footage?" I asked.

"What do you mean?"

"Did they only check the video around the time of the accident or did they go all the way back to say, six p.m.? The white van had to have come from somewhere." I pointed up to Haley Street, the next street intersecting State. "Did they check cameras on Haley or any of the other cross streets around here?"

"They'll get the make and maybe model of the van from the paint chips they found on the vic . . . that they found on Krista. As soon as they get the analysis back from forensics, they'll track down the vehicle and probably find the suspect." Grimes started walking east on State toward Joe's Café. "It's in the damn report. Read it."

"You just gave it to me." I followed Grimes, a step behind. "SBPD's a small force. Just want to know if there's some place we can fill in the gaps."

"There aren't any gaps." He shot me a look over his shoulder. "We're not partners. I'm lead on this investigation. Remember that when we talk to the witness."

"Aye, aye."

CHAPTER ELEVEN

WE ARRIVED AT Joe's at ten forty-five a.m. The steakhouse was a Santa Barbara landmark. Joe's maintained the red and white checkered tablecloths from its 1928 inception. The dining room was packed below vintage black and white photos of Santa Barbara on the walls.

We grabbed the last two empty barstools at a magnificent wooden bar backed by four dark oak arches that opened to another dining area. A petite bartender with fast-twitch movements dropped a couple menus down in front of us. Her name tag read Bree.

"Start you off with something to drink?" She smiled, but all my years in the restaurant biz told me her mind was whirring on the tasks she had to perform at the packed bar.

"Orange juice. Thanks." The six beers from last night had sucked me dry of moisture. I hadn't drunk that much in a long time. I hadn't been to Santa Barbara in a long time.

"Coffee, please." Grimes smiled at the bartender. I'd never seen him smile before. Even back when I sort of knew him on the force. Before he arrested me. The smile was pleasant. Disarming. A helluva weapon. "Can you send the other bartender down here for a second?"

"Sure." Bree smiled back at Grimes. A helluva weapon.

I watched Bree go down to the other end of the bar where a tall, rail-thin man poured Mimosas for two customers. Never too early to start in Santa Barbara. The man looked at us. Beach tan. Tall. Dark hair and eyes. Scruffy goatee. Must have been Dustin Peck. I didn't ask Grimes. The less talk between us the better.

The bartender finished with his customers, then grabbed the OJ and coffee Bree had poured for him and walked down to us. Eyes wide.

"Gentlemen." He set the beverages down in front of us.

"Dustin?" Grimes put on the smile and reached out a hand to Peck.

"Yes?" Peck shook his hand.

"My name is Jim Grimes and this is Rick Cahill."

I smiled. Not as high wattage as Grimes, but the best I could do. Peck stayed wide-eyed.

"I'm kind of busy with the brunch rush. What can I do for you?"

"We're friends of the family of the woman who died in the car accident you saw Monday morning. The family asked us to follow up on some things so we'd like to ask you a few questions."

Grimes was smart. Didn't introduce us as private investigators, which can make people as nervous as if we were cops. Using "saw" instead of "witness" when referring to the accident also made things sound unofficial. Less pressure. We weren't here to grill him about a police investigation, we just wanted to know about the accident.

"I already talked to the police twice." His head swiveled down the bar, then back to us. "I have customers to take care of."

"That's okay." Grimes smiled. Patient. Understanding. A convincing façade. "We wouldn't want to make things difficult for you at work. We'll wait until after your shift, so we don't have to come back here again and ask you questions while you're working."

The real Grimes lurked behind the pleasant smile and Dustin Peck just caught a glimpse of him. Talk to us today or we'll make your life difficult.

"I've got something to do after work." Peck's eyelids dropped to half-mast. He didn't like the real Grimes. I knew how he felt.

"It will only take a couple minutes. The family would really appreciate it. What time do you get off?"

"Twelve thirty. I guess I can give you a couple minutes." Peck walked back to his station at the other end of the bar.

"Let's eat." Grimes gave me a satisfied grin. I withheld judgment. What I'd just witnessed could have been a mirror shot of me manipulating people over the years in my tunnel vision pursuit of the truth. A good enough reason to keep avoiding mirrors.

I ordered huevos rancheros from Bree. Grimes had an All-American breakfast. I'm sure he thought it fit. We didn't talk while we waited for the food. No talk was small enough between the two of us. I looked over the police report while I ate. Big mistake. Photos of Krista were shuffled under the first few pages. I flipped them over after I accidently saw the first one and breakfast caught in my throat.

The right side of Krista's face was scraped raw. Her beauty in life gone in death.

The report by the Major Investigation Unit was thorough and contained the information Grimes relayed to me at the crime scene. It stated the facts as the detective writing it saw them. No gray area ripe for interpretation. No speculation as to why Krista was down on State Street at two fifteen on a Monday morning. There also was no mention of which direction she was walking when she was struck by the van. Just that the witness claimed he saw the van hit Krista head-on. According to Leah Landingham, Dustin Peck thought Krista was coming from her car, not returning to it, but there was no mention of that in the report. How had Leah come across that information?

I leaned into Grimes after we'd both finished breakfast so the civilian sitting next to me couldn't hear. "Leah told me that Dustin Peck thought Krista was walking away from her car. There's no mention of that in the report."

"What?" Grimes grabbed the report from in front of me and skimmed through it.

"Did she see a copy of the report or did she somehow talk to the witness?"

"I gave her a copy, just like the one I gave you. Nobody said anything about which way Krista was going. Just her orientation to the vehicle."

"I know what the report says. I'm telling you what Leah told me last night."

"I don't know where she got that. She must have misread something or let her imagination run wild."

"Let's ask Peck about it." I threw my eyebrows toward the other end of the bar.

"I'll question the witness, Cahill. You're here strictly as an observer."

"Leah hired me to ask questions."

"She hired you as an extra set of eyes and ears and to follow my lead. Not as an extra mouth."

That wasn't my interpretation, but I let Grimes play lead dog. If he didn't ask Peck the question about which way Krista was going, I'd blurt it out. What was he going to do, fire me? His signature wasn't on the check in my wallet. He didn't have a badge anymore, either. He just acted like he did. Seven years after his retirement.

I had a plan B of my own anyway.

Grimes kept sipping coffee, and I had another orange juice much to the dismay of customers waiting to take our place at the bar. I kept my eyes on Dustin Peck at the other end of the bar until he looked our way. Which he did every couple minutes, and more frequently, as the clock wound down toward twelve thirty p.m. Grimes eyeballed him, too. I wondered if he had the same thought I did, that Peck was going to try to lose us after his shift. I kept that to myself. I considered Grimes about as much of a partner as he did me.

I got off my stool at twelve twenty-five p.m.

"Too much orange juice for me. Don't know how you hold it."

"Mind over matter. You should try it some time."

"Right, coach. Don't start the interview without me."

I headed toward the Men's room and glanced at Peck as I rounded the bar. He avoided my eyes. Game on. I walked past the bathroom and made it out the front door of the restaurant. Grimes hadn't seen me. I circled behind the restaurant and found an alley that led to the back door where deliveries were made. I stood behind the door across from a couple dumpsters and checked my phone. Eleven twenty-seven. The stench wafting off the dumpsters reminded me of my restaurant days taking out the trash. And rats. Big rats.

A couple minutes later the door opened. Dustin Peck stepped outside with his back to me. He was wearing a backpack. Ready for home. Grimes was still in the restaurant practicing his mind over matter. I was outside practicing my own version.

"Where you going, Dustin?"

Peck jumped forward, then whipped around to face me.

"Shit." His eyes bigger than when Grimes talked to him in the bar. "Why'd you have to scare me like that?"

"Grimes is the scary one. I'm the nice guy." I gave him my version of a smile. "Where you going? You told the scary one you were going to stick around for some questions."

"I just had to throw something away." He looked down at his hands, then pulled off his backpack and searched around in it. He finally came out with a scrap of paper and threw it in the dumpster. Peck lied easily. Something to keep in mind.

"Lucky you found a container big enough to hold that piece of trash."

"Well, I . . ." He pulled the back door open, but I stopped it with my hand.

"Let's talk out here. It will only take a couple minutes."

"Okay." But he didn't look happy to extend our chat.

"What direction was the woman walking when she was hit by the van?"

"West in the crosswalk at Gutierrez where it crosses State." Peck didn't hesitate.

"You're sure?"

"Yes." Eyebrows and eyelids narrowed. He didn't look away. "Why?"

"It's not in the police report." I caught Grimes approaching us out of the corner of my eye. More mind over matter.

"Well, that's what I told the cops. Whatever they put in the report's not my responsibility."

"Gentlemen." Grimes planted himself between us, the folder with the police report snug under his left arm. "Were you skipping out on me, Dustin. I thought we had an agreement."

"I was just throwing something in the dumpster after my shift, and Mr. Cahill was out here so we started talking."

"Convenient." Grimes turned and gave me cop stink eyes. He turned back to Peck. "Tell me what you saw the night of the accident from the time you left the restaurant."

Peck ran through the incident without going into much detail. His story matched the police report.

"Which way was Krista walking when she was hit by the van?" I interrupted his monologue.

Grimes gave me double stink. I didn't care. Time for him to shut up and listen.

"I already told you that."

"Tell Mr. Grimes."

"I'm not sure, but I think she was going west across Gutierrez."

"You were sure when you told me a couple minutes ago," I said.

Peck's eyes pinballed between Grimes and me. Grimes made him nervous. I wondered if Detective Mitchell made him nervous, too, and he changed his story for him the night of the accident.

"Well, if it's not in the police report . . ."

"What?" Grimes spun to face me and his face squished into a fist. "You told him what was in the report?"

"I asked him about the discrepancy." I put my hands out and patted the air. "The report is supposed to be a documentation of what he told the police. I'm just trying to find out if something is missing from it."

"That's not a determination for you to make."

Peck pulled at the collar of his black Joe's golf shirt and looked for a place to hide.

I stepped in front of Grimes, faced Peck and commanded his eyes onto me.

"Dustin, which is it? Was she going west on Gutierrez or not?"

"That's what it looked like. I was kind of far away, but that's what I think I saw."

"Okay. Great." Grimes put on the charming smile again. "What were you doing here so late?"

"I'm the bar manager and I had to do inventory that night."

"Thanks, Dustin, if—"

I cut Grimes off. "Don't you do inventory at the end of the year?"

That's how we did it at Muldoon's, the restaurant I managed before I became a PI.

"I do the bar every month. The owners are real tight asses on pour costs."

"By yourself?" I asked.

"Yep. I really have to go. Anything else?"

"No. Thanks for your time." The Grimes handshake and smile. He handed Peck his business card. "If anything else comes to mind, give me or Detective Mitchell a call."

I shook Peck's hand, then we all walked out of the alley. Peck turned right on Cota Street, the opposite direction from State Street. Something from the police report percolated in the back of my mind.

"Headed to your car?" I asked over his shoulder.

"Yeah. Parking is a bitch around here. I can usually find something a few blocks away."

He kept walking and I took a couple steps after him.

"You park over there the night of the accident?"

"Always. Gotta go." Peck started jogging away. I let him go.

"Don't you ever pull that kind of shit on me again, Cahill." Grimes, red-faced.

"I played a hunch that he'd try to sneak away." Mind over matter.

"What was that last bit with Peck about?"

"Not sure yet." I grabbed the manila folder out from under his arm, flipped open the police report, and found the statement from Peck. He'd said he was on the sidewalk when he'd seen the accident. "Come on."

I hurried to the front of Joe's Café, stood next to the front door, and looked down State Street in the direction where Krista Landingham had been struck down. My view of the intersection was blocked by trees on the sidewalk that hung over the street. I walked out to the curb. Still blocked. I took a couple steps into the street and finally got a clear view of where Krista died.

I turned to Grimes to explain. He beat me to it.

"Peck was either lying about what he saw or where he saw it."

I walked back to Joe's and noticed the sign with the restaurant's hours next to the door. It only stayed open until eleven p.m. on Sunday nights.

"Or when he saw it."

CHAPTER TWELVE

LEAH LANDINGHAM LIVED on a winding street in the hills above downtown Santa Barbara. My recollection from our brief talks at cop barbecues years ago was that she worked for an interior design firm. Either the firm paid really well, she started her own business and was kicking ass, or she won the divorce battle.

Her home had a lot of glass and was set back on a rise from the street with a view of downtown and the ocean beyond. Not Montecito, but worth well over a million. Leah greeted me at the door in blue jeans, a white t-shirt, and no shoes. Blond hair pulled back in a loose ponytail. A relaxing afternoon at home if not for the dark circles under her bloodshot eyes.

Emotions still raw the day after burying her big sister.

"Thanks for coming up here." She opened the door wide for me to enter. "I don't feel like facing the public today."

"No problem." I'd called to meet her after Grimes and I split up at Joe's. He went to SBPD headquarters.

Leah led me into the living room with a cathedral ceiling held by sturdy wood beams. We sat down on one of two overstuffed sofas separated by a long hand-carved coffee table that held a plate of shortbread cookies and a cheese plater.

"Can I get you something to drink?"

"I'm good."

She looked down at the food on the table and sighed a laugh. "So many people brought food to my parents' house that they sent me home with platefuls. Please help yourself."

The cookies and the cheeses looked delicious but I was here on business.

"Thanks." I turned to face Leah. "I hate to intrude during this horrible time, but I need to dig a little deeper into what you know about Krista's death."

"Of course. I thought I already told you everything I knew, but please, ask me anything."

"How did you find out that the witness, Dustin Peck, claimed Krista was walking away from her car and not to it the night of the accident? It's not in the police report."

"I know it's not in the report." She folded her arms across her chest and pushed slightly back into the couch. Away from me. "Kenny Baines told me when he knocked on my door at six a.m. that morning to tell me Krista had been killed."

According to the police report, Kenneth Baines was the first officer on the scene of the accident. Not the usual personnel who'd deliver a death notice. That would be the investigating detectives.

"This was before a detective told you?"

"Yes. Kenny's a friend."

"And Dustin Peck told him that Krista was walking west across Gutierrez Street?"

"Yep."

"Did he tell you anything else that didn't end up in the report?"

"No. That was the only thing. I didn't even know it wasn't in the report until Jim Grimes gave me a copy yesterday."

"Did you tell Grimes about it?"

"No. He dropped it by here before the funeral. I read it after he left. Not the smartest thing to do before Krista's funeral, but I needed to feel proactive." Her eyes drifted in thought. "Anyway, I was going to pull Jim aside after the funeral and ask him about it. Then I saw you and changed my mind."

"How did seeing me change anything?"

"I hired Jim because Krista always thought he was a good detective and I figured he'd be able to get more information from SBPD than someone who hadn't worked for the department. And I was right. He got me the police report. But I was worried that he'd take SBPD's word as gospel. When I saw you, I knew you wouldn't take anything for granted."

"You had to know my history with Grimes. He was lead detective on Colleen's case. The cop who arrested me."

"I apologize." Leah blushed. "I should have told you it was him last night."

"Why did you think we could work together?"

"I didn't know whether you could or not." She leaned forward and put her hand on mine. Again. It was warm. Again. "This is going to sound woo-woo and weird, but when I saw you at the service, I felt calm for the first time since Krista died and I knew you were there for a reason. To help find Krista's killer. Crazy, I know."

"Not really. Sometimes we get feelings that we can't explain. Déjà vu, premonitions, foreboding. I'm not smart enough to know what they mean or stupid enough to ignore them." I'd felt a chill run through my whole body at 11:07 p.m. the night Colleen was murdered. The coroner put her death between ten p.m. and midnight, but no one will ever convince me it wasn't exactly at 11:07 on the night of April 18th, 2005.

"I know you agreed to just work today, but I'm hoping you can stay up here a bit longer. Obviously, I'll pay you." She picked up a purse off the floor below the arm of the sofa and took out a checkbook. "I can write you a check for five thousand. Is that enough to get you through the next few days? If you'd prefer not to work with Grimes, I'll ask him to step aside."

"Make it twenty-five hundred. That will get me through Friday." I needed the money, but I wasn't going to gouge Leah. "Grimes can stay. We need his connection to the department."

"Did you learn anything new from the witness? Mr. Peck?" She handed me the check.

"Yes and no." I put the check in my wallet. "He corroborated what Officer Baines told you he said about Krista walking away from her car. At least he did to me. He was less sure when Grimes asked him. I think he realized we thought this was an important observation and got nervous. I don't think he wants the responsibility of something meaningful hanging on his story."

"What do you mean by 'his story'? That sounds made up."

"Well, he made something up. He couldn't have seen the accident from where he claimed to be standing in the police report. His view would have been blocked by trees in front of the restaurant. It's possible that he heard the accident as he was leaving the restaurant, then ran out into the street and saw the aftermath. Maybe he guessed which way Krista was walking and didn't think it mattered until we started asking questions about it. Or he was in the middle of the street when he saw the accident and didn't want to tell the police for some reason."

"What did he say when you asked him about it?"

"I figured it out after we already talked to him. I'm going to question him again soon."

"Do you think he's lying?" Leah stood up and crossed her arms across her chest.

"Maybe. Whether he is or isn't, the accident reconstruction team probably got the logistics right."

"So, you're starting to side with SBPD's version of what happened?" She paced in front of the coffee table.

I understood her agitation. If Krista's death was the result of a random, drunken hit and run then it had no meaning. It was just bad luck. The wrong place at the wrong time. How could the death of the sister she looked up to her whole life be an avoidable accident? Krista's life was too big to end on a cruel twist of luck. It would be so much more fitting if she died because of some grand conspiracy hatched due to her dogged determination as a cop. There had to be a greater meaning.

Sometimes death has no meaning. Life is what matters.

"I'm not siding with anyone yet. I'm searching for the truth." One last time. "I need to talk to Officer Baines."

"He's coming by here tonight after work." Leah stopped pacing. "He gets off at nine. Why don't you drop by around nine thirty?"

"I don't want to interrupt." Just friends don't come over after work in the middle of the night. Boyfriends do. "If you can give me his phone number, that will be fine."

"You won't be interrupting anything." She smiled. No joy in it. "He's just a friend. He used to be my ex's partner and became more my friend after the divorce. He's been checking up on me since Krista's death."

Sometimes beautiful women, the kind that don't spend a lot of time in front of mirrors, don't realize the effect they have on men. Tonight, it would be to my benefit. Officer Baines might feel more comfortable talking to me with Leah in the room. Could be easier to cut through the SBPD inbred distrust and hatred toward me.

"One other thing. Did Krista ever talk to you about work? Cases she was working on or overseeing?"

"Very rarely. Sometimes she'd give me a broad outline if I asked."

"Did she tell you what she was working on before she died?"

"No. The last time we talked was at her birthday party here last Saturday night, and she didn't talk to me about work."

"Grimes told me she'd just started reinvestigating my wife's murder."

"Oh my God." Leah sat down. The hand. Warm. Again. "Did she learn anything new?"

Leah was still grieving the loss of her big sister. She probably would the rest of her life. The woman she'd put on a pedestal in life who would grow to more saintly heights in death. The truth about our night together would make Krista a mere mortal. The truth, my holy grail. Less than twenty-four hours on the case and already pain waiting to be inflicted.

"Not that I know of." Leah had been hurt enough by the death of her sister. I wasn't about to let the legend die, too. "Did she ever tell you why she thought I was innocent?"

"She said she knew in her heart that you weren't capable of murder."

I wasn't. Back then.

"Did she keep any files at home? Has anyone gone through her belongings?"

"There's a file cabinet in her office, but I haven't gone through it yet. Krista and Tom didn't have any children so she left everything to me and my brother. I tried to go through her house last week to get things in order, but I couldn't bear to look at pieces of Krista's life knowing I'd never see her again. Stephen wants to sell her house before we have to make too many mortgage payments, but I'm in no hurry to clean it out."

I'd moved out of our apartment after Colleen's murder. Like Leah, I couldn't bear to live in a home that Colleen would never be in again. I took everything left of her with me to my tiny new apartment. I hung her clothes in my closet and kept mine in boxes on the floor. I wanted to be able to smell her if I couldn't hold her. But her essence started to fade from her clothes so I sealed them up in plastic garment bags and allowed myself a whiff once a day.

Soon, even the plastic couldn't hold in her memory and I gave her clothes to her sister. Christy Kerrigan had once loved me like a big brother. When she came down from Mill Valley to pick up the clothes, she demanded that I not be in the apartment while she was there.

I still have photos of Colleen, a wedding album, a videotape, the first pair of shorts I bought her, and a Lake Tahoe t-shirt from our honeymoon. And her hairbrush. With a few long strands of her hair in it.

Some of my memories of Colleen have faded. Too many of the good ones, not enough of the bad. When I feel memories start to blur, I take out the remnants of Colleen, of our life together, and look at them and hold them in my hands and try to convince myself I can still smell her essence, feel her presence in my arms.

My quest in life since Colleen's death had been pursuit of the truth, but sometimes I could live with lying to myself.

"How would you feel about going over to Krista's house today?" I asked.

Leah stiffened and her blue eyes went big for an instant. Her eyelids slid back down and she let out a breath. "I can do that. If we're going to try to find something that will help catch Krista's killer, I can do that."

"We are."

CHAPTER THIRTEEN

KRISTA HADN'T GOTTEN the house I remembered from the cop barbecues in her divorce settlement with Weaver. Her new house was a mid-century modern ranch up Stagecoach Road, twelve miles northwest of Leah's home and much higher in the hills. No ocean view but a spectacular one of the Santa Ynez Mountains out the back. The street had a canopy of old-growth trees that gave each home a feeling of privacy. Seclusion.

Leah grabbed the mail from the mailbox on the curb and we went inside.

Krista had added finishes of old farmhouse rustic inside the house—in juxtaposition to the sharp-angled exterior. The soft edges and warm feel soon enveloped me in a cocoon. A beer on the backyard deck each evening watching the quiet of the mountains would be habit forming.

But I wasn't there to move in. I was there to find something. I didn't know what it was, or if it was. Just that something didn't seem right about the accident that killed Krista. It could have been as simple as Dustin Peck guessing which direction Krista was walking and then sticking to the story because he didn't think it mattered. Whatever Peck's motivation or his truth didn't answer the question of what Krista was doing down on State Street at two in the morning. Until I discovered that, her death would remain more than just a drunk driver hit and run.

I could smell Krista in her bedroom. Still wore the same perfume. More herbs than flowers, more cinnamon that sweet. I remember it from sharing a squad car with her and, later, a bed. Her scent brought her back to life. After thirteen and a half years of not seeing her or thinking of her very often, she was suddenly tangible and real to me again. But she was dead. I missed her more now than I did yesterday in a room full of mourners gasping their sorrow.

There were no clues to Krista's death in her bedroom. Just memories of her life.

Krista's office was a converted bedroom in the back with a spectacular view of the mountains. The office and desk, just like the rest of the house, were immaculate. However messy Krista's personal life may have been when we made our mistake, her work habits and organization had remained impeccable. But, something was missing. No computer. No desktop, no laptop. A printer sat on the right corner of the desk, so Krista used a computer there.

I didn't remember seeing a laptop listed in the effects found in Krista's car that Leah showed me.

"Did Krista have a computer?" I asked Leah

Leah had spoken the least amount of words it took in the car to direct me on the drive over from her house. The same inside the house, just pointing out rooms that I could have figured out myself. No small talk. Being in her dead sister's house was too big for small talk. She'd hugged herself into a tight statue, unresponsive.

"Leah, did Krista own a laptop or any kind of computer?" I asked again.

"Oh." She blinked a couple times. "Yes, she had a laptop. We did a girls' weekend trip to Palm Springs last year and she brought it with her."

"Was that the last time you saw it?"

"The last time I can remember."

"And it wasn't in any of the personal effects received from SBPD?"

"No. Just an extra set of clothes, coffee mug, and pictures of my niece and nephew."

"Did she ever send you emails?" I asked.

"Rarely."

"Do you know the password to her email account?" A long shot, but I wanted to see who Krista emailed the last week of her life.

"No. She had a Gmail account, but I don't know the password."

There was a tall four-drawer metal file cabinet next to the desk. It had a key lock in the top drawer that would unlock the whole cabinet. I tried the handle to the top drawer and pulled it open.

I sat at the desk and examined the files from the top drawer. Krista's financial history was neatly cataloged in multiple file folders in the drawer. Mortgage papers, investment records, bank statements, credit card statements, divorce papers. She had it all going back a decade. I skimmed through them looking for anything out of the ordinary. Nothing. Squeaky clean.

The next drawer held personal papers. Correspondence from her ex-husband, ex-boyfriends, friends and family. I'd remembered Krista as a pen and paper letter writer even as email took hold.

"We need to go through these and look for something recent that seems out of place or raises a red flag in your mind." I held four manila folders in front of Leah.

Leash hesitated a second, then nodded her head. "Okay. I can do this."

She took half the folders, sat down on the hardwood floor.

"You can have the desk." I stood up.

"This is fine." She smiled up at me, blue eyes suddenly dazzling.

I sat back down and started going through the correspondence, reading the most recent first. Most of the letters were at least five years old from friends and family, particularly her aunt back in Pittsburgh. The most recent I found was three years ago. Nothing with flashing lights that read, "Open me, I'm a clue."

"Did you find anything?" I asked Leah.

"No." She pushed the folders aside, then stood up. "But I think there was a letter among the bills I grabbed from the mailbox. Be right back."

She left the office. I waited. A minute. Then two. Nothing. Finally, I heard hurried footsteps down the hall and Leah emerged holding a letter envelope.

"I'm not sure this means anything, but it was mailed Wednesday."

She handed me the envelope. Handwritten address and return in black ink. The handwriting was blocky and looked male. I pulled out the letter and read it.

Dear Sergeant Landingham,

Thank you for coming all the way down to Oceanside to interview me. It gives me great comfort to know that you are following up on something that has bothered me all these years. Of course, if I had been able to report what I saw that night in Santa Barbara immediately, the whole situation might be resolved by now.

I don't want to be a pest, but I am hoping you will update me with whatever information you can. I know you are quite busy and it has only been a few days, but ironically after finally getting this off my chest, I am even more anxious about a resolution than before. You don't have to worry about me emailing or calling you. I am old, but I do know how to use such devices. However, I chose a letter so that you might read it at your leisure and not be interrupted while you're doing God's work.

If you're ever in Oceanside again on work or for any reason, this old sailor would love to take you out on the Lily Marie and show you the city from a different perspective. Maybe even sail down to San Diego for an afternoon. Your choice.

Yours,

Mike Richert

I reread the letter: "something that has bothered me all these years"; "what I saw that night in Santa Barbara."

My face suddenly flashed hot.

"What do you think this is about?" Krista was now standing, leaning over my shoulder.

"I don't know, but I'm going to track down Mr. Richert and find out." I couldn't say what I really thought. Not out loud. Not yet.

Krista started investigating Colleen's murder a week before she died. She went down to interview a man in Oceanside who'd seen something in Santa Barbara *all those years ago* and a couple days later someone ran her down in a van without braking. Before or after impact.

Colleen's death and Krista's death were linked. I felt it in my bones. And one person was responsible for both.

CHAPTER FOURTEEN

WE PUT ALL the old correspondence we'd looked at back in the manila folders and in the file cabinet. Except for two letters I'd read and set aside. I handed them to Leah. They were addressed to Krista from Leah and were mailed in the fall of 1999.

"You might want to keep those," I said.

She looked at the envelopes and her eyes started to tear up. She sat down at the desk and read each one.

"These letters are twenty years old and she kept them." She took a deep breath and wiped her eyes. "Whiny letters from her kid sister in college who was homesick during her first year away from her family and she kept them. God, I wish I would have kept the letters she sent me. They were so hopeful and encouraging. They really helped me through a tough time. I can remember the sentiment, but not the words. Why didn't I keep them?"

She stood up and looked at me. Her blue eyes shimmering in liquid.

"You'll always have the memories and now you have the letters that she kept all these years because they meant something to her."

Leah gasped a sob. I hugged her and we locked together for a solid minute. Her tears dampened my shoulder. Finally, she pulled away.

"I'm good." She wiped the last tears away. "What's next?"

"Let's see." I pulled open the third drawer and thought I'd found the jackpot. Copies of police reports. Cold cases. Murders. Not the complete files because they would take up the entire office and more. No three-ring binder murder books either. But what looked like copies of the original police reports and pages and pages of summaries of the progress made in the cases. It looked as if Krista had brought home information on all of SBPD's cold cases since she'd joined the Major Investigative Unit to work on in her free time. She'd always been passionate about the job, but this was next level.

Colleen's murder should be in one of the files. I pulled them out.

The first case went back over fifty years to the 1963 murder of a high school couple found on Gaviota Beach. The pair had wandered off from a high school senior ditch day. Notes in the file noted similarities to murders in the Bay Area claimed by The Zodiac Killer during the 1960s and '70s. The Santa Barbara Sheriff's Department, who had jurisdiction, even issued a press release in 1972 stating that there was a high degree of probability that the murders were committed by The Zodiac. SBPD had a file on the murders because there'd been a joint task force with the Sheriff's Department.

The next case was the 1993 rape and murder of a woman whose body was left on Hendry's Beach, about two miles from East Beach. DNA found at the scene had since been linked to that of the California Coast Killer, a serial killer who operated from 1988–2007 then suddenly stopped but remained at large. CCK was known to have murdered women in the Bay Area and as far south as Santa Cruz.

It wasn't until 2010 that law enforcement linked the Northern California murders with those that took place in Santa Barbara and other cities in Southern California in the 2000s. Once the connection became public, I hired a lawyer to try to demand that SBPD check all the DNA found in Colleen's case against that of CCK's. The department maintained that the only testable DNA found was my semen inside Colleen. We made love, in between arguments, the night before she was murdered. Her body had been washed in bleach, unlike CCK's victims, but maybe he changed his MO. I petitioned SBPD to search for more DNA using the additional advanced science available now. The department ignored my letters and calls.

Krista hadn't made any notes connecting Colleen's murder to the body found on Hendry's Beach.

The most recent case in drawer number three was a double murder in the Eastside area of Santa Barbara thought to have been a drug deal gone wrong in 2004. Colleen was murdered in 2005.

I opened drawer number four.

Empty.

CHAPTER FIFTEEN

I STARED AT the empty drawer. Metal rods lined both sides where the hooked green file folders would rest, but nothing else. Had Krista not gotten around to copying the police report or writing a summary of Colleen's murder? That didn't make sense if it was the first cold case she'd chosen to investigate. Maybe she kept it with her at the police station. But that didn't really make sense either since she'd have access to the entire file on Colleen there and not just her own summary.

"Shouldn't there be other cold cases in this drawer?" Leah asked, hunched over my shoulder.

"Yes."

I pulled out my phone, opened up a web browser, and searched "Cold cases Santa Barbara Police Department." Numerous search listings came up that had the cases I found in Krista's file cabinet, plus Colleen's and three other murders. A rape and murder of a UC Santa Barbara student in 2008, the murder of an elderly couple in 2011, and the murder of a bank executive in 2013. If Krista had made copies of all the cold case police reports, these, along with Colleen's, should have been in the file cabinet.

Why weren't they? She'd chosen Colleen's case to work first. Krista was a cop twenty-four hours a day. Was she down on State Street investigating Collen's death when she was killed? I stared at the file cabinet lock in the top drawer. There were a couple of slight scratches on the bottom edge of the keyhole to the lock on the file cabinet. It could have come from anything. One of those *anythings* could be a tension wrench used, along with a rake, to pick a lock.

"What do you think happened to the files?" Leah's voice woke me from my thoughts.

"Hand me Krista's key ring."

Leah handed me the keys. I found a short one and tried it in the lock of the top drawer of the file cabinet. It locked and unlocked the drawer.

"Maybe someone broke into the house and picked the lock on the file cabinet and stole the files along with Krista's laptop." I handed the key ring back to Leah. The file cabinet was unlocked when we found it. Made sense, since Leah lived alone. But she kept a key to the lock on her key ring, which meant she probably used it.

"Did you see any evidence of a break-in? I didn't, but you're more familiar with that sort of thing."

Leah didn't know how right she was about my familiarity with breaking into places where I wasn't invited. I couldn't be the only person in Santa Barbara who knew how to pick locks and had the tools to do it in the trunk of my car.

"See these scratches?" I pointed at the lock. "They could have come from someone picking the lock."

"Oh my God." Leah wrapped her arms around her chest.

"I think they found the cold case file on my wife's murder and took the rest of the files in that drawer so it wouldn't be obvious that any had been stolen. Merely an empty drawer that has always been empty."

I said it. I'd shown Leah my hole card.

"What does any of this have to do with your wife's murder?"

"I don't know, but Krista was the most dedicated cop I knew." I rubbed my fingers over the scratches on the lock. "Wouldn't it make sense that she was down on State Street at two a.m. following a lead? All the bars were closed. There's no residential housing there, so she wasn't visiting a boyfriend she might not have told you about."

"But why Colleen's murder?"

"Because Jim Grimes told me it was the case Krista starting investigating a week before she was killed. Whoever broke in found the cold case files and grabbed them along with Colleen's file and Krista's laptop. Maybe because of something she'd learned from Mike Richert when she visited him in Oceanside."

"Why do you think there's a connection between what Mr. Richert saw and your wife's murder?"

"The timing. Whatever Richert saw had been many years ago. Colleen was murdered fourteen years ago. He mailed the letter this Wednesday and said it had only been a few days since she'd talked to him, which puts the meeting after Krista started looking into Colleen's murder."

"Okay." Leah's posture, erect for the first time today. Her eyes, clear and zeroed in on mine. "If someone broke in and stole the files, why didn't they take all of them? Wouldn't that be better than just taking the ones in the last drawer? That way no one would ever know Krista brought the files home. Nothing would look like it was missing."

She had a point that had been itching at me since I realized Colleen's file was missing.

"I don't know. Maybe he didn't think beyond the one drawer. Maybe he was interrupted by something or only brought a backpack with them." I opened file drawer number three. "The files in here look like they'd easily fill a normal-size backpack and then some. Whoever took them probably thought he was being extra cautious by taking all of the files in drawer four and not just Colleen's. He probably figured no one would even care what was in the file cabinet."

"What do we do now?"

"Look for Krista's laptop."

We searched the entire house, Krista's car, the garage, even looking in ridiculous places like kitchen cabinets, under the sink, and in the trash. No laptop. No missing files.

"Well?" Leah asked as I closed the lid on the outside trash can. "What now?"

The sun had slid below the Santa Ynez Mountains, pulling night in behind it. I checked my phone. It was already seven twenty-five.

"Back to your house so you can get ready for Officer Baines."

"I told you, Rick." She put her hands on her hips. "There's nothing to get ready for. We're just friends. I'm just friends with everybody."

I fought down the sliver of joy knowing that Leah was unattached gave me. I had a rule about not getting involved with clients. Especially ones whose sister I had once slept with and had just been murdered. Still, the joy punched its way through all the layers of wrong I heaped on top of it.

We got back to Leah's at seven fifty-five. An hour and a half until Officer Baines was due. Leah got out of the car. I stayed seated with the engine running. Limbo.

"Come inside." She waved an arm at me. "I'll warm up some of the grief food. Otherwise, I'll have to freeze it or throw it away."

I didn't have to wait for a second invite. I got out of the car and grabbed the file that held the copy of the police report Grimes gave me and followed Leah inside. She got busy in the kitchen. I didn't offer to help. Instead, I tried to help another way. I dropped the police report on the coffee table and sat down on the sofa and searched Mike Richert and his address on a paid people finder website on my phone. I got a hit. He was seventy-three years old. Bingo. An old man with a boat. I called the phone number listed as his on the website. Someone answered after four rings.

"Hello?" Male voice. Sounded the right timber for a seventy-three-year-old. A slightly higher pitched echo of what may have once been.

"Is this Mike Richert?"

"Yes. Who is this?"

"My name's Rick Cahill and—"

"Rick Cahill?" My last name came out like an expletive. "Why are you calling me?"

Another Southern Californian who knew my past. And not the good parts.

"I'm a private investigator, and Krista Landingham's family hired me to investigate her death."

"What? . . . Her death?" I could feel Mike Richert slump through the phone. He didn't know. Why would he? He lived a hundred and seventy-five miles away. Shit. His letter made it clear he'd developed feelings for Krista from their lone meeting. I should have braced him for what I had to tell him.

"I'm sorry to have to tell you." Leah appeared at my side and mouthed "speaker" to me. I put the phone on speaker. "Krista was my partner when I was a police officer in Santa Barbara. She was a great cop and a great lady. Her family hired me to investigate her death and I—"

"How did she die?"

"Vehicular manslaughter. A hit and run."

"You think I had something to do with it?" Disdain.

"No. Of course not. I know she visited you in Oceanside last week about something you saw in Santa Barbara a long time ago. Whatever you told Krista might have some bearing on her . . . on the situation. Can you tell me what you talked about?"

"No. Why would I tell you?"

"As I've explained, her family hired me to investigate her death."

"You're not the police. I'm not going to tell you anything."

"Mr. Richert?" Leah spoke over my shoulder.

"What? Who's that?"

"I'm Leah Landingham. Krista's sister. I hired Rick to find the truth about Krista's death. Can you help us?"

"Is this a prank? Some kind of joke? How do I know Sergeant Landingham is even dead?"

"Search her name online, sir. Call me back when you're ready to talk." I said my phone number slowly twice, but I had the feeling he didn't write it down. He hung up before I finished the second time.

Leah sat down next to me on the couch. "Did I mess that up by jumping in?"

"No. He didn't like me from the start."

"Maybe it was my voice. I sound a little like Krista. That could have freaked him out."

"I wouldn't worry about it." But she did sound a lot like her sister. At least like the voice I thought I remembered.

I remembered Colleen's voice. Whenever I felt it fading, I put on the video of her at Fallen Leaf Lake up in Tahoe and watched and listened. And thought about all the lost tomorrows.

"What are you going to do if he doesn't call back? Call him again?" Leah put her hand on mine. Warm. But no joy. The warm didn't feel right caught up with my thoughts about Colleen.

"Drive to Oceanside to talk to him in person." I slid my hand out and stood up like I had somewhere to go. I didn't. I'd been running from my past for fourteen years. But even as memories of Colleen faded, the past always stayed within striking distance.

"Did you need something?" A slight blush in Leah's cheeks. Embarrassed that I'd recoiled from her touch? Had it been that obvious? What kind of bent signals was I giving this poor woman who'd just lost her sister?

"Bathroom?" My hands felt awkward at my sides.

"Down the hall. First door on the left." She smiled but her cheeks were still pink. "Dinner will be ready in ten minutes."

I turned and went to the bathroom. I stood in front of the sink and splashed cold water on my face. Leah Landingham needed my help, not my psychosis. Santa Barbara. Too close to the past. I waited a couple minutes, flushed the toilet, ran the water ten seconds, and went back into the living room.

Leah stood at the kitchen counter pouring precut mixed greens from a plastic bag into a salad bowl. She whisked some olive oil, balsamic vinegar, and Dijon mustard into a vinaigrette in a small mixing bowl. The smell of meat and cheese and Italian spices rose in the kitchen. Lasagna. Smelled good. Whoever brought the dish to Leah's parents' house knew how to cook.

"Are you going to work tomorrow?" I asked.

"I work from home but am currently between projects. Why?"

"I think it might help to have you with me when I drop in on Mr. Richert down in Oceanside."

"Are you sure? It didn't go too well on the phone."

"Yes." I nodded. "Unfortunately, he's going to see that Krista is gone when he looks her up online. Not only do you sound like her, you look a little bit alike, too. He'll see the familial resemblance and want to help. Especially since you will have come all the way down from Santa Barbara."

"Let's do it. What time do you want to leave?"

"Ten a.m. We'll avoid the LA rush hour."

"I'll be ready. Let's eat."

The mixed green salad was a nice palette cleanse for the rich lasagna that followed. We each had a couple glasses of red wine. The only thing missing was garlic bread. Leah and I settled on the couch after dinner and shared small talk in between bites of the shortbread cookies. Also delicious. We avoided talk of Krista. I sat far enough away from Leah on the couch to be out of reach of an accidental brush of her hand. The wine had warmed me enough. Any added heat might send the night and my entire Santa Barbara visit in a hazardous direction.

I learned that Leah's short-lived marriage had ended three years ago, one year before Krista's ended. Both women hyphenated their surnames with their spouses through marriage and dumped the extra name with the man in divorce.

Leah broke away from the interior design firm she'd worked for and started her own one-woman design consultation shop after the divorce. She'd managed to parlay a home redesign for a wealthy Montecito client into a word-of-mouth tsunami, the crest of which she was still riding. She and Krista became much closer after their divorces than they'd been in years. More than sisters, best friends. Krista's death had been a shock and shook Leah hard. The reverberations were still coming.

I liked Leah. More than just her striking beauty. Despite her burgeoning business rubbing elbows with some of the wealthiest people in the country, there was no pretense to her. She shot straight and liked it coming back the same way. She reminded me of Krista talking in the squad car during our endless hours of monotony broken up by occasional flashes of pure adrenaline. Like her sister, I felt Leah would be someone you'd want at your side if something nasty went down.

CHAPTER SIXTEEN

Someone knocked on Leah's front door at 9:25 p.m. Officer Baines. A tad early. Eager? Maybe. Who wouldn't be?

Leah got up and answered the door. A dark-haired man in jeans and a leather jacket, about five-ten, early thirties, walked into the foyer and started to turn back to Leah, then noticed me sitting on the couch. Surprise flashed across his brown eyes, then irritation. Officer Baines hadn't expected, and wasn't happy, to see me.

Baines turned back to Leah, his moment of stealing a welcome hug from her now passed. She stepped around him, an awkward smile on her face, and led him into the living room.

"Kenny, this is Rick Cahill. He was a friend of Krista's."

I stood up to shake Baines' hand. He'd regained his composure and gave me a firm handshake and a flat smile. I didn't read the usual hostility I expected when bumping up against law enforcement who knew my reputation. Baines was younger than I expected. He hadn't been on the force when the department kicked me off it. He did look vaguely familiar, though. I just couldn't place him.

"Nice to meet you, Kenny." I gave him back the handshake and a slightly friendlier smile than he gave me.

"You can call me Ken." He side-glanced Leah. I got it. Only the woman he was sweet on called him Kenny. I was more comfortable with Ken, anyway.

"You can call me Rick." I sat back down on the couch.

"I've got some lasagna warming in the oven for you, Kenny." Leah looked like now she didn't know what to do with her hands, so she walked into the kitchen.

Baines remained standing. "That's okay. I didn't know you had company."

"I'm actually here to talk to you," I said before Leah could jump in.

"Me?" Baines glanced at Leah then back at me.

"Like I said, Rick was a friend of Krista's and I . . ." Leah stood at the kitchen counter. "He's helping out Jim Grimes."

"I told you that was a bad idea, Lee," Baines said to Leah. Kenny. *Lee.* Maybe there was more to their relationship than she'd admitted to. "Hiring a PI. That could hamper the investigation."

"Look, Ken." I stayed seated and calm. Baines' building agitation was enough nerves for the whole room. "Jim Grimes and I aren't going to do anything to get in the way of SBPD's investigation. Anything new we find, we're giving to them. We all have the same goal. To find the person who killed Krista."

"I'll touch base with you tomorrow, Lee. Mr. Cahill." Baines nodded at me then headed for the front door.

"Kenny, wait." Leah walked over to Baines in the foyer. "You know I wouldn't do anything to hurt the investigation."

"Not knowingly." He looked at me on the couch. I pretended I wasn't paying attention. "But you never know what can happen when you bring in an outside entity. Private investigators are wild cards and have their own agendas."

I continued to pretend that I couldn't hear that my reputation had just been besmirched. Again. Water. Duck. Back.

"Kenny, please just talk to Rick." Leah took his hand in hers. I knew how that felt. Warm. "And even if you don't, at least eat the lasagna I have warming for you."

Baines' face didn't go Raiders of the Lost Ark, but I could still see him melt. His shoulders relaxed and he let out an audible exhale. Even from where I was sitting and still couldn't hear anything.

"Okay," Baines said. He and Leah returned to the living room.

"What would you like to know, Rick?" He stood in front of the coffee table, chest a little more puffed out than when he came in.

"Eat your dinner." I stood up and walked over to the dining area where Leah and I ate. "I remember how hungry you can get after a shift."

"I know you were a cop." Baines sat down at the head of the table. Bold. He'd been over for dinner before. "And I know all about your time on the force. I was at the service yesterday. A lot of old-timers remembered who you were."

That's where I'd seen him. The service. He'd been in his uniform. One of the stoics who eyed me without expression.

"Yep. They don't like me much and I don't give a damn." I sat kitty corner to Baines. I briefly considered taking the opposite head of the table but decided to hold off on the pissing contest. "Krista was my T.O. and then partner for a while. Unlike the old-timers who tugged your ear yesterday, she trusted me and believed in me. Hell, right now I'm working with Jim Grimes who arrested me for my wife's murder. He now knows I'm innocent. So, let's put the past and rumors behind us and work on finding Krista's killer. Deal?"

Leah set down a plate of steaming lasagna in front of Baines along with a bowl of salad. She went back into the kitchen and returned with a beer, which she set in front of Baines then sat across from me, diagonal to him He looked at the salad, then dug into the lasagna. Big mouthfuls. I let him enjoy the food for a few bites before I started in.

"Can you give us a rundown on what happened when you arrived at the scene?"

"How much detail do you want?" He put down his fork.

"All of it."

"Lee, maybe you shouldn't listen to this." He pushed the plate of half-eaten lasagna away from him.

"We can avoid some details." I said.

"I want to know what happened." Leah clasped her hands in front of her on the table. "Just not . . . her injuries."

Baines let go another loud breath and rubbed his face with both hands. "I was driving a U car, meaning I was alone on patrol, and got a call for a possible 20001 on the four hundred block of State Street at 2:17 a.m. I made it to the scene at approximately 2:22 a.m." He glanced at Leah, who nodded for him to continue. "I saw . . . the victim laying in the intersection of State and Gutierrez near the curb, on the east side of the intersection."

Baines stared down at the table. Nobody said anything. Cops aren't unfeeling automatons or callous bullies. Not the vast majority, anyway. They think and feel. Baines must have been reliving the moment when he realized the victim wasn't a stranger, but someone he knew. A fellow cop. Even worse, the sister of the woman he cared about.

Leah reached over and put her hand on top of Baines'. She smiled a sad smile when he let his eyes meet hers.

"Take your time, Kenny," she said.

"I knew it was Detective Landingham even before I got to her body. She wore a blue and pink running shoe. The other one was in the middle of the street. I—"

Leah pulled her hand away from Baines and gasped. She covered her face with her hands. Her voice came out halting and raw. "The shoes I bought Krista for her birthday."

"Yeah." Baines leaned over and put his arms around Leah. She started crying and Baines pulled her closer. I didn't say anything. Leah cried for a minute or so then pulled away from Baines.

"I'm okay." She wiped her eyes and exhaled. "Sorry."

"No need to apologize," I said.

"You sure you want me to go on?" A watery shimmer floated over Baines' eyes. He was in love with Leah.

"Yes. Please." No hand on his this time.

"I checked for vital signs, but she was gone." Baines wiped at his eyes. "I set up flares and secured the scene with police tape and called it in. The paramedics arrived at the scene and checked Krista's vitals even though we all knew she was dead. I called the watch commander and told him the victim was Krista. He told me that MIU had already been alerted and should arrive within ten minutes."

"Why would the Major Investigation Unit already be on the way if they didn't know that a police detective had been killed yet?" I asked.

"There's a team within the unit that investigates all traffic collisions, so they would have been notified as soon as I called it in."

"I thought Detectives Mitchell and Flora showed up. Do they normally handle 20001s?"

"No. Stack and Murphy normally do. Mitchell and Flora handle the high-visibility cases and anything involving a cop from SBPD. They came later and took over the investigation when they got there."

"When did you talk to Dustin Peck?"

"After I called the watch commander and told him that it was Krista."

"So before anyone from MIU arrived?"

"Right." Baines took a gulp from his beer.

"What did Peck tell you he saw?"

"It's all in the police report. I thought Grimes had a copy. Hasn't he shown it to you yet?"

"I read it. Have you?"

"No. Why would I?"

"Maybe you should." I got up, went over, and grabbed the manila folder with the police report in it and set it down in front of Baines. "Read the witness statement and see if it jibes with your recollection of what Peck told you."

Baines looked at Leah who nodded encouragement. He took the report from the folder and thumbed through until he got to the witness statement. Leah and I shared a couple glances while Baines read. She smiled at me like she hadn't at Baines. There was some sadness in it, but something else. A kinship with the hint of something more. The kind that could warm your hand without a touch.

"It's pretty much how I remember it." Baines set the report down.

"Pretty much?" I raised my eyebrows. "What's different?"

"Nothing important, really. Just that he doesn't mention which way Krista was walking. He told me she was crossing State on Gutierrez heading west when she was . . . when the accident occurred."

"That seems kind of significant to me. Her car was parked in an empty restaurant parking lot on the east side of Gutierrez, right?"

"Yes."

"So she would have been coming from her car at two in the morning on State Street instead of returning to it after a night on the town?"

"I don't know. I guess so."

"Did you check the area where Peck said he was when he saw the accident?"

"No." His face turned red. "I . . . I didn't want to leave Krista's body. I just took his word for it."

Liquid welled in the bottom of Leah's eyes. I understood Baines wanting to protect Krista's body even in death, but he made a mistake not physically verifying Peck's story.

"Peck couldn't have seen the accident from the sidewalk in front of Joe's Café," I said. "Trees block the view. He'd have to have been in the street."

"The witness had just seen something horrible. He probably got confused about exactly where he was."

"Did you happen to get a look inside Krista's car at the scene?"

"No. Why?"

"Do you know who did?"

"No, Cahill, I don't." He cop-eyed me. A pretty good one. "Now you answer my question. Why do you want to know what was inside Krista's car?"

Baines wasn't on my team, but he was on Leah's. Unless Krista's laptop was at police headquarters, someone stole it. The more I looked into Krista's death, the more my neck itched. Something wasn't right about it, and my bad experiences with all things cops, especially SBPD, made me question my agreement with Grimes to share everything we learned with them. Baines was one of them. But he was in love with Leah.

"We can't find Krista's personal laptop. It wasn't in her things SBPD gave to Leah and it's not in her home. I was just wondering if it had been in the car that night."

"Like I said, I didn't see what was inside the car. I don't know where the laptop is."

"Just so you know, I questioned Dustin Peck, and he told me the same thing he told you. Krista was walking in the direction away from her car. Why don't you think that's in the report?"

"How am I supposed to know? Maybe he didn't mention it because he didn't think it was important or he forgot about it. He'd just seen someone get run over by a drunk driver. That'll shake someone up who'd never seen it before. Why don't you ask Mitchell about what Peck said he saw? He wrote the report. Better yet, why don't you let MIU handle the investigation?"

"Because I hired him to investigate, Kenny." Leah's voice had a little bump in it. "He's asking you questions on my behalf. I just want to find out who killed my sister. If SBPD arrests the person, fine. But I'm not going to just wait around until they do."

"You said Peck had probably never seen someone get run down by a drunk driver. Is that the official unofficial story?" I pointed at the police report. "There's no evidence to that effect in there."

"Two in the morning. No skid marks. A hit and run. What else could it be?"

"That's what I'm trying to find out."

"I think all your wild speculation is extending Leah's pain and making her think about nothing but her sister's death." He lifted his hands off the table. "For what? What's your game? You trying to play hero? Maybe you can't be trusted just like the old-timers say."

"Kenny!" The bump in Leah's voice sharpened into an edge. "I told you, Rick is here because I want him to be. He's not making me think about anything. I'm in control of my own thoughts, thank you."

If Baines had had a crest, it would have fallen. He pushed away from the table with his head down.

"Thanks for dinner." He walked to the front door without looking at either of us.

"Kenny?" Leah's tone was softer, but Baines ignored her and left the house.

"Sorry about that, Rick." Leah poured herself a heathy glass of wine and held the bottle out for me.

"No thanks." I stood up to leave. "You know he's in love with you."

"I didn't see it until tonight."

CHAPTER SEVENTEEN

I CALLED GRIMES on the way back to the Best Western. We were supposed to be a team. One with questionable locker room chemistry.

"Yeah?" Elated to hear from me. Go team.

"I talked to the first officer on the scene and he recalls Peck telling him that Krista was walking away from where her car was parked when she was struck."

"You talked to Officer Baines?" He hadn't gotten any happier.

"Yeah."

"Who told you you could do that? I'm running this investigation. You should have contacted me first."

"It was by accident. Baines is a friend of Leah Landingham. He showed up at Leah's house while I was there."

"Why were you at Miss Landingham's house?"

"We agreed I'd ask her how she learned what Peck said that wasn't in the police report. Remember?"

"That's a simple phone call. Not a visit to her house."

"Grimes, neither one of us is wearing a badge anymore. I'll let you steer this investigation, but when it comes to questioning a witness, I'll do it my way."

"You're not *letting* me do anything, Cahill. And I'm not going to let you take advantage of a vulnerable woman who's grieving. I know your history. Especially with the Landingham family."

I was pretty sure Grimes was a Christian. And I was pretty sure he'd passed over the forgiveness part. My one-night indiscretion with Krista had done far more damage to my life than it had done to his police investigation, but he couldn't forgive me. Neither could I, but I'd leave final judgment to my maker. If he allowed me in his presence when the time came.

But some fights were best left internal. And the older I got, the thicker my skin grew.

"You want to know what else I learned today or would you rather stay up there on your high horse?"

"You're an asshole."

"I'll take that as a yes." Partners. "Leah and I went to Krista's house and had a look around. Did you know that Krista had files of cold cases in her home office?"

"She had copies of murder books there?"

"Not full murder books, but extensive summaries that looked like she'd written up on her own."

"I'm not surprised. She was in charge of the cold case unit in MIU."

"Yeah, but Colleen's file is missing."

"That's the case she was working on. The file's probably on her desk at Figueroa Street. No big mystery there."

"Well, this is a mystery." I told him about the cold cases in drawer three of Krista's file cabinet and empty drawer number four. "Come on, Grimes, doesn't that seem a little strange to you? Krista kept extensive, meticulous files and Colleen's case and the other cold cases that would fill drawer four of her file cabinet are all gone?"

"Maybe she hadn't gotten to those cases yet." His voice lacked its conviction of a minute ago.

"But you know she was working Colleen's case. If she was going to have copies of any cold cases at her house, that would be number one. Plus, her laptop is missing."

"That's police property. I'm sure SBPD has possession of it."

"Her personal laptop. We looked everywhere in the house and her car and Leah's sure it wasn't with Krista's personal items given to her by SBPD."

"Hmm."

"Plus, the file cabinet was unlocked despite Krista having a key for it on her key chain. The lock had a couple scratches on it that could have come from someone picking it."

I didn't tell him about my expertise in the field. There were some things you didn't even tell your partner.

"One other thing." I sensed Grimes was ready to take a ride on my natural suspicion for a while. "A letter arrived at Krista's house this week from a man in Oceanside thanking her for going down there to talk to him about something he saw in Santa Barbara a long time ago."

"What did he see?"

"I don't know. He wouldn't talk to me on the phone. That's why I'm going to pay him a surprise visit. I'm driving to Oceanside tomorrow."

Maybe I should have told Grimes that Leah was coming with me. Maybe he'd think I was taking advantage of a vulnerable woman.

Grimes didn't say anything. No doubt weighing whether to use his "I'm in charge speech" again. Finally, "Okay."

"What did Detective Mitchell tell you about the discrepancy between what Dustin Peck told us about which way Krista was walking and what was in the report?"

"Nothing. I didn't get a chance to talk to him. All communication has to go through Captain Kessler now. Supposedly word came down from the chief. According to Kessler, Police Chief Miss Transparency didn't like Mitchell trading information with some ex-cop PI." Grimes bit down hard on his words. I was glad his anger was directed at someone else for a change.

"What did Kessler say?"

"He wants me to put my requests, as he called them, in writing going forward. He's a politician. He'll stonewall me until they solve the case or until he can find a way to make himself and the department look good. In that order."

"What do we do with what I discovered today about the missing cold case files and the letter from the guy in San Diego?"

"I'll give it to SBPD. Our directive hasn't changed. We're going to continue to try to help find the killer. If the information only flows one way now, that doesn't matter. We don't have badges."

"Say I'm right about the missing files and the computer." Grimes wasn't going to like where I was going, so I'd try to have him lead me there. "Who do you think would know that she had the files and her computer might be important?"

"Quit playing games, Cahill. You're not that clever." His words less harsh than those for the police chief. He was warming up to me. "I know you think that it would have to have been someone from the department who took the files and the computer. If they were indeed stolen."

"So, do you think we should share that information with SBPD when we aren't sure who is friend or foe over there?"

"I may not yet know who the foe is over there, but I know who my friends are. That's why I'm sitting on a stool in Paddy's Pub right now."

Paddy's Pub was a cop bar on State Street when I was on the job. Chief Siems bought it after he retired.

"Mitchell's meeting you?"

"My sources are my own."

I ignored the opportunity to give Grimes my definition of a partnership. Maybe I'd use his from now on.

"I'll check in when I get back from Oceanside."

CHAPTER EIGHTEEN

OCEANSIDE IS ABOUT forty miles north of downtown San Diego. Snug up against Marine Corps Base Camp Pendleton to its north, it's a city of 175,000 people, the third largest city in the county behind San Diego and Chula Vista. As its name implies, it's on the coast but it stretches miles and miles inland, past Vista all the way to Bonsall. It has nice beaches like its neighbors to the south, but less million-dollar coastal homes. More Mission Beach than La Jolla or Del Mar.

The address listed on the envelope Mike Richert sent to Krista was in an upscale middle-class development five miles from the coast off El Camino Real. The home was a modern two story with a tile roof. An older model white Toyota Tacoma pickup sat in the driveway. I got the impression from the letter that Richert lived alone. A lot of house for someone living alone. Maybe I was wrong about that. Maybe I was wrong about the importance of the letter altogether.

One way to find out.

We knocked on the front door. Ten seconds later, a head peeked through the window next to the door. Male. Gray with a receding hairline. Early seventies. Tan leathery skin. He didn't look surprised but he didn't look happy, either. A second later, the door opened. The man stood about six feet tall. Lean, but square built. Big boned. Naturally strong, probably from years out on the ocean tending to sails.

"Mike Richert?"

"That's me." The same voice on the phone last night. He looked at Leah and his face softened.

"Rick Cahill. We talked on the phone last night." I turned to Leah. "And this is Leah Landingham. Krista's sister."

Richert looked at Leah but didn't say anything for a couple seconds. Finally, "I'm sorry for your loss. Your sister seemed like a fine woman."

"Thank you. She was."

Richert still didn't invite us inside. He looked at me and his face grimmed up.

"I don't appreciate you dropping by unannounced."

"I apologize, but we're here because it's important. We drove all the way down from Santa Barbara to talk to you. Krista was killed a week after she talked to you, and we need to find out if what you told her had something to do with her death."

"I read online that she was killed by a drunk driver. How could I have anything to do with that?"

"The person who killed her hasn't been caught yet. The drunk driver angle is pure speculation by the newspaper." And maybe a targeted leak by someone at SBPD. "Maybe they're right, but we want to find out anything we can to help catch the driver."

"If what I told Krista is so important, why haven't the police contacted me?"

"We just discovered your letter yesterday and started putting the pieces together. The police have the same information now." That is, if Grimes gave it to his source. "Hopefully, they'll contact you, too. But even if they don't, whatever you tell us we'll give to the Santa Barbara Police Department. We just want to find Krista's killer."

And I wanted to find out if Krista's death was related to her investigation into Colleen's murder.

"All right." Mike Richert opened the door and let us in.

CHAPTER NINETEEN

RICHERT'S HOME HAD a slightly feminine feel, like his wife did all the decorating. But he didn't have a ring on his finger. He led us into a living room that had a few nautical knickknacks to help offset the pale blue and white wallpaper. There was a painting and a couple pictures of sailboats but a lot more pictures of a beautiful woman as she aged over the years. Some with Richert in them, but most of her alone smiling at the camera that he was no doubt behind.

He led us to a sofa that matched the wallpaper, and Leah and I sat down while Richert stood next to a twill upholstered chair.

"Your wife?" I nodded at a photo of the woman on the coffee table between us. Judging by her age and the pallor of her skin, this was the most recent. A scarf covered her head. She'd obviously been ill when the photo was taken.

"Yes." His body seemed to shrink into itself. "She's no longer with us. Cancer."

"I'm sorry for your loss." Leah beat me to it. "She was beautiful."

I added my condolences.

"Thank you. It's been three and a quarter years, and I still expect to feel her next to me in bed every night." He pressed his lips together and shook his head. "I'm a little embarrassed about that letter I wrote. I never expected anyone but your sister to read it."

"There's no reason to be embarrassed." Leah leaned forward on the sofa closing the distance between the two of them. "We never would have read it if we weren't looking for clues to who killed Krista."

But I knew why he was embarrassed. He'd spent the last three-plus years grieving the loss of his wife. Stuck in a dark place, feeling he needed to stay there because of his love for her. And because it had been her, not him, who died. Then he encountered a beautiful, magnetic woman for a single day, and she reminded him of life's possibilities. It didn't matter that she was twenty-six years younger than him—she could have been ten years older. He invited Krista for a sail on his boat because he wanted to feel alive again. There may or may not have been romance connected to the feeling, but it was the life in Krista that mattered.

And now he felt guilty for feeling alive again when he should still be stuck in the dark place grieving for his dead wife.

Richert and I had more in common than he'd ever know.

"Can I get you all anything to drink?" Richert was still standing. The perfect host. "Ice tea? Water? A beer?"

Leah and I said no thanks in tandem, and Richert finally sat down in the chair opposite us.

"Before you ask your questions, I have one of my own." He looked at Leah.

"Sure." She smiled. "What would you like to know?"

"Why did you choose Mr. Cahill here to investigate your sister's death?" He continued to look at Leah and not at me. "I'm sure there were a lot of equally qualified private investigators to choose from."

I didn't take offense. As with Grimes, I was long past caring what people thought of me. I looked at Leah. Well, most people.

"Because Rick was Krista's partner a long time ago, and she always told me he was a good cop and a good man. And he's a damn good private investigator."

One for my side.

"So, you know about his wife?"

"Yes, and I know he didn't kill her."

"Hmm." Richert folded his arms and settled back in his chair, having performed his Good Samaritan deed. He couldn't help it if Leah didn't share his concern.

"My turn?" I smiled.

"Go right ahead." He flicked a hand at me.

"You mentioned in the letter that you'd told Krista about something you saw in Santa Barbara a long time ago. What was it?"

"I knew that's why you came all the way down here." He was looking at me, now. Not in a friendly way. "I'm going to tell you the truth. What I saw and what you already know."

The hair on my neck spiked and a shiver chilled my entire body.

This.

Now.

After all these years. The words stuck tight in my throat. Blocking off oxygen. I finally pushed them out.

"What did you see?"

"I better give some background first so it makes sense."

"Okay." I'd waited fourteen years. How much longer would I have to wait?

"I used to be a delivery captain and sail rich people's yachts from Santa Barbara, LA, or San Diego to Hawaii and back to the mainland. Rich folks like their boats available to tour around in when they're on vacation, but most of them aren't capable or don't want to sail them across the Pacific Ocean. Especially when they can go to and from in a mere six hours on a plane." Richert looked at the photo on the end table next to the sofa of his late wife sitting on the bow of a boat. "Lily went with me many times. She was the best first mate I ever had."

"Those must have been grand times." I needed to know what he saw. Now. "How does it tie in to what you told Krista?"

"Back in 2005 a man I'd worked for a few times hired me to sail his yacht from Santa Barbara to Honokohau Harbor in Kona. The Mirage, a sixty-foot Hinckley schooner in Bristol condition. I was anchored off of East Beach in Santa Barbara the night before we set sail." He glared at me, but I was way beyond his glares. I needed his truth.

East Beach was where Colleen's body was discovered on the morning of April 19, 2005. My heart raced. Had Richert seen her killer? He stopped talking and looked at me. Studying me. Torturing me?

"And?"

"And I saw you and another man dump something on the beach." He nodded his head and leaned back in his chair.

"What?" Leah whipped her head at me, eyes wide.

"Two people? You saw two people?" I asked Richert, realizing the trip down to Oceanside had been a waste of time. A wasted day.

Richert was making the whole thing up. There was one set of footprints walking away from the body. But they'd been obscured, like the killer had dragged his feet to make identification of his shoes impossible. It had worked, but it didn't stop SBPD from checking my shoes for sand. And they found some on my tennis shoes. Just like they'd find on the shoes of the 85,000 other people who lived in Santa Barbara at the time. Why live in Santa Barbara if you didn't stroll on the beaches?

Colleen and I did it often. In the beginning.

"That's what I saw. You and another guy." Defiant.

"Give me the specifics from when you first saw two men on the beach." I could feel Leah's eyes on me. Her uncertainty about me would soon evaporate after I exposed Mike Richert for the fraud he was. "Start from the beginning."

"Lily and the crew were asleep, but I always had a hard time sleeping the night before I sailed someone else's million-dollar boat across the ocean. I left the cabin about one a.m. and walked around the deck, making last-minute checks for the ninth or tenth time in the moonlight. The routine was the same every time we sailed.

Anyway, some movement on the shore caught my eye. A dark blob with four legs moving on the beach. I went down below to the navigation station and grabbed the binoculars. When I returned to the deck, I saw the backs of two men walking up the beach toward the road."

"So you didn't actually see them dump something on the beach."

"No." He raised his chin. "I didn't actually see you dump the body on the beach because the beach is on a rise and it was low tide. I could only see you and your accomplice from the knees up, but I could fill in the blanks. You two were carrying something that you dumped on the beach when I went to grab my binoculars. I'll swear to it in a court of law."

I ignored the accusation.

"What was the date?" Maybe Richert hadn't made the whole thing up but had just confused the date.

"It would have been early morning on April 19th, 2005."

He got the date right.

"How can you be so sure after all these years?"

"I'll show you why I'm so sure." He sprang from his chair quicker than I'd expected a man in his seventies could manage. He hurried down the hall of his home and came back with an old leather notebook a minute later. He snapped the notebook down on the end table and thumbed through it until he stopped on a page and pointed to handwritten notes. "See. Right here. April 19, 2005, 6:08 a.m. Set sail for Kona on Phil Russell's schooner."

"Where exactly on East Beach was this?"

Maybe he wasn't lying but was off a different section of the beach. Maybe two guys dumped some trash a quarter mile from where Colleen died and he was there to see it.

"Just west of the volleyball courts and Butterfly Beach. That's where we always anchored our boats in Santa Barbara. Quiet at night. Away from the hotels."

Colleen's body had been dumped near the volleyball courts, but he could have read that in the newspaper.

"Let's go back to the two men and what they were wearing. Did you see their faces?"

"No, but one of them was wearing a police uniform." More chin raising.

Many of the news reports at the time of Colleen's murder stated that I'd been alone on patrol that night and had an hour and a half of unaccounted time. Now I knew Richert was lying. He'd obviously gotten the cop angle off a news report. I wondered if he'd told Krista the same story. She knew the truth about my alibi and knew this guy was lying. The Krista I remembered would have called him out on it and set him straight. Yet, Richert had sent her a fawning letter a few days later. That didn't check.

"But you said by the time you looked through the binoculars at around one a.m. in the morning all you could see were the backs of the men. How can you be so sure one was a cop? There's no insignia or markings on the back of a police uniform."

"His belt. It was one of those utility belts with a gun holstered on his right hip." He folded his arms again and pushed back in his chair. "That's how I could tell it was a cop."

"How was the other man dressed?" Since I was obviously the cop in Richert's mind.

"In dark clothes. I think he had a watchman's cap on too."

"You mean a knit ski cap, right?"

"Yeah. In my day we called them watchmen's caps." Arms still folded, barely tolerating the killer he'd let into his house. "But I didn't get as good a look at him."

"Why not?" Because you hadn't fleshed out in your mind what he looked like because you were too focused conjuring up images of me.

"Because they left the beach single file and the cop brought up the rear."

A bolt of adrenaline shot through my body and ramrodded my spine. "What did you say?"

"They left the beach single file." Richert narrowed his eyes on me. "Like I said, by the time I got my binoculars, they were already walking away. I only caught glimpses of the man in the watch cap because he was taller than the cop and the cop looked like he was taking long strides and maybe dragging his feet. Each step brought his head down, and I'd get a glimpse of the other guy's head and shoulders."

My temperature spiked to fever level and my face blew hot. Sweat bubbled out of me. Richert was telling the truth. The foot-dragged tracks hadn't been in the media. The only reason I knew about it was because Grimes accused me of covering my tracks when he had me in the box. Unless Krista somehow let it slip when she questioned Richert.

Impossible.

If Richert was telling the truth, that meant at least one of the people who killed Colleen was a police officer. I'd suspected whoever stole Krista's files had been a cop, but this confirmed it. Made it real. A brother in blue. Did I know him? SBPD was a small force. Had I sat next to him at roll call? Shared a laugh at a barbecue? Tipped beer mugs at Paddy's Pub after end of watch? All these years of searching the internet for clues on my own, pestering the department for information and he'd been among them all along.

I tried to remember who had been at roll call the night Colleen was murdered. Yates and Seeger usually rode together when I patrolled alone in a U car. Had they been working that night? Martinez and O'Neal? They were a Dick and Jane team. Couldn't have been them. Carty and Scholl? I couldn't remember. Richert thought it was one man in uniform and one in civilian clothes. It couldn't have been a two-man patrol. Someone from the station on Figueroa?

Whoever it was, I had to know them.

"Fuck!" I slammed my fist down on the end table and shot up to my feet. The picture of Richert's wife tumbled onto the floor.

Richert threw his hands up to defend himself in his chair. Leah's eyes and mouth gaped round.

"Sorry." I paced back and forth in front of the couch.

"That's okay, son." Richert studied me and rubbed his chin. "It wasn't you, was it?"

"No."

"I'm sorry about the accusations."

"No need. You're not alone." I sat down and slid my hand across my brow and wiped the sweat onto my jeans.

"Losing your wife and then having people think you're guilty must be a terrible burden to bear."

My guilt was my burden.

"What did the police say when you told them what you saw?" I asked.

"Well, that's the thing, I didn't tell them until about five years ago."

"What?" My adrenaline red-lined. If Richert had spoken up at the time of the murder, SBPD might have caught Colleen's killers. Just like they might have if I'd given them my real alibi when they first questioned me and freed them to look for someone else.

"Like I said, Mr. Cahill." Richert twisted in his chair and a hint of pink hued through his leathery skin. "I didn't know at the time that it was significant. It was just two men on a beach like any other night. We set sail later that morning at six a.m. We spent a month in Hawaii then sailed the schooner to Tahiti and spent another month there."

"The case was still in the news two months later. It was the murder of the century to the *Santa Barbara Independent*. They did weekly updates." And harassed me almost daily. Phone calls to my unlisted number. Camping outside my apartment along with Channel 3

News. The press pushed me back to my hometown of San Diego as much as SBPD's suspicion.

"We didn't sail the boat back to Santa Barbara." His hands opened in front of him and his eyebrows rose. "The owner wanted it down in Newport Beach so we sailed it there. We were living in Seal Beach at the time but were only home about three months that year. The rest of the time we were sailing rich people's yachts around the world. I didn't even know about your wife's murder. In fact, the way I found out was by watching a *48 Hours* rerun on Investigation ID five years ago. When they gave the date of your wife's murder and where they found her body, I remembered that night off East Beach and realized the date fit."

"Who did you talk to at the police department?" Five years ago. Grimes had already retired and become a private investigator. The case had gone cold by then—no one would have been actively working it. Did Richert's call even go in the file?

"First I spoke to whoever answered the phone and told them I had information about Colleen Cahill's murder. He transferred me to someone, but I forgot his name. As I told Miss Landingham, I wrote his name down but can't find the damn pad I wrote it on. Either I or Lily must have accidently thrown it away. I feel badly about that because I could tell Miss Landingham thought it was important. I'm still looking for it."

"Did anyone from the police department ever call you back?"

"No."

"Did Krista say how she came across your name?"

"Yes. She said she found my name in a file."

"Did she already know what you reported to the police on your phone call?"

"No. I told her when she called me."

The information about what Richert reported should have been in the file along with the name of the cop who took the call. Why weren't they?

"Why did she come down here to talk to you in person?" Leah asked.

I knew the answer. Krista thought she might be able to get more out of Richert if she was physically in front of him. Take cues from his body language, maybe ask the right question that would unlock a memory hidden away through time.

"I told her I'd been waiting five years for someone to follow up on my call. I think she wanted me to know that someone was taking me seriously," Richert said.

Doubted it, but why burst a lonely man's bubble?

CHAPTER TWENTY

"Wow." Leah sat in the passenger's seat of the car and looked at me. "That was quite a story."

"Do you believe it?" I asked.

"I think I do." Leah pushed a stray strand of blond hair out of her eyes. "You might be right about Krista's death being related to your wife's."

"Yep." I knew I was right before we made the trip. But now, I had a pool of suspects. Cops working at SBPD the night Colleen was murdered. At least one of them.

"But I'm not sure one of the people Mr. Richert saw was really a policeman. I can't believe a policeman would kill your wife."

"Grimes did when he arrested me." I started the car.

"I guess you're right." She didn't look convinced. "What now?"

"Back up to Santa Barbara to tell Grimes what we found out."

Maybe he'd have an idea who Richert talked to on the phone at SBPD. Maybe he could get a look at Colleen's case file with Krista's updates after her talk with Richert. At least one cop knew her death and Colleen's were connected. And if Krista told him what she learned from Mike Richert, that probably got her killed.

"Can you call him instead of telling him in person? It would be nice to stretch our legs and get something to eat before we drive back."

Leah smiled but the sadness that had been in her eyes since Krista's service dug deeper. "It feels good to be out of Santa Barbara for a while. Even with what we learned today, I need a break from . . . from all the bad memories up there."

I knew how she felt, but I had the scent now, and it led back to Colleen's murder. I wanted to get a visual read on Grimes when I told him what we learned before he relayed it to SBPD.

"It might be best to head back now."

"Really?" Sad blue eyes that had felt too much sadness lately.

"I guess I could check on my dog and make sure my neighbor is okay with keeping him a few more days."

"I get to meet your dog?" Leah smiled, turned, and put her hand on my knee. "I love dogs."

"But you don't have one."

"I did. Had to put her down a year ago. Elfie. A boxer. Every time I think about getting a new one, I feel like I'm cheating on her. Discounting how much she meant to me."

"You are a dog lover." I patted her hand, still on my leg. It felt right there. Even though I knew it wasn't, it felt right. "We'll get something to eat and then I'll introduce you to Midnight."

"Yay! Can we get fish tacos at Rubio's?"

"We can get them at a number of places. San Diego is the fish taco capital of America."

"I want Rubio's." Smile still beaming. "My family used to go down to San Diego on vacation in the summer when I was a child. We stayed in Pacific Beach and always got fish tacos at Rubio's. The original one. Let's go there."

"Done."

The sun occasionally peeked through the haze on our thirty mile drive south from Oceanside. By the time we got to PB, the sun had burned off the gray and shone the postcard weather people from out of town associate with San Diego. They feel gypped when they arrive for vacation the first week of summer and experience June Gloom.

Even Paradise gets overcast.

We got to Rubio's a little after three, and I parked behind the fast-causal restaurant in the tiny parking lot. We picked a good time, between lunch and dinner. The original Rubio's didn't look a thing like its modern strip-mall offspring. A small stand-alone building with corrugated metal siding around the roof at the end of a block dominated by car dealerships. It had once been an Orange Julius. Before I was born.

We both ordered two taco plates of the original and ate our food under the straw tiki hut on the back patio.

"This brings back such memories," Leah said, taco in hand, white sauce smudged at the corner of her mouth. "Good memories."

I reached a napkin over and wiped the sauce off her lip.

"Thanks." She grabbed my hand as I pulled it away from her face.

"That was more for me than you. I don't want people to think I hang out with slobs. We're in my hometown now."

"No. Thanks for taking me here."

"I'm glad it brought back some good memories." Something we both needed as much as the food.

"I remember eating here and all the surfers checking Krista out. She'd lay out all summer and get golden brown. I thought I had the most beautiful big sister in the world. So did the surfers."

Her smiled faded and her eyes lost their gleam. She'd stepped out of the memory. Krista wasn't her teenage big sister anymore. She was the dead woman Leah'd seen put in the ground two days ago.

"Why did your family come all the way down here in the summer when you had beautiful beaches in Santa Barbara?"

"We lived in Buellton, an hour north of Santa Barbara. Land-locked. We couldn't afford to live in Santa Barbara when my dad was just a patrolman. He commuted an hour to and from SBPD every day. The hotels around the beaches here are cheaper than in Santa Barbara, plus you have Sea World and the zoo and lots of other things to do. Santa Barbara is tiny compared to San Diego."

"Where would you stay?".

"Best Western most of the time."

"My favorite."

"Huh?"

"Never mind."

"One year we stayed at the Catamaran Hotel when my dad splurged. Can we drive by there when were done?"

"Sure."

I paid for lunch. This one I wouldn't expense.

We drove over to the Catamaran, a landmark hotel right on Mission Bay with views of the ocean to go along with those of the bay. We walked around the grounds and the bay. Leah pointed out spots where Krista and she laid out in the sun and the spot where Krista bummed a beer from a twentysomething dude. She'd light up with a new story about an old memory every few minutes.

I was glad I'd taken her advice and delayed the drive north. Seeing Leah smile was suddenly important to me.

I took Leah to my home after we spent an hour chasing her memories. I parked in the driveway, and we walked next door to pick up Midnight. Leah knelt down and took all the licks to her face that Midnight could give.

"He's a love." She wiped her face and finally stood up. "How old is he?"

"Eight."

"He seems like a pup."

"He's a lab. They have extended adolescence." He did have the energy of a puppy, but the heart of a lion. He saved my life once. And saved me from debilitating depression more times than I could count. Plus, he loved the ladies and they loved him.

We walked back to my house, and I suddenly remembered the condition I'd left it in when I departed for Santa Barbara two days ago. The same condition it had been in for months since I lost the reins to my life. Didn't lose them, really. Just dropped them. When I picked them up again, it would be to steer my life in a different direction. My time as a private investigator was coming to an end.

Santa Barbara was my last case.

I opened the back door of my Accord and Midnight jumped in.

"Where are we going?" Leah stood next to the car but didn't open the door.

"Fiesta Island. On the other side of the bay from the Catamaran. There's a huge dog park there. I owe Midnight a swim."

"You're not going to give me a tour of your home first?"

"You and I have different ideas about interior design."

*   *   *

We got to Fiesta Island by five thirty p.m. Midnight chased after his buddy, a massive Great Dane named Brutus, and body slammed into him when he caught up. At eighty-five pounds of pure muscle, Midnight bounced off the beast, which was twice his weight. The Great Dane shifted a couple inches at impact. I waved at the Dane's owner down the beach and let Midnight cavort in the water and up a sandy berm and back again. And again.

Leah and I walked along the shoreline trailing behind.

"I never knew about this place when we came down to San Diego."

"Dog heaven. Especially for a water dog like Midnight."

"You've made a nice life down here, Rick. After all you've been through." She looped her arm around mine. I put my hand in my pocket to lock her arm in. Like I would with a girlfriend. Natural. Easy. Too easy.

The life she'd thought I'd made was a façade. Like the walls of my home hiding the mess inside. I didn't have a life. I had a quest. A hero's journey in quest of "the truth" as if it were something etched in stone. Bold print in black and white. It had turned into a fool's errand. Death, destruction, and empty dreams strewn behind me as I followed my quest. Was Leah the next casualty in my hunt for the one truth that mattered above all others? The truth about Colleen's murder. Leah had suffered enough with Krista's death. How could I bring her into my life, let her care for me, and then reveal who I really was?

When I found Colleen's killers and executed them.

"It's not as nice as it seems." I pulled my hand from my pocket and freed Leah's arm.

CHAPTER TWENTY-ONE

I LED MIDNIGHT through the side gate into the backyard when we got home. Leah followed. We didn't talk much after I disengaged on the beach. I felt badly about it. For me as much as Leah, but that's the way it had to be. Better to kill the relationship now before it mattered too much to both of us.

I washed Midnight with a hose and shampoo in the faltering sunlight.

"It's nice back here." Leah stood on the deck and looked out to the ocean barely visible miles away. "Peaceful."

She was right. The backyard was my sanctuary from the chaos of my life. I spent many a late night sitting on the deck drinking a beer and losing myself. Sometimes.

I unlocked the kitchen door to go in and fetch a towel to dry off Midnight. Leah followed me over. I turned to face her.

"Would you mind waiting out here?" I felt stupid as soon as the words left my mouth.

"Yes, I would." She shook her head defiantly. "I want you to show me your home."

"It's currently uninhabitable. Nothing to see but months of mess."

"I want to see your house."

Maybe it was the interior designer in her that made her persist. See the inside of someone's house and see their soul. Maybe that's what she needed to see. The disorder I'd been living in would be the final nick to sever any thoughts she had about the two of us.

I opened the door to let her enter then followed her into the kitchen. Ground zero for the mess my life had become. She looked at the sink overflowing with dirty dishes. The butcher block island covered in fast-food container detritus and newspapers. No expression.

"You want the whole tour or is this enough to get us back on the road toward civilization?" I swung my hand around like a *Price Is Right* model.

"You must be in so much pain."

Shit.

"No. I'm just a slob."

"Show me upstairs." Her blue eyes pierced my skull. Saw through the disorder, the walls, the desperation. And found the need. To connect physically. Emotionally. To feel something other than pain.

"Three bedrooms and two baths. Slightly less messy than down here but nothing special." I had rules that superseded needs.

Leah walked past me out of the kitchen and through the living room. She stopped at the staircase and looked at me, then went up the stairs.

I grabbed a towel from the laundry room and went back outside to dry Midnight.

I had rules.

When I got back to my house after dropping Midnight back next door, I thought about sitting in the car and waiting Leah out. But that was too much of a jerk even for me. I went inside. No Leah on the bottom floor. I went upstairs and checked my office, then the spare bedroom that I'd kept empty when I first bought the house. The nursery that Colleen and I dreamed about when we lived in the one-bedroom apartment in Santa Barbara. After a year, I finally gave up ghosts and made it a guest room for the living.

I found Leah in my bedroom. Fully clothed, sitting on the end of my unmade bed in the dark gray light of dusk. She was looking at a photo album I'd pulled out of a bottom bureau drawer the day I found out Krista was dead. It contained my cop career as documented by Colleen. No documentation of my final days on the job.

The album was open on Leah's lap to a photo from one of her sister's barbecues. Krista and her husband, Leah and her boyfriend, and Colleen and I stood smiling at the camera. We all looked truly happy. I had been happy then. Colleen and I hadn't hit our rough patch yet. The one we were still in when she was murdered. The one that had her tell a friend she was contemplating divorce. Maybe that's how we would have ended up. Divorced. But at least she'd still be alive.

A tear rolled down Leah's cheek as she stared down at the picture. I sat next to her and slowly pulled the album away and set it down on the floor. She put her head on my shoulder.

"I miss her so much," she said. More tears and gasps came.

I held her in my arms and stroked her hair. And fought back my own tears. For Colleen. For Krista. And for Leah, knowing that her tears will dry and eventually come less often, but the pain will never go away.

We sat quietly for a few minutes. Leah felt right in my arms and I was sorry for the circumstances. But not that she was in my arms. She looked up at me, then put her hand on the back of my neck and pulled my head down to her.

I forgot about the rules.

My lips to hers. Hers to mine. Tentative and soft, then eager and hard. She pulled off her blouse and unclipped her bra. I hesitated.

"I need you, Rick. Now." She held my face in her hands. "I need to know I'm alive and still human."

I took off my shirt.

* * *

"I have a confession to make." Leah rested her hand on my chest in the dark. "This has nothing to do with what just happened. But I had a crush on you when you worked at SBPD."

I had a confession to make, too. One I should have stated before we made love. Now I didn't know if I could say it. If I told Leah that Krista and I had had sex the night Colleen was murdered, would I be doing it to clear my conscience or did I owe her the truth? All of it. Would clearing my conscience be a fair trade for making Leah feel awful? Would not telling her be starting off whatever this was between us with a lie?

My rules weren't arbitrary. They came from wisdom earned through life's mistakes. And if I'd followed the most sacred of them, Colleen would still be alive.

"Thanks for telling me," I said. "But I understand that what just happened was something different."

"Yes, but it was more to me than that, Rick. I wouldn't have made love to just anyone who was with me today after going through all of this." She rolled her head onto my chest. "Yes, I had a crush on you way back when and still do. There, I said it. But I know that you're hurting like I am. In pain for Krista and Colleen. It may sound weird, but I wanted to connect with that pain. To merge it with what I'm feeling for Krista. To give it more meaning. Do you think I'm crazy?"

"No. I understand." And I did. Pain, even grief for a lost loved one, needs a greater meaning. Something so debilitating and lasting had to mean more than just the end of a life.

"Krista changed after Colleen was murdered. You weren't around much longer in Santa Barbara, but she changed. She never seemed as happy as she was before. Her marriage went to hell. Even all these years later, there wasn't enough joy in her life. I know she liked

Colleen, but I didn't think they were close friends. Yet her death really affected Krista."

I knew Krista felt some of the guilt for Colleen's death that I did from the last conversation we ever had. I guess I didn't know how much.

"Colleen's death had lasting repercussions for a lot of people. Her family never recovered." Although, her father did finally stop his annual call to me around Colleen's birthday to scream expletives and call me a murderer. Maybe that was part of his recovery.

"You know, Krista loved you." Leah propped her head up and looked at me.

"I loved her, too. We were brothers and sisters in blue. She taught me all I ever knew as a cop."

"Not like that. She *loved you* loved you." Leah studied my face. "She told me after you left Santa Barbara and came down here to live. But she felt guilty about it. Not just because she was married. I never thought she should have married Tom in the first place. She felt guilty because she fell in love with you and then Colleen was murdered. I think she somehow felt responsible."

"What else did she tell you?"

"What do you mean?"

"About us. Krista and me?"

"I didn't know there was a Krista and you." Leah sat up.

I sat up, too.

"There wasn't." I searched for her eyes in the dark. "Except for one night."

"What are you saying?" She folded her arms in front of her, covering her breasts.

"We had a one-night stand." I looked at Leah but she stared down at the bed. "It was a first for me. I'm pretty sure it was for her, too. I knew she was in a loveless marriage but she still honored it. Until that night."

Leah got off the bed and grabbed her clothes from the floor, pressing them against her body to conceal her nakedness. "Well, now you've fucked both Landingham sisters and it only took two one-night stands. Congratulations."

She ran into the master bathroom and slammed the door.

I jumped out of bed, went to the bathroom door, and softly knocked. "Leah, I'm sorry. I should have told you . . . before. I didn't want you to think less of Krista. Especially now. But tonight was about you and me. Nobody else."

The water in the shower went on. No doubt to scrub any remnants of me off her.

I had rules for a reason. Unfortunately, they only worked if I followed them.

CHAPTER TWENTY-TWO

I UNLOCKED THE gun safe in my closet while Leah was in the shower and grabbed a Mossberg tactical shotgun, a Smith & Wesson .357 Magnum, and a Glock 9mm pistol and three boxes of ammo. I hustled downstairs and put them into the trunk of my car alongside the Ruger .357 snub-nose I always had with me. If Mike Richert was right and two people killed Colleen, two cops, I had to be ready to go to war.

I would have been ready with just my bare hands but given the choice, I wouldn't be outgunned.

I packed a suitcase with a week's worth of clothes then showered after Leah left the bathroom, walking silently past me.

The silence continued for the first two hours of our drive north.

"Why just the one night?" Leah finally spoke after we got onto the 405.

"Why just one night what?"

"With Krista. You said it was a one-night stand."

I would have preferred another two hours of silence.

"I don't see the point in talking about something that happened so long ago."

"You talked about it less than three hours ago." Leah's eyes drilled into the side of my face. "Humor me."

"I think we both realized it was a mistake."

I did the moment I got out of Krista's bed and saw myself in her mirror. Someone I didn't recognize. A man who cheats on his wife with another man's wife. Another cop's wife. But beyond all that, I knew I'd lost the best person I'd ever known. Not just by my actions that night, but over months of taking Colleen for granted, for showing her my worst self instead of working to be a better person. I wanted her back. I wanted to be the man she fell in love with. The man that took the best of me to become. I wanted to give her the life she deserved. I vowed to myself right then to make it up to her. Even if I had to quit being a cop.

An empty oath to myself. The next time I saw Colleen she was on a coroner's table.

"When did it happen? The one night?"

"What difference does that make?"

"Because I remember how happy you and Colleen were when I first met you at one of Krista's barbecues. That would have been quite an acting job if you just screwed the host of the party. I want to know what kind of man I'm dealing with."

What kind of man.

"It doesn't make any difference when it was. I cheated on my wife. I cheated with the wife of another cop. That's who you're dealing with."

"So, it was when you were seemingly so in love with your wife. Good to know."

I didn't see the need to defend the indefensible. Argue over gradations of immorality. The mask was off. Leah saw me for who I really was. At least who I was back then. Maybe I was still the same man. Maybe I wouldn't know until I was tested in the same way again.

That was the end of conversation for the remainder of the drive. I called Grimes when we were thirty minutes outside of Santa Barbara to set up a time to meet the next day to tell him what I'd learned from

Mike Richert. Ideally it would be best for Leah to be with us in case I left something out. I doubted she'd be up for that now. I put the call on speaker.

"When can you meet tomorrow to discuss what we learned today?" I asked.

"Where are you now?"

"A half hour from Leah's house. Dropping her off then heading back to the Best Western."

"I'm downtown. I can meet you at Miss Landingham's in a half hour."

Not ideal. I'm sure Leah wanted to get rid of me as soon as possible tonight, but it would be best to talk to Grimes when our conversation with Richert was still relatively fresh in our minds. I muted the phone and looked at Leah.

"You want me to schedule something with him tomorrow?"

"No. Let's talk to him tonight." No anger in her voice. A relief. Her desire to find the truth about her sister's death trumped all else.

I unmuted the phone. "We'll see you in thirty."

We beat Grimes to Leah's and silently trudged inside her home. Not a word as we waited for him. Mercifully, the doorbell rang a couple minutes after we arrived. Leah went to the door and let Grimes in. He walked into the living room and spotted me at the dinner table. I wanted the formality of sitting at a table. Grimes and I needed to have a hard conversation.

"Cahill."

"Have a seat." I pulled out the chair at the head of the table.

"Can I get you gentlemen anything to drink?" Leah hovered, nervous. She felt the inborn tension between Grimes and me.

"No thank you," Grimes said and sat down.

"No thanks."

Leah sat down opposite Grimes.

"What did you learn from the letter writer?" he asked.

"His name is Mike Richert, and he thinks he witnessed Colleen's body being dumped on East Beach fourteen years ago."

"What?" Grimes shifted forward in his chair, bumping the table.

I told him everything that Richert told us. Leah filled minute details I missed or thought inconsequential. She didn't miss anything. And she hid her contempt for me brilliantly. Grimes' expression grew darker and darker with each new piece of information.

"And no one from SBPD called him back for five years until Krista did two weeks ago?" The creases between his eyebrows dug deeper.

"Yep. That's what he said."

Leah nodded to confirm my statement.

"Jesus." Grimes ran a hand over his face. "What the hell is going on over at East Figueroa?"

"Five years ago, the case would have been inactive for a while, right?" I asked.

"The brass stuck it in the freezer after Byers and I worked it for three years. Said we couldn't afford the manpower anymore. The only murder case I didn't solve in fifteen years as a homicide detective. I continued to work it every free minute I had for the next two years until I retired."

"And then you investigated it for John Kerrigan when you became a PI."

"For two years. Even he gave up hope after a while."

"What are the chances of you getting a look at Colleen's murder book?" I asked.

"I already have it at home. I made a copy before I retired and took it with me."

"I mean the version since Krista started working a week before she died."

"Zero."

"Even if you don't go through proper channels?"

"There are only proper channels. This is a murder case. Nobody's going to show me anything. Especially with the queen of transparency ruling from on high that MIU can't share anything with me."

"Does that include your talk with Detective Mitchell at Paddy's Pub last night?"

"I never said I was going to talk to Mitchell." Grimes stepping behind the thin blue line, leaving me on the other side.

"Whoever you talked to or didn't talk to, Colleen's murder is the key to Krista's death."

"You don't know that, Cahill. All we know is that someone saw a couple guys possibly carrying something on East Beach one night fourteen years ago. I agree that someone should have followed up with Mr. Richert after he called, but this doesn't prove anything. You can't jump to conclusions on a homicide."

I swallowed what my reflexes wanted me to say. That he and SBPD had jumped to the conclusion that I was Colleen's murderer and focused only on me. But I needed Grimes on my side. Or as close as I could get him to it. Besides, my own stupid actions or inactions had helped keep the department's focus on me.

"Let's look at the facts, Grimes. Mike Richert is sure of the date because he kept track of all the sailing jobs he took. He saw two men, one a cop, dump something on the beach where Colleen was found the night she died. Plus, someone stole Colleen's cold case file from Krista's office. I don't think I'm going out on a limb in believing that whoever killed Colleen killed Krista after she started investigating Colleen's death. Who would have access to the file on Colleen? A cop."

"Oh, you're way out there on a limb. All of this is sheer speculation, Cahill. We don't even know if there were any files there to be stolen. And we don't know if one of the men this Richert fellow thinks he saw on the morning your wife was murdered was a cop or just some-one in dark clothes. This is all supposition fueled by some need to get even with SBPD for arresting you and keeping you as a person of interest. This isn't about you, Cahill. You don't get to come up here and get Miss Landingham caught up in your grand conspiracies."

"I'm a big girl, Jim. Rick's not getting me caught up in anything."

"Somebody at SBPD killed my wife and fourteen years later he killed Krista." I snapped the words off. "You were on the right trail looking for a cop, Grimes. Just the wrong one."

The last sentence was a mistake. I regretted it the moment I said it.

Grimes cop-eyed me then looked at Leah. I wished he would have just continued to mean-mug me. "Did Rick tell you about his alibi on the night of his wife's murder?"

Grimes got up from the table and left the house without another word.

"What did he mean by that?" Leah looked concerned and tired. I'd let Grimes get under my skin and had to one-up him, forgetting that Santa Barbara wasn't about me. It was about Colleen, Krista, and Krista's sister.

"I don't know," I lied. Easily. Too easily. "He hated me before he thought I was a murderer and he still hates me even though he knows I'm not."

"What was your alibi, Rick?"

I could lie to her about something Grimes said and other things, but not about the alibi the night Colleen was murdered. That would cheapen Colleen's life. A throwaway lie thought up on the spot. Her memory deserved better.

I didn't say anything.

"Oh my God." Leah stood up and paced behind the table. "You were with Krista the night Colleen was murdered. Weren't you?"

I stayed silent.

"That's why Krista was so certain you couldn't have killed your wife. Not because she knew you were incapable of it, but because she was with you when it happened. She was your alibi. And that's why she felt guilty."

Silent.

"Why didn't you tell the police where you were? They never would have arrested you. Krista would have vouched for you. Were you trying to save her marriage?"

"I was protecting my reputation. I didn't want other cops to know that I broke the code and betrayed them. Or have Colleen's family and my own know that I cheated on her the night she was murdered."

"You were willing to go to prison for the rest of your life to protect your reputation?"

"I would have told the truth if the DA had decided to go to trial."

"Why didn't Krista go to Grimes on her own?"

"I talked her out of it. More for her marriage to the job than to Weaver. She'd be a pariah at SBPD just like I would have been if I told Grimes."

"Instead, *48 Hours* did a show on Colleen's death and half the country thought you killed your wife. Some probably still do. Was all of that worth it just to hide the fact that you slept with another cop's wife?"

"That's the rub, isn't it?"

"I'm glad you see the humor in it."

My life was nothing but laughs.

"I'll update you via email if I learn anything new. Otherwise, I'll leave the week's report to Grimes. Goodnight, Leah." I walked into the foyer and opened the door.

"Do you think Tom knew about you two?" Leah walked over to me. "Krista's marriage got even worse around the time Colleen died."

"Not unless Krista told him. Neither of us told anyone. You were not only her sister but her best friend. She would have told you if she told anyone. No way Tom could have known. He was out of town that night working a case."

"No he wasn't."

CHAPTER TWENTY-THREE

"What are you talking about?" I closed the door. "He was up in Fresno interviewing a witness on a drug bust. He drove up that day and stayed overnight."

"No, he was home that night. I saw his detective car in their driveway. My boyfriend at the time lived a few blocks from Krista and Tom, and I drove right by their house on the way to his." Leah put a finger to her lips. "Now the cop car makes sense."

"What?"

"The police cruiser I saw parked in front of Krista's house. That must have been you. So, you were on duty when you and Krista . . ."

"What time was this?" I asked.

"I don't know the exact time, but it was probably around ten p.m."

I'd stopped by Krista's on my dinner break around nine thirty p.m. We'd gotten into the habit of meeting for coffee and bitching about our marriages. The last couple bitch sessions had been different. Krista was flirtatious. Subtle at first, but more overt at the last meet. I'd eaten it up. The woman I respected more than anyone, even Colleen at the end, was giving me the attention I wasn't getting at home anymore. And I gave her the attention I wasn't giving at home anymore. There'd always been a hint of attraction that I tamped down like a married man should. But I'd let my ego out that night. I'd known Weaver was out of town when Krista invited me to swing by.

And I knew what it could lead to. What down deep, where my id roamed wild, I hoped it would lead to.

"How can you be sure this wasn't some other night?" I needed to know what other collateral damage Krista and I had caused that night. "Sounds like you had a routine."

"I probably wouldn't remember if I hadn't found out the next day that Colleen had been murdered." She frowned. "Something like that gives you acute focus about things surrounding it. Plus, there were two things that weren't routine about Krista's house that night. The police cruiser parked outside and Tom's detective car in the driveway. Krista told me that morning that he was out of town, so it was odd to see his car there that night."

"How do you know it was Tom's detective car? It could have been anyone's." But that would have meant some other detective was parked in Krista's driveway that night. If so, what did they see?

"Krista told me Tom always made sure he got the only black Crown Victoria. She thought it was kind of sad that he made such a big deal about it. All his cars had to be black. He'd never drive her car because it was white. All the cars she owned while they were married were white. I think she chose the color on purpose to piss Tom off."

The uneasiness of the night Krista and I were together came back to me. I'd felt a sense of dread mixed with sick excitement the whole time I was with Krista. I later came to associate the dread with Colleen's disappearance and then death. A sense of foreboding that something was wrong and outside of my control. But what if it was the sense of being watched? What if Tom came home early to surprise his wife in hopes of putting some romance back in his marriage and he saw me in his bed with Krista instead?

"You're a hundred percent sure it was the night Colleen was murdered?" I asked.

"One hundred percent." She nodded

"If that was Tom's car in the driveway, he was there when I was with Krista. And he wasn't there when we were done. He must have seen us. Where did he go when he left? He never came home later that night, and as far as Krista knew, he was still up in Fresno. No one at SBPD verified his whereabouts because no one considered him a suspect."

"Are you telling me you think Tom killed Colleen as some sort of sick revenge?" Leah's eyes went round.

"I don't know, but he has to be considered a suspect."

I was in bed with Krista from around ten to eleven. The coroner put Colleen's death between ten p.m. and midnight. I missed two calls from Colleen and a couple radio calls when I was in bed with Krista that left me unaccounted for during Colleen's death window. Tom Weaver was unaccounted for a lot longer.

"That's a pretty large leap, Rick. Why not just kill you and Krista right then? Or at least confront you? Tom isn't the kind of guy to just walk away."

"I don't know why he didn't confront me, but we both know his slick top was parked in the driveway while I was there and it was gone when I left around eleven p.m. When he was supposed to still be in Fresno."

"How would he even know where Colleen was that night? She wasn't murdered at home. Her body was found on East Beach."

"Yes, but she was at the UC Santa Barbara library until it closed at ten p.m. She was there every weeknight. We had a routine. I'd pick her up in my squad car and take her home every night around ten p.m. I didn't tell anybody at SBPD about it because I was breaking regs. The only person I ever told was Krista. What if she'd told Tom in passing and he remembered it the night he saw the two of us together?"

"I don't know." Leah shook her head. "Tom is capable of a lot of things, but I don't think murder is one of them. Maybe in a rage, but not premeditated"

"People can surprise and disappoint you." I'd already proven that to her today.

"But remember that Mr. Richert said he saw two people on the beach and one of them was wearing a uniform. You think Tom pulled some cop friend off his beat to help him dispose of Colleen's body after he murdered her? That's way out there, Rick."

"I don't know what to believe, but Tom has to be eliminated as a suspect first before we go any further."

"But if he murdered Colleen, then you're saying he killed Krista, too?" Leah's eyes blinked three or four times.

"I'm ninety percent convinced the two are connected despite what Grimes thinks. And I think you are, too."

"I'm not as sure as you are and even less so about Tom. I don't think he could kill Krista."

"Then let's eliminate him." I raised my hands, palms open. "Have you two remained close?"

"We were never close, but we're on friendly terms whenever we see each other."

"Okay. Call him tomorrow morning and ask him to come over." I shook my head. "No. Better yet, ask him to meet you at Krista's house. Say you need to show him something."

"What?"

"Tell him it would be better if he saw it on his own first. Can you do that?"

"I guess so." She nodded. "Where will you be?"

"With you. We're going to ambush him. Get him off balance and see how he reacts."

"Okay. I'll play along, but Tom can be pretty unpleasant when he's upset."

"That's fine. So can I." I put my hand back on the doorknob. "I'll be by tomorrow morning at eight to set everything up."

Leah put her hand on my arm. "You must be as hungry as I am. Let me feed you before you go."

We didn't stop for dinner on the drive up from San Diego. That would have just added to our silent time together. Now Leah invited me to stay. Not just from good manners. She'd forgiven me. And that mattered.

"That would be great."

"But only if you can stand lasagna again."

*   *   *

We finished with a second glass of wine after dinner on the couch.

"Why do you always take the hard way out?" Leah was genuinely curious, not angry.

"I'm not sure what you mean?" But I think I was.

"I accused you of some awful things after you told me about you and Krista." She set her wineglass down and inched closer to me. "Why did you let me believe the worst about you? That one night you spent with Krista ended up being the worst night of your life. Why didn't you defend yourself?"

"The facts don't change with the date of the adultery."

"You did an immoral thing. You cheated on your wife, but people do bad things and are forgiven. They move on with their lives. You haven't. You committed adultery a long time ago. You're a better man now."

"Colleen died because I was with Krista when I should have been at the library picking her up. Those facts will never change no matter how much I loved Colleen. She's dead because of me. She didn't get the chance to see whatever supposed better man I've become."

Leah took my hand and leaned close to my face. Her searing blue eyes pierced mine. "You have to forgive yourself, Rick. You can't change the past. You have to live your life. A new life."

Someone I loved told me the same thing once. That I was a better man and had to forgive myself. I never could. She married someone else and they're raising a daughter together.

"I should probably go." I didn't feel like defending my lack of defense. "Thanks for the lasagna. Still good on day two. And thanks for . . . well, just thanks."

Leah leaned forward and kissed me. I kissed her back, then stood up.

"It's been a long, hard day." Leah stood and held my hands in hers. "But it's still been the best day I've had since Krista died. I'm sorry I got upset about you and Krista. I overreacted. I apologize."

"No need." I didn't want an apology. That just made what I did worse. "I should have been more up front with you. I didn't expect things to go . . . where they went."

"Neither did I, but they did, and I don't want to change anything." She squeezed my hands and stared at me through eyes the color of the ocean just after sunrise. "Stay here tonight. I need . . . I don't want to be alone tonight."

"Okay." You can't unbreak a rule once it's broken. But you didn't have to break it again. Unless you were trying to start that new life.

Leah led me to her bedroom. She took off her clothes with her back to me, then got into bed. I took off mine and slid under the covers. She rolled over and turned off the light on the nightstand. I found her in the dark and held her from behind. She cradled my arm and gently kissed it.

"I just want to be held." Her voice, a whisper in the dark. "Okay?"

"Sure." I pressed my body against hers and felt her soft warmth, letting it flow through my body. Allowed myself to melt into it. Leah's breaths grew long and far apart. My own caught her rhythm and I fell asleep. And dreamed.

* * *

Colleen and I were walking hand in hand along Stearns Wharf under the stars. She looked at me, her blue eyes sparkling with joy. Content. Loved. The look that always filled my soul. Suddenly, I was on East Beach. Colleen lying bruised and beaten in the sand. Red ligature marks around her neck. Dead. I bent down to pick her up, and her eyes snapped open.

I woke with a hush, soaked in sweat, lying on my back. Still dark. Still night. Still in Leah's bed. The dread and guilt from the night Colleen died dug an endless pit in my stomach. I looked over at Leah sleeping peacefully on her side. Sister of the woman I'd cheated with the night Colleen was murdered. She was Leah down in San Diego, in my home where Colleen had never been. But here in Santa Barbara, where I married Colleen, she'd always be Krista's sister.

I quietly got out of bed, picked up my clothes, left Leah's bedroom, and slept on the couch in the living room. Or tried to. The couch was comfortable enough to sleep on, but my mind wasn't.

CHAPTER TWENTY-FOUR

LEAH CAME OUT of her bedroom in a robe at eight a.m. I'd put on a clean pair of jeans and a t-shirt I got from my suitcase in the trunk of my car. I hadn't expected to stay at Leah's home after we gave each other the silent treatment on the drive back to Santa Barbara from San Diego.

"There you are." Icy. "When did you get up?"

"A little while ago."

"Hmm." Anger shaded with disappointment in her eyes. "That's strange because I woke up at four and you were gone. I thought you'd gone back to the hotel."

"I wouldn't do that."

"Good to know that's where you draw the line."

I'd been in my own head so much that I'd forgotten why Leah asked me to stay. She needed me to be next to her when she fell asleep and still be there when she woke up. But I couldn't shake the feeling of betraying Colleen. Too late.

"I couldn't sleep so I came out here. I didn't want to wake you with my tossing and turning." I could lie easily on the small stuff. If it kept me from having to tell the truth about the big stuff.

"When do you want me to call Tom?" She didn't believe me. The truth would have been too hard to explain.

* * *

We got to Krista's house by nine a.m. Tom Weaver was due in an hour. Leah had persuaded him on the phone to come over. She was pretty good at lying, too.

We didn't include Grimes in our scheme because I didn't think he'd play along. He might call Weaver to warn him. Grimes was retired, but there was no question where he stood in relation to that thin blue line. And no question where I did, either.

Weaver arrived about ten twenty a.m. I hid in the guest bedroom while Leah escorted him into Krista's study.

"I think someone broke into Krista's file cabinet." Leah's voice. "There are some files missing and scratches on the lock like someone picked it."

"Why didn't you tell me that on the phone?" Weaver, gruff, irritated. "Why the big secret?"

"I was worried you might have been at SBPD and mention something to someone. I don't know who to trust over there."

"Why? Everyone's working hard to find Krista's killer."

"If you say so. Please, just examine the lock."

"All right." A huff. "I'll take a look at it."

This was my cue. Knowing Weaver had entered the office, I could stand in the doorway and block an easy exit.

"Morning, Tom."

Weaver startled and bumped his chin into the file cabinet near the lock, which he'd been examining. He straightened up and puffed out his chest. "What the fuck are you doing here?"

"I was in the neighborhood."

"Bullshit." He turned to Leah who stood on the other side of the desk. "What's this all about?"

"I wanted to see if you agreed with Rick's assessment that the file cabinet was broken into."

"Bullshit."

"No, she's serious," I said. "Did you see the scratches on the lock? Looks like someone went at it with a pick set."

"Those scratches could have come from anything. They could have been there when Krista bought the cabinet. What do you really want, Cahill?"

Weaver wasn't stupid. Or patient. I didn't have much time, but still had to be careful. I couldn't push him too hard too soon.

"I don't know if Krista told you, but she was reinvestigating my wife's murder." I looked at Weaver's face for a tell. Surprise. Faked surprise. Acknowledgment that he already knew. His face didn't change. Still wore the snarl he had when he saw me in the doorway. "She mention anything to you about it?"

"No." Weaver stepped around the desk and managed to squeeze another inch of puff out of his chest. "But everyone already knows who killed your wife, Cahill."

I got the implication. I'd seen it in many forms from too many people to count over the years. But Weaver was one of the few people who knew I couldn't have killed Colleen. He was now my only living alibi. And possibly Colleen's killer.

"Everyone's wrong." I shifted slightly to fill up the doorway. I wasn't going to really block his exit if Weaver tried to push past me. He was a cop. I wasn't stupid. At least not most of the time. But he didn't have to know that. "I know you were up in Fresno interviewing a witness for a case the night Colleen died. Do you know the name of the hotel you stayed in?"

"What?" Weaver scowled at me. "That's none of your business. What's this all about?"

"Just trying to establish where everyone was the night Colleen died. It's general practice to expense a hotel when you are out of town on an investigation." I studied Weaver's eyes. A hint of uncertainty slipped beneath the scowl. "Do you suppose SBPD still has a record of your expense report?"

"What are you implying, Cahill?" Weaver stabbed me in the chest with two fingers like he had at the funeral. "That I killed your wife?"

He side-glanced Leah to make sure she knew how angry he was that she'd set him up.

"I don't know. Did you? Because I know you weren't in Fresno the night Colleen was murdered. You here were in Santa Barbara."

"You're a liar!" Weaver stabbed me again and stuck his face into mine, nose to nose. He wanted me to push him away so he could arrest me. He probably already would have tried to put the cuffs on me if Leah hadn't been there.

"You're right about that. And an adulterer. They tend to go together." Time to flip over my cards. "But you already knew that because you came home from Fresno a day early to surprise Krista and found a different kind of surprise in your bedroom."

I saw the punch coming, shifted sideways, and slipped it. Except for the large ring on Weaver's hand. It caught the corner of my eye and ripped skin. I stepped backwards out of the doorway instead of clocking him with a right counter.

"Tom!" Leah's scream startled both of us and kept Weaver from pushing forward on me. She ran over and stood between us. "What's wrong with you?"

"I'll tell you what's wrong with me." He reached his arm around Leah and pointed at me. "This motherfucker. I knew you screwed my wife, asshole, but not because I was in the house when you did it. Krista told me all about it before we got a divorce."

I wiped the blood seeping from the corner of my eye. It stung. Weaver had a right to punch me.

If our roles were reversed, I would have done the same thing. A long time ago. But if he'd taken out his revenge on Colleen, I'd kill him.

No arrest. No trial. No verdict. Just the death penalty. But I had to be one hundred percent certain and I wasn't yet.

"Your car was in your driveway the night I slept with Krista. I have a witness who will swear to it." Leah and I hadn't gotten that far yet, but it didn't matter. And it never would, but Weaver didn't know that.

"Bullshit. You already admitted that you're a liar. I believe you about that."

Weaver was arguing his innocence with a two-bit private dick instead of leaving. Why? If he was innocent, why even bother? He was a cop, I was hated by cops. Especially in Santa Barbara. He should have welcomed my accusation so I could make a fool of myself at SBPD. Unless he was guilty. Or, at least, had something to hide.

"A witness saw your Crown Vic slick top in your driveway around ten the night Colleen was murdered. That's the same time I was in bed with your wife." I slipped my right foot back and flexed my knees in case he tried to cheap shot me again. Part of me wanted him to. Not to get him in trouble, but because every time I talked about being in bed with Krista, I remembered Colleen died because of it.

"How do you know your witness"—he air-quoted "witness"—"isn't mistaking that night for some other night? Why would he suddenly remember it now?"

"Because I didn't realize the significance of it until Rick told me he slept with Krista the night Colleen was murdered." Leah stared at Weaver like the roles were reversed and she had him in the square white room.

Weaver's face lost some color. It stayed hard, but he couldn't stop the blood from exiting his head. He tried to stay strong. "How could you possibly be sure it was that night?"

"Because it was the night Colleen died." Leah's blue piercers never left Weaver's face. "Where did you go after you saw Krista and Rick together, Tom?"

"I didn't go anywhere. I was in Fresno." He pushed past Leah and me down the hallway and out of the house.

"Oh my God." Leah slumped against the wall. "He's lying. He really could have done it. He could have killed Colleen."

"And Krista."

I was ninety percent there. Tom Weaver had as many days left on the earth as it took me to get to that last ten percent.

CHAPTER TWENTY-FIVE

LEAH CLEANED THE gash Weaver ripped in my face and applied a couple butterfly bandages from an emergency medical kit we found in Krista's bathroom. Krista was always prepared for the worst.

Except the night she was murdered.

Leah grabbed the mail from Krista's mailbox before we got into my car to drive back to her house. Bills. They chase you even after death. I backed out of the driveway and started to drive up the road, then stopped.

"What's wrong?" Leah asked.

"That house has a surveillance camera." I pointed at a camera mounted under the eaves of the house across the street from Krista's. "I didn't see it when we were here Sunday night."

"You think they might have video of someone breaking into Krista's house?"

"Let's find out."

I put the car back in gear and pulled into the home's empty driveway. I studied the angle of the camera before I knocked on the front door. It looked like it would catch anyone entering Krista's house. No one came to the door. I rang the doorbell. Nada. I went back to my car and grabbed a business card and pen out of the center console and wrote, "Please call me. Urgent!" on the card. I wedged it into the doorjamb just above the doorknob.

It's not every day that a civilian finds a private investigator's card on their door with an urgent message. I expected a call. The homeowner may not let me look at his surveillance video, but he'd call. Either out of curiosity or fear.

When we got back to Leah's house we plopped down on the sofa, and she tossed Krista's bills onto the coffee table. She reached over and gently touched my face below the butterfly bandages. "You sure you don't want to go to a doctor? It might scar."

"I'll survive." I gave her a squinty smile. "Even though my face is my moneymaker."

"I like your face." She touched my cheek again.

"Think of the character a scar will give it."

"I know it's not your first." She tugged the neck of my t-shirt down to the left revealing the scar below my shoulder. Then she pulled up my left sleeve exposing a scar on the outside of my bicep. "I saw these when we were in your bed yesterday. I didn't say anything at the time because I had other things on my mind. And body." She smiled. I would have blushed if I was capable of it. "How did you get those?"

I rubbed the cylindrical scar on my upper chest through my shirt. It was still tender six years after the fact.

"I took too long putting the pieces together on a case and almost got people I cared about killed."

"Someone shot you?" Her eyes went big like someone getting shot didn't happen every day.

"Yep." I wondered how much to tell her. We'd shared a bed and tragedies. That wasn't enough to tell her my whole story.

"What happened?"

"I lived and the shooter didn't."

Same story with the scar on my arm. Someone tried to kill me, but I killed them. I could live with those. And the others. But Leah didn't need to know about how many people I'd killed or that I wasn't done killing.

"What happened to the people you cared about?"

"They're mostly all right." One now walks with a cane, another married someone else, and the third got rich and famous. The survivors of my quest for the truth. Not everyone else survived.

"I guess *mostly* is okay." She studied my face, trying to see inside. Finally, she stood up. "Breakfast?"

"Sure." I followed her into the kitchen.

"No. You sit at the counter." She pushed me out. "I'm going to show you I can cook. Cheese omelet? I need to use up what's left of that cheese platter my parents forced on me."

"Sounds good." I sat down at the four-chair granite peninsula that right-angled the kitchen. "How well do you know Detectives Mitchell and Flora?"

"Not very." She cracked some eggs into a bowl. "I met them at a charity golf tournament once when I was married to The Idiot and at one of Krista and Tom's barbecues. Why?"

"The copy of Colleen's cold case file is missing from Krista's file cabinet. Only someone from SBPD would know she made copies of cold cases and kept them at home. Unless Mike Richert likes making up stories, at least one cop was present on the beach where Colleen's body was dumped."

My gut opened up again. The bodies of people you don't know are dumped like garbage. Not your own wife. No matter how far I tried to distance myself and treat this like just another case, I couldn't. But I wouldn't let that get in the way of my mission. Find the truth. One last time. And kill who's responsible.

"Whether that was Tom and some uniform abetting him or two other people we know nothing about, someone from SBPD was involved in both Colleen's and Krista's murders." I focused on the mission. "Agree?"

"I guess." She tilted her head. "But what are we supposed to do? We can't solve this without the department's help and we sure can't arrest anyone."

I didn't tell her arresting the murderer wasn't my goal. Or what I was going to do when I found him. The only person SBPD would arrest was me after I finished my mission. If I let them. And this time, the DA would put me on trial. Murder One.

"We gather as much information as we can until we have a solid case and then we find a cop we can trust and present our evidence." Another lie to someone I cared about in my quest for the truth. And now, my quest for vengeance.

"Okay. You're the boss," Leah said and plopped a couple omelets onto plates. She slid one in front of me.

"That's not how I remember it from my bed yesterday."

"Touché." She poured us each a glass of orange juice and sat down. "What's next?"

"I need to talk to Dustin Peck again." I took a bite of the omelet. Velvety with a tangy finish. Perfect. "This is great."

"You sound surprised." She cocked her head back. "I don't just decorate homes, Mr. Cahill. I know how to live in them, too."

"Touché."

"Why do you want to talk to Dustin Peck again?" Leah asked.

"Two things. What time he left work and where he was standing when he saw the accident."

"I thought we already knew he got off work at 2:15 a.m."

"The sign on the front door of Joe's Café states it's only open until 11:00 p.m. on Sundays."

"So? I don't understand." Her eyebrows pressed down.

"Peck told us he'd done an inventory of the bar that night. I assumed the bar closed at midnight or maybe one a.m. because it was a Sunday night." I turned to face Leah. "I used to do a yearly inventory of the restaurant I managed, and I could do the whole thing—meat, fish, produce, dry goods, liquor, and wine—in three hours by myself. Peck should have been able to do the bar and liquor storage room in an hour, hour and a half max. Let's say it took him a half hour to close out his bank and an hour and a half to do the inventory. That puts him at 1:00 a.m. What happened to the other hour and fifteen minutes until he saw Krista get . . . until he saw the accident?"

"Do you think he's lying about seeing the accident or what he was doing after work?"

"He has to be lying about one of them. I'm going to find out which."

CHAPTER TWENTY-SIX

"CAN I COME?" Leah asked.

Leah was smart, inquisitive, and beautiful. A good combination when interviewing a possible recalcitrant male witness. "Yes."

I rinsed the dishes after we finished breakfast and put them in the dishwasher. Leah grabbed Krista's bills off the coffee table and headed toward her office down the hall.

"I have to remember to cancel her cell phone service," she said to herself.

"Hey. Can you bring the phone bill in here?" I rinsed the fry pan and put it in the dishwasher.

Leah appeared around the corner of the kitchen.

"Here you go." She handed me an AT&T bill.

"I should have thought of this before."

"Should have thought of what?" Leah peered over my shoulder.

"Krista's phone was destroyed in the accident but not her call and texting records." I scanned the three-page bill and saw that the charges covered March 6th to April 5th. The last month of Krista's life. She died early on the morning of April 1st, so there should be a record of any incoming or outgoing calls from her phone the last night of her life. Maybe we could finally find out what she was doing on State Street at two in the morning.

And who the last person was she talked to on the phone before she died. I was pretty sure the two were connected. Fate didn't kill Krista. A human being with intent did. I was sure of it. Despite Grimes' warning about jumping to conclusions. I leapt at this one without a net.

"They don't send you the records with the bill." She reached over my shoulder and fingered the bill. "See."

"That's right. I forgot. They're online and you can look them up on your account."

"But I don't know the password to her account."

"You're the executor of the estate and responsible for paying the bills. You should be able to get access to her call records. Let's try."

We sat down at the dinner table, and Leah used her cell phone to call AT&T. After three or four frustrating minutes of pushing numbers and speaking to a recording, Leah finally talked to a human being. That took another four or five minutes of objections to getting access to Krista's phone call records. Finally, a supervisor told her that she could get access if she brought a copy of Krista's death certificate to the AT&T store in downtown Santa Barbara.

Getting a copy of Krista's death certificate wasn't a problem. As executor of Krista's estate, Leah had obtained a dozen copies to be safe. Eight days after Krista's death, she was down to four. When it came to death, no one took your word.

The AT&T store was located in La Cumbre Plaza, one of Santa Barbara's shopping malls. Santa Barbara had the quaint appeal of a small town with just enough big-city amenities to make life easy.

The manager of the AT&T store was young enough and with enough baby fat to be the manager of an ice cream store. Leah gave him the story and showed him the death certificate. Of course, it wasn't as easy as the supervisor on the phone said it would be. This was AT&T, after all.

The chubby manager had to make two phone calls that lasted over ten minutes before we finally got six pages of records of Krista's last phone calls and text messages. I had a hankering for ice cream after the back and forth with the manager so we stopped at McConnell's Fine Ice Creams on State Street on the way to Joe's Café. Midday on a weekday, there were only a few people ahead of us in line, and we managed to nab the last remaining open table against the brick wall opposite the counter.

McConnell's is a Santa Barbara institution. They produce their own ice cream, which can be found in grocery stores as far south as San Diego. The one taste of Santa Barbara I brought back with me to my hometown. They're mighty proud of their ice cream as reflected in the price, but they should be. It's the best ice cream I've ever had. And I've had a lot.

We looked over the last week of Krista's phone records while we ate the ice cream. Leah, a scoop of Salted Caramel Chip. Me, Dark Chocolate Chips and Nibs . . . and Vanilla Bean. Two scoops. Even better than the pints I bought at Vons.

Leah checked off all the numbers she recognized. Hers, her brother, her parents, and police headquarters. That left ten or twelve numbers she didn't know. We did the same with the text numbers. Krista didn't have nearly as many texts as phone calls, which was unusual nowadays.

"Why so few texts?" I asked Leah.

"She was old-fashioned. She preferred to talk to people."

"Or write them a letter on stationary."

"Right. That was my sister."

I thought about the one letter Krista mailed me seven or eight years ago. Upbeat and hopeful. For me. I never responded to it, but wished I had. More every day since I learned of her death.

I ran the phone and text numbers that Leah didn't recognize through a pay people finder website. Three belonged to women whose names Leah recognized as friends of Krista's, two to cops who worked on MIU, two to restaurants, one to a cable company, one to a bank, and one to Captain Kessler, her boss. That left one phone number that the website didn't have any data for. The final call that Krista received the last night of her life. Three and a half hours before she died. The call lasted four minutes. Longer than someone would leave on voicemail. Whoever it was, Krista had spoken to them.

Her killer?

We finished our ice cream, and I started heading back to the side street where I'd parked the car.

"Where are you going?" She stopped, still on the corner of State Street. "Joe's is just a couple blocks this way down State."

"I know. We have to go back to the car. We need a quiet, enclosed area to see if you recognize the voice of the person who answers at the one phone number we couldn't find any info on."

"Okay." Leah nodded, set her jaw, and walked with me back to the car. She was on her own journey to find the truth. For her sake and those she loved, I prayed it would be a short one.

I set up my iPhone to block caller ID, dialed the number of the last call Krista Landingham ever received, and put the phone on speaker. I let it ring eight times before I hung up. No answer. No voicemail. Unusual. Everyone had voicemail nowadays, even if it was only an automated response.

Who was on the other end of that phone number?

CHAPTER TWENTY-SEVEN

A HOSTESS GREETED us at the door when we entered Joe's Café.

"We have about a thirty-minute wait for lunch, but you can order at the bar. I think there are a couple seats open."

She was right. We found two seats separated by one guy in a suit who looked to be drinking his lunch. He moved over so we could sit together. No sign of Dustin Peck, but Bree, the bartender Grimes and I met the other day, was working.

"What can I get you to drink?" She slid a couple menus in front of us.

"I'll have a mimosa, please," Leah said.

"I'll have a water with some bubbles in it and one more of whatever my friend here is having." I nodded to the businessman who'd switched seats. I figured he might as well get lubed before he went back to the grind.

"Thanks, buddy." He patted me on the shoulder. I gave a half nod to close down any avenue for a conversation. The drink was more for the bar and the bartender than him. I was taking up space and wanted to pay my way. But I was on business as much as the businessman was escaping it.

Leah leaned into me. "I don't want you to think I'm a day drinker."

"I don't think anything." I drank myself into a sweaty stain on the floor for two months straight after Colleen died. I graduated to cocaine for about a year before I could get my hands back on the rudder. Everyone dealt with grief the best they could. There were no wrong ways.

Some were just more painful than others.

"I used to work in a restaurant." Leah looked up and down the bar. "We took the last two spots and we're not ordering lunch. I wanted to order an expensive drink to offset that."

Some people handled grief with more class than others. A lot more.

Bree came back with our drinks.

"My friend and I have a bet," I said to her, then smiled at Leah. "She thinks that everyone who works here has to fend for themselves when it comes to finding a parking space when they come to work. I bet that Joe's must have a deal for their employees with the parking garages around here."

"I wish." She put her hands on her hips in feigned disgust, then smiled at Leah. "Your friend wins. Parking is terrible around here."

"Then where does everyone park? East or west of State Street?"

"I think just about everyone parks that way." She pointed to the east. The same direction Peck said he always parked. "I don't know if that's east or west, but that's where everyone parks. Over in the residential area."

I reached for my wallet to pay for the drinks, but Leah handed Bree a credit card before I could draw. "We'll run a tab. Thanks."

"We're going to pass on lunch." I gave her back the menus. "Is Dustin working today?"

"That's how I remember you." She smiled and tapped the bar in front of me. "You and that cop-looking guy came in to see Dustin the other day."

"Yep. That was me." I tried my best smile. "Is he working today?"

"No, he works tonight at six."

"Thanks."

Bree tended to her other customers.

"Looks like we struck out." Leah set down her mimosa. "What now?"

"We gather information. Can you take one more for the team?" I looked at the mimosa and then at her.

She took a big gulp of her drink in answer. I did the same with my Perrier. We'd both finished our drinks by the time Bree made her next pass.

"Let's do it again," Leah said, a tinge of pink cresting her cheeks.

Bree set the drinks down in front of us a couple minutes later.

"You have a pretty extensive liquor assortment. How often do you have to do inventory?" I tilted my head like I was really interested. "I used to manage a restaurant and bar and I dreaded the yearly inventory. It was either stay late and ring in the New Year alone doing inventory while the world celebrated or come in early on New Year's morning with the first and worst hangover of the year."

Bree scanned the bar and leaned in. "Our owner is a real hard-ass about pour costs. We have to do inventory once a month."

"Wow. Are you the one who has to do it?"

"No." She shook her head. "Dustin usually does it, but sometimes I help him."

"I guess it wouldn't be too bad with two people." I looked at the back bar. "Probably wouldn't take you more than an hour."

"What's this all about?" Bree squinted one eye at me. "You seem to be pretty interested in our inventory process."

She caught me. One question too many. I could continue the ruse or be honest for a change.

"This is Leah Landingham." I opened my hand toward Leah. "Dustin saw her sister get killed by a hit-and-run driver last week after he got off work. She hired me to find whatever the police miss. You can help us find the truth."

I dropped my business card on the bar in front of Bree. She scanned it and looked back at me, then at Leah.

"I heard about that. I'm sorry for your loss." Back at me. "Dustin told me about it, and I saw something online. You don't think he had anything to do with it, do you?"

"No. What did he tell you he saw?"

"Why don't you ask him?"

"I did. Memories can change as time passes. I want to know what he told you when it was still fresh in his mind."

Bree rubbed the tattoo of a lotus blossom on her arm but didn't say anything.

"Please." Leah reached over the bar and gently squeezed Bree's hand. "Whatever you tell us won't get Dustin in trouble. I'm grateful to him for reporting it and talking to the police. We just want to get as much information as possible so we can help the police catch the person who killed my sister."

Bree patted Leah's hand then looked at the railed waitress station at the other end of a bar where a waitress stood with her hands on her hips eyeing Bree.

"I have to pour some drinks and check on my other customers. I'll be back in a few minutes." She hustled down to the other end of the bar.

My phone buzzed in my pocket while we waited for Bree's return. I pulled it out and checked the screen. Grimes. Shit. He'd ask me what I was doing, and I'd either lie to him or have to listen to him tell me he was running the investigation for the tenth time. I answered anyway.

"Cahill." A hoarse wolf. "Meet me at Figueroa headquarters forthwith."

"Did they give you your badge back? Because I'm not wearing a uniform, and I'm not going anywhere *forthwith*." I raised my eyebrows to Leah. "I can be there in about thirty minutes. What's so forthwith worthy?"

"Just get your ass down here and ask the desk sergeant for Detective Mitchell."

"Roger. In thirty minutes." I hung up.

"What was that all about?" Leah's cheeks were a brighter pink and her second mimosa was half finished.

"Grimes wants me to meet him and Detective Mitchell over at the station."

"Why?"

"I don't know, but he made it sound urgent."

"Do you think the police found Krista's killer?"

"No, he would have called you not me. He sounded even less chipper than usual. My guess is that SBPD has some kind of beef with me."

"I'm going with you."

"That's not a good idea. Guilt by association. Every law enforcement agency's default. SBPD is on your side right now. Let's keep it that way."

"I'm going with you."

Bree returned before I could come up with a more convincing argument.

"Dustin told me the same thing he told the police and that he probably told you. He'd just left work and looked down State Street and saw . . ." She looked at Leah and frowned. ". . . the accident."

"Did he tell you what time that was?" I asked.

"After work that night."

"Yeah, but what time?"

"It was probably around twelve thirty or one, I guess." Her eyes looked up to the left, searching her memory.

Leah and I exchanged a glance.

"He called the police at 2:17 a.m.," I said.

"Oh." Something clicked in Bree's mind. "What day was that again?"

"Late March thirty-first into the morning of April first."

"That was a Sunday night, right?"

"Yes." I stared at her, waiting for the significance. Instead, she turned and went to her register and came back with our bill and Leah's credit card.

"It's on the house." She put the credit card down in front of Leah. "I really have to get back to my customers."

"Wait," Leah said. "Why is Sunday important, Bree? What happened that night?"

"Nothing. I need this job. I don't want to get in trouble for ignoring my other customers. Sorry." She strode down to the other end of the bar.

"What was that all about?" Leah looked at me with a look as confused as the one I felt on my face.

"I don't know but I intend to find out."

"How?"

"I'm going to sit here and ask Bree over and over again until she answers me or I get kicked out of the bar."

"No. You can't do that." Leah furrowed her brow. "This is her livelihood. I don't want you to get her in trouble."

Leah's quest for the truth had boundaries. Decency. Mine didn't. And for an instant, I felt badly about that. For an instant.

"She knows something that might lead us to who killed Krista." And Colleen. "And I'm going to get it out of her."

"Not here where she works. We'll find another way." She took her wallet out of her purse and returned her card then pulled out a twenty and laid it on the bar. "Let's go to police headquarters and listen to what they have to say."

Leah was paying me. She was the boss. While we were together. Alone, I'd resort to the tactics that had always led me to the truth. No matter the damage.

CHAPTER TWENTY-EIGHT

THE HEADQUARTERS FOR the Santa Barbara Police Department is a two-story cement building with a tile roof that looks more like a school building than a police station. It's east of State Street in the upper downtown area smack in the middle of a mixed-use neighborhood.

The desk sergeant was a woman about my age. Sergeant Lance. She had a square jaw and a ruddy complexion that might have come from too much time outside in the sun or too much time inside a bar.

"Rick Cahill and Leah Landingham here to see Detective Mitchell," I said to Sergeant Lance at her cubbyhole just inside the front door.

"I'm sorry for your loss, Ms. Landingham." Lance looked at Leah. "Krista was a great cop and an inspiration to a lot of us on the force."

"Thank you." The mimosa-pink in Leah's checks went a shade darker and her lips quivered. She blinked glossy eyes.

Sergeant Lance picked up a phone and announced our presence. I pulled Leah a few feet away. "Are you okay? You don't have to go in with me. You can wait out here or I can take you home and come back."

"I'm okay." She tried a smile, but her eyes still threatened tears. "It's the damn champagne. It always makes me emotional, and I basically chugged two glasses."

"Leah." A man's voice behind me. "Are you doing okay?"

A man in his early forties, dressed in detective gear of slacks, dress shirt, tie, and blazer, approached us.

"I'm fine, Detective." Leah didn't give him a smile.

Detective Mitchell. My forthwith demander. He was a couple inches taller than me but leaner. I vaguely remembered him from my time on the job. He worked on the Special Enforcement Team dealing with gangs and probation violators while I worked patrol.

"Nothing that we can discuss just yet, but we are making progress," he said to Leah.

"Why can't you discuss it?" Her voice, a little too loud for the tiny lobby in police headquarters. "Krista was my sister and somebody ran her over. I need to know what you're doing to find her killer."

Sergeant Lance looked worried after Leah's outburst.

"You have to let us do our job, Leah. We're making progress." Mitchell side-glanced me. "Now, I need to discuss something with Mr. Cahill. You can wait here or I can have a uniform drive you home."

"Rick's investigating Krista's murder because I asked him to. Whatever you have to say to him, say to me, too." She folded her arms and raised her chin. "Everything he's done has been at my behest."

"This really is specific to Mr. Cahill, Leah." Mitchell's voice had a snip in it.

"Should I call a lawyer for Mr. Cahill, Jake." Leah out-snipped him. "Or would you rather have me join you for your talk?"

I was glad Leah was on my team and that I was on team Leah.

"Follow me." Mitchell regained his calm. Staying snippy would be admitting defeat.

He led us through a couple doors, up a flight of stairs, and down a hall into a room with a shingle outside the door that read "Master Investigative Unit." There were a couple sets of back-to-back desks with computers and files on them and a small office in the back of the room.

A detective-looking woman in her late forties stood next to Jim Grimes in the middle of the room.

"Have a seat, Mr. Cahill." Mitchell pulled out a chair from a desk.

"I'm good." I raised my hand, palm open to chest level, like Mitchell's statement had been an offer rather than a demand. "Everyone else is standing, I don't want to be odd man out."

"Very well." He gave me a smile that fell short of sincere, and I got a grimace from Grimes out of the corner of my eye. I hadn't been asked to headquarters for a pat on the back. "This is Detective Glenda Flora and you both know Jim Grimes."

Mitchell nodded to the woman. Dark hair and complexion with a crescent-shaped birthmark on her left cheek. She smiled at Leah and stone-faced me. Grimes glared at me.

"Mr. Cahill." Detective Mitchell couldn't conceal his contempt for me. "You made some libelous accusations against Detective Weaver this morning. Explain yourself."

Bingo. Finally, the reason I'd been forthwithed. Weaver must have come crying to headquarters about our chat.

"Why didn't you tell me you were going to ambush Detective Weaver?" Grimes jumped in and stared me down before I could answer Mitchell.

I looked at Grimes, but didn't say anything. This wasn't his show.

The door opened and Captain Kessler, in uniform, stepped inside and closed the door. He gave everyone his politician's smile. "Please, proceed."

"Mr. Cahill has it out for this department and is going to do his damnedest to make us look bad in the investigation of Detective Landingham's death." Mitchell back in charge.

"I don't give a shit about this department." I was already tired of the inquisition. "I'm here to do a job, and from what I've seen so far, you could use the help."

"Does your help include accusing a decorated detective of your wife's murder?" Flora got hers in.

"My *help* is to find the truth. And the truth is that Tom Weaver was in Santa Barbara at the time of my wife's murder, but he told everyone he was still in Fresno working a case. I'm guessing he falsified his expense report for that night or never turned one in."

"I'm confused." Captain Kessler from the front of the room. "What does Colleen Cahill's murder have to do with Detective Landingham's hit-and-run investigation?"

"Not a thing, Captain. Rick here is just trying to stir things up for personal reasons." Mitchell put his hands on his hips. "And he thinks he has the right to throw around false accusations about good cops."

"I didn't accuse Weaver of anything. I just stated the facts and wanted to know what he did after he saw me in bed with his wife on the night Colleen was murdered." Time to see what everyone knew and what Weaver's story had been when he complained to Mitchell about me.

"What!" Grimes' face flared crimson.

Mitchell's left eye staccato-blinked six or seven times and his jaw tightened. Kessler frowned and Flora gave nothing.

"What's this about Weaver seeing you and Krista?" Grimes still apoplectic.

"That's enough, Jim." Captain Kessler walked into our contentious circle. "You don't have a badge anymore. We've been more than accommodating in letting you piggyback on this investigation. We'll take it from here."

"All due respect, Captain, I worked Colleen Cahill's murder for three years and I just learned from Krista two weeks ago that this asshole had an alibi all along." Grimes pointed at me. "That's two people, one a good cop and one shitty one, who could have saved me valuable time and resources from going down a rathole investigation to nowhere. Now I'm finding out another cop knew Cahill couldn't have killed his wife and never said anything?"

"And is a possible suspect," I said.

"Shut up, Cahill." Mitchell's eyes cinched down on me and his lips turned white. "Tom Weaver didn't have anything to do with your wife's murder. He stayed at my house that night."

"You knew, too?" A flick of saliva flew from Grimes' mouth.

"Anyone not wearing a badge better shut their mouths right now." The politician in Kessler morphed into mob boss. "Or I'll find a reason to give them a two-night stay in jail."

Grimes' eyes bulged and he mashed his lips together. I didn't need to be told twice. I'd spent a week in the Santa Barbara jail fourteen years ago. That was enough for a lifetime.

"Now," Kessler continued with order restored, "Detective Mitchell, please explain your last statement."

"I will, but after the civilians leave the room." Mitchell eyeballed Grimes and Leah and me. "This is police business for police ears only."

"Unless what you're going to say jeopardizes an open investigation, Detective Mitchell, I suggest you proceed right now," Kessler said. "We have one very agitated ex-homicide detective here, who I think you know, will use all his resources to get to the bottom of this even if I throw him in jail. Proceed."

"I didn't know Tom had found this asshole in bed with Krista. He told me that he saw someone with his wife and split before he went crazy and killed them both. He didn't stick around long enough to get a good look at the guy. He got drunk and I gave him a place to stay and dry out."

"What time did he get to your house?" Grimes couldn't help himself. I suddenly respected the guy more than almost anyone I knew.

"Jim." Kessler was back to smooth politician. More dangerous than crime boss. "Are you trying to embarrass me in front of my command?

I just did you a favor by letting you stay and now you choose to disrespect me this way?"

"I apologize, Captain. It's just that I worked that case for—"

"Enough." Kessler put out his hand. "Now, Detective Mitchell, what time did Detective Weaver arrive at your house on the night Colleen Cahill was murdered?"

"Sometime after one thirty in the morning."

Grimes vibrated but kept his mouth shut. I had to fight to do the same. Using Mike Richert's earliest time estimation of what he saw on East Beach, after one thirty gave Weaver just enough time to leave Colleen's body on the beach and make it to Mitchell's house. Richert had said somewhere around one a.m. But there were two people on that beach. One in civilian clothes, like a detective might wear, Weaver, and one in a police uniform.

My stomach dropped and I glanced at Leah. She had no reaction. She'd missed what was jackhammering in my head. Two people on the beach. One dressed as a cop. The other not. Mitchell worked on SET when Colleen was murdered.

In a uniform.

"Sometime after one thirty doesn't give Detective Weaver an alibi, Captain Kessler." I hoped there was still some cop in Kessler underneath the politician.

"That's enough, Cahill," he snapped at me.

"Captain, this is really only for our ears. This concerns a man's reputation. A good cop," Mitchell pleaded.

"Judging by what I've heard today, his reputation is already in jeopardy." Kessler stared down Mitchell. "Speak up, Detective."

Mitchell blew out an angry breath. "Tom was in the Santa Barbara Jail in the drunk tank from eleven p.m. until I picked him up and brought him to my house."

"How did he end up in the drunk tank?"

Mitchell didn't say anything. He gave Kessler a look most cops wouldn't have the guts to point at a supervisor.

"Answer me, Detective." Kessler returned the look.

"He was pulled over by a sheriff's deputy for a DUI in Carpinteria."

"Hmm." Kessler pursed his lips. "I think I'd remember a detective from SBPD getting arrested for a DUI. That would constitute a suspension and possible dismissal."

"SBSO didn't charge him. They gave him a break because he was a cop. He gave them my name to call. He'd just seen his wife screwing another man, Captain. He blew a gasket like we all would. Please don't jack him up over this."

"Is there a record of this?" I couldn't help myself. It was all too convenient.

"I warned you, Mr. Cahill." Kessler, playing the bad cop.

"And does anyone know where Weaver was when Krista was run over?" I asked.

Kessler glared at me. "Detective Flora, handcuff Mr. Cahill."

CHAPTER TWENTY-NINE

DETECTIVE FLORA TWISTED my right arm behind my back and slapped a cuff on it so quickly she must have anticipated Kessler's command before the captain even said it.

"May I speak with the editor, Ms. Davidson, please?" Everyone looked at Leah. "Leah Landingham and I'd like the *Free Press* to know that the Santa Barbara Police just arrested a man for simply asking a question about the unsolved murder of his wife."

Detective Flora held onto my left bicep and looked at Captain Kessler. Just like everyone else in the room. Leah held her phone up to her ear.

"Detective Flora." Kessler raised his eyebrows and gave Flora a quick nod. Five seconds later my hands were free. "Ms. Landingham, please explain to whoever is on the phone that you were mistaken."

"I'm sorry. False alarm," Leah said into the phone. "I misread the situation."

She hung up after reading the situation perfectly. She'd been calm and smart under pressure and probably saved me from a night in the iron bar hotel.

"Detective Mitchell." Kessler, calm, like he was at a meet and greet with constituents, which was doubtless in his future. "Please escort our guests out of the station."

Mitchell squished his face into a fist. He was lead detective on a homicide. Not an errand boy or a gofer. Detective Flora looked at her shoes. Mitchell's face relaxed but he didn't move.

"Something on your mind, Detective?" Now an edge to Kessler's voice.

"Sir, no sir." Mitchell clicked his heels together and turned to us. "Come with me."

Mitchell hurried through the halls and down the stairs with Grimes, Leah, and me in tow. Santa Barbara PD's MIU was supposed to be their best of the best. Right now, it looked like a dysfunctional unit with command and morale problems.

Mitchell held the door open from the lobby leading to the outside for us and we filed out.

"Jim? This concludes our cooperation. You can direct all further inquiries to the community relations officer." He closed the door to SBPD headquarters.

"We need to talk." Grimes looked at Leah and me. "All of us. You hungry?"

"No," we said in unison.

"Well, I am." Grimes started walking and we followed.

He finally stopped in front of a sandwich joint called Pickles and Swiss in the Paseo Nuevo Shopping Center on State Street, a few blocks from police headquarters. The sandwich shop had a large arch-cased opening surrounded by green shrubbery growing up the wall like the ivy at Wrigley Field.

Leah and I sat outside while Grimes went inside to order a sandwich. Good. I needed a minute to talk to Leah alone.

"Any way your brother can find out if Weaver really was in the county jail drunk tank the night Colleen was murdered?" I asked her, then scanned inside the sandwich shop to keep tabs on Grimes.

"I can try, but why would Detective Mitchell make that up?"

"Mitchell wasn't always a detective. He worked the Special Enforcement Team back when I was a cop. He most likely worked nights when Colleen was murdered. In a uniform."

"Are you telling me that you think Mitchell was the cop on the beach Mr. Richert saw and Tom was the man in civilian clothes?" Leah's eyes went wide.

"I'm saying it's a possibility that has to be checked out. Mitchell is heading the investigation into Krista's death. He can steer it wherever he wants to."

"What about Detective Flora, his partner?" Leah's hands and eyebrows rose at the same time. "You think she'd cover for a murderer? Or all the other cops who are working the case?"

"Of course not. I'm just saying we need to eliminate Mitchell and Weaver before we move onto someone else."

Grimes walked out of Pickles and Swiss holding a small plastic basket with a sandwich inside and a bottle of beer. He sat down next to Leah at our table.

"You wanted to talk?" I said.

"Yes, I do." Grimes stuck his French dip sandwich into a Styrofoam container of au jous and took a bite. I waited while he chewed his food. Finally, "Why the hell were you holding out that Weaver walked in on you and Krista? This one-way information bullshit has got to stop."

"I didn't know about it until late last night. I found out by accident and asked Weaver about it this morning."

"Found out by accident? What the hell does that mean?"

I looked at Leah and nodded my head.

She told Grimes what she told me about Tom Weaver's detective car in the driveway the night I screwed his wife and Colleen died.

"And you're sure it was the same night Ms. Cahill was murdered?" Grimes asked. Maybe using her whole name or just her first one connected Colleen to me. I guess Grimes wanted to keep us separate. The good from the bad.

"Positive."

"But Weaver has an alibi for the TOD." Grimes looked at me. The bad. "He would have to have killed Ms. Cahill, wash her in bleach, dump her on East Beach, then get blotto drunk and picked up on a DUI all in an hour. Not doable."

"We only have Mitchell's word that he was in the drunk tank."

"What's your game, Cahill?" He set down his sandwich. "Are you more concerned about making good cops look bad or finding out who killed Krista?"

"I don't have a game." I tapped my finger on the table. "I look at the facts. And the facts that we know are that on the night Colleen was murdered two men were seen carrying something that looked like a body, which they left on East Beach in the exact area where Colleen was found. One was dressed in a cop uniform. Next set of facts: Tom Weaver was at his house at the same time I was in bed with his wife. Although he lied to Leah and me and said he wasn't, Detective Mitchell claims Weaver admitted to him that he had been home and had seen someone screwing his wife. His supposed claim that he didn't see who it was strains credibility. Thus, the reason I don't take Mitchell's story about picking up Weaver from the drunk tank as gospel."

"That's a nice speech, Cahill, but some of your facts are in question." Grimes air quoted "facts." "We don't have any corroboration of this Richert guy's story. He waited nine years to report what he saw. What kind of credibility is that? He could have remembered something he saw months before Ms. Cahill was murdered. Or maybe it was two years later."

"Colleen wasn't *Ms. Cahill*, Grimes. She was my wife." I'd had enough of him distancing Colleen from me. I'd failed her the night she died, but no one was going to erase me from her life. "And Richert is certain because he kept records of all his sails. I saw them."

"I wasn't finished. I let you talk; now it's time to listen." Grimes looked from me to Leah, perhaps in search of a better audience. "The other thing that bothers me about Richert's story is his claim that there were two people on the beach. There was no evidence that there was more than one person involved. That's why I think Richert mixed up the dates. The only DNA the techs found was Rick's and that was semen inside her."

"That's because the killers washed her in bleach," I jumped back in.

"Forensics is going to solve Krista's case, Cahill, not some story from a guy sitting in a yacht off East Beach fourteen years ago." Grimes cop-eyed me. "MIU got the forensics back on the paint from the van that killed Krista. It was a Chevrolet G20 or G30 Sports Van from sometime in the 1980s. They got every available cop tracking down owners of those make and models in Southern California. Can't be too many of those left after thirtysomething years. That's how they'll find Krista's killer. Not through whims, gut feelings, or wild speculation."

"How did they get the results so fast?" Forensic labs usually took months.

"Apparently, the chief has an in with a private lab that uses some new Belgian cutting-edge technology." Grimes pursed his lips. "So this case is about to be solved the right way."

"If they ever find the van, the owner won't be the murderer unless he's a cop at SBPD. The van will have been stolen. The killers are cops, Grimes."

He pushed away his sandwich and stood up. "You've got a vendetta against the department, Rick, and it's blinding you to other possibilities. Ms. Cah . . . Colleen's and Krista's murders aren't connected. The sooner you let that go, the better for you and Miss Landingham."

"You're letting your allegiance to SBPD blind you, Grimes. You're too good a detective for that."

"I'll continue to investigate as long as you'd like me to." He ignored me and looked down at Leah. "But I prefer to work alone from here on out. You don't have to make a decision now. Take a day and let me know."

He walked out of the mall.

"He could have been an asset, but after today SBPD will stop feeding him information anyway." I looked at Leah, but she still avoided my eyes. "I'm going to try to talk to Dustin Peck at Joe's tonight and hammer down his story about which way Krista was walking."

"Okay." She gave me a flat smile. "Can you take me home?"

We drove up to her house in the silence echoed from last night's drive back from San Diego. Leah opened the car door after I pulled into her driveway but didn't get out of the car.

"Can you call Jim?" She stared at the dashboard. "And see if you two can somehow still work together?"

"Grimes? You were ready to fire him Sunday if I asked you to."

"I know. That was before we met with Detective Mitchell."

"And?"

"I think Detective Mitchell was genuinely surprised when you told him Tom saw you with Krista. I was watching him carefully. He didn't know. I think he's telling the truth about Tom and the drunk tank. Maybe Tom really didn't know it was you with Krista."

"That's not the way I read it."

"I know." Leah got out of the car and walked into her house.

CHAPTER THIRTY

I HEADED INTO downtown Santa Barbara at five thirty p.m. to wait out Dustin Peck. I learned from Grimes Sunday that Peck drove a metallic green 2015 Kia Soul. When Grimes still had an in at SBPD and could still stomach me as a partner. I found a parking spot in front of a house a block and a half back from State Street where all the employees of Joe's Café supposedly parked. No sign of Peck's car. I watched and waited.

My phone rang at 5:47 p.m. I didn't recognize the number, but it had an 805 area code. Santa Barbara. I answered.

"Is this Rick Cahill?" Man's voice. Forties or fifties.

"Yes. What can I do for you?"

"Nothing. Apparently, you think I can do something for you. My name is Frank Cornetta. You left your card on my front door."

It took me a second to remember that I'd left my business card at the house with the security camera across the street from Krista's.

"Yes. Sorry. Thanks for calling. I'm working for the family of Krista Landingham investigating her death."

"She was a fine lady. The best neighbor we ever had." He cleared his throat. "But shouldn't the police be the ones investigating her death?"

"They are. I'm helping out with some peripheral investigating. If I find something that may raise questions, I turn it over to them." Not a lie two days ago.

"I thought it was an accident."

"It might be, but I'm tying up loose ends."

"Then I'm not sure how I can help. I was home when Krista was killed." Open, not dismissive. Workable.

"I was at Krista's house today and noticed your security camera. Does it work?"

"Yes, but Krista was killed downtown on State Street. I don't understand how my camera could have seen anything that can help the police."

"Well, it may have, but I'm not at liberty to discuss what we're looking for." I tried to sound like a cop. I'd almost forgotten how. "I'm sure you can understand the police can't divulge important information about an ongoing investigation."

"I certainly can. I was an MP in the United States Marine Corps for twelve years. But you're not a police officer. In fact, you're not even from Santa Barbara. Your card has a San Diego address."

A cop. Things had been going so well.

"You're right, but I used to be a cop on SBPD. Krista Landingham was my training officer, partner, and friend. I came up here for her funeral and her sister asked me to run a duel investigation to the police's. She thinks they're too narrowly focused on the drunk driver theory." At least she used to. "So do I. We discovered some things are missing from Krista's house, and I want to see if your security camera caught someone breaking into her house. I was working with the police, but they shut me out. I'm just trying to find the truth."

"Why didn't you just start with the truth from the beginning?" Some military in his voice that I missed at first.

"Because I was afraid you wouldn't help me."

"And yet, you just did tell me the truth right now."

"I see your point."

"I'm not sure you do, Mr. Cahill. You tried to coerce me into a decision to help you instead of letting me decide on my own. That's insulting." He was calm despite his words. A father trying to teach morality to his son. He didn't know I was a lost cause. "But Krista was a friend and a fine person. What do you need?"

"Thank you for helping, Mr. Cornetta." Genuine gratitude. Sometimes the truth works. "I'd like to get a look at footage from every day since Krista died through last Sunday. Do you have video saved back that far?"

"Yes. Come by here tomorrow morning at eight o'clock." He hung up.

I got out of my car and headed to Joe's Cafe. A minute into my walk, a metallic green Kia Soul passed me going the other way. I didn't get a look at the driver, but the car fit Dustin Peck's.

The Soul cruised slowly down the street, probably searching for a parking spot. After a couple attempts at parallel parking, the car snugged up against the curb between two SUVs. I slid behind a palm tree a couple blocks from Joe's Café and watched the driver exit the Soul. Peck. I waited behind the tree, then stepped out onto the sidewalk when he walked by.

"Shit." Peck jumped sideways. "Why the hell are you sneaking up on me?"

"I was in the neighborhood. Why did it take you so long to do inventory the night Krista Landingham died?"

"What?" He resumed his walk to work. More quickly now.

"I used to manage a restaurant. I did my fair share of inventories." I kept pace with him. "You could inventory that entire bar by yourself in an hour and a half at the most. What were you doing for the other hour and forty-five minutes before you left work?"

"I don't know what you're talking about." We were thirty feet from the corner of State Street and the entrance to Joe's. He only had to keep moving and wait me out another fifteen seconds before he could find sanctuary inside the restaurant.

Twenty feet from the corner, I noticed the Callahan building across the street from Joe's that housed Hotel Santa Barbara and remembered Bree, the bartender clamming up after she realized the night Peck had the late inventory had been a Sunday.

"Look." I grabbed Peck's arm and stopped his walk. "I don't care who you met at the Hotel Santa Barbara the night you saw the accident. I just want to know exactly what you saw and where you were."

Peck's eyes gaped wide and he yanked his arm free from my grip. "Leave me alone. I don't know what you're talking about."

"We can get this over with right now." I dropped the depth charge. "I don't want to have to ask your wife if she knows anyone who you rendezvous with on Sunday nights at the Hotel Santa Barbara."

"You're an asshole." He tried to push me out of his way, but I firmed up my two-hundred-pound frame and flicked his arms away.

"Just give me the truth about what you saw that night and this will be the last time we talk."

"I already told you. I looked up and the van swerved and hit the woman." The anger ebbed from his eyes as he recalled seeing something he'd never forget. "Knocked her like ten feet in the air."

"Where were you in the street?"

He blew out a breath. "I was right in the middle heading back toward Joe's."

"And the woman was walking west across State Street?"

"Yes. Heading away from the Casa Blanca." The restaurant where Krista had parked her car.

"I know you told that to the first cop on the scene, Officer Baines, but did you tell the detective who interviewed you later the exact same thing?"

"Not at first." Peck averted his eyes from mine. "I said I was on the sidewalk next to Joe's, but the detective told me I couldn't see the accident from there."

"Are you one hundred percent sure the direction she was walking? You weren't the other day when Mr. Grimes and I interviewed you."

"I'm sure. That Grimes dude gave me the creeps. I didn't want him to figure out what you did about me being at the hotel so I said I wasn't sure."

"Last question and I'll leave you alone for good. What was the name of the detective who questioned you?"

"Mitchell."

CHAPTER THIRTY-ONE

DUSTIN PECK WAS definitive. Krista was walking away from her car. And Detective Mitchell had left that off his report. An oversight or deliberate? Which way Krista was walking might seem like a minor point unless someone had contacted her about meeting them on State Street at that time of night. She'd received a call from an unknown caller three hours before she appeared on State Street and was run over. The last call she ever received. Had the call been to set up a meeting downtown?

If any other detective had interviewed Peck and omitted which direction he said Krista was walking, I probably would have written it off as on oversight. Not with Mitchell. The cop who was a friend of Tom Weaver and gave him the convenient alibi after he'd seen me in bed with his wife the night Colleen was murdered.

Another notch on the wrong side of the ledger for Jake Mitchell.

I got over to my car and fought the rush to head back to Leah's house and tell her what I'd learned. Instead, I drove to the Best Western on Cabrillo Boulevard. Leah had jumped ship and joined Grimes' team. Follow the facts as long as they were all lined up uniformly in a box.

SBPD held the box and two of their cops killed Colleen and Krista. And I was narrowing the remaining gap of certainty about which two.

I picked up a sandwich and a six-pack of beer from a grocery store/ deli on the way to the Best Western. I was glad I'd kept my suitcase in the trunk of my car after the drive back from San Diego. Kept me from having to awkwardly fetch it from Leah's house after I dropped her off. Our impromptu sleeping arrangement had an even shorter expiration date than I'd expected. I liked Leah. A lot. But I was on a quest. My last one.

The hotel parking lot was full, so I parked in a lot to another hotel behind it and grabbed my suitcase out of the trunk. Along with the Ruger. I left the other guns behind. The Ruger was habit, for self-defense. The mini arsenal still in the trunk would be used for war. If the time came.

I tossed the suitcase onto the bed and set the Ruger on the night-stand, then sat down at the desk and dug into my BLT and a pilsner. The sandwich and the beer went well together and I figured the beer would do well on its own. My work was done for the day. My budding relationship with Leah probably done for good. Beer for dessert seemed apropos.

I finished my sandwich, grabbed another beer, and went out onto the balcony. Although on the West Coast, Santa Barbara faces south, so the sun went down off to the right of me rather than directly over-head. Dusk settled over Stearns Wharf and a few sailboats bobbed beyond it.

I thought about Mike Richert sitting on a rich-man's yacht late at night waiting to set sail off East Beach in the morning. Watching two men dump something on the beach. Something used up and disposed of at their will. Just over a mile away from where I now sat but forever out of my reach.

I finished off the six-pack out on the patio. Feeling worse after each empty bottle. I was a little drunk but it was only eight fifteen p.m. I went inside and turned on the TV, turned off the lights, kicked off my shoes, and flopped down onto the bed. Some mindless distraction to keep me from thinking about Leah. And Colleen. And Krista. Sleep caught up to me before the bad thoughts could. At some point in the night I woke up and turned off the TV, shed my clothes, got under the covers, and fell back asleep.

My eyes snapped open and I held my breath. Someone was in my room. I sensed it before I saw it. Then a dark figure moved along the end of my bed. I grabbed for the gun on the nightstand. The figure spun and sped toward the door. My fingers bumped the Ruger and knocked it onto the floor. The door banged against the wall. I leapt out of bed, flicked on the light on the nightstand, and grabbed the gun off the floor.

I dashed out of the room and sprinted down the hall, naked except for the gun. Forty feet ahead, a figure in black clothes and ski cap. One arm tucked to the side. It spun to the right down the outside stairs. I hit the staircase and heard him pounding down the stairs below me. I leapt the last two stairs to the ground floor and whipped around the staircase.

A black lunge. Something hard crashed off my right arm. My gun bounced onto the ground. Another lunge. I twisted and threw up my injured arm to block it. A metal rod crashed off my forearm and across my face. Lightening flashed inside my head.

I opened my eyes. Sky. Dark. Blurry. I rolled over onto all fours. A jag of pain in my right arm when I put weight on it briefly subverted the thumping in my head. I crawled around searching for something. I'd dropped something when I got to the bottom of the stairs. I couldn't remember what it was. I couldn't remember why I'd run down the stairs. Something wet dripped onto my arm and ran down onto my hand as I searched in the darkness. I put my hand up to my face and felt the source of the wetness. Blood. Dripping from the bridge of my nose.

I must have fallen down the stairs. I sat back on the cement landing. It was cold on my rear end. Then I noticed I was naked. Had I sleepwalked out of my room and fallen down the stairs? No, I remembered running out of my room with something in my hand. Someone was running ahead of me. A man in black. I was chasing him with a gun in my hand. Then it came back to me. The dark figure in my room. The chase. Getting hit with something at the bottom of the stairs. Thin, cylindrical, and hard. I eased back onto all fours. My head pounded and I felt nauseous. My right forearm felt like it was broken. I couldn't find the gun.

I gave up after another minute. It was gone. Whoever ambushed me took it. Why hadn't he killed me? I was laid out, defenseless. He didn't have to use the gun, he could have cracked open my skull with whatever he used on my face.

I slowly stood up and ate the pain vibrating through my body. Blood trickled down into my mouth. Coppery and warm. I'd tasted it before. And had always made my attacker pay. Not always right away. But when the time came, I was swift and ruthless. That's where the man in black made his mistake tonight. He should have finished the job.

I turned to sit down on the stairs and saw a light glowing from the floor above. No one was staring over the railing at me, but I noticed the position of the room. Just to the right of the staircase.

Maybe that's why my attacker let me live. He'd seen the light flash on and escaped rather than be seen killing me.

Then it hit me. What had hit me. Long, thin, cylindrical, and steel. A policemen's baton. The shadowed physique of the attacker matched Detective Jake Mitchell's. He'd made his move. What if I wasn't his only target?

Leah.

I bolted upright. The pounding in my head almost knocked me back down. I steadied myself and slapped my hand against my thigh looking for a pants pocket and a room key. I didn't have either. No clothes. No key.

I staggered into the pool area, grabbed a towel off a lounge chair, and wrapped it around my waist. Blood curled over my lip and into my mouth. Nausea hollowed me out. I wanted to puke. I wanted to curl up into a ball and go back to sleep. But I had to make sure Leah was safe.

I did my best to steady my gait along the concrete path and walked into the lobby.

"Ugh!" The woman behind the counter thrust her hands to her face and backed up against the wall behind her. She was petite with big brown eyes that were now the size of saucers.

"I know I'm a bit underdressed and not at my best." I smiled and felt a drop of blood slide off my lip and splat down onto the floor. "But I locked myself out of my room when I went for ice. Could I have another key? Room . . ." I couldn't remember my room number. "My name's Rick Cahill. It's on the second floor, down the hall from the staircase. It's 2 . . . 219!"

"What happened?"

"Oh, you mean this?" I pointed at my face. "I stumbled out of bed on my way to the bathroom and banged into the dresser. Thus, the need for ice."

"I don't think I can do that. I mean, normally I would, but you don't have any ID or clothes on or anything. Maybe I should call 911. You look like you should go to the emergency room."

"I appreciate your concern, but I just want to go back to my room. If you want to follow me up to it, I can show you my ID inside. Look me up in your system. You'll see the room is comped because I'm a friend of a vice president in the Best Western corporation."

She rattled on the keyboard and looked up at me.

"I'll make you a key right away." Thirty seconds later, she handed me a key envelope with two keycards in it.

"Thanks." I turned to leave and staggered two steps before straightening out.

"Are you sure you don't want me to call 911, Mr. Cahill?"

"I'm fine. Thanks." I walked to the door and noticed a dotted blood trail on the tile floor from my walk into the lobby.

I made it to the elevator and went up one floor to my room level. The stairs were too tough. The new key worked, and I flung the door open and hurried to my cellphone on the nightstand. I found Leah's number and hit dial. Five rings. Voicemail. I left her a message to call me immediately and to not let anyone in her house. Especially anyone from SBPD. I called again. Rings. Voicemail. I sent her a text then threw on a pair of jeans, sweatshirt, and shoes.

I caught a glimpse of myself in the wall mirror when I walked over to the desk to grab my car keys. A gash across the bridge of my swollen nose leaking blood. Swelling around both eyes with red seeping into the skin. A knot half the size of a golf ball on my forehead above my left eye.

No time for a diagnosis or treatment.

I grabbed my car keys off the dresser and noticed what wasn't on the desk. My computer. I'd been right. Mitchell looking for info on my investigation. But I didn't know what I could do about it.

First, I had to protect Leah.

CHAPTER THIRTY-TWO

I CALLED LEAH three times with no answer on the fifteen-minute drive to her house. I could have made it sooner but briefly got lost when I made the wrong turn in her neighborhood because I couldn't remember her street name. I shouldn't have been driving but I didn't have a choice. Whoever ambushed me may come for Leah.

I slammed to a stop in her driveway. No other car there. All the lights were off in the house. I got out of the car, grabbed the Smith & Wesson from the trunk, and rushed to the front door. I hammered on the door and rang the doorbell. The neighbors' dogs next door started barking. Still dark inside Leah's house.

I pounded on the door some more and yelled her name. The lights went on next door, but not inside Leah's. More pounding and yelling. Finally, the porch light over my head went on.

Leah opened the door. "Rick! My God, what happened to you?"

She pulled the door wide and I went inside.

"Sorry. I had to make sure you were okay. I called but you didn't answer."

"I turned my phone off when I went to bed." She led me over to the couch and we sat down. The pain in my head bounced back through the adrenaline that had kept it at bay when I was afraid for Leah. "Wait here."

She ran into the kitchen. I heard a drawer roll open then slam shut and the same with the refrigerator. Then a few clunks. She ran back to me and gently moved my head back against the cushion and pressed a towel with ice against the bridge of my nose and the knot on my forehead. It focused the pain, but I knew the ice would help and that I should probably go to the hospital.

I told her about the break-in and the police baton and my stolen gun and missing computer. And my suspicion that Mitchell attacked me.

"Rick, you can't be sure it was Detective Mitchell. It could have been just someone burglarizing your room." Leah stared into my one uncovered eye. "Either way we should call the police and take you to the emergency room."

Someone pounded on the front door. "Police! Open up!"

Leah shot up and the towel of ice fell into my lap.

"Wait." I grabbed her arm. "He may not really be a cop or it could be Mitchell or Weaver. Go hide in the kitchen until I tell you to come out."

"Is that really necessary?" She pulled against my arm.

"Yes." I tugged back. Hard. "Go."

Fear flashed across her eyes. Maybe for the man outside. Maybe for me. She hurried into the kitchen.

More pounds on the door. "This is the Santa Barbara Police Department. Open this door. Now!"

I went over to the door, careful not to stand directly behind it, and angled my eye over the peephole. Two cops in uniform standing on either side of the door. Guns drawn.

I took a couple steps backward and yelled, "Be right there." Then went over to the table next to the couch and opened the drawer to stick my gun inside. And found another one already there. A Sig Sauer P226. I rushed over to the end table on the other side of the couch and put my Smith & Wesson .357 in its drawer.

I went into the kitchen and grabbed Leah's hand. "It's okay."

I led her over to the front door. The cop outside was into round three of pounding and yelling when I slowly opened the door.

Both cops had their guns pointed at me. One to the right of the door. One to the left. They held their guns in the Master Grip, fingers on the trigger guards and not the triggers. Thank God.

"Sir, step out onto the porch and get onto the ground. Now! Hands and legs out wide!" The cop on the right shouted.

"Officer, he's my friend," Leah said from behind me.

"Let us handle this, ma'am," The second cop said. "Please stay inside the house."

I took two slow steps out onto the porch and got down on my stomach as quickly as the pain in my head and arm would allow and spread out like a starfish. A knee compressed my back and a handcuff cinched around my right wrist. My right arm was yanked behind my back. Pain buzzed along my injured forearm. My left arm was pulled back to meet the right and my wrists were locked together. A single hand patted me down, top to bottom, front and back, along my crotch.

"No gun," the cop who patted me down said.

"My friend didn't do anything wrong." Leah, her voice a high crackle. "He was attacked at his hotel and came over here to protect me."

A black boot with a crepe sole passed in front of my face and another followed. Different male voice. "Ma'am, let's go into the living room where we can talk."

Footsteps faded away.

"If I sit you up, will you tell me what happened here tonight?" My hand-cuffer.

"Yes." Hands grabbed my arms and helped me up to a sitting position. My face left a smudge of blood on the porch and more trickled down my nose.

"What's your name, sir?" The cop's name tag read Armenta. Hispanic. Average height but built like an Olympic wrestler. I was glad he didn't accidently rip one of my arms out of its socket when he handcuffed me.

"Rick Cahill. I'm a private investigator." I realized as soon as I said it that being a PI probably wouldn't help me make my case.

"What brought you to this house tonight?" Officer Armenta took out a pen and pad.

"Someone broke into my room at the Beachside Inn about a half hour ago and jacked my computer. So, I chased after him." Now it got tricky. I had to be careful how much I told cops from SBPD, the department that employed the detective who attacked me. "He clocked me in the face with a baton or a blackjack and got away."

"Can you describe your attacker?"

"About six-two, six-three, one eighty. Lean but muscular. Dressed all in black, including a ski mask." I left out that he was a detective in MIU. I'd handle that on my own.

"Did you come over here with a gun and pound on the door shouting because you thought the suspect was here?"

"Ms. Landingham hired me to help former homicide detective Jim Grimes with a supplemental investigation of her sister's death. I'm sure you're aware of Sergeant Landingham, who was killed in a hit and run."

"That doesn't explain why you came here."

"This is her house. I've been asking questions around town and figured the person who broke into my room may have been the person driving the van that killed Detective Landingham." Another drop of blood slipped off my nose onto my sweatshirt. "I was afraid he might go after Leah since she's been with me on a lot of the interviews."

"Where is the gun you had when you arrived here?"

"Inside the house in the drawer of the table on the right side of the couch. A Smith & Wesson .357 Magnum. I have a concealed carry permit for it in my wallet." I tilted my head toward my right and back toward my right buttock. "It also covers the gun the suspect stole after he clubbed me."

"What?" Armenta stopped taking notes and looked at me. "How many guns do you travel with? You going to war?"

And he didn't even know about the Glock 9mm and Mossberg shotgun in the trunk of my car. But I had to tell the police about the stolen Ruger in case Mitchell or Weaver planned to use it on someone and set me up.

"All legally licensed."

"And where was the gun when your attacker stole it?"

"I dropped it when he hit me with the baton." I could have lied and said he'd taken it from my room, but I had other lies to tell and I wanted to keep the number down to a minimum. It's easier to remember the truth.

"So, you chased after the thief with a gun?" Armenta's voice went up a note like he'd never heard of an armed civilian chasing after a bad guy.

"Yes."

"Did you fire the weapon?"

"No." I stayed calm. Like getting mugged and having a gun stolen was an everyday occurrence.

The other cop, his tag read "Philips," appeared in the doorway. Tall, wide African American. Leah stood behind him with her arms crossed. Philips looked at me then nodded to Officer Armenta.

Armenta stooped down, unlocked the handcuffs, and took them off me. I stood up slowly. My head hammering from the inside and threatening to tilt me over.

The cops checked my permit against the Smith & Wesson inside the house and entered my stolen Ruger into their system. They took both Leah's and my phone numbers, told us a detective would follow up with us later, and then left in their squad car while Leah's next-door neighbors watched from their porch.

"Let's go." Leah put her shoulder under my armpit. "I'm taking you to the emergency room."

"Tell me about the gun in the side table next to the sofa."

"That was Krista's." She adjusted her position to get my weight better centered on her shoulder. "My brother wanted me to have it."

"Do you know how to use it?"

"Yes. Now, let's get you to the hospital. You probably have a concussion and that bump on your head doesn't look good."

No argument. I only played the hero when I didn't have any other choice. Tonight, I did.

CHAPTER THIRTY-THREE

I GOT OUT of the emergency room in just over an hour. Slow night. The doctor told me I had a concussion and a hematoma. No broken bones in my forearm, but it had swollen to twice its normal size. I was half a Popeye with a broken head and without the spinach. The doctor told me and Leah that I could sleep as long as I was coherent beforehand and to ice my head and arm for the next three days, plus bedrest, and recommended Tylenol for the pain.

I didn't tell him or Leah that this wasn't my first rodeo. This was probably my seventh or eighth concussion dating back to my football days in high school and college when there was no concussion protocol. I'd had worse but never with as much memory loss. Maybe they were starting to add up.

"Why didn't you tell the police officers that you think it was Detective Mitchell who attacked you?" Leah asked as she steered my Honda Accord out of the hospital parking lot.

"I can't prove it and I don't want him to know that I'm onto him about being involved in Colleen's murder."

"You don't know that, Rick. I think just the opposite. I believe the story Detective Mitchell told us at police headquarters yesterday."

"Why are you protecting them? Because they're cops on the same police force Krista was on?" I rubbed my head to ease the pounding. Denied. "You know what Mike Richert saw and told Krista. There was a cop in uniform who helped place Colleen's body on the beach. At the least he was an accessory after the fact. A couple days after Richert talked to Krista, somebody ran her over. Somebody at SBPD is dirty and we both know who it is."

"No, we don't." Leah's voice rose. "All we know is that fourteen years ago a man on a yacht a hundred yards offshore thinks he saw a man dressed in a uniform and another man walk away from East Beach after they may have been carrying something and he didn't report it to the police for nine years and that Tom saw someone in bed with Krista the night Colleen died and spent a few hours in the drunk tank at the time of Colleen's murder."

"Based on a story that can't be verified." I looked over at Leah. "Unless your brother confirmed Weaver was in the drunk tank."

"He hasn't called me back. But you have to look at all the facts we know, not just the ones that suit your theory."

"It's not a theory. It's what happened."

We made the remainder of the drive to Leah's house in silence.

Leah pulled into her driveway at five twenty a.m. Still dark but the sky was hinting at light. I got out of the car and walked around and met Leah on the driver side.

"Thanks." I stuck out my hand for the keys. "I can take it from here."

She put the keys in her jeans pocket, put her hands around my good forearm, and walked me into her house. She started to lead me down the hall to her bedroom. I stopped at the edge of the hall.

"I'm good out here. I don't think I can sleep. I'm not really tired. I fell asleep early last night." In a drunken haze. "You should try to get back to sleep."

"I'm not going to molest you, Rick." She frowned and shook her head. "I'm just going to take care of you for as long as you need taking care of."

I thought about the other night when I'd abandoned Leah in her own bed. She'd taken it as a rejection. It wasn't, but explaining why I left her in the middle of the night would sound like rejection just the same.

"I'm good to go now." I put out my empty hand again. "I appreciate all you've already done. I shouldn't have come over and gotten you involved."

"You came over here to make sure I was all right." She pushed my hand away. Her cheeks flushed and her eyes went narrow. "You have a concussion and a hematoma and you drove over here to make sure whoever attacked you and almost killed you wouldn't do the same to me. And now you're apologizing. What is wrong with you?"

"I just thought . . . I didn't want . . ."

"Why can't you give yourself a break? Why do you have to make things so hard?"

"I don't know."

"Well, you need to figure it out. You can't spend the rest of your life hating yourself. Or you'll always be alone."

She rushed down the hall into her bedroom and slammed the door behind her.

I took six Tylenol, iced my head and my arm, and watched the sun come up. I had to be at Frank Cornetta's house at eight a.m. to copy the files from his security camera.

I leaned back on the couch and wondered how much of what I told Leah she'd relay to Grimes. She had more confidence in his investigative abilities than in mine. The Tylenol hadn't kicked in yet and concentrating on how to deal with Grimes made my head hurt even worse.

I lay down with my head elevated and tried not to think of anything.

*   *   *

My eyes opened. My pocket was vibrating. I'd fallen asleep. I pulled out my phone and saw a phone number I didn't recognize. Then I saw the time. Eight fifteen a.m. Shit. I sprang up to vertical on the couch and my head reminded me that someone tried to split it in half last night. I answered the phone.

"We agreed on eight o'clock, Mr. Cahill." Clipped military voice. Frank Cornetta. "I have to leave here at eight thirty. Are you on your way?"

"Yes." I got off the couch and grabbed my shoes off the floor. "I can be there in fifteen minutes."

"Uh-huh." He hung up.

I put on my shoes and reached into my pocket for my keys. Shit. Leah had them. I tiptoed back to her room and eased the door open. I didn't want to knock and wake her up for the second time in six hours. The shades were open and I heard the shower running in the master bath. Her jeans hung over a chair next to the window. I rifled a pocket and grabbed my keys.

I didn't have time to wait for her to get out of the shower. I hustled into the kitchen and left a note on her notepad magnet on the refrigerator. "Meeting someone."

I called Mike Richert as I sped to Frank Cornetta's house. Looking for confirmation of what I already knew.

"Mr. Richert? Rick Cahill. Could the cop on the Santa Barbara Police Department you spoke to on the phone about what you saw on East Beach have been named Mitchell or Weaver?"

I held my breath and waited for another nail to hammer in both their coffins.

"No. Those names don't sound familiar."

I let go the breath, thanked him, and hung up. Maybe the tapes from Frank Cornetta's security camera would give me the confirmation I needed.

I pulled down Krista's street at 8:32 a.m. A white Ford F150 pickup truck backed out of the driveway across from her house. I pulled up alongside it, driver side to driver side, after it straightened out. A man in his late fifties sat ramrod straight behind the steering wheel. Bald on top with a trim ring of brown hair underneath. British lieutenant mustache. I rolled down my window.

He did the same.

"Mr. Cornetta? Rick Cahill. Sorry I'm late."

"By the looks of your face, you probably have good reason." Long R Boston accent. "I was just about to call you. I copied the files onto a flash drive and put it in the mailbox."

I took out my wallet, grabbed two twenties, and held them out the window. "Let me pay you for the flash drive."

"Keep it. Take care of yourself, Mr. Cahill." He rolled up his window and drove up the street.

I parked along the curb in front of the Cornetta house next to an old-fashioned mailbox. I got out of the car and pulled a small letter envelope with my name written on it. The envelope had a rectangular two-inch bump inside. I got back into my car and pulled across the street into Krista's driveway to execute a three-point turn.

My phone buzzed in my pocket. I pulled it out and checked the screen. Leah.

"Where are you?" Concern. "The doctor told you to lay low for the next couple days. In fact, he said bedrest."

"I'm taking things slow." As slowly as I could considering I had two murderers to nail down and kill. "I just picked up a flash drive with surveillance video of Krista's house."

"How's your head?"

"Not bad." Throbbing.

"You really should rest, Rick." More concerned than angry now. "I have to consult with a client for a couple hours. I'll call you when I'm done and meet you back at the house. Make yourself at home. I left a spare key in the large flowerpot on the porch."

She gave me the code to her home alarm.

"Okay, I'll head over there now and look at the security camera footage." I had planned go back to the hotel because I thought I was an unwanted guest. "Shit."

"What is it?"

"I forgot. My computer was stolen."

"I need mine for my appointment. Buy a new one and expense it. I'll cover the cost."

My kind of client. But Leah wasn't a client anymore. She was much more. Maybe too much more.

"That's okay. Call me when you're done."

"I insist, Rick."

"We'll talk about it later. Be aware of your surroundings."

"You, too."

"One last thing. What kind of car does Tom drive?"

"I think a Dodge Charger. Why? No, wait. It's a Dodge Challenger. The one that's more square looking. Why?"

"Black, of course."

"Yes. Why?"

"To see if he went by Krista's house after she died."

"I'll call you when I'm done." Clipped. She hung up.

For someone who didn't like the guy, Leah now seemed to be a defender of Tom Weaver. Maybe she didn't want to believe someone who her sister once loved would be capable of murdering her. Unfortunately, people kill their exes all the time.

Whatever Leah's concerns about her ex-brother-in-law's culpability didn't matter now. She could fire me today and I'd still pursue the truth until justice be done.

My justice.

CHAPTER THIRTY-FOUR

I BOUGHT AN Asus laptop at a Best Buy in Goleta and went back to Leah's house. Once I got the new computer up and running, I slotted Frank Cornetta's flash drive into a USB port. Cornetta had been thorough. There were seven dated individual video files. The Monday Krista died through last Sunday.

The first video I watched was from Sunday, the day Leah and I discovered the files missing from Krista's office. Each video began at 12:00 a.m. on the date listed.

I'd found out, grudgingly, from Grimes that Mitchell drove a white Jeep Wrangler. So, I had two targets. I watched the beginning of the video at regular speed to get a feel for the clarity of the image. Not a single car or movement in front of Krista's house appeared for the first five or so minutes. Finally, a dark SUV passed through the camera's view going down the street. The feed was in black and white, which made every dark car black. Not ideal.

I sped up the playback and looked for headlights and any movement at Krista's. Nighttime moved quickly due to lack of activity. After the sun came up and people began starting their days, I had to slow things down a bit. More activity meant more things to watch and more chances to miss something. I had to use the slowest fast-forward setting. Nothing suspicious happened. Finally, my car pulled into Krista's driveway at 5:47 p.m. It had taken me an hour and twenty-five minutes to get through eighteen hours of security footage. I had six more days to go.

This was the part of being a PI they didn't list in the brochures.

I went backwards one day to the day of Krista's funeral. Again, nothing suspicious. No black Dodge Challenger or white Jeep Wrangler parked in Krista's driveway or passed by her house.

Even though I'd improved my viewing process, I was burned out. My eyes felt like I'd cried for an hour straight and were all out of lubrication. And my head continued to pound.

My phone rang right as I cued up day number three. Blocked caller ID. I answered.

"Mr. Cahill, this is Detective Wilkens. I'm following up on the complaint you made early this morning to Officers Phillips and Armenta."

I hadn't really made a complaint until the cops finally figured out I wasn't a domestic abuser. Took him long enough. It was 2:12 p.m. Phillips and Armenta questioned me twelve hours ago. I was small potatoes. Probably more of an irritant with everyone focusing on Krista's case.

"What can I do for you, Detective? I don't have anything to add beyond what the patrolmen hopefully put in their report."

"Would you mind coming by the station so we can go over the report? It's missing a few details."

Despite 1,000 milligrams of Tylenol, my head throbbed and my eyes stung.

"Can't we just handle this on the phone, Detective? I'm a little sore from last night."

"I suppose I could come to you."

As much as my head hurt, there was one advantage to going to SBPD. I might get a glimpse at Mitchell or Weaver and measure their reactions when they saw me. Swollen nose, swollen head, swollen forearm, and black eyes, to boot.

"I'll be at the station in ten minutes."

CHAPTER THIRTY-FIVE

DETECTIVE JOE WILKENS was tall. Real tall, like six-six or six-seven. Thin and long-armed. Older than I expected, he looked to be in his late fifties. Retirement age for most cops. I didn't remember him from my days on the force. SBPD was a small department, and while I couldn't remember the names of everyone in it when I was there, I'd surely seen every cop in the department at one time or another over my two-and-a-half-year career. If you could call it a career.

After introductions, Wilkens led me upstairs to the second floor where Mitchell had taken Leah and me yesterday. But we turned into a room one door short of the MIU office. There were eight cubbyhole cubes jammed together in the center of the room. A female African American detective sat in the cube at the end talking to a white patrolman who stood at attention. A pale middle-aged doughboy detective sat reading a newspaper two cubes away. No one else was in the room. I didn't recognize either of the detectives. After my time.

Wilkens led me around to the other side of the cube bank and rolled a chair out from under a desk.

"Have a seat, Mr. Cahill." He sat down in the next cube facing me.

The detective stopped talking to the patrolman at the mention of my name and Pillsbury Doughboy prairie-dogged his head over his cubicle to get a look at me. Everybody at SBPD still knew who I was even if they didn't work there when I did. I sat down and now wished I'd taken Wilkens up on his house call.

"Now take me through exactly what happened last night, Mr. Cahill." Wilkens had a pen and pad out.

I told him everything that happened, starting with waking up to an intruder in my room and ending with a bump on my head and a missing gun and computer. I gave him the serial number to my stolen gun. The computer didn't matter. No one could get shot by it and blame it on me.

Wilkens filled out a form for the stolen gun and had me sign it. I didn't tell him about my suspicions that one of his compatriots was responsible. I had no proof. Other than what my gut told me.

Wilkens finished with me, and I exited the detective room, turned toward the stairs, and almost bumped into a cop going the other way down the hall.

Detective Mitchell.

"Whoa." He lithely sidestepped me, then stopped. "What happened to your face?"

Mitchell's body could have been a match for the silhouette I saw standing in my room in the dark and running down the hotel hall. I studied his face for a tell. A curled lip of enjoyment at the damage he'd done. A couple blinks to inadvertently admit his guilt. A tight mouth in disappointment for not finishing the job. He gave me none of that. A surprised look without empathy. Whether it was he or someone else who nearly cracked my skull, Detective Mitchell wasn't concerned about my health.

A detective walked by us, then down the staircase. No one else was in the hall.

"I thought you knew all about it." I stepped inside Mitchell's personal space. My swollen face three inches from his. The walls of SBPD fell away. All I saw was the man who covered for the man who killed my wife, conspired to kill Krista Landingham, and ambushed me last night. Just the two of us. He had a gun holstered on his hip. I had vengeance coursing through my entire body.

"What do you mean by that?" His demeanor turned hard. He stayed right where he was. Eye to eye.

I'd let my bloodlust override the need to be discreet. To let Mitchell know I was onto him. I could live with that. Maybe he'd get nervous and make a mistake. Or come at me head-on. I could live with that, too. Give me a chance for a righteous kill in the eyes of SBPD.

"I know word spreads pretty quickly around here. Next time I'll shoot first and worry about the rest later."

"Is that some kind of threat?" Mitchell lifted his chin a centimeter.

"Not unless you plan on breaking into my hotel room." I edged in closer, the pain in my head gone for the first time today.

"You'd better step off."

I didn't move. This couldn't end well for me, but last night hadn't either. Today the threat was right in front of me.

"Gentlemen." A stern voice behind me. The walls and the file cabinets in the hallway and the open doors to the detective rooms all filled back in. Still, neither of us moved. "Step away, Detective."

Captain Kessler came even with us. Dress blues, snap-creased. I saw him out of the corner of my eye as I continued to stare Mitchell down. He did the same.

"Detective!" Kessler wedged between us, facing Mitchell. "What is the problem here?"

Mitchell took a step back and finally looked from me to Kessler. The two detectives from the room I just vacated suddenly filled the doorway.

"You'll have to ask Mr. Cahill, Captain." His eyes lasered back on me. "He seems to think I *had* something to do with his face."

"Do you have a complaint to make, Mr. Cahill?" Kessler turned his attention to me.

"I already filed a complaint with Detective Wilkens."

"No suspect identified, sir." Wilkens aw-shucked his shoulders.

"That will be all, Detectives." Kessler put his hands on his hips and looked at each cop. The detectives retreated back into their room and Mitchell stormed off down the hall away from the MIU room. I started for the stairs until a hand on my shoulder stopped me.

"Rick." The politician returned to Kessler's voice. "Would you mind joining me in my office for a brief moment."

My adrenaline evaporated with Mitchell's exit and the pain in my head swooped in to take its place.

"I'm beat, Captain. I'd really just like to go back to my hotel and lie down."

"It will just take a minute. You'll be doing me a favor."

A favor. The currency of politicians. Maybe I could use a favor from Kessler sometime. Plus, I was curious about what he wanted.

"Sure."

"Great." He patted my shoulder and gave me the candidate poster smile, then led me through the MIU room and into his office in the far right corner. The back wall of the office had photos of Kessler's career going all the way back to when he drove around Chief Siems and before. Kessler was proud of his time as a cop. Maybe a bit too proud.

"Have a seat, Rick." He pointed to a chair in front of his immaculate desk. The desk was bigger and newer than the ones his detectives used outside his office in MIU. He closed the blinds on the windows facing the outside room. Either so his detectives couldn't look in or I couldn't look out. Neither option gave me the warm fuzzies.

"Seems like a lot of privacy for a one-minute talk." I tilted my head toward the blinds.

"I'm hoping the privacy will make you feel comfortable so you can be completely forthcoming."

"The last time I was here, you had Detective Flora cuff me for opening my mouth. Why do you want me to talk today?"

"First of all, I'd like to know what happened to your face and why you think Detective Mitchell is responsible."

Straightforward questions from a captain wanting to know if someone under his charge had committed battery. Fair enough. But I bet the politician in Kessler was looking for an angle. Always an angle with these guys.

But then again, I was looking for one, too.

"Has anyone corroborated Mitchell's story about Weaver being in the drunk tank the night Colleen died?" I asked.

"I'll ask the questions in this room or any other while I'm wearing a badge and you're not." His voice, calm, didn't match the harshness of his words. Almost like he was playing a part and hadn't yet found the character's motivation. Unusual for a politician as practiced as Kessler.

"I'm just looking for some reciprocity, Captain."

"Reciprocity comes after you tell me something. You haven't done that yet." He smiled a cigar smoke backroom smile that gave me hope he may actually tell me something about Weaver.

I told him about the 211 committed on me at my hotel.

"Sounds like a junkie looking to pawn something for his next fix."

Of course, he was right, but he hadn't connected the dots, yet. I had and there were only a few more to connect before I had a straight line to Colleen's murderers.

"Maybe. Or it could have been someone trying to find out how much I knew about Colleen and Krista's murders. The people who committed them."

"That's right. Two people, not one." Kessler smiled. Half campaigning politician smile, half cop smirk. Not a pleasant combination. "Jim

Grimes filled in the team on your theory after you spoke with an elderly gentleman down in San Diego."

"Oceanside."

"Right. Mr. Richert, I believe." The ugly smile. "And it doesn't bother you that he waited nine years to report what he saw on the beach?"

"He didn't learn about it until then." I didn't bother explaining. If Grimes filled in MIU, he probably told them why it took Richert so long to report what he saw.

"Don't you think it's possible, if not probable, that Mr. Richert, a man in his seventies, got his dates mixed up after so long?"

"Possible." I didn't expect to have SBPD on my side, but they still had access to information I needed to connect all the bloody dots I needed to justify my mission. Time for that reciprocity. "Have you been able to verify that Lieutenant Weaver was in the drunk tank at the jail the night my wife died?"

"Still on that track, Rick?"

"Just trying to nail down the facts, Captain."

"An officer-involved DUI is a tricky situation." Full campaign smile. "If a sheriff's deputy pulled over Lieutenant Weaver, they didn't write him up. No one will admit to stopping him that night because they don't want to get in trouble for giving a police officer special treatment. Especially in today's cop-hating environment. The same with the deputies on duty at the jail. No one's going to admit anything unless they're put under oath. I wouldn't read too much into the fact that Weaver's night in the jail can't be corroborated."

Kessler was toeing the company line as expected, but something else was bothering me.

"Did you know that Krista was investigating my wife's murder?"

"Of course. I command MIU. I know what all my charges are working on."

"Then why didn't you tell me when you brought up Colleen's death at Krista's service?"

"I didn't want to get your hopes up. Detective Landingham was just in the preliminary stages." He tilted his head and his eyebrows rose. "And, obviously, we have every police officer we can spare on Detective Landingham's vehicular manslaughter investigation. Even after we solve that, we'll be a detective short in MIU. I'm not sure when the chief will fill that spot. We won't be able to spare anyone on cold cases for a while. So, I'm sure you can understand why I didn't tell you about Detective Landingham's brief look at the case."

Bureaucrat.

"Sure."

"Anything else, Rick?" The political hack smile. "I think I've shown you some reciprocity."

I wanted out more than he wanted me to leave, but there was one piece of information I needed for the dots.

"Did you find out what Krista was doing on State Street at that time of night after she quit drinking six years ago?"

"No, but I have an idea."

"What's that?"

"I'm afraid she'd started drinking again." He pursed his lips and shook his head.

"Bullshit. Who told you that?"

"No one told me. I experienced it myself. You're the only person I've told, so please don't spread it around. We don't need anyone to think ill of a fallen police officer."

"What did her toxicology report say? Did she have alcohol in her system?"

"You know I can't give you that information."

"Was she drunk when the van hit her, Captain?"

"Next question."

"Okay. What do you mean you *experienced her drinking again?*" This went against what Leah knew about her sister. Or what she told me about her.

"Rick, I've given you enough information today." He steepled his fingers again. Sunlight broke through the clouds and backlit him through the window. He looked pious. All he needed to be a saint was for the window to be stained glass. "I can assure you Detective Wilkens will follow all legitimate leads in the investigation into your armed robbery. Now, if you'll excuse me, I have a lot of work to do."

Captain Kessler stood up and extended a hand across the desk.

"I appreciate that, Captain." I stood up and shook his hand. "But I'm baffled by Krista drinking again. Her sister was sure she hadn't backtracked. It would help if you could explain the incident you had with her."

"Like I said, Rick, there's no need for her drinking again to get out."

"I won't tell anyone. Not even Leah. But it might help me realize why Krista was down on State Street the night she died."

"Well . . . there wasn't an incident, per se. She called me at home a few nights before she died and was obviously drunk. I know you were a police officer, if just for a short time. You know any good policeman can tell when someone has had too much to drink. Even over the phone."

I learned as a child from my father. He was a cop, too, but I learned directly from him.

"Did she call you at home often?" This had to be the call on the Thursday night before she died.

"Very rarely."

"Why did she call that night?"

"She had a plan on how to run the unit better. She'd had too much and wanted to straighten her boss out. I didn't take it personally. Again, keep this just between us."

We shook and I left Captain Kessler's office with two important pieces of information that canceled each other out. First, SBPD hadn't been able to corroborate Weaver's supposed drunk tank stay. Second, that Krista may have been down on State Street for a night out on the town when she was killed.

Maybe Dustin Peck got it all wrong.

CHAPTER THIRTY-SIX

I GOT TO Leah's house around four thirty p.m. She wasn't home yet. I zombie-walked to her couch and sat down. The adrenaline of the chase evaporated somewhere on the drive between SBPD and Leah's. I wanted to go to bed and wake up in a week. Maybe my head would stop pounding by then. But the information about Krista drinking again made me reassess everything I'd theorized about Colleen's and Krista's deaths.

What if Tom Weaver really was in the drunk tank the night Colleen died, but no sheriff's deputy was willing to risk a reprimand or something worse to corroborate it? What if Krista was drinking again like Kessler said? Maybe I'd gotten so caught up in my lust for justice that I'd jumped way out on an unsustainable limb?

Mike Richert could be telling the God's honest truth and Colleen still could have been murdered by someone other than a cop. A lot of security guard uniforms look just like those of the police. Some security guards were wannabe cops who washed out of the academy for psychological reasons. What if Colleen had been murdered by a twisted rent-a-cop and a buddy and not the real thing? That made just as much sense, if not more, as a cop going bad and pulling in a brother in blue to commit man's worst sin.

I sat down at my new computer and dosed myself with another 1,000 milligrams of pain reliever and pulled up Frank Cornetta's security camera files. Day three going backwards from Sunday.

An hour and a half later Leah came home while I was in the middle of day four. Nothing of importance happened at Krista's house. Except Leah and her brother arriving at the house and staying inside for an hour. They came out with a couple boxes. The video wasn't very clear, but I could sense the anguish on Leah's face. She looked broken.

"Did you find anything?" Leah sat down next to me on the couch and set the leather satchel with her design notes and tools on the coffee table. She wore blue slacks with a cream blouse and looked very professional. And very beautiful. Her anger from this morning gone.

"Not yet. Three and a half days down." I thought about what Captain Kessler said about Krista's drunk dial. "Is it possible that Krista had started drinking again?"

"What?" Her eyebrows rose. "No. Why?"

"Captain Kessler thought she was drunk when she called him the Thursday night before she died." I thought of another possibility. "How about prescription meds?"

"There's no way she started drinking again. But . . ."

"What?"

"She hurt her back skiing over Christmas and did have to take Vicodin for a few weeks. There were still some in her medicine cabinet after she died, but the prescription was from January. I don't think she was still taking them. She wouldn't take them to get high. That wasn't Krista. She was proud of her sobriety. She didn't even want to take the Vicodin, but the pain was pretty bad."

"You're probably right. Thanks." But what people did when no one was watching could sometimes shock their loved ones. Maybe Vicodin explained Krista's call to Kessler. "Your brother call you back about Weaver being in the drunk tank the night Colleen was murdered?"

"Yes. He said he didn't know anything about it."

That didn't mean it didn't happen, but it didn't help Mitchell's story.

"How's your head?" Leah gently touched my forehead.

"Fine." The Tylenol had moved the arrow of pain from an eight down to a seven. Livable.

"I guess I should figure out dinner. Are you hungry?"

I hadn't eaten since breakfast.

"Leah." I turned toward her on the couch. "I appreciate the hospitality, but you don't have to take care of me. I got beat up on a case. I've been beaten up on a lot of cases. That's part of the job. You don't have to feel responsible for me. I'll head back to the hotel tonight and contact Grimes in the morning. See if we can work together."

"Do what you want, Rick." Cobalt blue eyes thrumming with intelligence and beauty. "Go ahead and make things hard on yourself. That seems to be what makes you happy. Misery is your joy. If you can't let someone help you when you really need it, you'll never allow someone to see who you really are. Your weaknesses. Your vulnerabilities."

"I . . ."

"I want you to stay." Leah's eyes bore into me. Not angry. Adamant. "I want to ease some of that misery, but I'm not going to beg you to stay. I won't be angry if you leave. I'll understand. I'll have my answer and life will go on."

Leah was on the other side of my shadow life, out of reach. I couldn't get there until my mission was complete. I owed Colleen justice. I owed myself vengeance. But maybe I could allow myself a glimpse of what life could be.

"What's for dinner?"

*   *   *

We settled back onto the couch after we'd consumed the last bit of sauce from Chinese takeout food containers. Moo shu pork, cashew chicken, and pot stickers. Leah gave me a second set of eyes on the last half of day four of the security tapes. Another blank.

I leaned back and rested my eyes for a couple seconds. Two hours later, movement on the couch woke me. Leah set my new laptop onto the coffee table and stood up.

"I made it through day five. I didn't see anything around Krista's house that seemed suspicious to me. I'm not as savvy as you, but I'm pretty sure no one broke into her house. No Dodge Challenger or Jeep Wrangler drove by. Black, white, or any other colors."

"Thanks." I sat up. "I'll get through the last two days tomorrow."

"You know, this house has three bedrooms. One is my office, but the other one has a bed. More comfortable than the couch and it has a lock on the door. First door down the hall on the right."

"The only doors I wanted locked are the ones to the outside. I wish I could explain about the other night . . ."

"You don't have to. Separate rooms make more sense." Leah studied my face, looking for an answer I hoped to be able to give her someday. "For now."

She lowered a hand to me. I grasped it and stood up. Warm. Like the first time we touched. She led me down the hall and into the room. The suitcase I'd left in the trunk of the car was sitting on the bed. There was only one thing missing. The Smith & Wesson for the nightstand.

"Thanks." I let go of her hand. "I just have to get something out of the car."

"It's in the drawer." She nodded at the nightstand to the right of the bed. I opened the drawer and saw the Smith & Wesson in its holster.

"My father always keeps a gun next to his bed. Even now when he's retired. I've never known a cop who didn't. The house alarm is set for the night, so make sure you disarm it if you go out for the shotgun."

She kissed me on the cheek and lingered. I turned my head to meet her lips but she'd turned away.

"Thanks for taking care of me."

"Goodnight, Rick."

CHAPTER THIRTY-SEVEN

MY CELL PHONE buzzed in my jeans pocket on the guest bathroom floor while I was in the shower. By the time I grabbed a towel and got out of the shower the call had gone to voicemail. I checked the screen. Grimes. Seven fifteen a.m. He started early. I listened to the message. Meet him for breakfast at Kimbo's on Cabrillo Boulevard at 8:00 a.m. No explanation. No ask. Just be there. I guess he thought I was in my hotel room down the street. Or maybe he didn't care where I was and just liked the food.

* * *

Kimbo's was an old-school diner that had been around for decades before Colleen and I used to eat early morning Sunday breakfasts there during the football season. She was a Raider fan and I rooted for the Chargers, back when it mattered. Made for some contentious Sunday afternoons, but breakfasts were always relaxed and easy and cozy. The world felt warm and inviting as I shared the *LA Times* with my partner for life. Even after things turned to shit before Colleen died, Sunday breakfasts were sacred to both of us.

The line was already ten people deep outside Kimbo's when I got there at eight ten a.m. Grimes had a booth by the window. I sat down opposite him. Neither of us said hello. He looked at my swollen face and took a sip of coffee.

"Aren't you going to ask me what happened to my face?" I smiled, which made the bridge of my nose ache. To add to the pain in my head. "That's right. I'm sure your buddy Detective Mitchell already filled you in about our encounter yesterday at SBPD."

"Tell me about the break-in." Flat eyes. Not the usual contempt. Something had changed. "Start from the beginning. Everything."

I told him everything. All the way back to drinking a six-pack of beer and falling asleep semi-drunk. Grimes listened quietly without interrupting. His expression stayed flat.

The waitress came by when I was done, and I ordered some pancakes. Grimes finally spoke after the waitress left.

"The 211 doesn't make sense. No junkie breaks into a room on the second floor of the cheapest hotel on the block to steal a computer and then lays in wait to ambush his pursuer. He would just keep running. Did you check with the hotel to see if any other rooms were burglarized?"

"No, but I think the detective who took my complaint did. I'm sure he would have told me about any other reported thefts at the hotel. That would easily disprove my theory."

The waitress brought my pancakes and the All-American breakfast Grimes ordered before I arrived.

"Whoever broke in wanted your computer because they figured it contained information on our investigation."

"I screwed up his plan by being in my room." I slathered the pancakes in too much butter and just enough syrup. "I had to park in the hotel parking lot behind the Beachside Inn. He probably didn't see my car and assumed I wasn't in the hotel."

"That makes sense, but it's not a smoking gun against Tom Weaver and Jake Mitchell."

"It doesn't help their case." I took a bite of the pancakes. No, just the right amount of butter. "Plus, Kessler admitted that SBPD hasn't been able to corroborate Mitchell's drunk tank story about Weaver."

"I'll never buy that Tom Weaver killed your wife as revenge for you sleeping with Krista. I can see him fighting you right there in the bedroom that night or even going out and getting a snoot full and ending up in a drunk tank, but not killing your wife to get back at you."

"What if he didn't intend to kill Colleen? What if he picked her up to tell her about what he'd seen at his home and things got out of hand? He makes a pass at her, she rebuffs him, and he gets physical. Colleen fights back. Now she's going to file a sexual assault complaint and his cop career is over and he could do time, all because I slept with his wife. So, he kills her. No Colleen, no rape charge."

"And he calls straitlaced Jake Mitchell for help and he risks his career and doing time by aiding and abetting after the fact? No way."

"Mitchell's already admitted to aiding and abetting Weaver that night. Just with the made-up drunk driving story. That shows he's inclined to cover for Weaver."

"Two completely different things. And all he did was pick Tom up from jail and keep his mouth shut about it. Any cop would do the same for another cop."

"Say somehow I'm wrong about it being Weaver and Mitchell. You know it still has to be a cop or cops who killed Colleen and then Krista when they found out she'd reopened Colleen's murder. Who else but a cop would know about our investigation? Only Krista's family and SBPD know Leah hired us. Hell, I'm not even sure her family knows, but everyone at MIU does. Which brings us right back to Detective Mitchell, head of Krista's death investigation and senior detective in MIU."

"Still not convinced, Cahill. Could have been a rent-a-cop and his buddy. Could have been UCSB Campus Police. Her last known whereabouts was in front of the UCSB library." He took a bite of hash browns. "Word is that you had a closed-blinds sit-down with Captain Kessler in his office after you and Mitchell pissed on each other's legs in the hall. What was that about?"

I gave him the highlights and lowlights from my talk with Kessler.

"Anything else?" he asked after I finished.

"A couple things. The first pokes a small hole in my theory." I'd finally gotten Grimes over to my side. At least one foot over. He'd been a homicide cop five times as long as I'd been a lowly patrolman. I couldn't waste his knowledge and deductive reasoning just because I thought his conclusion about new information may differ from mine. "Kessler claims that Krista fell off the wagon before she died."

I told him about the phone call Kessler had with Krista a couple days before she died. That he was certain that Krista had been drunk.

"I hadn't seen any evidence of Krista drinking again, but I only talked to her on the phone a couple times about Colleen's case. And she called me on those occasions. Doubtful that she'd be intoxicated while working a case."

"Krista could have just been closing down the bars that night and that's why she was on State Street. Did you ever see a toxicology report on Krista's body?" I played devil's advocate against my own theory to keep Grimes from getting there first.

"No."

"Kessler wouldn't tell me what was on it." I took another bite of heaven and good memories. "Any way you can find out what's on the tox report?"

"Doubt it. The scene at East Figueroa has changed since our chat with Mitchell in MIU. I'm sure your pissing contest with him didn't help."

"Probably not."

"Even if Krista was drinking that night, it doesn't mean she went down to State Street to bar hop." Grimes had the bone now and he was gnawing on it like a good homicide cop would. "And there's still the story from Mr. Peck about her coming from her car. Any change on that?"

"No. Peck is more solid than ever. He was actually crossing State going east from Hotel Santa Barbara when he saw the van hit Krista. A much better vantage point."

"What was he doing at the hotel?"

"I told him I wouldn't tell anyone."

"Well, that answers that. Infidelity is rampant around this case."

I let it pass. A reminder that while Grimes now seemed to be all in on my team, he still didn't like me and would remind me of my short-comings whenever he got the chance.

"The other thing I wanted to tell you is that Leah was able to get Krista's cell phone records from AT&T." I told him about the calls made to and from Krista that we were able to attach names to and the one phone that rang and rang and didn't go to voicemail that we couldn't identify. "SBPD must have them, too."

"Can I see the phone bill?"

"I'll email you a copy later today. It will have the notes we took next to the calls." I took my last bite of pancakes and pushed the plate away. "One other thing. A neighbor across the street from Krista's home has a security camera that picks up the front of her house. I got him to make me copies of the days between her death and the funeral. I've made it through five days looking to see if someone broke into her house and stole her cold case files. Nothing of interest so far. I'll finish them by the end of tonight."

"We still don't know for sure that she had a file on your wife's murder at home."

"I do. You should, too," I said.

"I thought I explained to you that you should never jump to conclusions in homicide cases." He took a gulp of coffee, set the cup down next to his empty breakfast plate, and leaned toward me. "The only time I ever did that in fifteen years as a homicide cop was with you. It was wrong then and it's wrong now."

"Why me?"

"The facts of the case at the time led me to you, to start. Not having an alibi, or, I should say, not giving me your real alibi, didn't help. Still, there wasn't quite enough evidence, but I convinced my lieutenant and he found a sympathetic judge to issue an arrest warrant even though the DA wasn't fully onboard."

"Why?"

"I felt I had to. I made the unprofessional mistake of convincing Colleen's family that you did it."

Colleen's father had delayed her memorial service for a month until after I was arrested. Probably to make sure that I wouldn't be able to be there to say a last goodbye to Colleen. The Santa Barbara DA ruined his plans by releasing me the day before the service after a week in jail. I surprised and disappointed everyone at the church by flying to the Bay Area and showing up for the service.

"Still, you must have known you didn't have enough to make the charges stick."

"I should have, Cahill." He shook his head and looked lost for the first time since I'd know him. "But I knew the story of your father being a bad cop, and I didn't like you from the first day I met you playing softball when you were just a boot. A cocky, know-it-all boot. I let all of that cloud my judgment and started connecting dots that were too far apart. That's what you're doing now. You're forcing every new piece of evidence to fit into the gaps of your theory. Confirmation bias. If the facts don't fit perfectly, you keep hammering them into the gaps until they do."

I got up and tossed a twenty onto the table for breakfast. "You need to get up to date on the facts about my father. Sounds like you forgot to wedge out some of the old facts you hammered in a long time ago."

I went outside where the Santa Barbara gloom pressed down hard on the morning and washed everything in gray.

CHAPTER THIRTY-EIGHT

LEAH WAS OFF to a new design job by the time I got back to her house. I was glad her life had gotten back to some normalcy. That she had something to do during the day that took her mind off the death of her sister. I'd kept busy for the last fourteen years. Unfortunately, that doesn't always work.

I went into Leah's office and found the file folder we'd put Krista's phone records in. I pulled them out and studied them, making sure the notes I'd written on them contained sufficient information to explain to Grimes what we'd learned. The notes next to the last call Krista received late that Sunday night on the last night of her life read, "Called. No answer, no answering machine. No name or address attached to a number found in search databases." I grabbed a pen out of a mug on Leah's desk and added, "Called numerous times night and day, same results."

I pulled out my phone and called the number one more time for good luck and let it ring ten times. No answer. I scanned the records and then forwarded them to Grimes' email. Maybe he'd have better results with the last number than I did. Maybe he could get someone at SBPD to run the number through their databases and come up with a name and address.

The pounding in my head now only rated a six on the pain meter without Tylenol. Progress. Livable, but I took a couple tabs because the hours I had to put into watching grainy video on a computer screen would push the meter higher.

I grabbed my computer and sat at the dinner table rather than the more comfortable couch. Viewing hours of the tapes made me drowsy and the couch was too willing to let me slump into slumber.

One more day down. Nothing. One day left until Krista's death and no one had breached her house. An itch in my gut began to grow into a sick feeling that maybe Grimes was right. Maybe no one broke into Krista's house and stole her file on Colleen because she hadn't gotten around to making one yet. Or, at least hadn't brought it home yet.

A dot missing that I'd leapt over to connect to my theory. Krista had found something incriminating on her ex-husband and Mitchell about Colleen's murder and they killed her before she could bring charges or go any deeper. What if I was wrong? What if Krista had gone down to State Street to get drunk or meet a new boyfriend who was closing down a bar and she'd been run over by a drunk driver? It happened all the time.

Maybe Krista hadn't made any progress on Colleen's murder. Maybe she saw something about Mike Richert that I'd ignored because I'd gotten a whiff of finding Collen's killers and a last chance at redemption. That Richert was a lonely old man and would say anything to please a beautiful woman who was giving him attention. Maybe there wasn't a file on Colleen at her house because she hadn't found anything to put in it.

I'd wanted some new information on Colleen's murder that I could grab hold of and feel and touch and worry into some truth. Some purpose for my life.

What if the person who broke into my room two nights ago was just a common thief and was in my room to steal whatever he could and grabbed my computer when I woke up?

What if I never found Colleen's killer?

One tape left to prove my theory. The last day of Krista's life. Monday, April 1st.

The video began at 12:00 a.m. like all the rest. I ran it on fast forward but at a slower speed than I had on the last one. No action from twelve to one. Krista's porch light was on as it had been in the other videos until Leah and her brother arrived at the house three days after she died and turned it off.

I looked at the clock on the video: 1:09 a.m.; Krista had just over an hour left in her life of forty-six years. 1:30 passed by. No movement around the house. Finally, at 1:59 a.m., Krista emerged from her house, got into her car, and took the last drive she'd ever make.

At least I now had proof of one thing. Krista had been home all night, not bar hopping on State Street, the night before she died. What made her go downtown at two o'clock in the morning?

The rest of the day zoomed by in a shuddering rush. No one approached Krista's house during the day except for the mailman. No black Challenger or Wrangler. Around six p.m., ten to twelve people gathered in front of Krista's house and put flowers by her front door. This went on for about an hour. Frank Cornetta set down a bouquet of white roses on Krista's porch at 8:23 p.m. when no own else was out on the street. The camera angle was from behind, but it looked like he raised his hand to his forehead in a crisp military salute. He held the salute for a moment, then turned and walked back to his house. And wiped his eyes.

I watched to the end of the tape. No one breached Krista's house and no Dodge Challengers or Jeep Wranglers drove by. I closed the security camera file and stared at the blank computer screen. Seven days of video viewing and I hadn't seen anything to confirm my theory that someone broke into Krista's house after she died and stole her file on Colleen's murder.

Then it hit me. *After* Krista died. What if someone broke into her house *before* she died? And whatever they found was the reason they killed her? I called Frank Cornetta.

"Frank, Rick Cahill. I'm hoping you can help me one more time."

"Did you find what you were looking for on the tapes? Are the police any closer to catching Krista's killer?"

"No, I didn't find what I'd hope to, but the police are making progress." And I might have to defer to them at some point if I didn't find any new evidence to get me closer to finding Krista's killer. And Colleen's. "I realized that what I'm looking for might be on your security camera before Krista died."

"And you want copies of those tapes?"

"Yes. Can you get me the security tapes going back a week before Krista died?" To when she reopened Colleen's cold case.

"No. Unfortunately, I can't. The cloud only holds the video for two weeks unless you make hard copies every night, which I don't. But, today's Thursday, so I should be able to grab the Friday, Saturday, and Sunday before she died. Will that help?"

"Yes. I'll take whatever I can get."

Another fool's errand that could be forever open-ended. What if someone broke into Krista's house on the Thursday where there's no tape? Or before? I didn't have a choice. Until SBPD found the killer, I had to get evidence to find the killers on my own and dispense justice or find enough evidence to disprove the connection between Krista's and Colleen's murders and let the other justice system play out.

"Can you tell me what you're looking for?"

Cornetta didn't have to give me the tapes. They were his property. He was doing me a solid in hopes I'd find Krista's killer. He deserved the truth.

"Evidence of someone breaking into Krista's house."

"I'm away from home right now and won't get back until ten or so. I'll copy them then. As long as I copy the Friday tape before midnight, we'll be fine. Meet me at my house tomorrow at eight a.m. And try not to get beat up between now and then so you can make it on time."

"Roger."

CHAPTER THIRTY-NINE

I GOT TO Frank Cornetta's house at 7:55 a.m. and waited in my car. He came out onto his porch and waved me inside at 7:56 a.m.

I stepped inside to an immaculate home that a drill sergeant wouldn't have anything to bark at. The smell of bacon and eggs permeated the air. Reminded me that I hadn't had breakfast yet or eaten much yesterday. A woman in her late forties, brown wavy hair, year-round tan, and sultry brown eyes, examined my broken face then stuck out her hand.

"Eve Cornetta." She was beautiful. "Nice to meet you."

Her grip was firm and eye contact direct. She fit right into what little I knew about Frank Cornetta's life.

"Nice to meet you. Thanks for letting me intrude so early."

"We've been up since five thirty. Breakfast?"

"Evie, the man's on a mission. Rick." He headed down a long hall past two doors.

"Thanks for the offer." I followed Cornetta into the last room on the right in the hallway.

If possible, Frank Cornetta's office was spit-shinier than the rest of the house. The room was decorated, but not littered with military keepsakes. A large shadow box hung on one wall. It had seventeen photographs of soldiers around a handcrafted metal Christian cross.

The pictures were of individual Marines; some looked to have been cropped from photos of larger groups.

I didn't have to ask what the solemn display meant. Frank Cornetta had seen death in his life. A lot of it. Friends lost to violence for valiant causes. So had I. But for much lesser purposes.

Some had yet to be avenged.

Cornetta sat down at his desk in front of an open laptop with a flash drive attached to the computer's USB port. I'd expected him to just hand me the drive. I'd brought $60.00 to pay him for it along with the first one he gave me.

"I took the initiative to scan through the video files last night and this morning. I hope you don't mind."

A Marine taking the initiative. Who would have thought? He had every right. The security camera was his, as were its images.

"Of course not. What did you find?"

"I'm not sure, but it might be something." He hit the enter key on the computer keyboard and a still nighttime image of Krista's house came up. No car in the driveway. No lights on inside the house. Just the porch light outside. Timestamped at 8:03 p.m. March 30. The last Saturday of Krista's life. Her birthday. Her last one of those, too. He hit another key and pointed at the screen. The video started on regular speed. "See? Right there."

Cornetta tapped the screen on the front window of Krista's house to the left of the front door. My recollection was that it was the living room window. The window was curtained. The lower part of the curtain appeared to suddenly turn a shade lighter, then went back to its dark color. It was almost imperceptible and made me wonder if I'd really seen a change. But Cornetta had seen it, or at least thought he had. And he'd convinced himself enough to highlight it for me.

"Run it again," I said. I stuck my face close to the computer screen.

Cornetta rewound five seconds and ran the video at normal speed. There it was. A two-second lightening. He rewound and ran it again, this time pausing when the curtain lightened.

"If the porch light wasn't on, we'd get a better contrast," Cornetta said. "That came from a light inside that house. Someone with a flashlight."

He was on the right track. This was the dot I was looking for that connected all the others.

But Jim Grimes' admonition crept into my head. Don't jump to conclusions.

"How do you know that's not just Krista turning a light on and off?"

"Well, for one thing she left in her car a half hour before this." Cornetta turned and looked up at me from his desk. Comfortable. In charge explaining his thought process to an underling. "And when she's home and turns on the living room light, the entire curtain lightens and is a lot brighter. You can see when you watch later while she's home."

"What about headlights from a car on a street behind her house shining through a back window?"

"There aren't any streets behind her. She has a clear view out to the mountains. No developments between here and there."

"But you didn't see anyone break into her house on any of the tapes?"

"No, but they could have approached from the back of her house. Parked a couple streets down where there's access to a hiking trail and veered off the path up to Krista's house."

"Where can I get a chair?" I asked and scanned the room. Cornetta was sitting in the only one.

"Take mine." He stood up. "Or, just take the thumb drive with you. It's all ready to go."

"No. Unless you're kicking me out, I want your eyes on the screen when I go through the whole night." On the hunt. This video put my teeth back in it. Then I realized I was in someone else's house, barely a guest, and I'd demanded more of his time.

Another useful pawn in my quest for the truth. "I mean, sure, I'll take the drive. And I'm going to pay you for this one and the other one."

"Grab a chair out of the kitchen. I'll cue this back up at the beginning."

Semper Fi.

I hustled out of Cornetta's office and down the hallway into the kitchen. Eve Cornetta sat at the head of the kitchen table reading the *Santa Barbara Independent*. She smiled up at me.

"Frank told me to grab a chair," I said.

"Help yourself." She set the newspaper down on the table. "Is Frank going to help you find Krista's killer?"

"He's been a big help so far." I grabbed a dark-stained wooden chair away from the table and started for the hallway. "Thanks."

"Good. I hope you catch that son of a bitch." She picked up the paper and started reading again.

I set the chair down next to Cornetta at his polished oak desk. I sat in it and saw that he'd cued the security video up to 12:00 a.m. Saturday, March 30. The beginning of the tape. The porch light was off so Krista must have been home in bed. We fast-forwarded through the night. No Dodge Challengers or Jeep Wranglers on the street. No one approached Krista's house.

Cornetta put the video on normal speed at 7:30 a.m. when Krista pulled her white Mustang out of the garage and drove down the street. The birthday party Leah threw for her that night was twelve hours away. Early exit for a Saturday. Krista didn't play golf when I knew her. Maybe she was headed for the gym. We didn't see her get into the car because she entered the garage through the house. All we could see of her in the car was her shoulder, her wavy blond hair, and her profile. She looked to be wearing a dark jacket, maybe a blazer.

A ball formed in my throat. Krista. Alive. The woman who was a part of the worst decision I ever made. The woman who'd been a mentor to me. Like a big sister until she morphed into something else. I'd forgiven her for her part in Colleen's destruction years ago. But I could never forgive myself. I'd pushed the memories I had of Krista before the night Colleen was murdered out of my life. Our betrayal, the lone memory I'd kept only as a reminder of my fatal decision. Now, I remembered the time before all that when Krista was my best friend and the smartest cop I knew.

All that remained was her profile and a splash of her wavy blond hair in black and white.

"I didn't see anything unusual during the day, but I'll run through it for you," Cornetta said.

He set the speed on a slower fast forward and we watched people begin their weekends.

Kids whizzed by on skateboards and scooters. Cars came and went. Not the ones I was looking for. Krista returned home at 3:43 p.m. and parked in the driveway. She got out of the car wearing slacks and a blazer. Detective wear. No gym bag slung over her shoulder. The athletic yet feminine walk I remembered. A sexy command presence. I'd never seen another female cop pull it off. Hell, I'd never seen a male cop do it either.

Her attire looked like she'd been on the job, but she was off duty that day. Working something on her own time? Colleen's case? Where did she go?

Oceanside. To interview Mike Richert. The timing fit. Richert mailed the letter to Krista on the following Wednesday. He mentioned that it had only been a few days since her visit. She was in detective attire and gone for eight and a quarter hours. The drive from Santa Barbara to Oceanside on a Saturday was three and a half hours, max. A seven-hour round trip left her over an hour to interview Richert.

Krista stayed inside her home the rest of the day. No one approached her house. I kept my eyes pinned to the screen looking for a black Challenger or a white Wrangler as the day spun by. Cars came and went, but none driven by Weaver or Mitchell.

Cornetta was right about the curtains in Krista's living room. At about 6:50 p.m. they lightened over the entire expanse of the window. They went dark again right before the porch light went on and Krista left her house at 7:35 p.m. She wore a black dress when she got into her car and drove away. Off to Leah's house for her birthday party.

Three minutes after Krista drove off, at 7:38 p.m., a black sedan cruised by her house going in the same direction. It wasn't a Dodge Challenger. I was tuned into that profile. I'd studied the last four years of models online after Leah told me the kind of car Tom Weaver drove. Something about this car was familiar. It might have been a Ford Fusion.

"Can you pause on the black car?" I asked Cornetta.

"Sure." He rewound and paused the picture as the car passed in front of Krista's house.

I studied the driver. Hard to get a good look at him at night. The nearest streetlight was three or four houses away.

"Can you zoom in?"

"Sure, but the picture will become blurry."

He zoomed in on the car. He was right. The image of the driver pixilated and no facial features were visible. However, it looked like the driver's face was turned away from the camera toward Krista's house and the sun visor was covering the upper half of the driver-side window.

Who has their visor down at night, much less positioned on the driver-side window?

Someone who was aware there was a security camera on the house across the street from Krista's and didn't want to be seen in the neighborhood.

"You see that?" I tapped the visor on the computer screen.

"Yes. He has the visor down."

"At night and covering part of the driver's window."

"He doesn't want to be seen by the camera."

"Right. Can you reverse the feed? I think we've seen that car before."

Cornetta started the video in reverse at regular speed. We watched the Fusion disappear backwards and Krista return to her house the same way. We kept watching at regular speed for a few minutes and nothing of interest appeared on the screen. We'd already watched it on fast forward once.

"Can you go to the next fastest speed?"

Cornetta clicked the toggle button on the screen and the speed of the image picked up. A black sedan appeared on the right side of the screen and passed Krista's house going backwards. Cornetta paused the image, but the driver was blocked by the passenger side of the car. It was the same car we saw earlier. A black Ford Fusion. The passenger-side sun visor blocked the upper half of the window. The time on the video read 6:42 p.m.

"That's the same car and he's got the other visor down," Cornetta said.

"Yep. Do you recognize it from the neighborhood?"

"No."

"Maybe this guy just likes driving around with his visors down." Playing devil's advocate to my own pounding heart.

"What's he doing in my neighborhood?" Cornetta restarted the video and played it forward once the car disappeared from the screen.

Again, no view of the driver. But there was something else about the Fusion. I'd seen a white version of the same model recently. In the Santa Barbara Police Department parking lot. Not the employee or visitor parking lots. It was in the lot where SBPD parks it's black and white cruisers. SBPD had replaced the old Crown Victorias with Ford Fusions. The angle of the camera didn't catch a license plate coming or going.

The car that passed by Krista's house the night someone flashed a flashlight from inside her house was a G ride. A slick top. A plain-wrap detective car. And it was black.

Tom Weaver's favorite color.

CHAPTER FORTY

WEAVER. HE'D BEEN in Krista's neighborhood thirty-one hours before Krista was murdered. Had he followed Krista to Leah's house the night of her birthday? Why? If he did, who was in Krista's house with a flashlight a half hour after Krista left for the party?

Weaver. He must have known about the birthday party and knew Krista would be leaving to attend it around seven thirty p.m. He staked out her house and waited for her to leave then went down to the trailhead a couple streets below the house and hiked up and broke in the back door. He needed time to get a look at whatever Krista had discovered about Colleen's murder since she reopened the case. The party would give him at least three hours to search Krista's house.

"Frank." I stood up and squared to Cornetta. "I have to go outside to make a phone call."

"Stay." He stood up. "I need to talk to the wife for a couple minutes, anyway." He left the room and closed the door behind him.

I called Leah's cell phone. She picked up on the second ring.

"Did you invite Weaver to Krista's birthday party?" I assumed their divorce had been contentious, but maybe time had healed the wounds. Until Krista reopened them by reopening Colleen's murder investigation.

"No. Why?"

"Did he know about the party?"

"I don't know. Probably. I invited a few of Krista's and his mutual friends. Why, Rick?"

"What about Mitchell?"

"No. What did you find out?"

"Not sure, yet. I'll call you back." I hung up. I didn't want Leah to try and convince me that Weaver was innocent.

I ran the security video ahead on the slowest fast forward until 8:03 p.m. when the curtains flashed lighter for an instant. I changed to normal speed and pushed my face close to the screen looking for any other sign of someone inside Krista's house. Five minutes passed and nothing caught my attention. Cornetta knocked and then opened the door a couple minutes later.

"All good. Thanks for giving me the privacy," I said.

"The wife thinks she's obligated to feed you now that you've been here for over an hour. I was in the Marines, but she's the one with the rules." He retook his chair next to me. "Plus, when she sees an injured man, the mother comes back out of her."

I didn't understand what Cornetta meant for a second. Could his wife see my damaged soul? I wasn't sure I still had one. Then my head started pounding again for the first time in the last hour and I remembered what my face looked like. My adrenaline spiked the instant Cornetta showed me the light behind the curtains in Krista's house. The pain quieted and my other senses took over. I had the scent again. The chase was back on and I was closing in.

"That's sweet, but I'm good. I'll just finish this video and get out of your hair."

We watched all the way until the tape ended at midnight. Krista returned home from Leah's at 11:55 p.m. No more Ford Fusions on the street and no Dodge Challengers or Jeep Wranglers. No one exited Krista's house with a backpack full of files and jumped into a getaway car. The intruder must have left the way he came and hiked back down to his car at the trailhead through the underbrush using his flashlight.

"That's that," I said. The first words either of us had uttered in the last half hour. "One last question. How long would it take someone to hike up to Krista's from the trailhead below her street?"

"Maybe fifteen, twenty minutes."

"But longer in the dark?"

"Of course." Cornetta leaned forward in his chair. "Why?"

"Just putting pieces together."

"What do those pieces have to do with the black Ford Fusion we saw?"

"Maybe everything."

"Rick, you seem like an intense, but decent, fellow." He looked at me with cop eyes. Military, civilian, they all looked the same. Asking questions in silence. "From the looks of the bump on your head and your black eyes I'm guessing you recently sustained a concussion and are probably still in pain. But you've never shown evidence of it. Your eyes stay targeted on that screen. Not just intense, but manic. You're focused on a mission. Tunneled in. I've seen it in enlisted men and COs. I'm worried you've lost your peripheral vision. You're target blind. Blind to everything but your target. Like a zealot. That's a dangerous way to live, Rick."

No argument. No defense. No explanation.

"Thanks again, Frank." I stood up, took out my wallet, and pulled out three twenties. "Sixty cover the two flash drives?"

"Consider this my contribution to your effort." Cornetta stood up and waved off my offer. "I believe you're on the side of the angels regarding Krista's death. If there's anything else I can do to help, call me. Anytime day or night. Just be careful and don't lose perspective."

He may have been right about being on the side of the angels. Only mine had fallen.

CHAPTER FORTY-ONE

I WALKED ACROSS the street to Krista's house and opened the front door with an extra key Leah gave me. The house felt emptier than when Leah and I were last there. Of course, because I was alone, but something else. I went into her bedroom and inhaled. Stale air. No hint of Krista's perfume that had still lingered just two days ago. I opened her closet and saw why. All of her clothes were gone. Stephen Landingham must have set in motion his plan to sell Krista's house with or without Leah's consent.

The last sensory memory of Krista now gone. I thought of Colleen's clothes that I'd kept wrapped in plastic after she died and the last day when I'd sniffed them and no scent of her remained. I felt her die all over again that day.

The bedroom had a door that led to the backyard. I opened it and went outside. The backyard had an overgrown lawn. Looked like no one had cared for it since Krista died. I checked the doorknob on the outside of the door. No evidence of tampering or picking that I could see.

The yard had six-foot-high redwood slat fences between Krista's yard and those of her two neighbors and a shorter version that faced the Santa Ynez Mountains behind the house. Nothing to obstruct the view or someone wanting to gain access to her backyard. I guess

Krista thought her guns and know-how would be enough to thwart any intruder while she was home. Hadn't worked when she wasn't. Or against a van going thirty-five miles an hour down State Street.

I stood next to the back fence and peered over it searching for footprints in the dirt or some clue to reveal an intruder. Kidding myself that I had any talent for tracking. It had been almost two weeks since someone broke into Krista's house with a flashlight. I didn't see any tracks in the dirt.

I went to the door that led into Krista's office and checked the knob for proof that it had been picked like I'd seen on the lock of the file cabinet inside. Nothing. Again. Maybe the intruder had his own key. Like some ex-husbands have for their ex's homes. The ones that still cared about each other. Could that have been Weaver until he decided he had to kill Krista?

One final door that led into the kitchen from the outside. I looked at the doorknob. And there they were. Two small scratches just like the ones on the lock of the file cabinet in Krista's office. This was where Tom Weaver broke in. I slid the key into the lock, opened it, and went back inside. The door led into the kitchen and with the open floorplan was a straight shot into the living room. And the curtains on the window facing the street.

Weaver picked the lock on the kitchen door and entered using a flashlight for illumination instead of the house lights. His one sweep of the living room was caught on Frank Cornetta's security camera at 8:03 p.m. Twenty-five minutes after his slick-top black Ford Fusion passed in front of Krista's house. After she left for her birthday party. Frank Cornetta thought it would take someone fifteen to twenty minutes to hike from the trailhead a couple streets below Krista's to the back of her house. Give Weaver two minutes to drive to the trailhead and three minutes to pick the lock and that left him twenty minutes to make the hike in the dark with a flashlight for guidance.

Easily doable. Another dot connected. Another step closer to justice for Colleen and Krista. The pieces were all falling into place.

I went over everything I'd learned since the day of Krista's funeral
in my head as I drove back to Leah's house. Mike Richert seeing two
men on the beach where Colleen's body was dumped on the morning
she was found. One in a police uniform. Tom Weaver's car in the
driveway of his house while I was inside screwing his wife. Mitchell's
story of picking Weaver up from jail where he'd supposedly been
when Colleen was murdered, but no one, not even SBPD, was able to
verify it. Krista's missing file on Colleen's murder. Someone with
Mitchell's physique breaking into my hotel room, stealing my computer, and assaulting me with a police baton. Finally, the black Ford
Fusion on Krista's street the night Colleen's file was stolen from her
house. The car SBPD detectives use. Black, the only color car Weaver
would drive.

I knew that, in Jim Grimes' terms, I was connecting dots that were
too far apart to fill in the gaps of my theory. Hell, I might even be
drawing dots out of nothing. But I knew I was right. If I took what I
had to the police, they'd never connect the dots. They wouldn't even
see most of them. Weaver and his accomplice, Mitchell, would never
be arrested. They'd retire with a pension in ten or fifteen years and live
lives of leisure on the taxpayers' dime instead of in a state hotel with
barbed wire and sniper towers.

I was almost there. I just needed a little more proof on another dot
or two. Confirmation that Weaver had taken home a black Ford
Fusion for the weekend before Krista was killed. A division's watch
captain was usually in control of the keys to the cars. For MIU that
would be my new friend Captain Kessler. The politician. I'd never get
that information out of him without some quid for his quo. He'd
need to know why I wanted to know who had the black Fusion detective car that night. If I told him and Weaver ended up dead, I'd have

laid enough breadcrumbs for even the weakest SBPD detective blood-hound to sniff up the trail right to me.

I needed to find a better way. I called Grimes when I got back to Leah's. "It's Cahill. Can you meet me at Leah's? I need to show you something."

"What is it?"

"It would be much easier to show you."

A long, angry exhale. "I guess I can get there in about an hour."

Grimes knocked on the front door about an hour later. I cued up the Saturday night security tape to just before the black Ford Fusion went by Krista's house the first time and let him in.

"Have a seat in front of the computer at the head of the table."

Grimes sat down and I hit "play" on the laptop keyboard and stood behind. The Fusion passed by Krista's, the passenger-side sun visor flipped down.

"That car look familiar to you?" I asked over his shoulder.

"Could be an SPBD slick top or it could be a civilian ride." He turned and looked at me. "I can't see the plate. Why?"

"It passed by Krista's house the Saturday before she died." I stepped around Grimes and ran the tape backward until the car passed in front of Krista's the wrong way and hit pause. "The night of her forty-sixth birthday party that Leah threw for her right here. See anything unusual about the car?"

Grimes moved his face closer to the computer screen and studied the image on it. He didn't move or say anything for maybe a minute. Finally, "It looks like the sun visor on the passenger side is down and across the window, not the windshield."

"Bingo."

"Bingo what?" Grimes turned and looked at me. "Somebody drives during the day and has their visor down against the setting sun and leaves it like that. The next time they get in the car, it's still down. Big deal. Where'd you get this video, anyway?"

"From a neighbor who cared about Krista and wants her murderer caught."

"And the killer will be caught eventually. Is this all you have?"

"Keep watching." I ran the tape on fast forward until Krista left for her birthday party, then paused the video when the Fusion passed by in front of the camera.

Grimes gave me a dirty look and studied the image.

"So both visors are down. Same argument I just gave you."

He was making this difficult. I'd expected easy confirmation. Maybe he just didn't like validating any new evidence or theory that I came up with. Because he was Grimes and I was Cahill.

"The driver's head is turned away from the camera. He's got the visor down and is turned away to make sure the camera doesn't get a good shot of him."

"We don't even know if the driver knows there's a security camera in the neighborhood. You are tunneling in on this car because it's the same make as the slick tops SBPD detectives drive. You're still trying to pin Krista's death on Tom Weaver, aren't you, Cahill?"

"I'm looking at the evidence and following where it takes me."

"So what's your theory? Tom Weaver followed Krista for thirty hours and then ran her over on State Street in a white van he doesn't own?"

"Nope. He didn't follow her Saturday night."

"Then why are you showing me the Fusion?"

"I'll show you." I hit play on the keyboard then fast-forwarded to just before the flash of light in Krista's living room at 8:03 p.m. "Watch the bottom of the curtains in the living room window."

"Now what?"

"Just watch." I hit play and the light flashed for an instant and disappeared. I rewound the tape then paused it when the light hit the curtains.

"How do you explain that?"

"What? The light?" Grimes gave me his best or worst squint. "Easy. Probably from a car on a street behind the house."

"There aren't any streets behind the house, but there's a trail back there. The trailhead is a couple streets below Krista's."

"Enough with the puzzle pieces, Cahill." Grimes folded his arms and looked at me. "Explain your latest theory so I can move on with my day."

"The driver of the slick top knew about the birthday party Leah threw Krista here." I sat down at the table diagonally from Grimes. Putting us on the same level. "He stakes out her house until she leaves for the party. He knows she'll be out of her house for at least a couple hours, so he drives down to the trailhead and hikes up to the house and picks the lock on the kitchen door into the backyard. I already checked it. Scratch marks just like those on the lock on the file cabinet. The flash of light is when he opens the door and scans the room with a flashlight. The kitchen door is straight across from the living room window."

"And your theory is that this mystery driver picked the lock on the file cabinet and read Krista's notes on Ms. Cahill's file and found something that incriminated him in the murder?" Grimes kept his arms folded, a scowl on his face.

"More or less," I said but he didn't look convinced.

"Then why wait?"

"What do you mean? Why wait to go to SBPD?" I had my reasons but I couldn't tell him. Or anyone.

"No. Why did the killer wait to run down Krista thirty hours later? Why not just stay in the house and shoot her when she comes home? Take a few things. Make it look like a robbery. Or shoot her and bury her body somewhere where it will never be found. She would just disappear. Or stage a suicide. She just had a birthday. Divorced, alone, nothing but the job to get her through each day. Why take a chance that she'll get a warrant for his arrest?"

"Maybe he wasn't one hundred percent convinced that she was on to him, yet."

"What changed in the next thirty hours?"

"I don't know, but someone broke into Krista's house and stole the file she had on Colleen's murder. Only a cop would know she copied files and took them home. And only someone in MIU would know she reopened Colleen's case. That would be Mitchell, Weaver's alibi that no one can corroborate for the night Colleen was murdered."

"You never would have made detective if you stayed on the force, Cahill. Your logic takes more leaps than a cricket on crack."

I didn't need Grimes' validation on Weaver and Mitchell being the killers. I was ninety-five percent convinced. I guess I wanted that last five percent to come from someone else to do what I had to do. If I was going to play judge, jury, and executioner, I had to be one hundred percent certain before I carried out the sentence.

"All right, forget my theory. Do some investigating on your own. Find out of if Weaver had a G ride the weekend Krista died. Show me I'm wrong. If he didn't have a black Ford Fusion from the SBPD lot the night of Krista's birthday party, I'm full of shit."

"Cahill, I'm not investigating Krista's death to prove or disprove whatever bullshit theories you come up with. I'm doing it because her sister asked me to." He walked toward the front door then turned back toward me. "And because Krista was a good cop who deserved better than to be murdered and left to lie on the street for hours while MIU investigated."

"Then find out what really happened and don't take MIU's word for granted," I said. But he'd already walked out the door leaving me alone in Krista's sister's house chasing ghosts on a video.

CHAPTER FORTY-TWO

LEAH CALLED ME at six p.m. Dinner with a new client. She didn't know when she'd be home. I knew that when she did come home, I wouldn't be there. Time to separate. Better this way. Better that we didn't go a few more steps down a path that couldn't have a happy ending. Better that Leah didn't ever see the true darkness that lived inside me. She'd seen some of it. The gray around the edges. Mild symptoms but not the disease. No one still living had ever seen my black core.

Tom Weaver would soon.

I gathered up my clothes and my gun and put them in the trunk of my car. I left a note with the key to the house Leah'd given me on the dinner table. The note said, "Went back to the hotel. Will send a report tomorrow."

I stopped by a laundromat on the way to the Beachside Inn. I didn't know how much longer I'd be in Santa Barbara but I was reaching the end of my clean clothes.

My phone rang at seven twenty p.m. while my clothes were in the dryer. Grimes.

"Don't get all heated, Cahill, but I found out Weaver was on call the weekend Krista died, which means he'd have a G ride."

"A black Ford Fusion."

"I don't know what color, but either way, it's not proof of anything."

I knew the color. Black. Like every car he ever drove. Tom Weaver killed Colleen and Krista.

One hundred percent.

And I was going to kill him. One hundred percent.

"You're right, it's not proof. Without seeing the license plate or the driver of the car, it's all supposition." The more I zeroed in on Weaver and Mitchell, the less certain I had to seem to be to everyone else. I'd already showed Grimes my hole card on my belief that Weaver killed Colleen and probably Krista and that Mitchell was an accomplice either before or after the fact. When they ended up dead, I'd be a suspect. A plan to deal with that was already percolating in my head. "You find anything else out from your mole in the department?"

"As a matter of fact, I did. A burned-out van with a large dent in front and a cracked windshield on the passenger side was discovered in an abandoned warehouse in Carpentaria last night."

"Did they get a VIN?"

"My guy tells me that the VIN number was removed from the dash before the van was set on fire."

"Cars have VINs in a number of places. On the chassis, door jamb, under the handle. Probably a bunch more."

"Most older models don't."

"Could your guy confirm that it was the same van that ran down Krista?"

"He wouldn't go that far. Just that it was from the '80s."

"This new info doesn't really narrow things down then, does it?" I was thankful that Grimes was back sharing information, but the van didn't add up to a plus or minus yet.

"Maybe. The inside edge of the passenger door still had a few flecks of paint on it."

"White?"

"Yep." Grimes nodded. "The flecks are on the way to the lab."

I folded my freshly laundered clothes and put them into my suitcase. I was only a few blocks from the hotel, but I had another stop to make before I spent the night in a room that had been breached by a killer. I had to head back in the other direction to get there.

A long way back.

*   *   *

Tom Weaver's Dodge Challenger was in his driveway. The house where I'd taken Colleen to barbecues when I was a snot-nosed cop and a raw, unrefined husband. I never got the chance to be a seasoned cop or sand down my rough-husband edges. The Spanish mission-style house sat back from the street up a winding hill similar to the street Leah lived on a few miles away.

I sat in my black Honda Accord across the street. Camouflaged by the night, the color of my car, and the lack of a streetlight on Weaver's block. A pavestone deck sat over a tiny one-car garage that was too small for anything but a sports car. A mission wall encased the front lawn where Tom and Krista held their cop barbecues.

I remembered the first barbecue Colleen and I attended there together. I was only three weeks out of the academy and Krista was regaling Colleen, Leah, and her boyfriend at the time, about a foot pursuit we'd engaged in earlier that week. We were patrolling the barrio and rolled up on a petty drug deal. I was the last rookie in my class without an arrest and I was hungry. The buyer bolted and instinct kicked in like a dog chasing a ball. I sprinted after him even though I should have stayed with my partner and the buyer, who got a late start running in the other direction because I heard Krista yell at him to stop.

A foot pursuit is not like you see on TV. You don't pull your gun and yell, "Police! Halt or I'll shoot!" What are you going to do when the suspect keeps running? Shoot him, unarmed, in the back for buying a two-five rock of crack? It can happen. But usually it's a scared psychologically deficient cop who should have washed out in the academy, who pulls his gun when his wits and command presence should have been enough to get the job done.

I was still working on my command presence as I chased the buyer down an alley, but I was athletically arrogant and desperate for the taste of that first bust. Even if it was just a penny-ante drug buy. I tackled the suspect and was on top of him with one wrist cuffed when a 10-33 from Krista came over the two-way radio on my shoulder.

"Officer needs immediate assistance."

I was one wrist and a walk back to the car away from finally getting on the board. No time. There was a chain-link fence at the end of the alley I could have cuffed him to, but that would have taken an extra ten to fifteen seconds.

I sprang off the suspect and bolted to Krista's twenty. Her location. I found her in less than thirty seconds. On the dirt lawn of a shanty house with her suspect lying at her feet. Krista'd made the bust, but eight or nine of the suspect's crew encircled her throwing gang signs and Mexican insults. Krista had her hand on the grip of her holstered service weapon and was shouting for the gang to back away.

I broke the circle and stuck my face up at the biggest banger of the crew. I was six feet and a fit two hundred pounds and the guy dwarfed me. Six-four or more, two-fifty plus of prison tats and steroid muscles in a body shirt under a bald dome. I smiled up at him.

"You and me. Three minutes. I win, you all walk away and we take your boy in. You win, we uncuff him and he can get back to slinging crack."

Krista was silent behind me. I took that as consent. The mass of muscles in front of me didn't know that I'd fought Golden Gloves as a teenager and won all my seventeen fights. All but one by knockout.

It wouldn't have mattered if he knew anyway. I'd called him out in front of his homies. He didn't have a choice. He looked happy not to have a choice.

"You know what you're doing, boot?" Krista whispered to me as I handed her my holster, gun, and radio. "Backup is on the way."

"Yep."

"'Cause if this goes bad, you just turned your probationary period into a washout."

"I just lost my first bust because of these assholes. Big Boy's tasting dirt."

I stepped toward the tattooed granite slab and put my hands up. His crew surrounded us, giving us about six by six square feet to ma-neuver. Seemingly an advantage for the larger man. Seemingly.

He charged and predictably launched a haymaker. I blocked it and caught him with a straight right that split his lip and staggered him. But he didn't go down. He lunged at me with his hands open. A quick learner, he knew he had no chance fist to fist. I knew I had no chance in arm to arm. I slid to my right to avoid him, but one of his crew shoved me back at him.

He got me in a clinch; his right arm tied up my left and his left hand squeezed my throat. My Adam's apple became a golf ball wedged in my throat. I hammered six uppercuts in a row to his solar plexus. Puffs of air blasted from his mouth with each punch. His grip eased, and I slammed three overhand rights to his jaw. He released me and staggered backwards. I stayed in front of him and pistoned a straight right into his nose. Snap. Blood. Broken.

He fell backwards, but his crew pushed him back at me. He stag-gered. I didn't want to hit him anymore. My hand hurt. I'm sure his face did, too. Along with his ego. I'd beaten him.

No point in beating him down. Except to show him and his crew that you don't fuck with Santa Barbara Five-O. Especially me or my partner.

I snapped a left jab into his broken face and a right cross to his temple. He went down like a wronged Jingo puzzle. My hand felt like someone dropped a sledgehammer on it. His crew picked up his pieces and shuffled off, throwing a few half-hearted mean mugs over their shoulders as they left.

Krista finished the story by saying, "Here he was, breaking his cherry and hooking up his first bust and he drops everything to save me." She finger quoted "save." "Lost his cuffs when the suspect ran off while he was playing Rocky with the biggest, baddest banger of the bunch. I felt sorry for him so I gave him my bust. He'd earned it. But the damndest thing about your husband, he wouldn't take it. Said he didn't want charity. Had to bring down some baddie on his own for real. And he still thinks he hasn't broken his cherry, yet. This boot is one stubborn son of a gun. Good luck, Colleen."

I'd won Krista over the day of that foot pursuit. And lost a small piece of Colleen at the barbecue. I didn't realize it at the time. But Krista had exposed a side of me to Colleen that she'd never known existed. My recklessness. Risking the life we were building together unnecessarily.

Colleen became quiet and withdrawn after Krista's story and remained that way for the rest of the barbecue. We left after only an hour. Before the food was even ready. She stayed quiet in the car on the way home. She didn't speak until we were back inside our small apartment.

"Why did you do that?"

"What? Help my partner when she was in a jam? That's the job, Colleen. You know that. Krista would do the same for me."

"No. That's not the job, and she wouldn't do that." Colleen's face flushed and her eyes went soft with welled tears. "You should have waited for backup instead of that macho show you put on for Krista."

"I didn't put on a show for her." But the thought slipped into my head that maybe I had. I definitely wanted to show my partner that, despite the fact that I hadn't made an arrest yet—which was by happenstance, not incompetence—I could more than handle myself and be a partner who had her back. I would have abandoned the bust and ran into danger for any partner, not just Krista. But would I have challenged a giant to a fight in front of a male partner? Or any other cop but Krista? I couldn't lie to myself and say that I would have.

"Are you committed to this marriage, Rick?" Tears ran from Colleen's azure eyes. I saw doubt in them for the first time since we met at a party in college four years earlier. It scared me. We'd only been married for six months, and I'd already given her reasons to doubt me.

"Yes." My own eyes welled.

"Then why did you risk it and your life on some stupid stunt? That's not the man I married. Not the man I fell in love with."

I knew in my heart that she was right. The six months at the academy and three weeks on the street had changed me. No, they hadn't changed me. I'd changed me. I'd puffed myself up and pushed out some of the humanity that had made me who I was. Insecurity and arrogance, fused together into an inert block, took humanity's place. I was the son of a cop who'd been deemed dirty. A bag man for the mob. I had to prove I wasn't tainted. Beyond that, a super cop. I had to prove that a knee injury that destroyed my college football career was just a minor blip. That I was physically and mentally whole again. Strong. The toughest motherfucker on the street.

A bad combination for a healthy marriage. A healthy human being.

I didn't have an answer for her. We cried and hugged and made up. I spent the next year trying to prove to Colleen how important she was to me. How much I loved her. And I did love her, more than anyone I ever had in my life. But there was a crack in the foundation of our marriage. I'd plastered it over for as long as I could keep the darkness in me from coming to light. But the crack was still there and it would grow into a fissure a few months before Colleen was murdered. It never got a second chance to heal because of the man in the house across the street from where I now sat.

Somewhere behind the wall inside the house where I slept with his wife and ignited the tragedy that ended Colleen's life, but never ended for me, sat Tom Weaver. Unaware that the number of his days left on earth were being counted down by someone else.

CHAPTER FORTY-THREE

SOMEONE KNOCKED ON my hotel room door at eight fifty-five p.m. I answered, expecting to see Jim Grimes. Figured he'd learned something new, good or bad, about Krista's death and wanted to tell me face-to-face. Probably something bad, something that didn't jibe with my theory of her murder. He'd come to tell me once and for all that I was completely wrong about Tom Weaver.

I answered the door. Leah.

Stunned, I didn't say anything.

"Can I come in?" Weary.

"Sure." I opened the door wide and stepped aside.

"So." She scanned the room. "You like this place better than my house?"

"I thought this would be a better base of operations."

"You left me a Post-it note on the refrigerator? Two sentences? Ten words? That's what this past week has meant to you?" The hurt went deep into her eyes.

"You're right. I should have waited until you came home."

"I thought we were in this together." She walked over to the desk and looked down at my computer. The report I was just about to send her was on the screen.

"We were." I couldn't tell her that we couldn't be anymore. That by being in, she'd be aiding and abetting and I couldn't allow that to happen. "But the investigation is about to close down. SBPD found a burned-out van in an abandoned warehouse that may be the one that struck Krista. It's just a matter of time before they track down the owner."

"Wait? What?" She shook her head. "What happened to Tom and Detective Mitchell? I thought you had it all figured out."

"It looks like I was wrong." I forced myself to look into her eyes. To sell the lie. I'd gotten good at lying. Especially to those whom I cared about.

"What changed?"

"Nothing really changed. I just took a step back and tried to look at everything as if I didn't have a personal attachment to the case. What a more professional PI would do. What Grimes has done."

Leah tilted her head and squinted one eye at me. Maybe I wasn't as good at lying as I thought.

"What did you see that you missed before?" Her half-closed eyes burned into me like the moon eclipsing the sun. "That changed your opinion?"

"Weaver's drunk tank alibi, for one."

"I thought you didn't believe Detective Mitchell's story about Tom being in a drunk tank."

"You, yourself, told me that you believed Mitchell."

"Yes, but you didn't and now you do?" Laser squint. "What about the two men Mike Richert saw on East Beach the night Colleen died? One in a police uniform and the other in plain clothes."

"Those could have been any cop and a buddy. Hell, it could have been a rent-a-cop and his friend." I didn't look at her this time, but felt the blue eclipse burning into my skull. "And who knows if Richert saw what he thinks he saw? It was nine years after the fact. People manufacture memories. It happens all the time. He sailed a bunch of yachts from Santa Barbara to Hawaii. He could have missed the date by a year."

"All of a sudden you sound like Jim Grimes and Detective Mitchell, Rick. There's something you're not telling me."

"No, there's not." I stared into her eyes this time. This grieving woman. The first person I'd really fallen for in years. Someone searching for the truth, just like me. And I lied to her. "I'm just trying to be objective for a change. Taking my need for vengeance out of the equation."

My need for blood.

"So, you're quitting?"

"I agreed to investigate Krista's death to find the truth. I let my emotions taint what I saw. I almost even had you convinced, but you were able to take a step back and see things as they are. The police are close to solving the murder. That's what we both want." I took the second check Leah gave me from my wallet and offered it to her. "I didn't earn this."

"Were you even going to call me or just send me a report?" She ignored the check in my extended hand.

"I'm driving home tomorrow morning." I could lie to her about the case, but not about the two of us. Away from everything else. She wouldn't want a future with me if she knew what I planned to do and who I really was.

"Keep the stupid check. You earned it." She waved her hand. "I don't know what you're up to, Rick, but I don't believe anything you just told me."

"It's the truth. I'm leaving tomorrow. I'm sorry."

She slapped me across the face. Hard. "Don't you dare apologize."

My face stung, but not enough. I wished she'd hit me harder.

"I'm not some fling that didn't work out. You're just too cowardly to take a chance on happiness." She strode out of my hotel room and slammed the door behind her.

CHAPTER FORTY-FOUR

I STOOD UNDER a tree and the cover of night in a park on the corner of East Yanonali Street and North Soledad in the Eastside neighborhood of Santa Barbara. Eastside was home turf to a vicious criminal gang and an area known for drug dealing when I was on the job. Based on what I saw tonight, nothing had changed.

Forty yards away from me a teenage kid was slinging crack out of a backpack at his feet. He wasn't my target. The 1963 Chevy Impala lowrider across the street and up half a block on North Soledad was. I pressed my arm against my chest and felt the Smith & Wesson in its shoulder holster.

Two bandanaed bangers in the Impala watched two other homies in a 1978 Monte Carlo lowrider fifty feet from the kid. Every so often, someone would stumble up to the Monte Carlo and stick their hand in the passenger side and then hustle over to the park and the kid. He'd pull something out of the backpack at his feet and hand it to the visitor, who'd then shuffle off.

Pay the men in the car and get your junk from the kid while the muscle watched from the other car and made sure no one got ambitious. The muscle had what I needed.

I'd watched for a half hour and no SBPD cruisers had passed by. Maybe crack wasn't a priority anymore now that all the federal dollars were aimed at opioids.

I didn't care about drugs or anyone taking them. It's a free country. Mostly. Everyone should have the right to screw up their lives however they want as long as they don't hurt innocents and don't expect me to clean up their mess. The war on drugs had done about as much to stop their consumption as Prohibition did to stop drinking in the '20s and '30s. All it had done was help create gangs that were even more brutal than the Italian, Irish, and Jewish mobs that Prohibition birthed. Where there's demand, there's a market. You can cleanse it in the sunlight of the free market or push it into darkened parks and let muscle in lowriders run it.

Tonight, I was happy for the black market. A means to my ends. And someone else's.

I needed something the bangers in the Impala had or knew how to get. For a price. I could try to buy one from the muscle, but theirs wouldn't be for sale. Even if it was, I'd have to show my face. If the dots were ever connected by the police and they questioned the men in the Impala, the muscle could identify me. That would defeat the whole purpose of my mission tonight.

I hopped over a fence on the south side of the park into a T-boned alley that led into East Mason street. I hustled down Mason and turned right on North Soledad. The Impala was about fifty yards ahead on my side of the street facing away from me. I grabbed the black ski cap from the pocket of my black leather jacket and pulled it down over my face. The only holes in the wool cap were for my eyes. Dark blue jeans and black gym shoes finished my ensemble.

Dress for the job.

My wallet and phone were both on the nightstand of my hotel room. No ID and no cell phone to ping off nearby cell towers. If someone suspected me of what I was about to do, all evidence pointed to me being snug in my hotel room.

I edged forward, slipping behind trees for cover. I pulled the Smith & Wesson from the holster in my black nitrile-gloved hand and sidled up against a tree trunk fifty feet behind the car and waited.

And tried not to think. But the harder I tried, the more I thought. And the one thing that kept popping up in my mind were the words of Irene Faye: What kind of a man was I? The answer grew worse every day.

Movement next to the Monte Carlo grabbed my attention and pulled me back into the present. Someone shuffled up to the car. Too dark to tell if the hooded person was a man or a woman. Just that it was a junkie. Time for the buying ritual to begin. Time for the muscle to earn their keep and hawk-eye the transaction to make sure the junkie didn't try to rob the cash car. Their focus was straight ahead.

I got low and pressed along the two parked cars between me and the muscle. I stepped behind the right ear of the passenger in the Impala and slipped my gun through the open window.

"Don't move!" I commanded in a harsh whisper.

The passenger jerked forward and the driver's hand went under his seat.

"Hands behind your head!" I took a half step forward so the driver could see my gun.

The passenger leaned forward and put his hands behind his head. The driver slowly brought his hands up from the floor. I held my revolver in a Master Grip and cocked the hammer back with my thumb until it locked with a metallic click. For effect, not necessity. The click worked. The driver swallowed and put his hands behind his head.

I uncocked the hammer and opened the passenger door. The interior light went on, and I could see fear in both men's eyes. Boys really, just barely men. But the weapon the driver had reached for gave a finality more powerful than wisdom to whomever held it. Just like I wielded now.

"Turn off the light with your right hand and keep the left behind your head." I crouched down. He did as told and returned his right hand to his head without instruction.

"Malo? Everything okay?" This from the bank car.

"Answer," I whispered.

"Just do your job, vato," the driver yelled out his window at the bank car, then turned back to me. "Ese, we don't have any money or drugs. You're making a mistake."

"Just do as I say and everyone lives tonight." I kept my eyes on the driver and calmly took hold of the passenger's hoodie and gently pulled him out of the car. "Lie down."

"You don't have to do this, man." The passenger's voice, a whispered wail. Afraid of what I might do.

My stomach flipped over and acid ran up my esophagus.

"Lie down." Firm with a growl. I swallowed the bile. "This will take thirty seconds and no one gets hurt."

The passenger lay down on a patch of dirt next to the curb. I put one knee on his back, with my gun and eyes still on the driver, and blindly patted down the prone man. I pocketed a large flip knife and dumped his wallet, cellphone, and weed onto the ground. No gun.

"You," I said to the driver. "Lie across the seat and keep your hands behind your head."

He just looked at me. My eyes had readjusted to the night, and I could see hate and defiance in his eyes.

"Heroes don't live very long, ese. Lie the fuck down!"

He slowly lay down onto the Impala bench seat, mean-mugging me as he went. I patted down his torso with one hand. Nothing. I couldn't reach his legs without putting myself in a bad position or running around the car to the driver side. I shoved my hand under the passenger seat and searched while I kept my eyes on the driver. Nothing. I opened the glove compartment. No gun.

"How many guns are in the car?"

"None." His voice came up from the seat.

"Bullshit. There's one under the driver's seat."

"One."

"What about the trunk?"

"Just the one under the seat."

"Malo? What the fuck are you doing? Are you sucking off Cheesy?" A laugh from across the way.

I grabbed Malo's hoodie and pulled. "Slide out on top of Cheesy," I said.

He army-crawled out of the car and lay on top of Cheesy. I patted him down and pocketed another knife.

"Don't move. I'm getting into the car, but my gun is still on you, Malo." I stepped around the pile of hard boys and got into the car on the passenger side and slid across the seat. My gun and eyes stayed on Malo as I slid my hand under the driver seat and came out with a Colt Super .38 or a Browning .45. Didn't have time to check. Either would do the job I needed it for.

I holstered my Smith & Wesson inside my jacket, grabbed the keys from the car's ignition, stuffed my new weapon into my coat pocket, then jumped out of the driver's side and ran down the street in the direction I'd come from.

"Hey!" This from the other car.

Doors clanked open and slammed shut. I dropped the car keys and kept running. No car ignition behind me. The bank probably went to check on the muscle. I turned right on East Masson and jumped into my car three houses down from the corner. I ripped off my ski mask and sped down to South Voluntario Street, made a hard right and then a left on Quinientos, and geared down to the speed limit and calmly drove away like a citizen making a late-night run to a convenience store.

Sweat cascaded down my face. Adrenaline continued to pump as I headed to the freeway.

For the last seven months I'd clung to the notion that there was still some humanity left in me. That the things I'd done last year had been to keep myself and others safe. Most of that had been true. But I'd been the one making the decisions. I'd been the judge of what was right and what was wrong. Outside of the law and the courts. My sense of justice was paramount. The actions I took, backed by what I considered good intentions, had made me the final say. Enforced with violence.

I had to do what I did for the greater good. Isn't that what all megalomaniacs say? Did the fact that I recognized what I'd become give me a chance to change? A choice? Yes. And I'd made my choice. I slipped my hand into my coat pocket around the grip of the gun I'd just stolen at gunpoint. Armed robbery. It didn't matter that I'd stolen the gun from gang members who sold drugs and probably committed murder to maintain control of their turf.

I'd made my choice.

Tom Weaver and Jake Mitchell had to die. And despite the self-doubt, I could learn to live with what I'd become.

CHAPTER FORTY-FIVE

I MADE IT down to the Walmart in Ventura just before it closed at eleven p.m. My shirt still damp with flop sweat. One item left to procure. This one legally.

Ventura was a thirty-minute drive south along the coast from Santa Barbara. Just far enough away to be able to find a Walmart. I paid cash for a metal cash box with a key lock. The kind waiters used as banks when I managed Muldoon's Steak House.

I pulled the gun out of my coat pocket when I got back to my hotel room. I studied it for the first time since I stole it. My first assessment had been correct. It was a Colt Super .38. Shiny stainless steel. A gun favored by the Mexican cartels even though modern handguns were more efficient. They'd found a home with Mexican Mafia affiliate gangs in the States.

I'd just robbed some truly bad dudes who had friends in low places. That was my last trip to that part of town. At least in Santa Barbara. I prayed there wouldn't be other towns where I'd drive the mean streets looking for untraceable guns to impose justice.

My justice.

The weapon looked to have been recently cleaned and oiled. I removed the magazine and ejected the cartridge in the chamber and field stripped the weapon, removing the barrel bushing, the mainspring, and finally the barrel to get a look at the floating firing pin. It looked to be in working condition. I reassembled the gun.

I would have liked to take the gun to a range or a secluded area and test it out, but then I'd be seen with it and have to buy more ammunition. Another chance to be seen and traced. A dry fire was the best I could do. I aimed at the dresser under the TV, pulled the trigger to check the action. An easy pull and a pleasing click. A few rapid pulls. I'd fired enough weapons to know that the gun was mechanically sound. I was certain of it.

When I pointed it at another human being and pulled the trigger, it would do what it was designed to. If it didn't, I'd probably die.

Fortunately, the serial number had been filed down. There were ways to recover filed serial numbers, but my guess was that the gun had had many owners and no sales receipts or transfers of ownership, except maybe the very first one.

I picked up my phone off the nightstand and checked for texts and messages that might need to be returned. In today's world of twenty-four-hour instant accessibility, messages unreturned within an hour could make people wonder where you were and why you hadn't replied. I didn't want anyone wondering. Not now and not in the next twenty-four hours.

No texts, one phone message. From Grimes at 9:42 p.m. Two hours ago. Shit. I didn't want to talk to Grimes, but I didn't want him to wonder why I hadn't returned his call. I hit play.

"Cahill, I found the phone connected to the incoming call to Krista at 10:49 the night she was killed. It's a pay phone on State Street, maybe one hundred . . . it's a couple blocks from where she was run over. I need to check something out. I'll get back to you later."

A payphone? Not many of those left. Whoever had called Krista two hours before she left her house on the night she died had made the call from a pay phone on the street where she'd later be run down.

Had to be the killer. Had to be Weaver or Mitchell. What did Grimes have to check out? What did he know that I didn't?

I tapped his number. No answer. Voicemail. I left a message to call me as soon as he could. I hoped it wouldn't be too late. I had to try to get some sleep. Tomorrow was going to be a long day.

I lay back on the bed and went over everything I had to do. A lot. And many miles on the road. If I got caught and the police were able to backtrack my day, they'd find plenty of premeditation. I'd be charged with first degree murder. Even so, with that dark cloud hovering over me, Grimes' voicemail message kept pushing through my thoughts.

I sat up and listened to the message again.

A pay phone on State Street. He said, "Maybe one hundred . . ." and then said it was a couple blocks from where Krista was run over.

Maybe one hundred what?

I checked the time. Five to midnight. I needed sleep, but knew I wouldn't get any until I found the payphone.

I grabbed a hand towel from the bathroom and wrapped the Colt Super .38 in it, then locked it inside the cash box.

One stop to make before I searched for the payphone on State Street.

CHAPTER FORTY-SIX

I GOT TO the 400 block of State at about ten after midnight and parked in the same restaurant parking lot Krista had on the night she died. The restaurant was closed down for the night and there were plenty of spaces. I walked to the corner of Gutierrez and State and peered down the street toward Joe's Café. Grimes and I had already walked north on State from this side and I didn't remember seeing a payphone.

I crossed over State to the west side. A few people passed me on the sidewalk. A couple snuggled together in the brisk spring Santa Barbara night. A handful of college-age bros venturing out of the university town of Isla Vista for a night in the "big" city.

A cigar lounge, tattoo parlor, dive bar, but no payphones on the first block. Next block, a Japanese restaurant, a pizza place, and Paddy's Pub but no payphones. I passed in front of Hotel Santa Barbara, where Dustin Peck cheated on his wife, then crossed Cota Street.

Passed a couple retail stores, then there it was. Next to a bus bench and a trash receptacle.

A payphone. An anachronism from another time. But now, a clue. I pulled out my cell and called the number I'd called at least ten times since I found it on Krista's cell phone records. Three seconds later the payphone rang. I picked up the receiver and held it to my ear just to be one hundred percent certain. I said my name into my cell phone and heard my voice through the payphone receiver pinned to my ear.

One hundred percent.

I looked across the street and estimated the distance that I now knew Grimes was referring to when he said "Maybe one hundred" on my voicemail, then stopped himself.

One hundred feet. I squared myself even with the payphone and started walking south on State Street, taking long, even strides. Past the retail shops, across Cota, past Hotel Santa Barbara, and stopped in front of the door to Paddy's Pub. Thirty-six steps. A shade over one hundred feet.

Grimes didn't want to make the connection to the cop bar. Rather, didn't want me to make it. Why not? Is that what he had to investigate? I called him on my cell. Voicemail again. I left another message to call me ASAP. Maybe he was still in the middle of his investigation or maybe he didn't want to talk to me. Both made sense, except that he called me, originally. Sleep didn't matter anymore. I was on the hunt for the truth and Paddy's Pub was connected to it.

I peered through a window of the pub. I couldn't see much. Dark inside. Definitely for an older crowd. Millennials liked their bars bright and cheery and loud. Paddy's had none of that. No music thumping through the door. Cops and ex-cops like a cozy dark spot where you can sip amber whiskey and slowly erase the day. Unless you were raw and inexperienced like I'd been when I was on the force. Then you wanted to rehash overhyped heroics while standing at the bar chugging beer and shots so the waitresses could hear you when they loaded their trays with whiskey to take to the old hands secluded at dark tables in the back.

I entered the bar. It hadn't changed much in the fourteen years since I'd spent a few nights a week standing near the waitress station spouting off. Red brick flooring around the bar and up the walls. Ancient thin slatted hardwood made up the main floor. Sports memorabilia hung on the walls. A private lounge upstairs. There were still probably a couple grills and picnic tables out back. The only difference between now and then was that ex–police chief Lou Siems was behind the bar pouring drinks instead of on the other side drinking them. He gave me a mini-nod, which was about the best I'd ever get from law enforcement anywhere. I returned it.

Three young bucks stood at the bar, chugging shots and backslapping each other. No good memories there and not who I was looking for. The tables around the outside of the room were manned by the older crowd. Detective-looking types.

I spotted them at a table in the back. Both of them. Looking comfortable and at home. Like they stopped in for a drink every night. For years. Unfortunately, Tom Weaver spotted me, too. He leaned over the table and said something to Jake Mitchell, and they both looked at me. I'd gotten the information I needed. Either one of them could have been the person who called Krista on the payphone and lured her down to State Street the night she died. But I'd been spotted. Time for plan B.

I smiled at both of them and walked over to their table.

"What the fuck do you want?" Weaver flashed to rage in an instant.

"I came in for a drink, but that seems like a bad idea now."

"You're damn right it is." Weaver rose to his full height in his chair. "So piss off and go back to the hole you crawled out of."

Mitchell watched me calmly and stayed silent.

"I understand why you don't like me." I looked at Weaver and feigned remorse. "I've given you plenty of reasons not to. I doubt you'd accept an apology from me at this point, but I'll just tell you that I may have jumped to some conclusions that I shouldn't have. Jim Grimes has convinced me that Detective Mitchell here and his unit are closing in on Krista's real killer. I'm heading back to San Diego tomorrow. Let me buy you a round on my way out as an apology you might accept."

"Fuck you, Cahill." Weaver's rage hadn't abated. "Keep your wallet in your fucking pants where you should have kept your dick a long time ago. Stay away from me, or I'll finish what I started the other day."

I backed away from the table without another word, turned, and headed for the door. Lou Siems caught my eye behind the bar. He gave me his trademark life-is-good smile then nodded down at an empty stool opposite him. An invitation? Maybe he wanted me to sit at his bar so he could tell me to get the hell out. I took the bait.

"Chief." I sat down.

"What are you drinking, Rick?" Flat smile. "It's on the house."

I'd never gotten to know the chief very well when I was on the job. Wasn't around long enough for that. We met when he swore in my rookie class of five in 2002. Even at that size, I wasn't the top of my class or the bottom. Right in between.

The chief had smiled and looked each of us rookies in the eye when he shook our hands.

Gave a nice speech. Everybody seemed to like him. I'd only spoken "hellos" to him the two and a half years I was a cop before I went in front of the disciplinary board and lost my badge. Even after the DA dropped the murder charges against me, they took away my badge. Presumed guilty in the court of public opinion. And behind the thin blue line.

He looked me in the eyes that day, too. But he didn't smile.

Thus, I was a bit confused by the smile tonight, no matter how flat and devoid of joy.

"Jameson. Neat."

"Of course." He poured me two fingers of the Irish whiskey and two for himself. "True to your roots."

"I guess if you'd been true to yours, this place would be a German stein house and we'd be listening to polka music right now." I took a sip of the Jameson. Smooth. Hints of vanilla and honey and a pleasant burn down the back of my throat. I hadn't sipped whiskey in a long time. Life hadn't slowed down long enough for that.

"Wanted to keep everything the same when I bought the place. Most cops don't like change. Besides, I've got a bit of the blarney on my mother's side."

"Erin go Bragh." I raised my class and he clinked his off it. We both took sips.

"I always thought you got a raw deal at SBPD, Rick. Your separation from the force wasn't my idea. It was political. There was a lot of pressure from the media, the mayor's office, and the city council after that *48 Hours* ran." Siems' eyes drooped. "And from outside forces."

I knew all about the pressure from the media and the city government. If I hadn't known the truth, I would have thought I was guilty, too, after watching *48 Hours*. But I'd always suspected there was another entity vying against me behind the scenes as well as in front of the TV cameras.

"Was that other force John Kerrigan?" Colleen's father. No one in my life had ever disliked me more. And that was before he thought I murdered his daughter.

"Yep." Siems solemnly nodded. "A man with that kind of wealth can do a lot of damage."

"Yeah, but I understand his point of view." I drained my glass. Siems filled it up again.

"Still, just some bad luck for you, son. Bad luck for your wife, too. I'm really sorry about what happened."

"Me, too." I didn't know about luck, bad or good. Maybe there had been some luck the night Colleen was murdered, but it had all been on the side of evil.

"I saw you talking to Weaver and Mitchell over in the corner. Detective Weaver didn't look too happy."

"He has his reasons not to like me, too." I didn't know how much ex-police chief Siems knew and I didn't feel like bringing him up to date.

"And you have yours for not liking him? I always thought he was a hothead."

An opening I hadn't expected. A chance to further sow the seeds of my newfound doubts about Weaver's guilt in my wife's and Krista's murders.

"I thought I did, but I was wrong." Turned out it was time to get Siems up to date. "I don't know how much you know about the investigation into Krista Landingham's death."

"Well, I was once the chief of police. That allows me certain access that other civilians never get." Siems took a sip of his whiskey. "I know that Leah Landingham hired you to investigate along with Jim Grimes. And I know that you think your wife's murder and Krista's were done by the same person."

"I used to think that. Grimes helped me to see the light. That's why I came in here tonight. I wanted to apologize to Weaver." I glanced over at Weaver's table. He continued to mean-mug me. "That didn't go over too well, but he must be happy to know that I'm heading back to San Diego tomorrow. Grimes convinced me that the forensics from the vehicle paint chips found on Krista's clothes has MIU narrowing down suspects and that an arrest will come from it."

"I think you're right about that." Siems leaned over the bar and turned his voice down low. "You find anything out that would make me doubt that outcome? I know you and Weaver got into an altercation the other day. Something about someone sleeping with Krista the night of your wife's murder."

Siems was definitely dialed in. Probably by his former driver and gofer, Captain Kessler. If that was the case, he might know about my two-cop theory on Colleen's murder. I didn't know Siems' angle. Maybe he did think I got a raw deal from SBPD. Or maybe he was just bored and missed the action of running a police force.

"A misunderstanding." I pulled back from the bar. "Thanks for the talk and the free drinks, Chief. It's nice to know someone was in my corner a while back when it seemed I was all alone."

I just wish he'd fought harder in that corner, but I'd put myself in it and had no one else to blame.

"Safe travels, young man." Siems gave me a smile and wiped down the bar. "We'll take care of things up here."

Grimes and the hundred feet from the payphone to the bar popped into my head.

"Was Jim Grimes in here tonight?"

"Briefly." Siems stopped wiping. "Why?"

"He left me a message, and I haven't been able to track him down." I glanced over at Weaver and Mitchell. "Did he talk to anyone?"

"No. Just had a drink at the bar and left."

I'd already convinced myself that I was one hundred percent on Weaver killing Colleen, with help from Mitchell after the fact, and that the two of them killed Krista. When it came to a man's life, there was no reason not to get to one hundred and ten percent.

"One last thing. I've been thinking about the night Krista died and how the crime scene was protected and how everything went down. I know Detective Mitchell got to the scene well after everyone else. That surprised me. He's a pretty by-the-book cop. I'm wondering why he was late. Were he and Weaver here drinking that night? Maybe he had to wait a while to sober up before he went to the scene. I'm sure he had a good reason, but that's always bothered me about this case. Maybe I'm thinking too much."

"No. As a matter of fact, they were here that night. They are most nights."

"What time did they leave?"

"Around midnight. That's when we close on Sundays. Why?"

"Just curious whether Mitchell had to sober up before he went to the crime scene." I flinched my shoulders like it wasn't that important. The next question was. "Did either of them leave earlier? Maybe just for a little while a bit before eleven?"

The call to Krista from the pay phone.

"I don't think so." Siems squinted at me. "Why?"

I'd pushed too hard. I didn't have a good answer to why. The question itself would point a finger at me when Weaver ended up dead tomorrow night.

"Someone thought they saw Mitchell outside the bar around that time." I smiled. "Just doing my due diligence for Leah Landingham. She's very thorough. That wraps it up for me. Back to San Diego tomorrow."

"Safe travels then, young man." He gave me a flat-eyed smile. "We'll hold down the fort up here."

I left the bar praying that Siems didn't tell Weaver and Mitchell about my interest in when they'd left the bar the night Krista died.

CHAPTER FORTY-SEVEN

THE TRAFFIC WASN'T bad the next morning when I left Santa Barbara at six. Saturday, no rush hour. I hit Los Angles about seven thirty and stopped for gas at a Shell station just off the freeway in Culver City. Normally, I'll fill my tank with gas before I begin a trip of over two hundred miles. I could have probably even made it home with the gas I had in the tank, but I wanted to document my location. A couple security cameras hung from the corner eaves of the mini convenience store. Bingo. One facing the pumps above the door.

Just what I needed. I took off the Padre ball cap I wore on long drives because I wanted the camera to get a good shot of my face. Even if the camera's footage was in black and white, my black eyes would show up on the video.

I got out of my car, used a credit card on the gas pump, put the nozzle into my tank, and went inside the store to buy a bottle of water. There was another security camera above the cashier. I put the water bottle on the counter and grabbed a Hershey's Almond Bar from the candy display and paid for it and the water with the same credit card I'd used for gas.

Location established.

I only drove about fifteen miles before I made another stop. This one in Inglewood, and I did my best to avoid any security cameras. I got off the 405 on Manchester and parked on Isis Avenue, a few hundred feet north and across from a mini mall with a 7-Eleven convenience store. There was an industrial park on the other side of the street. Probably security cameras over there, but I was mostly blocked by a couple of trees. I got out of my car, opened the trunk, and pulled out the duffle bag wedged in the spare tire well.

My black bag. It held the tools I used when I worked on the wrong side of the law like last night. I pulled out a black t-shirt and a Los Angeles Rams cap, plus five twenty-dollar bills from a wad of cash I kept in the duffle.

I changed into the black tee, pulled the bill of the Rams cap low, and walked over to the 7-Eleven. I kept my head down for the exact opposite reason I took my hat off at the gas station. I didn't want to be seen or noticed and a man with two black eyes would be remembered. The store kept its prepaid cell phones behind the counter. The phone might be an unnecessary risk, but one I felt I had to take. I bought one and went back to my car. When I was sure no one was looking, I changed back into the shirt I'd worn earlier and stashed the black t-shirt and Rams cap back in the hidden duffle bag. Back to my real identity. I wanted to be seen as much as possible for the next few hours.

I didn't stop again until I hit a Walmart a couple miles from my house. No ball cap on when I went inside and was caught on more security cameras than I could count. Me being me, restocking groceries after being away from home for a week. Fire away cameras. Cheese. I made one purchase that I hadn't in probably fifteen years. Coke. Coca-Cola. Three twenty-ounce bottles that I would use for something other than consumption. I used the same credit card I'd used to buy gas in LA.

I parked in my driveway and unloaded the groceries then went next door to retrieve Midnight. He vibrated with excitement when he saw me, leaping up and bouncing off me and yelping. We'd never spent that much time apart before. Unfortunately, our reunion would be short-lived. I hoped I'd be able to make it back for another one.

We went home and I was reminded again about how badly I'd let my life roll away from me. My house, still a mess. An outward reflection of internal turmoil. But the turmoil had eased. I had a new mission now. A last mission.

I grabbed a trash bag from my pantry and shoved it full of pizza boxes and to-go containers. Another trash bag for the empty beer bottles and weeks of newspapers. Order. Control. I had some of both back. I went to the sink and scrubbed out pots and pans and rinsed off dishes and glasses and silverware and loaded my dishwasher to the limit.

The clock was ticking down on my mission, but I did have time for the one constant in my life. The one being who loved me unconditionally. I led Midnight into the backyard and we played ball. He tore across the lawn after the tennis ball. Wild, determined, free. We played for a solid half hour until his tongue was dragging just above the top of the grass. I couldn't remember enjoying the game more. I couldn't remember a better half hour I'd spent in years.

Fourteen years.

I checked the time on my phone. Twelve thirty-five. Time to get things rolling. I took Midnight inside and went up to my bedroom. The only valuables I had in my house, aside from mementos of Colleen's life, were in the closet. In the gun safe. I punched in the code that opened the four and a half feet high, two feet wide safe. A derringer was the only gun left inside.

I grabbed two envelopes from the top shelf of the safe. One a letter envelope bulging with its contents, the other a six-by-nine-inch manila envelope. I tossed the letter envelope onto the bed and opened the manila one. Its contents hadn't changed since I first put the fake driver's license, fake passport, unused credit card in the new name, and spare wallet inside it almost two years ago. They'd cost me a lot. Cash. In a Vegas hotel room well off the strip. The untraceable gun I bought from the same man on the same day had already been put to its intended use last year. And been broken into separate pieces and scattered in trash bins across San Diego.

Today I'd use the fake ID toward the same result.

I slipped the new ID into the wallet and shoved it into the back pocket of my jeans. I emptied my old wallet of all its cash and tossed it, along with my real ID, into the safe. The traceable gun would remain in the safe. I had an untraceable one waiting for me.

Midnight sat upright just outside the closet and watched me. Ears at full alert. Nose sniffing the air. He sensed danger or something wrong. My actions were calm. My heartbeat steady. No perspiration. But Midnight could sense a change in me. A tell I didn't even know I was giving off.

I told him to stay and hustled downstairs to my car and opened the trunk. I pulled the duffle bag from its hiding place and grabbed the Mossberg, Smith & Wesson, and the Glock. I went back up to my room. Midnight backed up on all fours turning his body to his side like a horse shying. He didn't like guns. I quickly stashed the guns in the safe and locked the door. He stood in the corner, his tail close to his body.

"Come here, buddy." I kneeled down and he slowly walked over to me. I stroked him from his shoulder to his tail with my hand like his mother would have done with her tongue when he was a pup. "Everything's okay. I'll be back tomorrow, and we'll get back to a normal life."

A new normal.

I put an extra day's worth of clothes in the duffle bag, then loaded in a pair of cotton navy-blue sweats. Dark. Disposable. Twins to clothes I'd worn last year for a similar purpose.

I took a quick shower, got into a clean pair of jeans, a white t-shirt, and grabbed my bomber jacket. I opened the envelope from the gun safe for the first time and counted its contents. Five thousand dollars, in twenties, fifties, and a few hundreds. If I was successful in my mission, I wouldn't need any of it. If not, I'd spend the rest of my life on the run. Five grand would be enough to start.

I stuffed the envelope into the inside pocket of my coat, grabbed the duffle bag, and headed downstairs with Midnight on my heels. I made a ham and cheese sandwich on sourdough from the groceries I'd bought at Walmart while posing for my close-up. I tried not to wolf the sandwich down, but my stomach was already on the clock. The last train going north out of the Old Town Depot wasn't for another two and a half hours, but my body was already in mission mode.

After I finished the sandwich, I grabbed the three twenty-ounce Cokes I'd bought at Walmart and emptied their amber fizz down the sink, then rinsed them with water. I shook the excess water out as best I could, then found some duct tape in my kitchen junk drawer and took it along with the bottles to the butcher-block island. I grabbed a bread knife with a serrated edge from the knife block and cut three inches off the bottoms of two of the plastic Coke bottles.

Next, I placed one of the bottles inside the other, being careful to align the mouth openings perfectly. The bottles snugged together about an inch and a half from where the top of the bottle tapered. I wrapped a piece of duct tape where the edge of the first bottle touched the outside of the inserted bottle. I checked the hole alignments with the knife block's sharpening steel. Still aligned. I wrapped another piece to completely secure the bottles, then inserted the last bottle, still intact, into the opening of the second bottle. Aligned, then secured with tape. After triple-checking the alignment of the holes, I sealed the entire construction with layers and layers of duct tape, then put it and the duct tape in the duffle bag.

I walked Midnight over to the sliding glass door to the backyard, pulled back the curtains with my hand, and opened the door. We both went outside and I left the door open. A light breeze pushed the curtains deeper inside the house. I made a brief sweep of the backyard, making sure the padlock on the gate was locked. Midnight stayed pinned to my side during the entire circumnavigation.

He followed me into the house. I pushed the curtains aside and let them fall back into place. The breeze through the open door billowed them inside. I wished I'd put in a doggie door, but Midnight had been an inside dog ever since a murderer nearly killed him by throwing poisoned meat over the fence six years ago and broke into my old house. The only killers I had to worry about now were in Santa Barbara.

And they should be worried about me.

I went over to the kitchen counter and set my iPhone down on it. I wouldn't use that phone again until I got home tomorrow. If I got home.

I filled Midnight's water bowl to the brim and set it down on the kitchen floor. Next, I filled his dinner bowl with two meals' worth of dog food. Per schedule, my neighbor had already fed him his breakfast. Dinner didn't usually come until five thirty p.m. I'd trained Midnight well and trusted him with my life in dangerous situations. In fact, he'd already saved me from death once. But he was a Lab and, thus, a chowhound. He'd eat anything you put in front of him and some things you didn't. Setting the bowl down and commanding him to watch the clock before he ate half of the food was well beyond my capabilities as a dog trainer.

Nonetheless, I set the bowl down on the kitchen floor.

"No." I pointed at the bowl and walked out of the kitchen. He followed me. He'd probably retreat into the kitchen and eat the entire bowl after I left, but I'd take that over him missing a meal and going hungry. I grabbed the duffle bag and walked to the front door, Midnight my shadow.

"You be a good boy." I looked down at him at the door. "I'll be back."

He looked up at me with sad eyes that knew too much for a dog. Too much for a human. He had the faith in me I'd lost in myself. If things went wrong tonight and I managed to stay alive and not get arrested right away, I wondered if I'd have enough time to get back home and grab the most important being in my life before I started my life on the run. If I didn't or if I died, I knew my neighbor would take good care of Midnight. He'd have a good life. But what would mine be like without him when I needed him most? A risk, selfishly, I couldn't take.

I went over to the kitchen counter, picked up my iPhone, and tapped Moira's number.

"Have you come back to your senses?" The machine-gun voice.

"I know you don't owe me anything. I owe you plenty that I'll probably never be able to repay you." I looked into Midnight's sad eyes. Into his pure soul. "If I call you late tonight or early tomorrow morning, can you go over to my house and pick up Midnight and meet me with him somewhere? Maybe Needles or Barstow?"

"Jesus Christ, Rick. What have you gotten yourself into?" More quaver than machine gun.

"Nothing yet. Better for you not to know anything. This is the last favor I'll ever ask. Hopefully I won't even have to ask it, but will you do it if I call?"

"Where are you?"

"I'm safe and haven't done anything wrong." Yet.

"What are you going to do?"

"What I have to. Will you do it?"

"Yes."

"Thanks. You'll have to go right away."

"I get it. Now tell me what you're mixed up in?"

"If I call, it will be from a number you don't recognize. I won't be answering any calls or texts on this phone after I hang up."

"Jesus, Rick."

"You've been a better friend than I could ever deserve." I ended the call.

Midnight stared up at me. I kissed him on the head and left my house, locking the door behind me.

CHAPTER FORTY-EIGHT

I SCANNED MY neighborhood before I took off down the sidewalk. I didn't want to be seen with a duffle bag walking away from my house. Clear. I walked to the end of the street and turned down Moraga Avenue, which ran down a long hill to Balboa Avenue. A car passed by me, but I didn't recognize the driver. Good, then he probably wouldn't recognize me. Balboa was less than a mile away, and it took me about ten minutes to get down to it. In another five minutes I reached the Union 76 station on the corner of Balboa and Mission Bay Drive. I gave the clerk behind the counter five bucks to call me a cab.

Uber would have been quicker and cheaper, but with a taxi, I didn't have to worry about names and GPS on my phone. I was just some dude at a gas station with a duffle bag. The cab picked me up and deposited me at the Old Town Train Station by two twenty p.m. Plenty of time before the Pacific Surfliner arrived on its journey north.

I had to show an ID to board the train. Which I did, my fake one. Or, more accurately, the one with a different identity that matched the credit card in my wallet and the passport in the duffle bag. Timothy Francis Wright. Resident of Alhambra, California, in Los Angeles County.

The train arrived in San Clemente at 4:07 p.m. I could smell the ocean in the small seaside town when I got off the train. Colleen and

I had spent a night there while we were in college after a weekend in San Diego. We walked on the beach hand in hand at sunset. I told her I loved her that night for the first time as we lay in bed listening to the waves lap up onto the beach.

The beach and quaint seaside hotel we'd stayed in were on my left when I got off the train. I turned right and walked a mile to a Hertz car rental. I gave the rep my license and credit card. I told her I'd pay cash when I returned the car so the credit card was only used as a deposit. She offered me a Ford Fusion to rent. Black. She told me it was a popular car. Not to me. I rented a black Toyota Corolla and used their landline to check messages on my cellphone's voicemail. Nothing.

I got onto I-5 and headed north arriving in Santa Barbara a little before 8:00 p.m. Weaver's house was a ten-minute drive. Instead I got off on Laguna Street, turned left on East Cota and right on Santa Barbara Street. I drove past the Santa Barbara Historical Museum, the county courthouse, Alameda Park, and finally parked alongside the Alice Keck Park Memorial Garden.

The botanical garden was less than a mile from the apartment where Colleen and I had lived. We used to walk over with a picnic basket and spread out on a pristine lawn near an arch where wedding ceremonies were held. We'd watch young children run around the garden and comment that our kids would be better behaved, then laugh.

I got out of the car and walked onto the path that led over to a pond. A small gazebo with a metal railing and latticed sides hung out over the edge of the pond. I stopped at the gazebo and looked around. The garden had a few lights along the path, but the gazebo was pretty dark. I saw a couple walking in the distance and waited for them to clear. Once they did, I darted down the slight embankment below the gazebo. I shoved my hand under the structure where it hung out over the water and found my target. The cashbox I'd wedged up under it last night. Still there. I pulled it out, tucked it under my arm, and headed back to my car.

I drove a few blocks away to a dark residential street and unlocked the cashbox. Gun still inside. I'd taken the extra precaution of locking the gun in the box in case someone somehow found it. I could live with killing a murderer in cold blood, but I wouldn't be able to if some kid found a gun I'd hidden and accidently killed his sister or himself.

I flipped the toggle switch for the overhead light to the off position and got out of the car in the dark. I took my duffle bag full of crime tools from the trunk and got back in the car. Still no one on the street, but I hurried to my task.

I put on a pair of black nitrile gloves from my burglar's duffle bag and went to work.

First, I unwrapped the Colt Super .38 from the Beachside Inn hand towel. I checked the safety. Still on. I popped the magazine out and checked to make sure there wasn't a cartridge in the chamber. Clear. I wiped down the gun and the magazine with the towel and set them all down on the passenger's seat.

I took the two-foot-long edifice I'd constructed in my kitchen, along with the duct tape and a penlight flashlight out of the duffle bag. I turned on the flashlight and put the handle between my teeth, then ripped off a couple strips of tape and hung them from the car's steering wheel. Next, I placed the bottle device between my knees with the drinkable opening facing upward, then put the barrel of the gun against the opening of the bottle. The slide of the gun was too big to fit inside the opening but the muzzle was thin enough to center in the middle of the hole. I wrapped a pieced of tape around the slide of the gun and the drink opening of the bottle. Two more until the Coke bottles felt secure on the end of the gun. Another check of the alignment. Centered.

Many more strips of tape until the connection was solid. Unmovable. I now had an untraceable gun with a rudimentary suppressor. An assassin's weapon. I loaded the magazine and put the gun in the duffle bag, which I hid in the trunk in the spare tire well. I got back behind the wheel. Ready to stalk my prey.

This was the man I'd become.

CHAPTER FORTY-NINE

I GOT OFF the freeway a few blocks from Tom Weaver's neighborhood at eight forty-five p.m. and parked in the alley behind a closed tailor's shop. No one in the alley. No security cameras either. I quickly got out and removed both license plates from the rented black Toyota Corolla and put them in the trunk next to the duffle bag.

The remainder of the trip to Weaver's house was along residential streets with limited streetlights. Weaver's driveway was empty and his small, old-fashioned garage wasn't big enough to hold his Dodge Challenger. Not home.

I parked across the street and five houses up from his home. The home he used to share with the woman he killed fourteen years after he killed my wife. My adrenaline kicked in. It rode on top of the fear and anticipation already roiling in my stomach. Fear that I might die. I might get caught. I might fail. The anticipation oozed from my primordial past. The hunt. The kill. Vengeance.

I'd killed before. In self-defense, on impulse, and with premeditation. None were victims in life, only in death. They'd all murdered people to advance their self-interests. Most took pleasure in the act. Most, if not all, would have killed again. All deserved to die. Maybe they would have gotten life in prison if they'd been caught and tried by the justice system.

I'd give them my justice. Death. I told myself that I was different from them because I was saving people's lives and I gained no benefit from their deaths. That made it right.

To me.

But this was different. Tom Weaver might never kill again. Maybe he was remorseful for an act he probably committed on impulse. Maybe he wasn't. Maybe he got a thrill out of it and he relived it over and over. Didn't matter either way. He was going to die for what he did to Colleen. And to me. No chance for remorse. No chance for redemption. Only death.

I waited up the street, perched in my lair. Anxious. I needed to be calm, thinking clearly. When Weaver got home, I'd let him go inside, then I'd drive down and park below his house. I'd wear my ski mask up on my head like a beanie and knock on his door. He'd know it was me when he peered through the peephole. I'd be tilted slightly to the side with my suppressed Colt Super .38 hidden from view. I'd smile. His ego wouldn't allow him to pass up an opportunity to tell me what he thought of me. He'd open the door and I'd shoot him once between the eyes.

The homemade suppressor wouldn't work as well as the real thing, but hopefully the three chambers would dissipate the gases exploding from the barrel enough to deaden the noise so that it wouldn't sound like a gunshot. I had one shot. The slide recoiling after the projectile exploded from the barrel would rip off the suppressor. A second shot would be loud and recognizable.

I'd pull down the ski mask and hurry to my rental then calmly drive a few blocks on the back streets and park behind a Western wear store and put the license plates back on the Corolla then drive to the Andre Clark Bird Refuge and throw the gun into the middle of the lake. I'd change my clothes and drop the old ones near a homeless encampment next to Santa Barbara City College, then drive back to

San Clemente, rent a room using my fake ID, return the rental in the morning, take the train back to Old Town, a cab back to the Union 76 station on Balboa and the mile walk back to my house.

I'd go on living my life for a year or so until I made another night-time drive to Santa Barbara in a rented car and killed Jake Mitchell.

I checked the time on my phone. 10:47 p.m. No Weaver. I'd been above his house for two hours. Paddy's Pub, Chief Siems, and Weaver and Mitchell popped into my head. Siems had said that Weaver and Mitchell spent most nights in the bar. That's probably where Weaver was now. Just another night that would be his last.

Could I wait another two or three hours on his street for him to come home? Someone would notice the Corolla if they hadn't already. I could move the car a street away, hike back to Weaver's house, and pick the lock and wait inside. But he might have an alarm and the longer I stayed in his house, the more DNA would slough off me.

Plan B.

I drove the side streets to the Western wear store and parked behind it. I quickly screwed the license plates back onto the car and drove down to State Street. I cruised the southern end, a couple blocks down for Paddy's Pub, knowing there weren't any security cameras on that end of the street.

Bingo. I spotted a late-model Black Dodge Challenger parked in the same restaurant parking lot Krista did in the night she died. It was after eleven p.m. The restaurant was closed. Weaver was probably up the street at his watering hole huddled with Mitchell. But it really didn't matter where he was. I had his car. He had to return to it sometime.

I found a parking space about a quarter mile away on Gutierrez Street. I parked, grabbed my murder kit from the trunk, and walked quickly back to the parking lot. The Challenger was still there.

I found a decent hiding spot behind a hedge on the sidewalk next to the parking lot. It was about twenty-five feet from the rear of the

Challenger. Not ideal, but workable. I'd have to move fast and quietly to get close enough to make sure the first shot, the only shot, was lethal. Far enough away from the street lights to hide in the dark behind the hedge No businesses open on this end of State or Gutierrez. I had cover. I had time. I had a mission. I unzipped the duffle bag and slid my hand around the grip of the Colt Super .38 and arranged it so I'd be able to clear it and the suppressor easily from the bag.

I still wore the black nitrile gloves and the black beanie to go with my dark clothes.

More waiting. Fifteen minutes in, I heard footsteps approaching down State Street. A man in his late twenties wearing black pants and a white shirt walked into the parking lot. I watched him through the leaves of the hedge. He got into a Chrysler PT Cruiser and drove away.

I let go a long breath.

Over the next hour, three more people picked up their cars in the parking lot and drove away. That left two vehicles in the lot. Weaver's black Dodge Challenger and a late-model Silver Jeep Grand Cherokee.

Maybe luck would be on my side and the driver of the Grand Cherokee would arrive at the parking lot before Weaver did. Then it would just be me and Weaver and less chance of a witness walking up. A killer hoping for good luck. At least I didn't pray for it. But what if I was unlucky and a witness happened by at the wrong time? Would I put down an innocent to save myself? A murder to advance my self-interest?

No. I could live with the others, but not that. Innocents were to be protected from men like Weaver and Mitchell. And me.

Voices wafted down State Street. A man and a woman. Too far away to understand the words or identify the male. It could be Weaver. If it was, I had to find a plan C. Even with the ski mask pulled down over my face, I couldn't let the murder be witnessed. That would cut my escape time and limit my options to bad choices. And I'd have to call Moira to meet me with Midnight.

A life on the run.

No. I'd go back to Weaver's house and knock on his door after he got home. I couldn't risk tailing him this late at night. Mine would be the only headlights in his rearview mirror. Even if he went somewhere else, eventually he'd have to go home. When he did, I'd be waiting.

"The DA cut him loose." The man's voice. Tom Weaver. My heart double-tapped. I took a deep breath and let it out slowly to control my breathing, but my heart couldn't be tamed.

"After you caught him snorting a line off the hooker's breasts?" The woman. Vaguely familiar.

"Yep. Said we didn't have probable cause to break into the bathroom. Chickenshit."

I bent down and pulled the silenced Colt .38 Super out of the duffle bag, held it down along my leg, and peered through the hedge. Weaver and the woman entered the parking lot. When I saw the woman, I realized why her voice was familiar. Sergeant Lance. The desk sergeant from Leah's and my trip to SBPD headquarters a few days ago. Her red hair was down and she wore slacks and a sweater that accentuated her curves, which had been hidden under a desk when I met her.

"Well." She put her arms around Weaver's neck and looked around. "The coast is clear. Your place or mine?"

She kissed Weaver on the mouth like she'd done it before, but with enough lust that it might still be a new experience.

"Mine."

Shit. Justice delayed. Again.

Weaver walked her over to the Grand Cherokee. They kissed again and he opened the SUV's door like a gentleman. A disguise of the monster who strangled the life out of Colleen and ran down Krista in the street. He had to die.

Now. I pulled the ski mask down over my face.

My breath turboed up to match the pounding in my chest. I stepped around the hedge and raised the Colt, only camouflaged by the night. The bulk of the Coke bottle suppressor blocked sure aim. Weaver walked to his car twenty-five feet away from me. If I charged him for a close head shot, Sergeant Lance would see me and spring from the Jeep, gun blazing. One shot center mass wouldn't guarantee death. A second shot would guarantee a gun battle with Lance.

Weaver got into his car and turned on the ignition. I retreated behind the hedge and stuffed the gun back into the duffle bag and crouched down.

Lance pulled out of the parking lot first followed by Weaver. I watched his taillights disappear down State Street.

My target. My mission. My absolution.

CHAPTER FIFTY

I ZIPPED UP the duffle bag and walked back to my rental car. No point in heading over there just yet. Sergeant Lance didn't go to Weaver's house for a nightcap and then a drive to her own home. They'd have sex—his last—and she'd probably stay for the night. At the least, a couple hours. The longer I sat on Weaver's house the more likely I'd be noticed by a neighbor. It was twelve forty-five a.m. I'd drive by his house at three a.m. If Lance's jeep was still there, I'd come back at six a.m. Still dark, but close to dawn. If Lance was still there, I didn't have a plan D yet.

I only knew that Weaver would die before I left Santa Barbara.

I got onto State Street and made the short drive to Stearns Wharf. I parked on Cabrillo Boulevard and walked onto the long wooden pier. All the businesses and restaurants were closed for the night. A lone homeless man slept on the boardwalk a hundred yards from the entrance. I walked to the end of the 2,300-foot-long edifice, passing darkened restaurants and curio shops. The last quarter of the wharf juts diagonally to the west and is flat as the deck of an aircraft carrier, unencumbered by buildings. A favorite spot for fishermen and women, but clear this late.

Fog and night limited visibility of the ocean, but couldn't silence the sound of water lapping against the wharf's two-thousand-plus pilings. I stood next to one of the tree logs set along the edge of the pier and stared into the black mist.

Colleen and I had stood at this very same spot early in our marriage staring out at our future. I'd promised her children and new dreams to come. I'd given her death and an empty nursery in a house she never lived to see.

I checked the time on my phone. Ten after one. Almost a full two hours until my next chance to murder Tom Weaver. Too much time to think. And remember.

I pulled the burner phone I'd bought from the 7-Eleven in Inglewood this morning from my pocket. Except it was already the next morning. I stared at the phone. My cellphone sat on the kitchen counter at home in San Diego. I hadn't checked messages since my stop in San Clemente. Had I missed any calls? Any texts could be passed over. Those would be from friends and I didn't have enough of those to worry about. The phone calls mattered. They were from strangers or friends who'd followed up their texts because something was urgent.

Or former enemies who still weren't friends but were partners out of necessity. Like Jim Grimes. Someone who would wonder why a call hadn't been returned. Someone who might connect dots later when it mattered.

If I activated the burner phone and called my cellphone at home to check for voicemails, my phone records would show an incoming call from Santa Barbara just a few hours before Tom Weaver was murdered. SBPD wouldn't be able to prove that I was in Santa Barbara and made the call, but they might think I'd hired someone to murder Weaver and he called me before he did the deed. But they'd need a whole lot more evidence than a random call from Santa Barbara to make an arrest, much less take me to trial. There'd be no other calls from that phone. No money trail to anyone.

Suspicion, yes. Arrest, unlikely. Trial, remote.

Still, I had to weigh whether that minute risk was worth the reward of checking my calls. The absence of my returned calls might be as dangerous as an inbound call from Santa Barbara. Someone might wonder why it took me eighteen hours to return a call in today's world of instant access.

I had to know if someone called me.

I dialed my cellphone number and tapped in the code number to access my voicemail. If no one called me, the phone call would be so short it might just show as a hang-up if someone bothered to check.

My voicemail came on. Five messages. Shit. I rarely got five phone calls in a week, much less in eight hours. I had to check the messages. The first one was at 8:37 p.m. Leah. She asked me to call her right away. Another from her at 9:30 p.m. I needed to call her now. Her voice anxious.

What could be so urgent? I started the long walk on the pier back to my car. Maybe Leah was in trouble. Or worse. I needed to drive by her house. I pressed the phone against my ear and listened to the next message as I quickened the pace.

10:15 p.m.

"Rick, where are you? Call me back. Please!" Frantic.

I upped my tempo to a swift jog and continued to listen to the messages.

10:55 p.m.

"Rick! Tom really was in the SBSD's drunk tank the night Colleen was murdered. He couldn't have killed her! Where are you? Why won't you call me back? God, I hope you didn't do something bad."

I stopped dead run and almost dropped the phone. Weaver really in the drunk tank? Bullshit. A con. A made-up story. Where was the proof?

The last message came on. Leah again.

11:30 p.m.

"Rick. You have to call me. Tom is innocent! Call Stephen. He has proof about the drunk tank." She recited her brother, the Santa Barbara Sheriff's Deputy's phone number. "Call him when you get this message. He doesn't care how late it is. Call him and then call me. I'm worried about you. I'm worried about what you might . . . Talk to Stephen, then call me." She recited his phone number one more time and hung up.

I stared at the burner phone and repeated the phone number in my head and debated whether to make the call.

No.

Leah knew I was going to kill Weaver. She'd figured it out and hadn't bought my backtrack story from last night in my hotel room. She'd seen the darkness in me after only a week together. And she still cared about me. She didn't want me to spend the rest of my life in prison for killing the man who killed my wife and her sister.

Leah wanted justice. I wanted revenge. She believed in the rule of law. I was my own law. She didn't have the bloodlust that vibrated throughout my body.

She made up the story about the drunk tank and co-opted her brother to help convince me of the lie. She must have. If I called Stephen Landingham for his part in the lie, the caller who called my home in San Diego from Santa Barbara would be identified as me. In Santa Barbara two or three hours before Tom Weaver was killed when everyone thought I was home in San Diego. I couldn't risk it for false information. Nothing Stephen Landingham could say would dissuade me from what I had to do.

Everything pointed to Weaver. At the house when I was with Krista. Lying about being in Fresno when Colleen was killed. Two cops on the beach where Colleen was dumped. One in plain clothes, he a detective at the time, and his buddy Mitchell, a patrolman in uniform back then. The black Ford Fusion passing to and fro in front of Krista's house the night before she died when he'd checked out the same exact detective car from Santa Barbara PD. The flashlight in Krista's house after the exact time it would have taken him to hike back to her house after he made his last pass in the car.

Weaver killed Colleen. Krista found his connection to her murder when she reopened the case and he killed her. Case closed. Judgment determined. Execution imminent.

Leah had tried to save me, but she didn't know that my salvation could only be measured in blood. Weaver had to die. Whether I killed him tonight or a year from now, Leah would know I pulled the trigger. I could live with that. She'd have to decide if she could live with it, too.

I threw the phone into a trash can and sprinted the rest of the way to my car. The phone had served its purpose. I wouldn't make any calls or check any more messages.

I drove up Tom Weaver's street ten minutes later.

CHAPTER FIFTY-ONE

SERGEANT LANCE'S JEEP Cherokee was still in Weaver's driveway, right next to his Dodge Challenger. They'd been at his house for less than an hour. Not long enough if they were in the early stages of a relationship when what happened post-coital was still important.

I stopped in front of Weaver's house. My heart jackhammered. The blood rushed audibly up into my head. I wanted to break into Weaver's house and shoot him in his bed. In the same bedroom where he should have shot me instead of tracking down Colleen and taking out his vengeance on her.

But Sergeant Lance was an innocent. I wouldn't make her pay for Weaver's crime. Weaver would die, but not in exchange for my freedom. I'd wait him out.

I parked on Cabrillo Boulevard and this time remained in the rental car with the assassin's gun in the trunk. My hands, still wearing black nitrile gloves, clasped the steering wheel. I thought of Colleen. The only images my brain would reveal were of Colleen on the Santa Barbara coroner's table. Purplish white skin and a red indentation around her neck where she'd been strangled. Death was all I had left of her. I pushed hard to find other images. Our wedding, the first time we met, the night she told me she loved me the first time. Every memory morphed into her death mask.

I sprang out of the car and started walking. Running. Sprinting. Down the street, toward Stearn's Wharf. It didn't matter the direction, only the movement. I hit the entrance to the wharf and turned up it. Pushing. Long, deep, wet ocean, breaths to fill my lungs, my body with the tang of life. Taste, smell, touch. Anything to push out the last memories of the only woman I'd ever given everything to.

Would my act of revenge cut through the horrible memories to retrieve the good or would I be left with neither? Just my twisted act of redemption. Was killing Weaver retribution for Colleen or just blood from a body that would never absolve my sins? A cloak I could wear to try to fool myself that I'd squared my failings with Colleen.

Sweat boiled off my forehead in the cool night. My breaths machine-gunned in and out of my mouth. I tried to slow them and swallow the ocean air, to pull myself into the present. Into another life. But there was no other life. My past was my present. This was the path every decision I'd made in my life, good and bad, had led me down.

I stopped walking. Right in front of the trash can where I'd tossed the burner phone. The voicemails from Leah. Her desperate pleas to stop me from doing what she'd figured out I was going to do. Needed to do. Wanted to do.

Leah. My last chance at a real life. A lifeline floating atop my sea of turmoil. Was such a life even possible? By letting a killer walk free? Leaving it up to a failed justice system if it even got that far? My life would never be fulfilled without righting its one great wrong. My great wrong. Even after I did, could I go forward?

One last call. One last chance at that real life. One last shot at saving my soul?

I ran Stephen Landingham's number through my head again. Got it. But I couldn't use the burner again and connect it to me. I needed another phone and I knew where to find one.

I drove over to State Street, made a right onto Cota, and parked in an empty restaurant parking lot. The pay phone that someone used to call Krista Landingham on the last night of her life was across the street, half a block up. The clock inside my rental car read 2:37 a.m. Too damn late or too damn early to call anyone. Too damn bad.

I hustled over to the payphone, put two quarters in the slot, and punched Stephen Landingham's phone number on the square metal numbers. It rang. And rang. And went to voicemail. I put in the last two quarters I had. The phone rang four times and someone finally picked up on ring number five.

"Hello?" Groggy and pissed, like you'd expect from someone awakened in the middle of the night.

"Stephen. Rick Cahill. Leah left me a message to call you."

"At two thirty in the fucking morning?" Awake now. And a lot pissed.

"Leah told me to call you about Tom Weaver being in SBSO's drunk tank the night my wife was murdered. She said I could call late." I wanted to hear the lie he'd concocted or Leah fed to him. Maybe he was groggy or pissed enough to go off script.

"Like I told Leah, I don't see how this is any of your business, Cahill."

Playing hard. Not the delivery I'd expected. I thought he'd just parrot whatever Leah told him to say, hang up, and go back to bed.

I suddenly realized I'd made a big mistake by calling. Landingham wouldn't give me anything that could come close to convincing me that Weaver was innocent. Weaver shows up dead tomorrow and Landingham tells SBPD that I called him asking about Weaver's fake alibi the night my wife was murdered. When SBPD checks the call to Stephen Landingham and sees it's from Santa Barbara, my own alibi is dead.

I'd have to wait. Weeks. Months. Until Stephen Landingham forgot about this phone call, and I had a clean alibi again. I bit my lip. Until I tasted my own blood. It was a poor substitute for Weaver's. My brain had been on fast twitch ever since I realized Weaver killed Colleen. I'd spent the last fourteen years without an answer. Investigating on my own at first, then hiring a private detective until I couldn't afford to pay him anymore, then finally coming to grips with the likelihood that I'd never have an answer, and let Colleen and her memories and her justice slip out of focus. Still with me, a part of me forever, but now difficult to find the edges to grab onto.

Until I came back to Santa Barbara. The city of lost tomorrows where I came to mourn a lost friend. In her death, Krista showed me the way to my vengeance. Now I had the target in sight. In reach. The man who killed Colleen and killed the rest of my life. Each extra second he breathed made each new breath of my own painful. Desperate.

"Then why the hell did she tell me to call you?" I'd shoved myself back in the furnace for this? "First you tell her Weaver wasn't in the drunk tank the night Colleen was murdered, now you say he was. Which is it? Which time were you lying?"

"Fuck you, Cahill." Wide awake. Venom wide open. "You were a cocky boot who didn't deserve your wife and now you're fucking up my last remaining sister's life. Stay the fuck down in San Diego and leave Leah alone."

"So, I guess Weaver never spent a night in your drunk tank. Strange that Detective Mitchell would say that he did." Time to backtrack on my motive. "I don't really give a shit anymore. Leah wanted me to call and I did. I don't care what Weaver does with the rest of his life. I didn't volunteer to investigate Krista's death. Leah asked me to. As far as I'm concerned, it's over. Hopefully, SBPD will do their fucking job and find her killer. And when they're done with Krista, maybe they'll finally put a little effort into finding Colleen's murderer. I don't give a shit about Weaver. I just don't like being lied to."

"Nobody lied to you."

"Look, I know Weaver didn't kill my wife. I jumped to some stupid conclusions, but I know he wasn't in the drunk tank the night Colleen died, either."

"You don't know shit, Cahill. You never did. Tom was there from about eleven thirty to one thirty."

"Were you at the station that night?"

"No."

"Then how do you know?"

I didn't understand why Landingham was still fronting the lie. I'd given him the out. I guess he didn't believe that I didn't see Weaver as a suspect anymore. Maybe I should wait a year before I killed Weaver. My face flashed hot. A year. I didn't know how I'd make it through tonight, much less next year.

"'Cause a buddy of mine who worked the jail told me about it the next day." He blew out an angry breath. "I don't know why the hell I have to explain myself to you."

I did.

"Why didn't anyone at the sheriff's department tell that to SBPD when they inquired in the last couple days?"

"We don't rat each other out up here."

"You've known all these years and never said anything?"

"Said anything about what? That my brother-in-law was picked up for drunk driving and we cut him a break? That's the way it works on the right side of the thin blue line, Cahill. I guess you weren't a cop long enough to figure that out. Tom's spending two hours in the drunk tank fourteen years ago had no significance until you started calling him a murderer a couple days ago. And the only reason I'm telling you now is because my sister called me crying tonight saying she thought you were going to kill Weaver because you were convinced he killed your wife. Well, he couldn't have, you asshole. He was behind bars."

Stephen Landingham hung up.

I dropped the phone and slumped to my knees.

CHAPTER FIFTY-TWO

WEAVER. INNOCENT.

My mind flashed back to staking out his house, then his car in the restaurant parking lot. Waiting for him to arrive with my hand on the grip of the assassin's weapon. The barrel aimed at his head. What if he'd been alone when he returned to his car? No *what if.* He'd be dead.

I would have murdered an innocent man.

Nausea swarmed inside me. Cold sweat blanketed my body. My lungs hyperventilated uncontrollably. I fell forward to all fours and wretched. The last bit of undigested food in my stomach fire-hosed out of my mouth. Again. Bile spewed out after all the food was splattered on the sidewalk.

I rolled away from the puke and stared up through the mist into the night. My breathing calmed, the sweat dried, and the nausea melted away, its memory echoed in my raw throat.

The horror of what I'd almost done receded to the edge of my thoughts. Something less destructive but still damaging to my psyche took its place. If not Weaver, then who? I'd convinced myself I'd found Colleen's killer and overlooked the facts that didn't fit to feed my bloodlust. To finally lead me to the redemption I'd been seeking for fourteen years. Twisted and malevolent though it was, it would be my salvation. Retribution. Revenge. Murder.

Now I was back at zero. But with the taste, the taunt, of redemption in my mouth.

Minutes away from finally freeing my soul by further blackening it. God's cruel joke or my deliverance? The only person saved tonight was Tom Weaver. My soul remained irredeemable. I rolled over onto all fours. My left knee landed in the pile of vomit I'd splashed out onto the ground. I pushed myself up to my feet and walked back to my car. I opened the car door and noticed the black nitrile gloves still on my hands. Assassin's gloves. I pulled them off, along with the ski mask atop my head and tossed them into a trash can.

I got into my car and started driving without a destination. My instincts were tainted. Counterfeited. The hunches I'd bet my life on and those of others could no longer be trusted.

I was rudderless.

Colleen's killer was still walking the streets a free man.

I'd added up the pieces and forced them to fit the puzzle I was desperate to put together to solve Colleen's murder. To put a frame around her killer so I'd have a bull's-eye to aim at for redemption. One shot to unlock my life. A villain to take my place.

Weaver had to be the killer and die so I could live.

My head whirled. The stench of vomit filled my car. I got onto 101 and drove south. Ten minutes later I pulled up in front of Leah's house. I didn't remember exiting the freeway or turning onto her street. I didn't have a plan. I rolled down the window and reclined the driver's seat.

* * *

"Rick?" I floated above the car in a dream watching Leah jiggle my shoulder. "Rick?"

I opened my eyes. Leah stared at me through the open window. Wrapped in a bathrobe, the sky a blue gray above her.

"How long have you been out here?" She opened the car door. "Come inside."

I got out of the car, stumbled, and steadied myself with the door. My body felt like it weighed one thousand pounds with all the bones and muscle removed. No scaffolding left inside me. I needed sleep. Something more than a fitful nap.

"Are you okay?" Leah put her arm around my waist. She sniffed my fouled air. "Are you sick?"

"I'm okay now." I gently removed her arm from my waist to let her drift away from my stink. "Do you mind if I got a couple hours sleep in your spare bedroom?"

"Of course not." She stayed at my side as she led me up to the house, ready to catch me if I tumbled again.

Thanks to her phone calls to my voicemail, she'd already caught me once tonight.

*   *   *

I rolled over and looked at the clock on the nightstand. It read 8:40 a.m. I didn't know what time Leah took me inside her house, but I figured I'd been asleep for three hours.

I got out of bed and noticed the jeans, t-shirt, underwear, and socks I'd packed in my duffle bag hanging over a chair next to the window. Leah was efficient, but I wasn't getting into clean clothes until I had a clean body. The night camouflage clothes I'd worn last night were not in the room. Leah must have thrown them in the washer, the trash, or poured bleach over them. I hoped she burned them.

I went across the hall into the guest bathroom. I didn't seek Leah yet. I needed to scrub off the last twenty-four hours first. The shower was hot and short and vigorous. I chased it standing under thirty seconds of cold water.

Awake. Without a plan or a destination, but alive.

I went back into the bedroom and put on the clothes Leah laid out from the duffle bag.

The duffle bag.

Leah.

I shot out of the bedroom, down the hall, and saw Leah sitting at the dinner table. The duffle bag was in the middle of the table. Right next to the Colt .38 Super with the water bottle suppressor. And a lock pick set, mini flashlight, binoculars, box of nitrile gloves, duct tape, plastic zip tie handcuffs and envelope stuffed full of cash. My felony kit and murder one gun.

"I guess I know why you didn't return my calls." Leah's hands were splayed out on the table. A predator ready to pounce or a disillusioned woman trying to contain her anger.

"I . . . I left my phone at home in San Diego." My arms hung limp at my side.

"Because you didn't want there to be cell tower evidence that you were in Santa Barbara when you killed Tom." Her face flushed red. "You planned the whole thing. You convinced yourself that Tom killed Colleen and felt that gave you the right to be judge, jury, and executioner. You were going to kill him cold blooded and make your escape so you wouldn't have to pay for your actions. It wasn't heroic. It was vengeance."

"But I didn't kill him."

"I know. I called and woke him up two hours ago when I found, this . . ." She pointed at the gun. "This thing. I came up with a stupid lie for the call so I didn't have to tell him that I was checking to make sure you hadn't murdered him."

"Your calls to my cellphone saved his life." I didn't have an excuse and didn't know of an apology to absolve cold-blooded murder. I didn't know of one when I was a cop and still didn't now that I was on the other side. "You saved me, too."

"I don't think I did, Rick." She relaxed her hands and her whole body slumped. Tears welled in her eyes. "I don't think you can be saved. I don't think you want to be saved. You're trapped in a death spiral that you created. Good versus evil."

I stood clothed, but fully exposed.

"There's a good man inside you. I've seen him. I was falling in love with him." She wiped a tear away from her eye. "But I think he's losing the fight."

"You can give the clothes to Goodwill or just throw them out." I picked up the gun and the burglar tools and put them in the duffle bag. "Thanks for taking care of me and figuring out the person I really am quickly enough to keep me from doing something I wouldn't be able to live with. The man inside me losing the fight was falling in love with you, too."

I loaded up the duffle bag and walked toward the front door.

"Where are you going?"

"Home."

"Could you . . . I can't . . ." Leah shook her head.

"What?"

"I haven't been able to get a hold of Jim Grimes. It's not like him not to return my calls." She wrapped her arms across her chest. "It's not fair of me to ask now after . . . after the things I said."

"I'll go by his house and try to track him down." I let go a breath. "I don't have a phone to try to contact him or to let you know what I find out." I'd left the burner phone in a trash can by Stearns Wharf last night.

"Wait." Leah ran down the hall and came back with an iPhone. "This is my backup for work."

She handed it to me and our fingers touched when I took it. A bolt of electricity shot through me and buzzed both men fighting inside me.

We looked at each other. The silence between us acknowledging what we both felt. Warmth spread across my chest and, for an instant, I felt the good man inside me was winning.

CHAPTER FIFTY-THREE

GRIMES. HE HADN'T returned my calls after I received his message about the payphone Friday night. I'd pushed it to the back of my priorities when I plotted Tom Weaver's murder. I called his number as I headed over to the address Leah had given me for him. No answer. The call went straight to voicemail but the mailbox was full. Shit. It sounded like Grimes hadn't returned anyone's calls since he left me that voicemail.

PIs working a case don't ignore calls from the person that hired them. Jim Grimes was laid up somewhere. In a hospital or in his car in a ditch. Or he was dead. The odds, unfortunately, favored the latter.

I thought of Midnight waiting for me at home and called Moira before I got to Grimes' house.

"Jesus Christ, Cahill, you were going to call me last night." Her hole punch voice frenzied.

"Only if something went wrong. Everything's okay." Not if Grimes was dead. A bridge yet to cross.

"Everything's okay doesn't tell me what I need to know, Rick."

"What do you mean?"

"Don't play stupid. I know you and what you're capable of. When you tell me to prepare to meet you in the middle of the night with

Midnight, I know what you were planning to do." A deep, brittle breath. "Did you do it?"

"No. And I'm not going to." As far as I knew. "But I'm not exactly sure when I'll be home." I thought of Grimes and the unreturned calls. "It could be later today or a couple days. My neighbor is going out of town. Could you go by and pick up Midnight? His food is in the pantry."

"Midnight is fine. I'm already at your house. I couldn't just wait around for you to call. Where are you?"

I didn't have many friends, but I had one no one could replace. "Santa Barbara."

"What the hell are you doing up there?" She knew my past.

"I'm not sure anymore." I ended the call.

Grimes' house was on West Micheltorena Street, just a few blocks from the apartment Colleen and I lived in for our too-short time together. The house was a small cottage with light blue shiplap on a block with a view of the Santa Ynez Mountains through old-growth trees.

No car in the driveway. I parked in front of the house and peeked inside the garage. The rear wheel and side of a dark sedan were visible. Grimes drove a dark blue Chrysler 300. Shit. If his car was home that meant he should be too.

Home. Not answering his phone. Dead.

I walked over to the front door and knocked. And held my breath. No noise inside. Another knock followed by the doorbell. Nothing. I didn't expect Grimes to answer, but prayed he would. I tried the doorknob. Locked. I walked over to a wooden side gate and went into the backyard, then into the garage. The car inside it was a blue Chrysler 300. Grimes' car.

I looked inside. Thankfully, he wasn't in there. I tried the door leading into the house. Locked. I went out into the backyard. The lot dropped away in the back and the house had a wooden deck. I went up the stairs and tried the sliding glass door. Locked. The drapes were drawn over the back windows. Next, the kitchen door. Locked.

I went back out into the front and scanned the street. Clear. No one that I could see staring out windows either. I opened the trunk of the rented Corolla, opened the duffle bag, and slipped on a pair of nitrile gloves and grabbed my lock pick set. It was right next to the modified murder weapon I almost killed Tom Weaver with. I went back through the gate and into the garage. The door into the house was easy. I wiped it down with my shirt to erase my prints from my earlier attempt to enter the house and unlocked the door in forty-five seconds.

I'd gotten good with the pick set. I used it whenever there was a locked door between me and finding the truth. I used it following hunches without consideration of the law. My father's credo. Sometimes you have to do what's right even when the law says it's wrong. I'd become the sole determiner of what was right and wrong. Even when my gut, my hunches, my certainties were wrong.

Today I hoped they were. The second I opened the door into the house, I knew they were right. The hint of death floated in the air. Cloying and putrid. Early in its hunger for decomposition, but un-mistakable. Grimes or somebody else was dead inside his house. I shut the door and stared at it. I had to call the police. A call to dispatch about the smell of death from someone who'd smelled it before would be enough to get a squad car to Grimes' house. I didn't have to go in-side and contaminate a crime scene to confirm.

Except I did. Grimes and I weren't friends, and we were barely part-ners, but we'd both worked to try to bring justice to Krista. Him within the law, me whatever it took. Different tactics, but the same goal. The truth. He might have gotten closer than I did.

Maybe that was why he was dead. I had to see his body. To get a look before a police department I still didn't trust did. I owed Grimes that much.

I held my breath then opened the door and closed it quickly behind me. The door opened into a small laundry room with a stacked washer/dryer. I went into a galley kitchen and then into a living room.

And found Grimes. He sat in a leather chair in front of a TV. The TV was off. So was he. Permanently. His body slumped to the left. Left arm dangling below the arm of the chair. Dried thick black blood matted his gray hair above his right ear and ran down his neck, frozen like river runoff in an Alaskan winter. A black winter. A handgun lay on the floor a couple feet to the right of the chair.

Grimes and I had spent most of the last fourteen years as enemies. We still weren't friends even after working Krista's death together, but I think we'd developed grudging respect for one another. At least, I had. I'd never know now how he felt about me. He'd been a cop and a PI. He'd dedicated his life to finding the truth. He deserved better than an anonymous death. Body decaying, waiting for someone to discover it.

I let go the breath I'd been holding and inhaled death with my next one. I didn't want to get any closer to inspect the body. The manner of death would be an easy call for the medical examiner. Another ex-cop eats his gun. Or in this instance, shoots himself in the temple. A shock, but the statistics would say, not a surprise. Except that it wasn't true.

I hadn't known Grimes well, but I knew a bulldog on the scent. That's what he was the night he left me a message about the payphone. That's what he'd been the whole time he investigated Krista's death. We may not have agreed on everything, but he was on a quest for the truth as much as I was.

His death looked to be over a day old. That would put it back to the night he called me about the payphone. When he left a message that he had to check something out.

Whatever it was had gotten him killed. Which meant that Krista and Colleen's killer had gotten onto him and maybe onto me. I may have been wrong about Weaver and Mitchell, but I hadn't been about Krista's killer not being some random drunk driver. He was out there covering his tracks and the real reason he killed Krista.

I scanned the living room for a computer. None. I searched the rest of the house. No computer. I went back into the garage and searched the Chrysler 300, even popping the trunk. No computer. No notebooks. No evidence of what Grimes found out the night he died.

I unlocked the front door, opened it, and went outside. I took off my gloves and closed the door behind me, careful to use my bare hand on the doorknob.

With Grimes dead inside his house, I knew my mission wasn't complete. It just had a new target. One I couldn't see yet.

CHAPTER FIFTY-FOUR

A TWO-MAN SQUAD car pulled up in front of Grimes house at ten fifteen a.m. Ten minutes after I called 911. And twelve minutes after I wiped down everything I'd touched inside the house except the front door and put the homemade supressor in the trash can of a home five houses down from Grimes'. The gun was still in the duffle bag. I might need it before I left Santa Barbara. For self-defense. Or something else.

The police would need a warrant to search my car and didn't have probable cause at this point. But all it would take was for someone to peek in my duffle bag in the trunk and fudge up some PC.

I could explain the gun. Not the silencer. I found the gun on the street downtown. I didn't even notice its serial number was filed off. I was going to turn it in to the Santa Barbara PD on Figueroa Street after I checked up on Jim Grimes who wasn't returning calls.

A silencer was used for one thing. Killing humans. No story could spin that.

I told the police officers on the scene the truth, but not the whole truth. My usual practice. That Grimes and I were investigating the death of Krista Landingham for her sister, Leah, and that neither Leah nor I had been able to get a hold of Grimes for a day and a half. I stopped by his house to check on him and went inside when I tried the front door and it was unlocked.

The unlocked door was part of the whole truth I left out. Actually, a lie. SBPD didn't need to know that I broke in. If I hadn't, no one would have discovered Grimes' body for days, maybe weeks, evidence decaying with the body.

The patrolman asked me to stick around for the detectives to arrive. I knew I didn't have a choice and sat in the back of their squad car with the door open while they put up crime scene tape around Grimes' house.

I called Leah.

"I've got bad news about Grimes," I said.

"He's dead, isn't he?" A quaver in her voice.

"Yes. I'm sorry. How did you know?"

"A man like Jim Grimes doesn't just disappear and stop returning calls." She let out a deep sigh. "I hoped I was wrong. How did he die?"

"It's set up to look like a suicide."

"Set up?"

"He called me and left a message on my voicemail after you came to my hotel room the other night. He said that the last call Krista received the night she died was from a payphone on State Street and that he had to check something out. I called him a couple times, but he didn't return my call. That was the last I heard from him."

"You're telling me this now?"

"You're right. I should have told you about the payphone Friday night."

"But you were too busy planning Tom's murder, weren't you?"

I didn't say anything. No more lies and I didn't want to say the truth out loud.

Leah hung up without another word. The warm touch of our hands together this morning seemed a long time ago.

Ten minutes later a white Ford Fusion G-ride drove up. Detectives Mitchell and Flora got out of the car and walked over to the patrolman manning the crime scene. Great. Detective Mitchell, who I'd accused of breaking into my hotel room and assaulting me. Shouldn't he be busy working Krista's case? He walked under the tape and inside the house.

Detective Flora peeled off and walked over to me in the patrol car. Good. Maybe Mitchell realized that he should recuse himself from dealing with me. Not that a cop had to. This wasn't the federal government.

I got out of the squad car before someone decided to close the door and lock it.

"Cahill." Flora stuck out her hand and gave me a curt smile.

I shook her hand.

"Can you tell me what happened, beginning with why you came by Jim Grimes' house?"

I gave her the same ninety percent truth that I gave to the patrolmen earlier.

"Why did you go inside the house?"

"I knocked and rang the doorbell and no one answered and I just naturally tried the doorknob. It turned, so I went inside."

"Did you touch anything inside the house?"

"No. As soon as I opened the door, I smelled . . ." I'd smelled death too many times in my life. As a private investigator. As a cop. And as a husband.

"Smelled what, Mr. Cahill?"

"Death."

Detective Mitchell walked up behind Detective Flora. The man who had been second on my kill list.

"Where were you yesterday?" Maybe Mitchel didn't buy the suicide. Good. Maybe he saw me as a suspect. Bad.

"In San Diego."

"Why are you back in Santa Barbara?"

"I didn't like how things ended with Leah Landingham." That part was true.

"Shit." Mitchell looked over my shoulder. "What's he doing here? There's not even a TV truck here yet."

"Jake!" Detective Flora nodded at me then looked back at Mitchell. He'd cracked out of turn and revealed his true feelings about a fellow brother in blue in front of a civilian. Though I hardly qualified as a civilian and nothing surprised me when it came to cops. Especially those in Santa Barbara.

I turned and saw a Black Ford Fusion pull to the curb beyond Mitchell's car. The car Grimes confirmed that Weaver drove while on duty and the car I'd convinced myself that he drove by Krista's house the night before she died. I wanted so badly for the piece to fit that I'd ruled out the hundreds of Black Fusions in Santa Barbara owned by citizens quietly living their lives.

I thought Weaver and he were buddies. And Weaver didn't strike me as the kind of cop who liked to step in front of a TV camera. Just the opposite. The door to the Fusion opened and the driver got out. Now I understood Mitchell's comment.

Captain Kessler strode over to us. Blond hair jelled back in a perfect wedge, beach volleyball sunglasses, business suit tailored perfectly to show off his fit body. He should be strutting down a catwalk not up to a crime scene.

"Rick. Detectives." He put his hands on his hips. "What have we got?"

Mitchell stared at the ground while Flora filled in Kessler on what I'd told her.

"So, Rick, the door was unlocked and you just walked right in?" Kessler's lips pulled tight, his wraparound sunglasses hiding his eyes.

"Yes."

"Are you sure the door was unlocked?"

"How else would I have gotten inside the house?" What was Kessler's game? Did he suspect I'd picked the lock? Why?

"However you got inside, you committed an unlawful entry." Kessler was suddenly playing hardball. He'd been more politician when we had a private talk in his office. Showing off for Mitchell, a detective he knew didn't respect him?

Mitchell glanced at Kessler and furrowed his brow.

"Grimes was a friend." He might have become one after we cracked Krista's case. "He hadn't returned my or Leah Landingham's calls since Friday night. I was concerned about him, so I opened the door and went inside."

"Detective Flora and I are done with Mr. Cahill, Captain. I was about to send him on his way." Mitchell somehow coming to my defense. If he'd only known what I'd planned for him before I learned the truth. "We have his contact info."

"I'd like to question him back at the station," Kessler said.

"Are you arresting me, Captain?" Reflexes stiffened my body.

"No." A reptile smile beneath the insect eyes. "As a courtesy to me and the department and the memory of Jim Grimes, I'm asking you to follow me down to the station where we can talk in a less hectic environment."

I didn't know Kessler's game. Didn't matter. Jim Grimes was dead. My duty now was to speak for him.

"Sure."

CHAPTER FIFTY-FIVE

KESSLER WALKED ME through the police station, up the stairs to the MIU, and into his office. He pulled the blinds down again and sat behind his desk. I took the chair opposite him.

"What happened to your car?" Kessler asked.

"What do you mean?"

"I thought you drove a Honda Accord."

"It's in the shop." How did he know what car I drove? Had he caught onto my original plan for driving the rental?

"How well did you know Jim Grimes?"

"Better than I used to. I don't think he'd kill himself in the middle of working a case."

"People surprise you. You were a cop once, Rick, you should know that."

"Is that why you wanted me to come down to the station, Captain? To ask how well I knew Grimes?"

"No." Kessler leaned forward. Sculpted face intense. "I made you come down here so we could talk alone. Away from people who might want to hear our conversation."

"You mean Mitchell?"

He nodded.

"How's your investigation into Detective Landingham's death going?" Eyes keen and hard. "You still have questions about Detectives Mitchell and Weaver?"

Now's he's interested. After their alibi for the night Colleen died had been confirmed.

"No. They've been cleared."

"By whom?" He snapped his head back.

"By me. Their alibi checks out for the night Colleen died. They weren't involved so they wouldn't have a reason to kill Krista."

"What alibi?"

"The Santa Barbara jail drunk tank. Weaver was there when Colleen was murdered and Mitchell checked him out."

"Who told you this?"

"I can't say."

"What if I compelled you to say?" Kessler's cop eyes boring into me.

I didn't owe Stephen Landingham anything. Except that he saved me from killing an innocent man.

"Then we'd have a problem."

Kessler glowered a bit, then his face shapeshifted into a politician's running for office. "You're still convinced that your wife's and Detective Landingham's deaths are related?"

"I'm not convinced of anything anymore." Except that Colleen's and Krista's killers were still free and were probably cops. And that, if I could find the truth and get up my nerve again, I was going to kill them. "Except that Weaver and Mitchell are innocent."

"And that includes neither one of them assaulting you at the Beachside Inn?"

"Yep."

"What are your plans now?" Kessler crossed his arms and leaned back in his chair.

"I'm heading back to San Diego." But I'd be back.

"Today?"

"That was my plan."

"I'd like you to stay here another day just in case we have some more questions about Jim Grimes' death."

The office door flew open behind me, and I turned to see ex–police chief Siems rush in and fling the door shut behind him.

"I just heard—" Siems saw me and his eyes went wide and he snapped his mouth shut.

"Lou." Kessler stood up. "Mr. Cahill discovered the body."

I stayed seated and watched the two of them. Tense. Guarded. Hiding a secret? Kessler held sway in the relationship. His steely eyes on Siems, who looked to the side.

"Oh." Siems' eyes shot over to Kessler, then back to me. "Hello, Rick. Sorry to interrupt. We can talk later, Ted."

"I was just leaving." I stood up. "If you need to reach me, Captain, I'll be at the Beachside Inn. But I'm leaving tomorrow afternoon."

"Thank you, Rick." Kessler smiled a lockjaw smile.

I walked to the door and noticed Kessler's glory wall of photos and commendations that chronicled his career. The back of my neck itched. I stopped at the end of the photo gallery. I could feel one of the pictures staring at me. I scanned the wall.

"Something else, Rick?" Kessler over my shoulder.

Then I spotted it. The picture I'd seen the other day that hadn't meant anything to me then. It did now. It was around fifteen years old. Chief Siems, in civilian clothes, leaned against a Crown Victoria detective car with his arms folded and a smirk spread across his face. Lieutenant Ted Kessler stood near the hood of the car, ramrod straight in his SBPD uniform.

Everything clicked into place like a racked cartridge in a shotgun.

Kessler and Siems.

My gut flipped inside out.

Kessler was Chief Siems' gofer and unofficial personal driver. Most police chiefs wore their uniforms to work, but Siems always wore civilian clothes. The press sometimes called him a man of the people and that morphed into Chief of the People. He never drove in a squad car, always a slick top. And Kessler often drove him. Especially around the time Colleen was murdered.

In a uniform.

Kessler, a perfect physical match for Mitchell, also for the man in black who broke into my hotel room and assaulted me with a police baton. Kessler drove a black Ford Fusion detective car like the one in the surveillance video driving past Krista Landingham's house the night before she died. The captain of the unit investigating Krista's death. With access to the police report and every facet of the investigation.

Also, captain of the cold case unit when Krista started investigating Colleen's death.

Krista had reopened the case and found new evidence. As her captain, Kessler would have access to her file on the case. The phone call she made to Kessler three nights before she died that he claimed was a drunk dial. Was it something else?

Lou Siems, owner of Paddy's Pub. The bar just one hundred feet from the phone booth that made the last phone call Krista ever received on the night she died. Where Siems admitted Grimes had been the night he disappeared.

Where were Kessler and Grimes when Krista was run down? Where were they the night Colleen was murdered?

"Rick?" Kessler. I turned to look at him. A cheerless smile on his face. More like a predator showing his teeth. "Something interest you on my wall?"

"Just looking at your past. You know where you can find me." I left Kessler's office.

CHAPTER FIFTY-SIX

I CALLED MIKE Richert. He answered on the third ring.

"Mr. Richert, Rick Cahill. Could the name of the cop you talked to about what you saw on East Beach have been Kessler?" I held my breath. Wasn't easy when I was fighting not to hyperventilate.

"That sounds familiar." A burst of energy in his voice. "I think that might be it!"

I hung up without explanation.

Jim Grimes' house was still sealed off by yellow police tape when I pulled up. I needed Grimes now more than ever but he couldn't help me. My gut, my instincts, the acid taste in my mouth all told me that Kessler and Siems killed Colleen and Krista and Grimes. But I'd been wrong, almost tragically, before. I needed someone who could get inside SBPD. Or someone who was already there.

Colleen and Krista deserved justice. Even if it wasn't mine alone.

I walked up to the yellow crime scene tape stretched across Grimes' front yard. One of the patrolmen who'd been first on the scene stood sentry. He was young, buzz cut showing below his hat. Watchful, arms crossed behind his back in a military parade rest posture. His name tag read Ochoa.

"I need to speak with Detective Mitchell," I said.

"Detective Mitchell is investigating a crime scene and can't be disturbed right now."

"You know who I am. I discovered the body. Tell him it's urgent."

"Detective Mitchell is not to be disturbed while he's investigating a crime scene."

"Tell him I have information about the victim." I did. Tangentially.

The patrolman glared at me, then shook his head. "Wait here."

Officer Ochoa took a few steps away from me, turned his back, and spoke into his shoulder radio. I couldn't hear what he said. He shook his head and walked back to me.

"Detective Mitchell is busy right now, but he would like you to wait for him."

"How long?"

"He didn't say."

"I'll be in my car." The one with the unregistered, filed-off serial number, handgun in the trunk.

Ochoa nodded.

I sat in my car and waited and let my mind run. For too long and too far. My stomach turned in on itself. Not from the certainty a half hour ago that I was standing in a room with Colleen's killers. From uncertainty. What if I was wrong again? Could I ever trust my instincts again?

Kessler and Siems. What possible reason could they have had to kill Colleen? They only met a couple times. My swearing-in ceremony and a big banquet dinner a couple months before she died. They'd probably said hello and shook hands twice.

I don't think she ever even met Kessler. I barely knew him when we were on the force together. I was working the streets while he was driving Chief Siems around on them.

Ten minutes. No Mitchell.

I Googled Santa Barbara Police Chief Lou Siems. Not surprisingly there was a Wikipedia page for him. He'd been police chief for twenty years. In today's celebrity-starved world, that would get you a page. I searched for anything that could give hint to his capacity for murder. Nothing.

All positive including the nickname Police Chief of the People.

His daughter Megan was mentioned and had a link to her own page. She was an actress known for her roles on a couple soap operas and made-for-TV movies. She was also a graduate of UCSB. I remembered her being an undergraduate when Colleen was studying for her master's in education. Chief Siems had put up flyers around the headquarters about her starring role in some play at UCSB around the time Colleen died. The joke by the rank and file was that Kessler was jealous because Siems never put up a flyer about him.

A half hour later, Mitchell strode up to my car, glowering. I got out of the car to greet him. He didn't smile.

"What's this about, Cahill?" He put his hands on his hips. "You know I'm busy with a crime scene."

"Right. Crime scene. You don't think Grimes committed suicide?"

"Officer Ochoa told me that you told him you have information about Grimes." Mitchell punctuated each word with a finger jab at the air between us. "Is that a lie?"

"No. The same people who killed Krista killed Grimes. And my wife."

"Get the fuck away from my crime scene or I'll have you arrested for interfering with a police investigation." More air stabbing.

"Grimes called me the night before last and left a message that the last phone call Krista received was from a payphone just down the street from Paddy's Pub."

"What? I don't remember a call from a payphone on Detective Landingham's phone records."

"It's there. I have a copy of it."

"I don't have time for this, Cahill." Mitchell yelled over his shoulder. "Officer Ochoa, please escort Mr. Cahill from my crime scene. If he refuses to comply, arrest him."

Looky-loos milling behind the police tape looked over at me.

If Mitchell was serious and Officer Ochoa arrested me, the booking sergeant would discover my fake ID, and I'd be looking at a fine and a max of a year in jail under a misdemeanor and up to three years in jail for a felony conviction, plus suspension of my driver's license for up to three years. I don't know what would constitute a felony use of a fake ID, but using one to rent a car might put me on the path there. If Mitchell wondered why I'd chosen to use a fake ID to rent a car and drive to Santa Barbara, he might start digging deeper. Get a search warrant for the rental car and find the unlicensed gun with altered serial numbers.

Still, I had to get Mitchell to see what I saw. Or thought I saw. I'd already played the great avenger on my own and almost killed an innocent man because of it. I needed help now. From the police force least likely to give it to me. But if I didn't risk jail now, how much longer would Colleen's killers be allowed to walk free?

"I know I've given you plenty of reasons to hate me." I caught Ochoa out of the corner of my eye hustling toward us across the street. "But I also know you care about the truth. Did you see Grimes Friday night?"

"Sir, please exit this area." Officer Ochoa's expression, not as polite as his words.

"Two more minutes of your time, Detective," I said.

"Give us a minute, Officer," Mitchell said to Ochoa.

Ochoa walked back across the street.

"I did."

"Did he look like a man who was about to kill himself?"

"People kill themselves all the time for all sorts of reasons and ninety-nine percent of the time, their loved ones are surprised."

"Did you talk to him?" I asked.

"No. Is that all you have, Cahill?"

"Did he talk to Chief Siems?"

"Time to go."

"Did he? Was Captain Kessler there?"

"What are you getting at, Cahill?"

"Grimes said he had to check something after he discovered Krista's last call came from the payphone on State Street. He probably asked Siems if he saw someone leave the bar around ten forty-five p.m. the night Krista died and return a few minutes later."

"Why?" Mitchell looked skeptical but at least he was asking questions. "What's the significance of that?"

"The call to Krista from the pay phone was at 10:49 p.m. The last call she ever made or received. Three hours later she's run over on State Street a couple blocks from Paddy's and three blocks from the pay phone."

"So, you think whoever ran her over called from the pay phone and lured her down to State Street to do the deed?" Mitchell sniffed and shook his head. "On this flimsy evidence?"

"Yep. A cell call would be traced to the nearest tower in the area. Unfortunately, Grimes asked exactly the wrong person about the phone."

"Wait a second." Mitchell waved his hands in front of himself. "You think the chief killed Grimes? You are out of your fucking mind!"

"Chief Siems or Captain Kessler or both."

"Officer Ochoa!" He nodded at me. Ochoa jogged back across the street.

"Find out if Kessler drove Siems to UCSB to watch his daughter in a play the night Colleen Cahill was murdered." I opened my car door.

"The Chief of Police is on call 24/7. The department has to know where he is at all times. There must be a log from that night. Find out where Siems and Kessler were that night. And check the last phone call Krista received on the Sunday night before she died. If I'm right, you'll close three murder cases."

I got into my car, rented with a fake ID, with the gun I'd committed armed robbery to obtain in the trunk, and drove away.

CHAPTER FIFTY-SEVEN

I GOT ONTO 101 and drove north nine or ten miles to the Santa Barbara airport. The airport is miniature and looks like an early California mission. A wealthy mission, with high arches and vaulted wood ceilings. I pulled into the Hertz car drop-off and grabbed my duffle bag from the trunk.

The attendant, a kid in his early twenties, looked at my paperwork and explained that dropping the car there instead of San Clemente was going to cost me a lot more. I told him I'd handle it at the counter inside. I needed a new car that Kessler hadn't seen and didn't want Hertz to charge the credit card that I'd opened a couple years ago under my fake identity name. That would open up a line of bread crumbs I didn't want anyone to find.

The girl behind the counter inside was also in her early twenties. Perky and pretty and eager to help me save money by explaining to me that it would cost much less if I just kept the Corolla I'd already rented in San Clemente and returned it there. I paid her the $323.17 in cash and didn't bother with an explanation and rented a white Mazda 3 on a day-to-day basis.

I picked up a Subway sandwich and got back to police headquarters on Figueroa by three fifteen p.m. The station's personnel parking lot entrance was on East Anapamu Street behind the station. There weren't any parking spaces on the street so I took wide circles around the block until one opened up in front of a house a half a block east of the station fifteen minutes later. The spot gave me some cover and I still had a decent view of the parking lot's gated entrance.

A handful of black and white patrol cars came and went from the parking lot over the next hour and a half. No black Ford Fusions. Captain Kessler may not drive the car home each night as Detective Weaver sometimes did. I walked by the parking lot and saw a few civilian cars behind the electric gate. One of them could have been Kessler's. Or, he might use the Black Fusion that was also in the parking lot.

I went back to my car and waited. I tried to find Kessler's home address from a paid people finder website, but nothing came up. He may have had it blocked from databases. A captain in a police department could hold that kind of sway.

A couple civilian cars, a Ford SUV, and a Chevy Malibu exited the parking lot around five thirty headed west on Anapamu. I was too far away to tell if either was Kessler. Even with my binoculars, all I caught was the back of their heads blocked by headrests.

Finally, at six forty-five, the Black Fusion exited the parking lot and turned left on Anapamu and headed toward the middle of town. Dusk had pulled down the first layer of night, and I couldn't even make out if the driver was male or female. Didn't matter. I had to jump now and hope.

I followed the Fusion from a block behind through town and onto 101 North for seven or eight miles into Goleta. It exited on Calle Real heading north. I hung back to blend in with the headlights and followed the Fusion onto Bradford Drive, a residential street of mid-century modern homes.

The Fusion pulled into a driveway of a home with drought-resistant plants instead of a front lawn like most of his neighbors. I drove past and turned my head to the left to avoid Kessler spotting me as he got out of his car. I drove a couple blocks then did a three-point turn into a driveway and doubled back toward Kessler's house. I parked three houses down and on the opposite side of the street.

No movement at the house for the next hour. I wasn't even sure what I was looking for.

Maybe Chief Siems would show up. What if he did? What was I going to do about it? Nothing. But I didn't see another option. Until Detective Mitchell got onboard, the best I could do was watch and take notes of any comings and goings or anything unusual.

Another hour passed. Nothing. Leah's phone rang at 9:04 p.m. I checked the screen, not sure if I should answer if it was one of Leah's clients. It wasn't. Leah.

"Rick, I need my phone back." Urgent.

I didn't want to leave my stakeout.

"Can I bring it by in the morning?"

"No. I need it now. There's information in it that I need for a client."

"Can I access it and email it to you?"

"No. I need the phone." Shrill.

The damage I'd done to our relationship must have been irreparable.

"I'll be by in twenty minutes."

I started the Mazda and drove past Kessler's home. Quiet. He could have been inside murdering more people, and I wouldn't be able to tell. The night, the trip back up to Santa Barbara, had been worthless. I'd come up certain about who killed Colleen and a night later I still felt the same way. Only problem was that they weren't the same people. Were Kessler and Siems the real killers or would it be someone else tomorrow? And someone else the next day?

CHAPTER FIFTY-EIGHT

I ARRIVED AT Leah's and knocked on the front door, her phone in hand. She opened it, her eyes wide in the porchlight.

"Here." I proffered the phone. "Thanks for letting me use it."

"Come in." She didn't take the phone but opened the door wider and stepped back.

The back of my neck prickled. I stayed on the porch. "Are you okay?"

Chief Siems stepped into the foyer from the other side of the door, pistol zeroed on my chest. My neck hit full spike and so did my heart.

"Inside, Rick," he said.

The gun wasn't close enough to me to try to dislodge or redirect. I could bolt off the porch and hope Siems missed me. He probably wouldn't, but even if he did, Leah would be left alone with Siems and his gun. She'd probably be dead by the time I got the gun from my duffle bag in the trunk of the car.

I went inside.

Siems took a step back. "Shut the door."

Leah did as told, and that left the two of us three feet apart and five feet from the barrel of Siems' gun. He kept it trained on my center mass. I still had Leah's iPhone in my hand. A limited, but potential weapon.

"Set the phone down onto the bench and follow Leah into the living room. Both of you sit on the sofa."

I set the phone down. I was running out of options. I needed to be ready if Siems made a mistake. Sitting on a sofa would lessen my reaction time. Then I remembered Krista's Sig Sauer that Leah had put in the side table next to the sofa.

I followed Leah into the living room and could feel Siems behind me. Leah got to the sofa first, but I grabbed her arm to subtly steer her to the far side so I could be next to the side table that held the gun.

"No, Rick. You sit on that side." Siems' voice behind me. He'd seen what I'd tried to do. I hoped he didn't figure out why.

Leah and I sat down on our prescribed sides. I needed to keep Siems' thoughts on me and not the table.

"Afraid of having me close, Chief? Afraid your reflexes aren't what they used to be, and I might get to you before you got a shot off?"

Siems sat down in the chair nearest Leah and diagonal to me. He kept his gun, a Glock 9mm, pinned on me. If Siems wanted us dead, he should have started shooting by now. Was he getting up his nerve?

"Shut up, Cahill." He scowled at me. "If you would have just gotten with the program and let SBPD do its job, no one else would have gotten hurt."

Siems wasn't going to kill us now unless I made a mistake. He was waiting for his partner. But as soon as Kessler walked in, we'd be dead.

"You mean after you killed Krista? I showed up after that." My heart pounded in my ears, but I tried to slow everything down. And speed up my brain. "But she was Kessler's idea, right? Just like Grimes."

"Shut up, Cahill." He raised the gun to target my face for emphasis.

"I know you meant the things you said at Krista's service, Chief." Leah's voice was soothing, consoling. "I could hear the emotion in your voice."

"Krista was a good cop." Siems' voice low, raspy. "She didn't deserve to die."

"Kessler killed her, didn't he, Chief?" I tried to match Leah's voice. "And he killed Grimes. That's why you came into his office today, wasn't it? You were surprised when you heard Grimes was dead. You weren't in for either of those murders, were you, Chief?"

"Krista couldn't leave well enough alone." Siems shook his head. Tears welled in his eyes. "Once she found Mike Richert's name buried in Colleen's murder book, the die was cast. Some reserve officer who answered Richert's call must have put it in there after Ted handled the old guy. Krista told me about her meeting with Richert at her birthday party. She planned to go directly to the chief to get approval to send Colleen's fingernail clippings to a forensics lab with a new DNA retrieval method after Ted shut her down with a bullshit story on budget cuts. We couldn't take a chance on the DNA."

"Krista respected you, Chief," Leah said, leaning forward and to the right slightly. She was angling for the gun in the side table. I could give her the moment she needed if I drew a shot from Siems.

I took a deep breath and began a count to three. The front door opened on one, and Kessler walked in holding a gun. My Ruger .357. Eyes empty.

Outgunned. If I moved now, we'd both die. If I waited, we'd both die.

"Good job, Lou," Kessler said and looked at me. "I spotted your tail as soon as I left the station, Rick."

He walked around Siems' chair to the right near me.

"We need to talk, Ted." Siems kept his eyes and his gun aimed at me.

"I know." Kessler raised my gun and shot Siems twice in the chest. Siems slumped wide-eyed, and his gun fell into his lap.

I sprang off the sofa and caught Kessler in the chest with my shoulder. Another gunshot as I drove him into the floor. Leah screamed.

The air blew out of Kessler. I grabbed at the gun. The barrel burned a crease into my hand, but I held on and slammed my forehead into his nose. He released the gun and went limp.

I yanked the gun free and rolled off him to the right and jumped to my feet. His eyes were closed and blood seeped from his broken nose.

"Leah!" My eyes zoomed to her. Sitting on the floor rocking against the sofa. Her right hand clenched around her left bicep, blood dripping from a wound between her fingers. "Are you okay?"

"Yes." She was crying. "But it hurts."

I glanced down at Kessler. His eyes fluttered open. He'd be conscious in seconds. I pointed the gun at his head. One trigger pull and he'd no longer be a threat. Not to Leah. Not to me. Not to anyone else.

And my absolution would be complete.

"Don't, Rick." Eyes pleading louder than her voice. "That's not who you are."

"Yes, it is."

"No." She picked her phone up from the coffee table and pushed three numbers. "My name is Leah Landingham, and I live at 1609 Lasuen Road. I've been shot and a man is dead. I need an ambulance."

Kessler blinked a couple times and stared at me from the floor. My flex cuffs were in the duffle bag in the trunk of the Mazda.

"In the arm. Please hurry." Leah spoke to the 911 operator. "Rick Cahill and the man who shot me and killed ex–police chief Siems is Captain Kessler of the Santa Barbara Police Department."

"Get up and sit in the chair," I said to Kessler. "On your hands."

He sat on his hands in the chair opposite Siems.

I slammed the grip across Kessler's nose. Blood spurted from a gash on his already broken nose. He thrust his hands to his face.

"Put them down! Sit on your hands or I'll hit you again."

"Rick!" Leah. "No. Everything is okay," she said into the phone. "Just get here fast." She ended the call and put the phone down. "The

police will be here any minute. You don't have to do anything more."
Fear in her voice

Blood ran down Kessler's face.

"Tell me what happened the night Colleen died," I said to Kessler.
"I'll kill you if you lie."

"Rick!" Leah tried to stand up but slumped back against the couch.
She'd go into shock soon.

"I drove Lou to his daughter's play at UCSB." His voice thick with
blood. "We took her out to dinner afterward then dropped her at her
apartment in Isla Vista. Lou saw your wife sitting on a bus bench, and
we stopped to offer her a ride. She recognized the chief and got in. He
knew Colleen was your wife. It wasn't the first time we stopped to
pick up women. Lou made an excuse to drive by his house before we
could drop Colleen off at your apartment. His usual routine. He got
your wife to go inside his house. I waited outside. Fifteen minutes
later, Lou ran out of the house frantic. Your wife fought him and he
strangled her."

Tears boiled out of my eyes and ran down my face. Colleen, alone,
and scared and fighting for her life because I'd betrayed her.

"Why didn't you stop him?" I stood over Kessler, the gun aimed at
his face.

"Rick! Stop!" Leah.

"I didn't know he'd get violent. He never had before. Not like that."

"But you helped him destroy evidence instead of arresting him.
You were there when he bathed her in bleach to get rid of any DNA,
weren't you? Your career meant more than giving Colleen the justice
she deserved?"

Chief Siems suddenly coughed and jerked in the chair. I snapped
my head toward him.

Kessler lunged up at me, the crown of his head slamming into my
face. Stars. The gun slipped from my hand, and I slumped down to

one knee. Darkness pushing in on the sides.

Leah screamed, pulling me back awake.

"She was still alive when I found her, but unconscious." Kessler's voice above me. I looked up and saw the barrel of my own gun staring me in the face. Above it, tears ran down Kessler's cheeks. "I was an accessory. I couldn't let one mistake ruin the career I'd planned out. Be a fucking errand boy to the chief for all those years for nothing. I was on my way. I didn't want to kill her. Siems never even knew she was still alive. He thought he'd killed her, and suddenly, I had leverage. I didn't want to—I had to."

I leapt at him. Gunshots. Darkness.

*   *   *

Colleen smiled up at me as she handed me her camping breakfast specialty. Scrambled eggs and bacon straight off the Coleman stove. Her impossibly blue eyes bright with love and promise, matching the color of Fallen Leaf Lake behind us. The first morning of our honeymoon. Our first morning as husband and wife.

The happiest day of my life.

EPILOGUE

"I wish I had better news, Ms. Landingham."

Sobs and sharp breaths.

Darkness. I opened my eyes. Still darkness.

"Although the bullet missed the optic chiasm, its concussive force caused swelling in the area and, thus, resultant blindness." The male voice I'd learned to associate with Doctor Morizi. "But since there was no direct damage to the area, blood flow returned fairly quickly. There is a chance that Rick's vision will return. When, and how completely, are anybody's guess. But, all in all, he is a very lucky man. A millimeter difference in any direction and the outcome would have been far worse."

I was lucky. And I was blind.

I closed my eyes and searched my memories of the only vision I had left.

A hand on my head. I knew it was Leah's by the touch. I'd felt it often over the past few days. It comforted me, even without words. I'd grown dependent upon it.

Lips on my forehead. Then something wet. Tears.

*   *   *

Detective Mitchell's voice startled me one morning in my hospital room.

"You were right, Cahill. Kessler and Siems were responsible for your wife's death." I heard an exhale. "Kessler steered the investigation into Krista's death where he wanted to. I thought he big-footed his way in because he knew the death of a cop would get a lot of press and he was looking for some help to climb up the next rung on the career ladder. I should have known something was hinky when he jumped in to take responsibility for obtaining Krista's phone records before I could assign a junior detective to do it. He cut out her last incoming call from the payphone on State Street. And he convinced me that Dustin Peck was an unreliable witness. I should have put the pieces together. If I had, maybe you . . ."

"Regret's a horrible thing, Detective. It poisons your soul and stops you from moving forward in life. You did the right thing when your number was called. That's all anyone can ask."

"Maybe." I heard a sigh. "Anyway, we have Kessler dead to rights. The burned-out van we recovered was once owned by a man, now deceased, who lived next to the ranch owned by Thom Murphy, Kessler's stepfather. The van and the property had long since been abandoned. Apparently, Kessler stole it and got it running . . . so he could kill Krista."

"What about Siems?"

"He died on the operating table."

Detective Mitchell never talked to me again, but his visit had served its purpose. For both of us.

Leah's shoulder healed nicely, although it did scar. I felt it etched into her arm. I often caressed it after we made love. A reminder of the new life we led in San Diego. An imperfection I couldn't see. I had a new scar, too. On my left cheek. Cylindrical and deep. I only touched it when I knew I was alone. It made me think of Colleen.

Kessler survived Leah's gunshot to his abdomen. She saved us both when she grabbed Krista's gun from the side table and shot Kessler. A millisecond after he shot me.

As much as I wanted Kessler dead, I was glad he survived. He would easily go down for Krista and Siems' murders, but I wanted justice for Colleen. Not my justice. The law's. Humanity's. I stayed on the Santa Barbara DA until she agreed to prosecute.

The trial was set for September of next year. The month Colleen and I were married. I wanted people to hear about Colleen before she was a victim. When she was alive, not a statistic and a sad story. I wanted the world to know she'd been a real person, living a real life. With dreams and goals.

And infinite tomorrows.